LUCKY BABY

A SMALL TOWN ENEMIES TO LOVERS ROMANCE

CRESCENT COVE
BOOK 11

TARYN QUINN

RAINBOW rage
PUBLISHING

Lucky Baby
© 2021 Taryn Quinn
Rainbow Rage Publishing

Cover by LateNite Designs
Photograph by Lindee Robinson Photography
Models: Shannon Lorraine & Junior

First print edition: September 2022
ISBN Print edition: 978-1-940346-77-9

ACKNOWLEDGMENTS

Sometimes a book doesn't go exactly as planned. For us, that's actually most of the time. We are always wondering if this time it just won't come together.

And then here we are once again! Another book finished and a happy couple full of laughter, love, and all the shenanigans our readers can handle.

Thanks to our crew for always being excited to get an advanced copy, for our wonderful team Tori & Kim. And also an extra thanks to the Word Wenches for making up such a fun community.

Sometimes we make up fictional places that end up having the same names as actual places. These are our fictional interpretations only. Please grant us leeway if our creative vision isn't true to reality.

For those without family.
Found family is just as amazing.

ONE

THIS MOMENT WAS PERFECTION.

The suspicious part of me wondered if it was *too* perfect.

Leaves crunched under my boots as ghostly swirls of steam rose from my oversized mug of coffee. The hazelnut blend, with whatever secret ingredient Brewed Awakening's mistress had added, was my favorite way to start the day. Even if I never quite got the milk to coffee ratio magic Macy seemed to do so effortlessly. However, it was *my* coffee blend alone.

That thrilled me more than it should, but I could own it in my own head, if nowhere else. Since my particular genius turned into one-of-a-kind car and motorcycle parts, it was only right I got a kick out of someone else's talents when it came to my coffee. Especially considering the liquid gold was my soulmate.

Coffee had kept me alive even when food had been scarce. Being a woman in the car business wasn't for the faint of heart, and I'd had to claw my way up to a living wage before I'd been able to start calling my own shots. Fast forward ten years—with quite a few crash and burns—and here I was, making an actual home in a little nowhere town as quaint as a postcard and just as family-centric.

Maybe a little too family-centric. I was tempted to get an IUD and

1

birth control. My doctor had actually laughed when I'd tried—until she looked at my address.

Crescent Cove was legion when it came to babies.

So not in my ten year plan, thanks.

I flipped my collar up on my battered motorcycle jacket against the wind racing off the water. The sun peeked from Crescent Lake's still surface, turning the sky gold and misty blue. The air had a chilly bite that warned of the long winter coming, but the burn in my lungs made me smile over the rim of my mug. It was almost as good as the cigarettes I'd miss until my dying day.

Okay, not *as* good, but it was definitely invigorating.

I picked my way across the uneven spots of my lawn—*my* lawn. God, that felt good to say. Apartments and hand-me-downs or thrift finds had been my life for twenty-six years.

A year ago, I would have been happy with that. I never stayed in one place long enough to care about what I plunked my ass on or laid my head on at night as long as it was clean. I'd lived a transient life by choice. Job in Seattle? Yep, I was there. Car show in Miami? Sure, I could make it. Sturgis Rally? Hell yeah, I'd be there.

Now I was one-third owner in an actual company. People came to me now instead of me doing guest spots in various shops. I'd been in demand before I was legal to drink. I had an uncanny ability to fabricate just about anything. If a client dreamed up something, I could pluck it out of their mind. For years, I'd worked with any and all machines at my fingertips to make it happen. Now I had my own fabricator I'd created, down to the proprietary specs.

And I'd patented it. I'd learned the hard way that loyalty was for dreamers, not for the cold hard reality of business.

That lesson had been tattooed on my back with a blade, leaving a bonus scar that I hadn't seen coming.

But those moments had only made me stronger. Now I could charge whatever the hell I wanted for jobs. And I did. Shamelessly. I even had a company begging to license my machine. They hadn't quite come up to my number yet.

To be fair, I had a disgustingly high number in my head. I had a feeling Ramsey Inc. would get there eventually. He had a serious hard-on for Hilda, my baby.

I had a waiting list three years out to get time on my bench. They were all curated projects suited to me. I said no to people all the damn time. Did I feel bad about it? Nope. I'd worked hard to create a name for myself since I was sixteen years old.

And now I had two workshops I could outfit however I wanted.

Part of my contract with Dare and Gage Kramer had included absolute autonomy when it came to how I worked. Unique jobs were eighty percent of our income at Kramer & Burns Custom, but Dare had a special affinity for the town so we still took care of the locals.

The Kramer boys had been involved in NASCAR in a former life. Now they were happily settled with kids, but our combined reputations had resulted in a constant stream of clients and word of mouth that had only grown with each car that rolled out of our bays. Our customs had blown up so much we were looking to take over the building behind the garage to extend the space and hire on a few general mechanics. But getting Dare to move on anything was like asking a glacier to put some hustle into it.

Mostly I didn't care about that part of the company. I was more involved with the specialty projects than the everyday labor of tows and oily fingers. Unless you asked me to rebuild a British motorcycle, then I was more than willing to get my overalls on.

Like the sweet '69 Triumph Bonneville sitting in my home garage right now. I'd spent the last few months acquiring the perfect pieces, tools, and even a lift to make my home garage as effective as the one in town. To be truthful, it was the only thing I'd actually completed in my fixer-upper farmhouse.

My bedroom was as bare bones as a clichéd bachelor pad. It included my mom's old dresser my dad had shipped me, a mattress, and the badass four poster bed. Admittedly, I'd overpaid for it from August Beck, a local carpentry artist. It was a damn work of art, and I didn't mind paying for the unique, especially since sleeping was my favorite hobby.

I was still eating off a TV tray in front of my seventy-inch television in my living room three months later. My house echoed it was so damn empty, but that was a problem for future Tish.

Right now, I was going to enjoy the view and my coffee. I climbed up on my picnic table and sat on the uneven slats of the top. It was rickety as hell and probably wouldn't last the winter. Because dear God, this town was no joke when it came to winter.

The blazing summer had been full to the brim with work and somehow October had snuck in with its cool mornings made for warm coffee, and silence save for some badass birds. Just how I liked it.

I'd impulsively bought this property on the lake thanks to a little bit of right-time-right-place. Mr. and Mrs. Slide had been tired of the snow and bitter cold of Upstate New York and looking to sell the house to someone who would appreciate it. I'd lucked into the whole damn thing because I'd fabricated a hard to get part for Gary Slide's pristine all-glass hatch Pinto.

A Pinto, for fuck's sake. No one made parts for that damn car anymore, but the guy loved it—maybe even more than his wife. I was pretty sure she knew it too.

I'd volunteered to make the crazy part after he and Dare had tried to find it from one of the parts dealers we worked with. The look on the old guy's face had broken me. Actual tears because they couldn't find the rare hydraulic kit for his baby.

I'd made an exception and let him bump the line, then spent seven hours creating a new kit and actually improving the seal on the weirdly shaped glass hatch that made up the trunk. It ended up being a fun project, probably one of the best decisions I'd ever made.

Because Gary couldn't stand to be away from his baby, he sat with me as I worked on it. Once my annoyance cleared about being watched, I'd settled in and been treated to his life story.

It should have been boring, but Gary was a born storyteller and entertained me well into the night. Over a pair of hoagies from Jersey Angel's, he told me about wanting to sell his property.

After the way he'd described it, I'd ended up offering him a cash settlement for the damn thing. And now here I was, with a view that most people would kill for.

Arthur Maitland had raged at the bank as I was signing my papers. Evidently, I'd ruined his plans for another set of condos on the lake courtesy of Maitland Enterprises.

My gaze skimmed over the water to the east side where condos had been in progress for the last six months. I was pretty sure Maitland was still having a kitten about me buying up this piece of land.

I couldn't say I minded. The man was a dick.

A little meow was my only warning before a ball of fluff leaped onto the table beside me. I gave my cat a quick scratch under the chin before Dusty sprawled onto his back to play with the fringe on my jacket.

I waggled the fringe above his head and laughed at his crazy eyes and Wolverine-esque nails trying to catch them. The wind kicked up, reminding me I really did need to get a proper winter coat before the first snowfall.

"Keep Ya Head Up" blared out of my jacket pocket, startling Dusty. He flew off the table and headed for the garage for safety.

I laughed and pulled out my phone. Only one person had that ringtone. My older brother loved 2Pac.

"What do you want?"

"I can't call my baby sister?"

I spun on the picnic table and stretched out my legs, praying I wouldn't end up with a splinter in my ass. "Nope. You text, not call. Why you're usually my favorite brother."

Ezra Burns was the eldest of the Burns pack of wild dogs—my dad's name for us, not mine. But truly, he wasn't far off. Especially when we all got together, which had been harder and harder to do over the years. All of us had scattered to the four corners of the country.

"Glad I still have favorite status."

His whisky-dark voice rolled through me. A pang hit my chest like a kickback from a wrench. My brother really didn't call unless something was going on. "Depends on how this conversation goes, Ez."

"Guess I can't check in either."

I crossed my legs at the ankle. "Is that what you're doing?"

"You know me too well, Ging."

I winced. "Really?"

"You're the only redhead in the bunch."

"Because I'm the special one." The usual back and forth seemed a little forced and nerves skated up my neck, leaving bunched muscles in its wake.

"Yeah, we'll go with special."

I picked a piece of leaf off my jeans. "Not like you to try to do the small talk, bud."

He sighed. "Yeah. I suck at it."

"Indeed."

"You bought a house, right?"

I sat up and swung my feet back onto the faded wood bench. "Yeah. You gave me nothing but grief about it."

"Roots aren't for me, Ging."

"I didn't think so either." I glanced out on the lake. "They don't seem so bad these days."

Ezra was quiet for a moment. I could hear something on the other end of the line as if he'd muffled the speaker. My shoulders hunched and I braced my elbows on my knees.

I was not getting a good feeling.

"How would you feel about all of us crashing there for Christmas?"

I sat up straight. "God, why?"

He laughed. "Well, you're the first one to buy a house. You win."

"No. That's not how this works. Besides, weren't you the first one to bust my balls about my 'money pit', as you called it?"

"Well, it is."

I glanced over at the old house. The porch had seen better days, but the inside wasn't too bad. Just dated. It probably hadn't been updated since the seventies. And while I enjoyed the music, I did not love the decor.

"It's a work in progress."

"Well, can it be ready for the week of Christmas?"

"Since when do we *do* Christmas?" I pinched the bridge of my nose. Ez was being far too friendly. He had a soft spot for me, but my eldest brother was usually moving at warp speed, and niceties weren't his forte. "What happened?"

"Nothing. Well, not exactly."

"Ezra David Burns."

"Jeez."

I could see his shoulders hunching in my head. My brother was a famous photo journalist, but I was one of the few people who could crack the whip on him. Not that he'd admit it.

"Look, it's not a big deal. Don't freak out."

"Freak out?" I put my mug down, jumped off the picnic table, and stalked down to the rocky shore off the lake. "Why would I freak out?"

"I said *don't* freak. I can hear you stomping from here, you know."

"Then just tell me. Is it Dad?" The mere idea of my larger than life father being sick had me bending at the waist to drag in a breath.

"No, it's not Dad."

Relief left me with black dots in my vision.

"Breathe, Ging."

"I am," I growled before I took a deep breath. "Then what's going on?"

"It's Cohen."

Every terrible scenario blasted through my brain. My middle brother was a smoke jumper in California. He'd always been the daredevil in our family, even more so than Ezra. He'd channeled that into saving people instead of doing stunts on his dirt bike on the dangerous tracks he'd rode on during his teen years. He'd always picked out the most challenging ones to give us all nightmares.

"He's okay?"

"He's fine, Tish, I promise. Just a little messed up." He went quiet for a moment. "Okay, more than a little. He lost Jimmy on the job."

"Oh, God." I fell back on my butt on the rocks. The flash of pain up my tailbone had nothing on the vise around my heart.

Immediately, I pictured Jimmy's cocky swagger with his sunny hair flowing down his back. Those thick, myriad shades of blond strands had been my favorite thing to tangle my fingers in.

And then to pull when the hot fever of need had blown wild and fierce between us for that secret month in July.

"Not Jimmy."

He'd been my brother's best friend since they'd met during smoke jumper training. They were the youngest guys to be added to the Alpha team for his unit.

Jimmy and Cohen had been inseparable until that summer we'd had a *very* ill-advised fling that had ended in a blade I hadn't seen coming. I'd nursed the wound alone in the mountains of Colorado.

My family didn't know what he'd done. Now they never would.

And it didn't matter.

I sucked back the sob that was trapped in my chest like a frightened bird. The only thing that mattered was my brother.

Ezra's voice dragged me back from the past. "Cohen isn't doing great. We had to kick his ass to even get him into rehab."

Get it together, Burns. "Why the hell didn't you call me sooner?"

"He didn't want to worry you."

"Damn idiot." They still treated me like I was twelve. "How bad is he?"

"Just a busted leg, but it was a serious fracture so he's gotta do the whole physical therapy thing. He should be done the first week of December. I figured your place would be a good place to plant him for awhile."

"Of course."

The words came out before I could think better of it. I mean, of course I'd take in my brother and my family, but my place was definitely *not* ready for them.

At all. And neither was I.

I pushed away the memory of Jimmy's startlingly blue eyes. His laughter and the arctic chill of his deception vied for dominance. I slammed those memories back into the metal box I'd put them in years ago then hauled myself to my feet and crunched my way back over the shoreline stones to the grass strewn with leaves.

The half acre of land between the water and my house was a quick trip. It wasn't a large farmhouse by any means. In fact, it was only a three-bedroom place. Not nearly enough room for all my roughhousing brothers. Even if one was laid up and probably hurting far more than he'd let on.

"We won't need much."

"Ha." I snorted. "Right."

"Hey, you're the one who was crowing about how amazing your house was. Now I'm going to hold you to it."

Relief warred with sorrow as I tried to get my mind working again. "Yeah, yeah." I wished I could say I hadn't. But being the baby of the family and being the first to buy a house had left my ego a little unchecked. "Is Dad coming too?"

"Yep. The Burns family will be back together, baby. I'll check in later, Ging."

"Okay. Talk soon."

I shoved my phone into my pocket then tipped back my head. Tears threatened, but I wouldn't let them fall for Jimmy. Not ever again. I had one focus right now. And it was a freaking big problem because there was no way I could get this place in shape for them in less than two months on my own.

The old barn beside my garage caught my eye.

I'd had plans to call in my chip from Lucky Roberts in the spring. The dude owed me for his harebrained last minute scheme for his best friend's proposal last month.

The man was obnoxiously loud, had *player* stamped on his forehead in neon green, and was far too attractive for his own good.

He thought he could charm his way out of any problem. I knew firsthand how charm could hide a person's dark side and could even make you think you'd imagined things that weren't there.

But I needed Lucky—well, not Lucky specifically, just his hands and his carpentry skills. I preferred a budget, but I figured I'd be tossing money at this place like I had an endless bank account.

It would be the perfect place to house my brothers, otherwise known as the animals. And fixing up a guest room for my dad in my house was doable with a bit of spit and grit.

I held open the door for my cat as he zipped around my ankles. Even he seemed uncharacteristically feisty.

Did he sense that change was in the air?

No. No change. This was just a temporary speed bump. I could handle this. My brother needed me, and it just so happened I wanted to fix up my place.

If that meant I needed to deal with Lucky to get it done, then that was what I'd do. I'd make up a plan, get supplies together, and thank God I'd already started the ball rolling when it came to permits.

Now I just had to go inform Lucky it was time to pay up.

TWO

I DECIDED TO KILL TWO BIRDS WITH ONE MOTORCYCLE. QUEENIE, MY Triumph, needed a test ride to see if my tweaks on the engine had fixed the noise that was driving me crazy.

They had not.

In fact, it was freaking louder. I swung my leg off the bike and resisted the urge to kick it. That rarely solved the problem. Queenie was a refined sort. Brute force wasn't her thing, and finesse wasn't my finest quality.

I toed down my double kickstand as I flicked open the chin strap on my helmet and gave a disgusted huff before I tugged it off. The crisp fall air felt good, even if my hair was now all over the place. I should have put it in my usual braids, but my brain had been offline since Ezra's call.

Dammit, I was normally a planner. I didn't do things impulsively. I wasn't even sure where to go to find Thor aka Lucky. He wasn't quite as bulky as the screen version of the god of thunder, nor did he have the pretty factor, but he did have the hair and drinking aptitude. And to be honest, I wasn't into pretty boys.

Not that I had time for them—or guys like Lucky—right now.

I had a barn to remodel in less than six weeks. I was pretty sure even the Property Brothers would give me grief about that, and they had a huge crew as well as the magic of television.

I was watching DIY shows by the dozen and still *not* working on my house. There was a small amount of shame for the fact that I had the Pinterest app on my phone, iPad, and a perpetually open tab on my computer at this point. I could pin like no one's business, but doing the actual work?

Yeah. Fuck.

I was stuck in the planning stages, lost in a jumble of ideas that had no cohesive vision. I could design a car from the tires up, but ask me to pick a paint color and my pits tingled. Now time was up and I couldn't make excuses any longer.

I stepped onto the sidewalk outside of Gideon Gets It Done's shop. I was pretty sure that wasn't where I'd find Thor, but John Gideon usually knew where his people were. As it was, I should have been at the shop, but I could juggle my projects for a few days if need be.

I'd called Dare to let him know I'd be out of pocket today. Not that he was my boss, but he liked to think he was. His brother Gage and I let him think so because it made our lives easier.

Tucking my helmet under my arm, I stepped inside. Macy was sitting on the counter with her legs wrapped around Gideon's hips. His fingers were twisted in the belt loops of her jeans, and they were going to town like a pair of teenagers.

The sounder over the door was a screeching bat, which made both of them jump. I dropped my helmet and ducked. "What the hell?"

Macy's peal of laughter made me straighten. "That's your doing, I imagine?" I grumbled.

"Halloween season!" She slapped Gideon on the ass.

He groaned. "The sound effects are everywhere. Every doorway, every place of business between us. She'd add them to every project site if I let her."

She gripped the front of his shirt and dragged him closer. "Oh, would you?"

He gave her a quick kiss. "No."

12

"Spoilsport." Macy pushed him back and hopped down. "I'll let you work. Missed you this morning, Tish."

I picked up my helmet by the strap. "Family stuff."

"Oh, I know how that is. My house is chaos."

"*Your* house?" Gideon leaned his hip on the counter and crossed his arms.

"Ours. Jeez, so touchy." She came around the counter and passed me. "It's mine during fall. He's just grumpy because I had an awesome new *noisy* delivery at the house and the Haunt." Macy sailed out the door with a cackle as the bat screamed again.

Gideon shook his head. "Good thing I love her."

I rolled my eyes. "Gross."

He grinned. "Wait until it happens to you."

"Dear God, no." I set my ruby red helmet on the counter. "I'm looking for a man to do only one thing for me."

"Father a baby?"

I would not even dignify that with a response.

"C'mon, it's Crescent Cove. Gotta wonder." He plucked the pencil behind his ear out of his dark curls. "What can I do you for, Tish?"

"Tell me where to find Lucky."

He tucked his pencil back in its perpetual spot and smiled wider. "I thought you weren't looking for love."

"Hell no. He owes me a bet, and I'm ready to collect. It's a sizable job, so I may need to hire a few of your guys to help out if that's possible."

"We get pretty booked out. How fast are you looking for?"

"ASAP."

He whistled. "Fall is a slower season, but it's still not easy to shuffle things in a hurry."

I bit my lip. I didn't like using emotional blackmail, but I was desperate. "Look, my brother was in an accident."

Worry instantly furrowed his brow.

I held up a hand. "Not too terrible, but it jacked up my timetable for the renovation I had in mind." Sure, we'd go with that. I'd definitely had no plan. "He's in rehab right now for the injury, but he'll

13

be dropping in on me for Christmas and staying indefinitely. My house isn't ready, and he probably can't do stairs anyway." I sucked in a breath. I was pretty sure this was more words than I'd ever spoken at once since I'd lived in this town. "I bought the old Slide house."

"Oh, right. On the lake." He whistled. "That's a nice property. We're nearly neighbors."

I patted my helmet and resisted the urge to twitch. *Neighbors* wasn't a word I threw around. I rather liked that my house was secluded, and I didn't want to start doing cookouts or some shit. "Yeah. I can't believe I own property, to be honest. But the old barn would be a good rec room-slash-guest house for my family."

"A great idea. But if I remember right, that place is…" He rubbed the back of his neck, clearly searching for a nice word for my new home.

"Hellish? Yeah, it needs to be gutted. I already made some calls and have a dumpster coming tomorrow accompanied by some burly football players from the high school who wanted to make some quick money destroying shit."

His eyebrows shot up. "Wasting no time."

"Nope. I have a small window of opportunity. Lucky owes me, so I'm collecting."

"He'll be thrilled."

"I bet."

"No, he actually will. Lucky might look like a frat boy on steroids from the 80s, but he's one of the best designers and carpenters on my payroll."

"Well, that's promising. I was just hoping I would have a decent area to frame out to put my brother in there. Maybe a few electronics to keep him occupied."

Gideon reached for a folder, then pulled out his keyboard and started typing. "What's your budget?"

"I don't have one."

He glanced up, one eyebrow spiking. "As in you expect him to do it for free?"

I laughed. "No, I mean no limits. I have money to throw at the project to get things moving faster. Over the last three months, I've started proceedings on permits and all that."

"Huh." He scribbled something on the folder, then went back to his keyboard. "Well, that makes things easier. Shoot me what you have, and I'll take care of whatever else is needed to get the ball rolling. Permits are a pain in the ass."

"I did some custom work for Earl Jennings over at City Hall. Should make permits a little easier."

"Impressive. Maybe I should have Macy create a special blend for him so I could get my permits easier too."

"Would help if Earl drank coffee. A Lipton tea bag dunked in hot water for about ten seconds is more his style."

He curled his lip. "Fitting," he muttered.

I pressed my lips together against a smile. "But he loves his cherry Oldsmobile Cutlass. The engine could take a cop car after what I did to it." I folded my arms on the counter. "Just don't tell the Chief."

Gideon shook his head. "The things you learn." He tapped a few more keys and pushed a form in front of me. "This covers the start to the project. I'll put Lucky down as project manager. He's over at the Olsen's house on Elm Street doing a fence install." He slapped down a sticky note with an address. "If you want to take a ride out and talk to him, you can."

A twinge of something like worry niggled between my shoulder blades. "Give out details on your employees so easily all the time?"

Gideon crossed his arms. "Word of mouth is king in a small town, but this is mostly a little payback. Lucky losing a bet makes me giddy. Especially since he still owes me forty bucks from our last poker game."

"Sucks at poker, huh?" Good to know.

"He's actually usually cleaning us out, but Joe, one of my guys, may have doctored his drinks with double shots."

I laughed. "Sounds like my brothers." I scrawled my signature on the contract. "Thanks, Gideon."

"Don't thank me yet. Overtime gets expensive."

"Worth it." I pulled out my phone and took a photo of the contract, then tucked my copy into my inside jacket pocket. Another thing I'd learned long ago—keep paperwork organized. Especially the kind with signatures. I grabbed my helmet. "Talk soon."

Gideon gave me a salute, and I rushed out the door. It was only a little after ten in the morning, but I'd been on the phone all day already trying to pull this insanity together. And okay, maybe I'd put off talking with Lucky for last, but it was time to face that blond-streaked, large, brutish fire.

So brutish wasn't the best word for him. He was just a big, affable steamroller. But I was ready to do some rolling over of my own.

That had sounded better in my head.

I fastened my helmet and kicked Queenie's engine to life. The throttle was off and maybe the timing belt. Nothing that would be earth-shattering for a quick ride out to the suburbs of Crescent Cove. I flicked up my kickstand and eased into the moderate traffic on Main Street. Colorful awnings used throughout the summer for some shade were in various stages of breakdown. Bright pots of mums and pumpkins and the occasional cheerful scarecrow framed out the doorways.

Drinking stations for the dog-friendly shops shone with fresh water and shop owners waved customers in off the street. School was back in session, leaving the daytime pedestrian traffic a little lighter as well. Sugar Rush had a tower of cupcakes in the window with a huge selection of carved pumpkins surrounding them like a freakish crowd at a concert where the main attraction got eaten. A new store, Vintage December, had quietly opened up with repurposed clothing. Mannequins were decked out in concert T-shirts from the late 80s and ripped jeans had been patched with colorful matching bandanas.

I was tempted to pull off and and have a look. I had a soft spot for faded jeans that were already broken in the right way, not in manufactured evenly spaced rips and frays.

A delivery truck blocked the road, giving me a few more minutes to take a closer look. Nope, those were the kind that had been carefully frayed with a razor during times of boredom or creativity, depending on the day.

Alas, new denim wasn't on the agenda today.

Finally, the diesel-belching truck in front of me shuddered forward. I flipped my visor down against the smoke and eased around the death trap when his flashers went on again. A horn behind me had me opening up my throttle to make tracks. The wind off the water sliced through my leathers. Pretty soon, it would be time to put my bike away for the winter.

I'd picked up a beater at auction for the off-season. No way was I driving my convertible Lucille in the sleet and salt-heavy months of Central New York.

I eased around the bend and took a side street shortcut to get out of the increasing truck situation. The more picturesque gold and burnt orange array of trees replaced stores as I hit Lake Street. Sun glinted off the water, reminding me why I'd settled here. Day-trippers were clogging up the shoulders of the road, eager to park and look out on Crescent Lake.

The mansions and foliage were a good stopgap for snacks and a little shopping on their way to the mountains for even more views, but I didn't mind so much. It kept the town alive.

I'd lived in plenty of smaller towns on their way to seedy and rundown. Drug dens and meth labs usually followed pretty quickly thereafter. I much preferred the quaint aspect of the Cove, even if I had to slap a smile on my face more than I was comfortable with.

It was better for business and why I usually left customer service to Gage whenever I could help it. He was the charming one of our unit—well, at least usually. Now and then, he pulled out his inner growl and reminded people how he'd dominated back in his racing days.

About ten minutes later, I pulled off the side of the road to check my maps app on my phone. I was definitely close to the burbs, complete with little cul-de-sacs and driveways crammed with SUVs. Some still had lakefront views, but for the most part, this was a maze of endlessly circular streets with an army of high-end minivans marching along at exactly fifteen miles per hour. Safe blues and silvers with the occasional pop of sassy burgundy seemed to be the color palette of choice.

Holy boring. My skin itched to turn around and get out of there. Most seemed to be coming and going with moms, and a few dads, in errands mode.

"Need some help?"

I flipped up the visor on my helmet. "Sorry?"

The cherubic woman in one of the minivans I'd been careful to avoid gave me a dimpled smile. An improbably perfect head of blond ringlets spiraled around her face. Wig? Extensions? Curling iron influencer on Facebook? "Need some help? It can get a little confusing in here. A lot of the roads have the same name with east or west tacked on. Super original, I know."

"Right." I unearthed the sticky note. "You probably don't—"

"Oh, honey, I know everyone here. I'm the head of the HOA."

I didn't know what that meant, but it sounded terrifying. "Okay. I'm looking for the Olsen house on Elm."

"Oh, Kimberly. Yes." Her voice went a little sly. "She's got that handsome handyman working on her fence." She fanned her face. "All the girls have been making excuses to go over and watch him dig the post thingies. Then he uses this handheld mixer thing to make cement. I've never seen muscles like that outside of watching *The Bachelor*. My husband isn't anything to sneeze at, truth be told, but nothing like that."

I resisted the urge to roll my eyes. "I'm sure he's enjoying the attention."

"Oh, do you know Lucky? Of course you do, you look like..."

I tightened my hold on the handles of my bike. "I look like..."

"Um, well, you look like the kind of woman who would go out with a man like him."

Being insulted took too much energy, but it certainly threatened. Lucky and I didn't fit in any shape or form. He was the Jason Momoa sized key to my non-standard-sized lock.

Then again, with Lucky, you'd probably need an expandable one if he was built to scale all over.

I huffed out a breath. Already I was experiencing suburbia-induced psychosis.

"He's working on my house next." Why I felt the need to explain, I had no clue. I'd been learning that some sugar was easier than the vinegar that flowed through my veins on most days. I pasted on a smile—as much as I could with the foam insides of my helmet pressing on my face. "So, you know where the house is?"

"Why don't I just drive there and you can follow?"

God save me from nosy neighbors.

"Oh, I'm Bethany. You are?"

Of course, she was a Bethany. "Tish."

"Well, Tish, let's get you over to Kim's house. She'll just die." Her voice lowered and she peered over the window to scan the length of me. "Are those leather pants?"

I lifted my boot onto the foot peg and revved the engine. Maybe this wasn't exactly the best idea. I glanced around at people craning their necks to check us out. I was going to be talked about during dinner tonight for sure. "Leather from top to bottom, Bethany."

She probably figured that included underwear. I was obviously a rough and rowdy chick the likes of which these suburbs had never seen.

My plain cotton would kill all her secret dreams.

"Wow." She shook her hair back and straightened her shoulders so her mom rack was on display.

Not sure what she thought it was going to do for her. Or maybe she was hot for my leather. Go HOA lady. "Ready?"

"Oh, yes. Of course." She brushed her hair away from her face and put her hands on the wheel at ten and two. She put her blinker on and then eased onto the street.

A few people came out of their houses and even a few bold ones ended up on the lawn to get a good look at the chick on the motorcycle. I resisted the urge to gun the engine. All it took was a tiny tap of my boot, but I didn't want to give anyone the vapors. That and Queenie still needed some adjustments before I could do fancy maneuvers on her.

TARYN QUINN

Three minutes later after traveling through a maze of sameness, we turned off and a dizzying circle of houses in the exact cookie-cutter house plans greeted me. How could anyone handle this? The only differences were the fonts on the mailboxes. Twenty to one, that had to be approved by Bethany.

The meaning of HOA finally clicked in my brain. I'd bet Bethany liked to lord over her little dominion—with a smile and brownie, of course.

Two cars were in the driveway. Instead of honking her horn and moving along after she pointed to Kimberly Olsen's place, she parked beside the perfectly manicured lawn.

Great.

I eased behind the Beemer with the vanity plate, Bethany1. She'd probably had that plate since her sixteenth birthday. Hell, probably got it with her first car, thanks to daddy.

I tamped down the snarling bitch that lived in my chest. Bethany and her privilege were just a part of life. I was here to call in a marker, not judge suburbia rules of etiquette.

I hooked my helmet to the handlebars and leaned down to shake out my hair, then flip it back. Bethany was staring at me again. Kinda like I was an alien. Maybe I was in this part of town. I tugged down my fitted motorcycle jacket and dropped my double kickstand to the unmarred blacktop.

Late morning sunlight fought its way through the huge oak trees that canopied the boxy modern house. A stone pathway led to the side of the house where a bright white fence stood. A wheelbarrow and bags of quick cement were stacked beside a bed of fall flowers. A trio of pumpkins and a scatter of gourds artfully framed the small hand-painted sign decreeing that The Olsens had been established in 2012.

Shoot me in the forehead.

Maybe I just should have texted Lucky.

"Are you coming?" Bethany was standing at the gate.

"Shouldn't we ring the doorbell or something?"

She laughed. "Why would we do that?"

"Why indeed." I carefully stepped over a pink bike crossing the

20

wide gray pathway. A squeal from the backyard nearly had me running back to my bike. Shouldn't the kids be in school? Ugh.

"Kimmie! Are you here?"

Yeah, I should probably just go. Before I could turn around, another small blond stuck her head around the corner. "Hello." She was of an indeterminate age, but probably not old enough to go to school. I was pretty sure she wasn't big enough to ride the bike I'd stepped over.

"Hi."

"I'm Abby."

I wiped my palm on my hip. "Tish."

"Your hair is pwetty."

"Um, thanks?"

"I like your pants. They're shiny."

"Protective leather for riding my bike."

"I think my sister needs them. She falls down a lot on hers."

I pressed my lips together against a laugh. My fall would be a bit more intense, but the kid was quick, I had to give her that.

She wasn't so bad. Maybe there was just the one. A high-pitched squall had me wincing. I'd never had any luck, why would today be any different?

Before I could back down the path, the little girl stepped up to me and took my hand.

"It's okay. It's just Gus. He cries a lot because he has a toof that won't come in. Drools a lot too." The loud whisper shouldn't have been adorable, but it was.

"Is that right?"

"Yeah, he's chewing on everything. It's 'esgusting. Misty, our cat, won't come out from under my bed."

"I wouldn't either, kid."

She laughed. "You're funny. I like your voice too. It's so…different."

Smoking like an asshole through the better part of my teens and early twenties had deepened my already husky voice. "Different is good, right?"

"Yeah!" She dragged me behind her as she headed for the backyard.

"Mom! We have a vis—vis…" She glanced back at me with a furrowed brow.

"Visitor?"

"Right. That. Visitor!"

Bethany and a slightly harassed looking brunette were on the deck. Three other women were sitting at the table with Brewed Awakening cups scattered around with a bakery box from Vee's part of the café.

They didn't seem to care about my appearance in the least. Then again, their attention had zeroed in on a certain long-haired construction worker.

Lucky had lost his plaid shirt, leaving his shoulders glistening with exertion. A white ribbed tank stretched across his back, smeared with dirt and cement debris. His arms were a grid of flexing muscles as he used the hand-mixer in a large white bucket.

His hair was up in a messy man-bun with his aviator sunglasses perched on the blade of his sharp nose. A red bandana was wrapped around one wrist and a leather cuff draped over the other.

He was outrageously fit. I had to fight not to do some staring of my own.

Make that a *lot* of staring.

My first instinct was to head for the gate and jump on my bike. I could totally find another builder. Maybe even hire Gideon without Lucky.

I definitely shouldn't have come.

But then he switched the mixer off and turned to put it on the flatbed cart with his tools. The cart was splattered with old cement and his discarded red plaid shirt fluttered in the breeze like a flag.

He spotted me and put his sunglasses on top of his head. His gaze skimmed down my body without a single hint of remorse. His mouth went from a grinning slash to a wide smile. His eyetooth was slightly crooked, and I had the most ridiculous urge to lick it.

Where the hell had that come from?

Maybe escape really was the answer.

Possibly a lobotomy.

He hauled a large piece of wood off the pile on his cart and muscles I didn't know the name of shifted under his bronzed skin. Objectification station had one more gawking female.

Checking him out was one thing. That was natural, and hell, it had been a damn long time since I'd even looked up from my fabricator. I was human, after all. Much to my consternation sometimes.

But Lucky Roberts was definitely not going to be added to my already full slate of complications.

Look but don't lick was officially my new motto.

THREE

Lucky

I HADN'T SEEN MY REDHEADED VALKYRIE IN A DAMN LONG TIME. SHE'D been playing hide and seek with me since we'd made our pact during the insanity that was Caleb and Luna's engagement.

Well, more hiding than seeking in my damned opinion.

I'd barely seen her since that afternoon in September. I was hella disappointed that she hadn't taken me up on the favor she'd threatened me with. Now that my best friend was on easy street with his girl, Luna, I'd been bored as fuck.

Gideon was ready to sell me on Facebook marketplace because I wouldn't stop bugging him for jobs to keep me busy. Luckily, we usually had more work than men to cover, but I was pretty sure he was down to giving me the shit jobs until a few bigger ones came up in the schedule.

Problem was, I didn't like to spend the night alone. Add in the endless weekends and I was going nuts.

Of course I could've sought out some company of a personal nature. I wasn't exactly hard up for dates. I just didn't seem to want any.

It wasn't as if my flagpole wouldn't raise anymore. No, sir, it was fully operational. The mental side of things was what was slowing me up. I had gotten pretty particular lately.

Hell if I knew why. Or would admit it, which was almost the same thing in Lucky land.

Deny, deny, deny.

So, I worked. I told Gideon I'd take anything—even the jobs with back-breaking physical labor. Like this job in cookie-cutter nation, Cove Gardens. Putting a fence up on my own was doable, but it wasn't ideal. A bevy of MILFs watching me didn't suck though.

I didn't poach on married ladies. Even I had some limits when it came to women, but I didn't mind showing off for them. Their excuses for stopping by were getting more interesting. Most of them included baked goods and the occasional apple-laden treats or spiked cider, which was my personal fave. Kimmie was usually exasperated, but I was pretty sure she enjoyed the adult conversation. Her day consisted of a kid strapped to her chest and the little blond devil child twirling around the yard. Abby, the devil, asked many, *many* questions about my process.

Pretty sure Kimmie was glad to unload question time to me for a few hours. As long as the kid stayed behind the big pink chalk line I'd sprayed in the grass, I was cool with it. I figured it was good practice for when my goddaughter or godson showed up.

Caleb had promised me I was first in line to be the kid's godfather. Which was a rather official and scary title but I intended to use it as cred all over town.

At least I had before the psycho chick at The Mason Jar had slowed my roll and I'd gotten super selective when it came to the dating scene. I wasn't sure which sucked more.

I was usually proud of my easy standards. I looked at it as a Lucky loves the ladies benevolence program.

Now it was more Lucky loves his right hand.

Tish was in Abby's line of fire right now. She was circling her like a shark. I couldn't hear the questions, but her little bow mouth was flapping so I was sure there were a lot of them. Kimmie kept trying to corral her, but the kid would not be deterred.

Kimmie gave up and ate a brownie from today's bounty. I wondered if they were the macadamia nut ones Mrs. Jones made last time.

Absently, I rubbed my belly. I'd definitely been working up an appetite.

Maybe I could get the Valkyrie to go to dinner with me. All friendly like.

I could have female friends. It was doable, right?

Maybe.

My shoulders hunched at the squawking shriek coming from the deck. I spun around fast enough that the bucket of cement splattered upward, dousing the front of my jeans. "Awesome," I muttered.

I glanced back at the women and found Tish smirking at me. Her hands were on her hips, showing off the delicious line of her leather-clad legs. Goddamn, she was magnificent. I was no poet, but her hair was that kind of red that made a man think of black silk sheets.

I didn't have silk sheets, but I'd damn well get them if she deemed me worthy of a tumble.

A *friendly* tumble.

Another shriek of mom voice broke my little daydream. I shoved a rogue curl back into the knot of hair on top of my head. Some days cutting off my hair seemed like a good idea, but then again, it was my best feature according to the ladies—so, it always stayed.

Kimmie was running around the table up on her porch. I couldn't hear what she was screaming about, but I had a feeling the kid was to blame since she was trying to hide behind Tish.

And honestly, what kind of grown woman still called herself Kimmie? It reminded me of a doll covered in pink sparkles—which I only knew about because of the baby boom in this town. I couldn't count the number of times I'd had to go buy a gift card for baby shit.

In the end, I wasn't the one who had to shout "oh, Kimmie" out in the middle of the night. Nope. Her dude had that honor. And since she was knocked up again, I was pretty sure the Crescent Cove water was working way out here in the burbs too.

I couldn't imagine having two under the age of drool. Hell, I couldn't imagine *any* in my life. I liked the practice rounds of making a kid, not the reality.

Tish's exasperated face as Abby interrogated her made me laugh. She was one woman I'd like to practice on—to infinity. Even if she usually looked at me as if I was a bug on the bottom of her badass boots.

Not that I had time to think about that right now. I was losing time on the mix and didn't want to waste it. Gideon would kick my ass if I had to order more for this job. I hauled the five-gallon bucket of cement to the next post in the lineup.

I glanced over my shoulder one more time. Just what was Tish doing at my job site? Hopefully, she'd hang out until I was finished enough to take a break.

The quick set cement needed to be poured so it could cure overnight and I could come back to put in the rest of the slats. I didn't have a lot of wiggle room to go over and see what was up.

However, I wasn't above using some extra attraction points. I set down the pail, yanked out my hair tie, and let my hair tumble over my shoulders. I could hear the sighs from the moms on the porch. They really liked when I did that. Tish didn't seem as impressed.

Ah, to heck with the friends crap. What would it take to get her to see me as bangable material? I could not get a read on that woman. Generally, I didn't have this much trouble with the opposite sex. Becoming choosy didn't mean I still didn't have skills.

Just not with her.

I scooped up my hair on top of my head and quickly fastened my frayed hair tie around the curly mess. I realized not everyone was my catnip and vice versa, but I knew there was something between us. Especially since she was extra surly when we did see one another. And not in the I'm-going-to-serve-you-a-restraining-order kind of way.

I figured if we got naked then maybe things would ease up. As it was, I was spending any of my extra money in Brewed Awakening, hoping for a glimpse of her.

She and Macy seemed to have a semi-friendship. At least when it came to coffee and food, they gave each other the same kind of grief that Caleb and I did. Back when I used to get to spend time with Caleb anyway. The wedding was in two months, and the only thing he and Luna ever wanted from me was to build shit or to nag me about getting fitted for my tux.

I really missed having a beer with my bro.

With a sigh, I lifted my sledgehammer and slammed the post into place with more force than was necessary. But then I heard the new blond lady give a clutching pearls sigh and decided it was worth it. Even if Tish seemed to be bored with the whole deal.

What the hell was she doing here? This didn't seem like her scene at all.

I poured another bit of Quikrete over the post and measured to make sure it was centered correctly. I had five more to do, but I'd have to mix up some more since it set so fast. Maybe I could even get some more of that amazing lemonade Kimmie made.

I dropped my hammer and stepped around the bucket when I heard a small whimper. The weeds and brush at the edge of the lawn were one of the reasons the Olsens had contacted us. They were afraid of ticks and all manner of wildlife beyond their property line.

Another housing development was also in progress and the devil was a curious sort. Crescent Cove was a booming area for families. Maitland Enterprises was making a killing all over town, even out here in the burbs. This was a new developer though, which I was happy to see. FHK Property Group. Never heard of them.

Whimpers turned into a pathetic whine. I frowned and crouched down. Two little sad brown eyes glowed from the underbrush. A little snout was half hidden in leaves and mud.

"Hey, buddy." I dug out my phone and turned on the torch light.

The little bundle of fur scrabbled back, and the wet cardboard box collapsed around him. Frightened, he—*it*—tried to get its face free, but its little mouth was tied shut by a piece of dirty clothesline rope.

"What the fuck?"

"Language!" Kimmie shouted from the deck.

I ignored her and crouched lower. My shoulders wouldn't fit under the small space. Branches snapped and a thorn sliced along my neck. My fingers were shaking with anger, but I kept shoving my way in. I blew out a slow breath and forced my voice to gentle. I fisted my fingers for a moment to get them to stop shaking. "It's okay, I'm not gonna hurt you."

Humans were pieces of shit. How long had the little dog been tied under there? The cardboard box was degrading in the perpetual wet of fall. The dog was filthy. Last night had been cold as hell, and the ground was boggy with moisture.

I tried not to flash the light in his eyes, but I needed it to see. The rope had dug into his fur, and his eyes were fierce and fearful. I gentled my voice and flattened myself on the ground. Dirt, leaves, and God knows what else stuck to my beard. I spit it out and sent up a silent prayer it wasn't shit.

The little guy flinched. Slowly, I reached under the mangled bush to get closer. The rope was tied to the trunk so the small dog couldn't get away.

Whomever had tied the dog here had left it to die.

My muscles locked with anger, but I forced my voice to stay soothing. The little guy seemed to know I was upset and couldn't decide if I was friend or foe. Finally, I got to his tiny foot and I lightly stroked it with one finger. The dog was shuddering, but couldn't pant since its poor mouth was tied shut.

"Everything okay?"

My skin prickled at the sound of *her* voice. Now was not the time for that, but my dick had an auto-response to this woman. All hard, all the time.

"Someone tied a little dog to the underbrush."

"What?" She pressed her hand to my lower back and crouched down beside me. "You're kidding."

She smelled spicy. Like cinnamon and leather and fabric softener all wrapped up in a sexy package. I hadn't been this close to her before. Then her hair slid along my shoulder and my dick decided muddy leaves were a just fine spot for a seduction. "Nope. Hey, it's pretty gross down here. Dirty and—"

"I'm a mechanic and metal worker, Thor. I can handle some mud."

I twisted my shoulder enough to get a look at her. "Goddamn, you are so hot."

She rolled her eyes. "Dog?"

"Right. Sorry." I inched to the side to give her some room and the little dog jumped, then tried to scrabble back, but he was out of options.

"Careful."

"I know," I growled. "He's tied."

"How do you know it's a he?"

Exasperation dented my lust haze. "I'll let you know when I get it untied, how's that?"

"Touchy."

I could not get any closer to the little guy. I winced as thorns dug into my arm.

She let out an exasperated huff. "Can I help? My arms are skinnier."

"Not in that jacket, they aren't."

"I can take it off." She dropped onto her hip on the ground beside me.

"I think I'm good. Can you get my knife out of my holster?"

"Holster? Seriously?"

I tried to relax as the pup shook uncontrollably. "It's sharp. Would you rather I sliced open my leg every time I bent down?"

"Good point." Her long fingers slid along my belt then grazed my skin. "Where the hell is it?"

"Other side." My voice lowered and I focused on the little dude in front of me, not the fact that my dream woman was in my space for the first time.

She grunted and leaned over me. Her scent was gonna end me. I wanted it all over my skin. And then there was her hair. It was dripping all over my shoulders and tickling my sides. Her fingernails skimmed over my lower belly and I nearly groaned.

"You're killing me here."

"I can't find the snap. There it is. Oh…" She cleared her throat. "I got it."

31

She tried not to touch me, but our closeness made that impossible. Her curtain of glorious, soft, fistable hair draped over me. I really wanted to revisit this scenario very soon.

Preferably without our clothes and the mud. Though that might work in an entirely different fantasy...

Focus on the trapped dog, Roberts.

She finally collapsed next to me. "Okay, got it."

She nearly sliced my arm, but my quick reflexes left leaves as the only fatality. "Watch it."

"Kinda a cramped situation here."

"Yeah. More cramped for this little guy." I hacked at the branches to make more space. "So what are you doing here anyway?"

She leaned against me to see what I was doing. "You should cut over there."

"Thanks, Captain Obvious."

"Dick."

"Language," I mumbled.

"You too?"

I grunted and broke off another branch. "Kimmie is a drill sergeant."

"I'm getting that."

"So?"

"So what?"

"Why are you down here in the mud with me?" I hissed as a thorn sunk into the side of my hand. "Bastard."

"Language."

"Jerk."

"Bitch."

Her immediate reply made me turn toward her. "Sexiest woman in the Cove and watches *Supernatural?* We should get married."

"Not in this lifetime."

I grinned and went back to work. "Did you come here looking for me? Or are you friends with the mom squad?"

"Dear God, no."

I huffed out a laugh. "Are you finally calling in your chip?"

"Yes. I talked to Gideon, and he told me where to find you."

"I'll have to buy him a case of beer."

"He says you owed him money."

The other guys on Gideon's crew were tired of me winning at poker and had gotten me shitfaced at the last guys' night. They couldn't handle my natural aptitude. "Fucking cheaters."

"Language!" Came a chorus of voices just behind us.

I turned to look at Tish and her face was way too close to mine. More of that cinnamon goodness came from her dark red mouth. Her deep brown eyes were intense and damn if they didn't dilate a bit. Maybe it truly wasn't one-sided on this attraction thing after all.

The dog let out a pathetic growl, dragging me back to the reason I was laying facedown in the mud. I flicked my very sharp knife through the cord tied to the trunk and dragged the little guy close enough for me to scoop up before he could disappear into the thornier tangle of brush.

I lowered my voice to a rumbly whisper. "Hey, there. You're okay now."

"What's going on?"

I glanced over my shoulder to find Kimmie and the herd of moms hovering just behind the pink line in the grass. Abby was practically vibrating with the need to get closer.

I wiggled out from the mud onto my knees. "It's okay. Someone tied a poor dog to one of the bushes."

"Are you kidding?"

"Who could do that?"

"I'm going to make flyers to find its owner!"

The women were ready to be suburban warriors for the dog, but I was pretty sure no one would be looking to collect the shaking bit of muddy fluff.

I caught Abby's eye. "Could you go get me a towel?"

The little girl's eyes nearly popped out of her head as she nodded excitedly and took off.

I turned to help up Tish, but she was already on her feet, brushing debris off her leather motorcycle pants. She paid special attention to her hips and ass, which made my tongue about two sizes too big for my mouth. For once in my life, I opted for silence.

I struggled to my feet, cradling the dog in the crook of my arm. Tish gripped my upper arm to balance me, her short black nails digging into my skin. Our gazes collided before hers slid away, and she took two big steps back.

Abby came running back with a huge beach towel in her hand imprinted with a grinning Harry Styles.

"Your sister is going to kill you," Kimmie said with a sigh.

Abby shrugged and held up her phone, video obviously engaged. "Harry will save the puppy. Melly can put it on TikTok later."

I should have thought of that, but the animal was way more important than a viral video. Even though I was pretty sure this would definitely provide a million clicks minimum.

I took the towel and wrapped it around the shaking dog. He was matted with mud and leaves and I didn't even want to think about the fleas or insects. The tiny dog burrowed into the crook of my arm and rested its tiny snoot on my forearm.

"Sweet baby," Tish cooed.

My eyebrow rose.

"What?" She wrinkled her nose.

"Nothing."

She crossed her arms over her spectacular chest. "Animals are better than people nine times out of ten."

"Can't fault you there." I tucked the blanket more securely around the little bundle of near bones. "I want to get this rope off his mouth."

She chewed on the corner of her lower lip. "Maybe we should take him to the vet. It looks pretty dug in there."

I frowned. "Yeah, maybe you're right."

"The clinic isn't too far away."

I gave her another arched eyebrow.

"What? I have a cat. They were nice to me. The vet there is super capable. Hot too."

My jaw clenched.

Her lips twitched. "Anyway, I guess we should bring in the dog."

"You're coming with me?"

The ladies were watching our conversation as if we were the Wimbledon playoffs, their gazes bouncing back and forth between us.

She jammed her hands into her jacket pockets. "Well, you need someone to hold him, right? Or I can drive and you can hold him —*her*. Whatever."

I dug my keys out of my pocket and tossed them to her. She had quick reflexes—even snatched the keychain out of the air without a fumble. "Since you know where the clinic is, I guess you're up. Unless you can't drive stick."

"I've been driving stick since I was eleven." She grabbed my shirt off the cart and handed it to me. "Let's just go."

"Need me to cover up?"

Her dark eyes went shark flat. "No. You're a muddy mess, jerk. I'm saving your upholstery."

"Right." I wasn't sure why her smart mouth made her even more attractive to me. I did have a twisted side when it came to strong women.

She stalked away from me, her exceptional ass swinging with each long stride.

"I'm probably going to marry her." I wasn't sure why that flew out of my mouth again. I definitely wasn't going to marry her. I did want to get under those leather pants though.

The new blond that joined the party clutched her hands together under her chin. "It's like a book I just read."

The dog snuggled into the towel and stopped shaking for the first time. My heart did a little somersault. I stroked his little nose, careful not to touch anything that was bleeding. "So, did it have any juicy parts?"

The blond nodded and smiled. "Lots of them."

"You chicks always get the good books."

"You should try romance novels. They might even make you blush, Mr. Handyman."

I laughed as I swayed with the small bundle in my arms. "Name's Lucky."

35

"Bethany." She reached out and touched my arm, then snatched her hand back. "Sorry, I don't know what got into me. I've never seen an arm so muscled in real life."

I flexed a little. "Want another feel?"

She curled her fingers into her hand. "No. Well, maybe just one." She squeezed my biceps and gave a twittering laugh. "Wow."

"Move it, Thor!"

My gaze tracked to the gate I'd finished putting in yesterday. Tish held her head high and her warrior princess hair whipped on the breeze. I took another moment to admire her head to toe leather with a red racing stripe down one arm and leg.

Damn, what a woman. Maybe I *would* be marrying her.

FOUR

How the hell I'd ended up driving Lucky's battered Ford truck into Kensington Square, I did not know.

Okay, so the pathetic dog had hit me in a weak spot. His face—and Thor's face as he worried over the tiny ball of dirty fur—were too much to handle.

I did not have any defenses against animals. Especially hurt ones.

Thor cooed over the little dog in his lap. He kept stroking its small head, telling him how brave he was. I didn't quite have the heart to tell him I didn't see any itty bitty doggy twig and berries when he pulled it out of the mud.

Then again, there had been a lot of mud.

The little dog preened, even with its poor nose all crusty with blood and dirt. The tiny tail stuck out of the towel and wagged with each rumbling tumble of Lucky's stream of conscious conversation.

"I think I should call him Butch."

"Butch? Dear God, why?"

"Well, he's—"

"Might be a she."

Lucky hunched his shoulders protectively. "Whatever. It doesn't matter. The little guy is Butch. Look how brave you are." Lucky lowered his nose to the dog's. "You're a brave little guy, aren't you?"

The dog was a maximum of six pounds—mostly fur.

"Couldn't find a better name for him or her? Like Athena the warrior dog? Or how about Xena?"

He picked up the dog, towel and all, to look at it in the eye. "Nah. Butch."

I rolled my eyes and downshifted as we came to a light. Kensington Square wasn't far from suburbia nation. The clinic was barely out of the Cove and with the boom of families, it did very well, good enough to be open around the clock. It was almost noon and I had a bad feeling we'd be doing a whole lot of waiting to be seen.

Based on the dog's situation, I imagined we'd be doing a whole lot of paying too. Not that it mattered. Animals would always win out when it came to my wallet.

"Just a few more minutes."

Lucky snuggled the dog up against his chest. "Getting cold, little buddy? Should I boost the heat?"

"It might be a bit gross, but if you put him against your skin, he'll —" Now he had me calling it a him. "*It* will warm up."

Lucky grinned at me. "Even you think he's a little dude." Without hesitation, he tucked the dog into his tank top.

"I hope it doesn't have fleas."

Lucky stilled, then shrugged. "Guess we'll both get a flea dip, hey?"

My lips twitched, but I managed not to smile.

Lucky gave me some side-eye. "I almost saw a smile."

"You did not."

"I did." He snuggled down in the seat and inched him over to the middle of his chest. "She likes you, buddy." He lowered his voice. "Think she likes me too."

"No."

Lucky snorted.

I shrugged. "The dog, maybe."

He crossed his legs at the ankle. "Then why were you at my worksite?"

"You know why."

"You could have texted."

"I didn't have your number. And I wanted to explain the expedited situation."

"Expedited situation?" One bleached brow rose, and there was an intriguing scar through the arch.

Focus, Burns. There was nothing intriguing about this guy.

"Sounds interesting," he added when I remained silent.

He laced his long fingers together over his little bundle. The smudge of mud striping his cheek was not cute, dammit.

I gritted my teeth together. I would not be swayed by a hot guy with a dog. Nope, not at all. Ever.

Keeping my gaze straight ahead, I turned off the dirt road that always snuck up on me. The clinic was a converted farm with a ton of land, but it was rather remote. A horse was grazing in the fenced off area to the side of the building, his ragged tail twitching happily. Maverick was a rescue from a shitty owner, and the vet, Grant Thorn, had nursed him back to health.

I knew that because when I'd nearly killed Dusty—since the stupid cat loved to lay in the middle of the damn road, and I'd clipped his tail swerving away so I didn't kill him—the vet had been unloading the horse when I rolled up in a panic. Now I was the proud owner of a cat with a slightly crooked tail, and it looked like Maverick was living his best life.

I downshifted to gently roll over the tire ruts from the last good rain. Dirt became gravel the closer we got to the large horse stables. A little girl with a lopsided ponytail was chasing a tripod dog around the opening of one of the bays.

Someone must have been looking out for us since there were only a handful of cars in the parking lot. I parked and the little girl came running over to us.

Penny? P…something.

"Hey, Miss Dusty. Everything okay with your cat?"

Lucky stepped down from the truck.

Priscilla? No…she was a flower name. Poppy! "Hi, Poppy. Dusty is doing really well, but my friend's dog not so much."

"Oh, no." Her huge eyes glittered with tears immediately. She rushed to Lucky, showing absolutely no fear toward the six-foot-four long-haired stranger.

I should probably talk to her dad about that.

Lucky crouched down to the kid's level. "Are you the vet?"

The little girl's tears dissolved away with a giggle. "No. I'm not big enough yet. Someday though. I'm gonna be just like my daddy."

"I'm sure he'll be proud. Think you could find your dad for me? My friend here could use some help." Butch peeked out from the side of his shirt, the end of the rusty red rope frayed from Lucky's knife.

"Oh, no." Poppy's eyes went fierce. "You didn't tie his mouth shut, did you? We don't use those kinds of muzzles, sir!"

"No. Not at all. We found him like this. It looks really painful though. We want to get him all fixed up."

I resisted the urge to rub my chest. My heart was doing funny twirls and I really didn't like it.

"I'll go get my daddy. He's having a tuna sammich, but I'm sure he'll stop his lunch for your doggie." She tipped her head and lifted a corner of the towel snaking out of Lucky's shirt. "Is that Harry Styles?"

"Harry is taking good care of Butch, yes."

Poppy giggled. "You're funny. Okay, I'll be right back."

Lucky glanced up at me. "Cute kid."

I swallowed. "Yeah, she is." I cleared my throat. "Anyway, let's go in. Dr. Thorn is a bit different, but he's a damn good vet."

"Hot too, right?"

I flushed and stalked past him. "Yeah, well, I have eyes. It was just an observation."

A huge white sign hung next to the black door. Thorny Paw Clinic was open rain or shine, day or night. It had a few block sliders to say which vet or vets were on the premises. I was relieved to see Grant's name there.

It was a rotating roster, but I knew Grant Thorn did good work. I opened the door for Lucky and resisted the urge to roll my eyes at the guy behind the desk.

Snooty Steve was manning the desk today. Great.

"Hi, we have an emergency."

He didn't even look up when we walked in. "Everyone has an emergency. We're a clinic."

I curled my fingers into my palm, hiding it beneath the half wall that divided the small vestibule.

Lucky came up behind me, his cedar scent with a side of dog curling around me followed by a wall of warmth. A cool fall day had nothing on his ability to pump out a disturbing level of heat from the furnace of his upper body. He wasn't even wearing a coat, for God's sake.

"I have a hurt dog we found tied to a bush. It's an emergency."

Steve's gaze tracked up and his bored face cleared to attentive. "Right. Fill this out and I'll go check with Dr. Thorn."

I glanced over my shoulder at Lucky. "I had it."

Butch peeked out from Lucky's jacket, a little snaggle tooth peeking out from the dirt caked on him. Dammit, he was so sweet even with that damn rope around his face. I gently stroked his nose. "Dr. Thorn will fix you right up, buddy."

Lucky angled down to look at me, his voice still rumbly. "I've never seen you so soft, Ruby."

I frowned up at him. "Did you hurt your head?"

His eyebrow rose in question.

"Ruby?"

"Hair, racing stripe, helmet on your bike. Rich, dark ruby red." His lids lowered to half mast over those dark green eyes of his. "Ruby."

"Tish," I reminded him.

"More of a Ruby to me."

I didn't have time for his nonsense. "Anyway, it's a defenseless dog. I'm not an asshole."

His lips kicked up at one corner, showing that slightly crooked incisor. He matched the dog. I refused to find that endearing. "I really like when you're grumpy."

"You're weird."

"The doctor will see you. Janice will show you to stall three."

I stepped back and spun, almost taking Janice out. "Sorry." I flipped my hair over my shoulder. "Which way?"

Janice blinked and took me in, then Lucky behind me. Being female and almost six feet tall was definitely not something I could forget. But it wasn't often that a guy was taller than me to the extent Lucky was. The tech was barely over five feet tall. We probably looked like freakish giants—with a teacup-sized dog.

How was this my life?

Janice hugged the iPad against her chest. "Right. Um, this way, please."

We headed past the waiting room as a few grumbling patients watched us walk by and down a hallway into the repurposed barn. Instead of horses, the large stalls were sectioned off with old sliding barn doors on glossy black rollers. Each door was a different color. A well used chalkboard hung from a nail in the center of each door and gave quick stats about the pet's name and breed.

The first door was dark red with Larry the Macaw scrawled in chalk. The next was a whitewashed natural color with Baxter the Collie chilling inside, and the last one was navy with a blank chalkboard waiting for our details. Yellow caution signs signaled a freshly scrubbed cement floor. The sharp scent of bleach couldn't quite cut the scent of many different animals even with the front and back of the barn open to give a cross-breeze. There was only so much the crisp fall day could do to clear the air with animals in various stages of fear or injury.

The yip of a dog followed by a chorus of responding canines echoed through the barn. The back of the clinic was also a boarding and adoption center. Grant had a big heart when it came to getting animals taken care of.

I might have donated a chunk of money to his vet practice. It was a good write-off for the business, and did I mention I was a sucker for animals?

Poppy came ripping around the corner. Her ponytail was a tad higher, but that was probably more out of annoyance than from help from a brush. Dr. Thorn brought up the rear mostly because his daughter was dragging him along. His white lab coat flew behind him over his typical faded black thermal shirt, jeans, and sturdy boots.

The three times I'd been in for Dusty he'd been wearing something similar each time.

He gave us a harried smile. "Poppy tells me we have a special case. Nice to see you again, Tish." The lilt of Ireland teased like the breeze. There, but not at the same time.

"I wish it was under better circumstances."

"Me too."

Lucky stiffened behind me. I wasn't sure if that was his little growl or one of the dogs in the kennel. Considering the sound seemed awfully close, I chose to go with ignorance.

Grant's dark hair fell forward as he gave me a rueful smile before tugging on his daughter's ponytail. "Why don't you go help Janice set up so we can take a look at our patient?"

"Okay." Poppy dashed off to door number three.

"What have we got?"

Lucky stepped around me, then peeled back a corner of the towel to reveal Butch and his predicament.

The vet hissed in sympathy before muttering something under his breath. Lucky was blocking me so I couldn't hear exactly what he said, but I could infer. Grant's personality bordered on a miracle in patience, but he definitely wasn't happy.

"I was putting in a fence for a family in Cove Garden and found him tied to the trunk of one of the bushes."

"Bastards." His Irish was thick and sharp.

"Think you can help him?" Lucky's voice was rough with more gravel than I was used to hearing out of him. "I just want to get that rope off him. Ruby said we should do the vet thing instead of doing it ourselves."

I crossed my eyes at his broad back. Honestly? Not my name. I clenched my fists inside my jacket pockets.

"Glad that you came here first. Looks like it's pretty dug in there. We'll do what we can to get him...?"

Lucky nodded.

I peeked around him. "We're not sure if it's a girl or boy."

Grant gently stroked the dog's head. "Either way, we'll get you all fixed up." He glanced up at Lucky. "I'll need to give him or her a bath to see what's what. There's a farm sink in there we can use. Might need your help since we're pretty booked at the moment."

Lucky nodded. "Just tell me what to do and where to go."

"Good." The vet nodded decisively. "Let's do this."

The next forty minutes revealed that Butch was, in fact, a girl, and was actually a creamy white color under all the mud and muck. I felt very unnecessary and chose to stay out of the way along the one wall.

Poppy came up beside me and held my hand. "My daddy is very good at this."

I frowned down at the little girl. "I know. Why we're here, sprite."

She shrugged. "You looked worried."

I dropped my shoulders and ordered my muscles to loosen and relax. "Thanks, kid."

"Welcome," she said brightly. But I let her keep holding my hand. She seemed to need it.

Okay, I needed it. I went on my toes, but I couldn't see over the shoulders of the two males. The dog was not thrilled with the situation and let them know it with pitiful cries. Poor thing probably had never seen a bath in her life.

Lucky was endlessly patient and focused as they both slowly washed her matted fur. Once they got most of the dirt off, Grant started the equally painstaking process of removing the rope.

Butch wasn't having any of that. Grant had to send his daughter out of the room because she was getting so upset by the dog's whines. I wasn't faring much better, but that stupid piece of rope needed to come off. I peeled off my jacket and waded into the fray.

I had strong hands and stopped her flailing back legs. Grant's ever soothing voice finally dented the terror in the dog's little body. He was speaking a language I didn't know, but the rolling sounds seemed to do the trick to calm Butch down.

However, we were all soaked by the end of it.

Her terrified whine would sit with me for a damn long time. Fucking humans. I was far better with machines and animals.

The raw welt around her little nose had me dabbing at my eyes. Lucky gave me a fierce look, but there was definitely some red rimming his green eyes as well.

"There's a lass. I know, we're almost done, I promise." Grant finally straightened, cracking his neck as he stretched. "All in all, she's in good shape. It's a bit cold for fleas, so she was saved from that, though I won't know about the ticks until we get her blood panel back."

Lucky sniffed and gathered her close in a fresh towel. Harry was fairly destroyed, but I tucked the pop star towel in a plastic bag the tech laid out. Butch seemed to freak out when I tried to throw it away.

Her tiny black nose poked out of the towel, but she only had eyes for Lucky.

"Looks like you've got yourself a dog, Mr. Roberts."

"Lucky."

"Yes, you are."

Lucky laughed. "No, that's my name." He gave a choked laugh and sniffed. "But I think I'm pretty lucky too."

"Not even a second thought? I would be disappointed of course, but I could find her a home."

Lucky settled her closer into the crook of his arm. "Nope. Butch is mine."

I shook my head as I used one of the towels Janice offered to dry off my shirt—not that it really helped. "Still going with Butch? Not Xena? Come on."

He shook his head. "You like Butch, right?" The little dog wiggled in his arms and popped her head out to lick his face. "See?"

Grant tapped something into his iPad. "Butch Roberts it is. I'm just going to give her the shots she's probably never had and you'll need to put this cream on her nose three times a day. It'll take some time for her fur to grow back, but as long as you keep her nose clean, she'll be in good shape."

Lucky gently lifted her out of the towel and up to his eye level. "Any idea what she is?"

"She's a bit of a mutt, but I'm pretty sure there's some Pekinese and Chinese street dog in there. Not sure how she ended up over here, but there's a lot of illegal dog breeding in every corner of the world." He took the dog back from Lucky.

Butch wasn't thrilled. She squirmed until she could see Lucky. I was pretty sure there were little hearts bubbling around her head. Lucky stroked his big ol' finger down her paw as the vet quickly gave her shots. The dog didn't even notice—she was too busy mooning over her new dad.

When Grant stepped back, Butch leaped off the table and Lucky caught her like a football. She was still wet and squirmy, but she quickly scrabbled her way up to press her small face against Lucky's.

I laughed. "Looks like you have a new bit of Velcro in your life."

Lucky grinned and perched her on his shoulder. Butch decided that was almost as good. She curled up there and stuffed her little face into his hair.

"Don't think you have to worry about her running away."

"I forgot to check if she was chipped." A loud buzz came from Grant's belt. He lifted his phone and glanced at the notification. "Shoot. Another emergency. Bring her back in about ten days?" He tapped on the iPad. "Have the front scan her to see if she has a chip. If not, we'll take care of that next visit."

Lucky nodded. "Sounds good. Anything I should watch for?"

"Dogs have a higher temperature than humans so if she feels a little warm, that's okay. But if she is panting a lot and feels super warm, give me a call. She might have an infection. I'm writing a script for a general antibiotic that should cover the usual suspects. I'll check the bloodwork after my next patient and contact you if there's anything out of the ordinary."

"Thanks, doc." Lucky held his hand out. "I'm grateful."

Grant shook his firmly. "Best kind of client." He waved at Butch. "Take care of your new dad."

"She will." Lucky nuzzled the dog.

"Wow, you are sunk," I muttered.

Lucky's cheeks pinked up. "She's sweet and just needs love."

"Kinda cute, Thor."

Lucky's eyebrows waggled. "I know."

The large barn door squealed on the rollers as the tech stuck her head in, interrupting my epic eye-roll. "They need you doctor."

"Right. Okay, Janice will check you out." He turned his attention to his assistant. "Check if the dog has a chip too, please."

"Yes, Doctor."

Then he was gone.

Lucky followed Janice out, his crooning voice full of soothing words for his charge.

I gathered up the bags and meds, following behind him like some idiot girlfriend. He moved like his nickname suggested. For once, I had to trot to catch up with them. I overheard Lucky asking if they did payment arrangements in a low tone.

My eyes burned again.

How many times had I needed to ask that same thing in my life? Living paycheck to paycheck was more commonplace than not. And as I'd recently paid an emergency fee myself, I knew it was going to be cringeworthy.

A chorus of barks and howling cat screeches met us as we came around the corner. An orange and black cat was zipping all around the waiting room, leaping from the table to the turtle enclosure, its back arched, teeth bared. A black puppy in the Labrador family was happily chasing the cat from surface to surface.

The turtle enclosure was a Plexiglass tank, but oversized puppy feet jumping up against it were no match for gravity. It slid off the large farmhouse end table and crashed to the floor.

Turtle dude went onto its back, flapping his feet wildly as the puppy changed from the cat chase to a whole new point of interest.

The dog licked the turtle's face exuberantly as its owner tried to drag him away.

The door to a cat carrier was wide open and the cat flew back inside. I was pretty sure that was the only time a cat had actually willingly gone into a carrier. The puppy gave a happy bark and tried to climb in with it.

Janice ran forward with Steve huffing out an exasperated sigh before slowly following. Another dog was curled up under the table on the other side of the room, its nose tucked under its body to make itself smaller.

"Turtle, come out from under there."

Well, that was a fitting name.

A slashing paw must have finally made contact because the black puppy whined and backed out of the carrier batting at its nose. The dog's owner was shrieking uselessly from the sidelines. A smear of blood streaked the floor before the puppy stumbled away from Janice and its owner. The puppy made a beeline for the front door.

Another pet owner was backing through the door, utterly oblivious to the chaos he was walking into.

"Oh, shit." I dropped my bags and jacket, then sprinted toward the door and made a grab for Wiggles, the trouble maker. I managed to scoop him up around the middle since the devil must have slipped his collar. I landed on my butt with a tongue bath across my face for my trouble.

The puppy knocked me onto my back, covering me in kisses and slobber from neck to hairline. "A little help here?"

Steve finally made it over to me and hooked a contraption around the dog's neck. He hauled him off me. "Down, Toby."

I craned my neck to narrow my eyes at Lucky. "Thanks for the help."

Lucky shrugged and cuddled Butch closer. "I had faith in you, Ruby."

I collapsed back on the floor. "I hate you."

He moved closer and peered down at me. "Sure you want to lay on that floor?" He held his hand out and I slapped it away. He tried again as I struggled to my feet.

"I got it."

"Of course you do."

I picked up my things and tried not to think about what had been on the floor. Maybe I'd just burn these leathers, to be safe.

Janice and Steve had restored semi-order to the waiting area, but now everything was backed up time-wise.

I slapped my credit card down before Lucky could ask about payment plans.

"You're not paying for my dog." His voice was tight.

"I'll just take it out of your fees for doing the remodel."

He frowned. "No."

"Look, Thor. This is just easier. You can pay me back if you want or I can just make it part of your remodeling fee."

"My fee is covered for helping Caleb."

"That's a damn big favor for a friend."

"So? I only have one best friend and he's worth it."

My gut churned. I didn't have one of those. I had my brothers, but I'd never really had a best friend. Gage and Dare came close, but they felt more like another set of brothers. I was surrounded by them, for God's sake.

"Whatever. It's just easier. And the dog is worth it too."

Lucky huffed out a growl. "I'll pay you back."

"Fine." I slid the card closer to Janice. "Ring it up. Oh, and Grant wants us—Lucky—to come back in ten days. Could you make him an appointment?"

"Sure thing."

The little dog was now *his* problem. I had enough of my own.

FIVE

Lucky

Surprisingly, I didn't even try to take my keys back from Ruby. I just got back into the passenger seat.

I could count the number of times someone other than me had driven my truck on one hand. Not that it was surprising she'd be the one. She was magnificent. All that red hair had been scraped back with a rubber band she'd stolen from the checkout counter. It made her angular face even more arresting. She'd stalked to the truck without even a second thought about having me drive.

Some guys would be offended, but a strong woman always got my dick heading for the happy land of paradise. Probably because I'd learned over the years that women were just as capable as men, if not more so. Ruby had *capable* stamped all over her in freckles.

The conversation back into town was nonexistent. She handled the truck like she did everything else—assertively. It was late afternoon and I really needed to get back to the site and clean up.

I'd left everything where it lay after I found Butch. The oily discomfort hit me squarely in the gut. I knew most people saw me as a good time guy without responsibilities, but over the last few years working for Gideon, I'd found my place. I was dependable when it counted. And the job site was one place I could be counted on.

I dug out my phone and found a few texts from Gideon. Wincing, I texted back that I'd take care of what I'd left behind.

But instead of being angry, he just asked about the dog via Kimmie. I grinned at the dog on my lap and snapped a photo to send back to Gideon. Then I told him I'd clean up and finish the job tomorrow.

"You're not posting your new dog, are you?"

I looked up. "That's an idea, but no. I was just checking in with Gideon."

"Oh, right. Yeah, we did kind of just scram."

"Yeah, but it's under control." Sort of. But I didn't need to bother her anymore today. This woman hadn't even thought about saying no to taking care of Butch. From driving to the clinic to paying for her, there had been no hesitation.

"I'll pay you back, by the way."

She didn't take her gaze off the road. "Not a big deal. Just glad it wasn't worse."

"Agreed." The dog was settled in my lap in a shrimp formation, her nose tucked under her fluffy off-white tail. The vet had to shave a few spots that were too matted to clean, but overall, she looked perfect.

Far too perfect to be a street dog, or whatever he'd called her. Chinese street dog? I stroked a finger along her head. "I wonder if dog DNA works the same as humans?"

"Why are you a mutt too, Thor?"

"Probably. I don't really know."

Her gaze whipped to me. "You don't know?" Those expressive brown eyes were questioning, but a bit softer than I was comfortable with.

I shrugged. "Dad was MIA, mom was about the same. I lived with my gram for a little while before I hitched a ride out of town. I was around twelve. Can't really remember. Been on my own ever since."

I hadn't meant to share all that crap. I wasn't ashamed so much as I didn't like the looks I usually got—very close to the one she was giving me. Sorrow and pity were not the emotions I wanted between us.

"I have three brothers and a dad."

"Wow." I couldn't imagine having that much family. "Wait, did you say three?"

The corner of her mouth lifted in that almost smile that made my chest tight. "Yeah. All wildly different." Her affection and exasperation were obvious on her otherwise poker face. "Actually, that's why I came to see you. My family is coming for Christmas, with one of my brothers staying indefinitely."

"I'm assuming this is unplanned?"

"Understatement."

Unused to the passenger seat, I crossed then recrossed my legs. Room was definitely at a premium, and Butch wasn't happy with my constant moving. He kept twirling around in circles to get comfortable. "Okay, so you talked to Gideon?"

She nodded. "Started the paperwork there. I already got some permits, but he's checking to see if I missed anything."

Impressed, I laid my hand over Butch's tiny frame, settling her with a few pats. "Did your homework. Makes my life easier. What are we looking at?"

She downshifted and came to a stop where Lake Street crossed Route 23. "Probably easier if I just show you. Mind if we go to my house?"

"Now?"

"If that's okay."

My to do list had just lengthened. I really needed to get back to my work site, but I owed her—on a number of levels at this point.

Butch popped up since we were stationary and climbed up to poke her nose against the window. I scratched the top of her head. "Want to make a pitstop at Ruby's house?"

Her feather duster of a tail swished excitedly and her whole body vibrated.

"Guess that answers that." I hooked my arm around Butch and settled her back on my lap. Were there dog seats like a kid seat? I'd have to check. "I just need to contact Kimmie and reschedule the end of that job."

Ruby's face scrunched. "Who goes by Kimmie?"

"Right?"

She smiled at me—the full deal. It transformed her serious lines and reminded me that she was actually a few years younger than me. Maybe more than a few. I'd crossed the thirty bridge last summer. The last fun summer I'd had with Caleb and the boys. Now everyone was shackled with kids and rings, sometimes in that order. It sure was for my boy, Caleb.

Now he was asking me to stand up in a monkey suit and give him away. Well, not exactly that but it sure felt like it.

Absently, I tucked Butch up on my shoulder so she could see a bit better. We rounded the bend and a modest farmhouse came out of the fog off the lake. The perpetual gray of Central NY had taken some getting used to when I'd first moved here. Either it was a cloudless sky with perfect lake days or eternal steel gray swollen with rain or snow depending on the righteous mood of Mother Nature.

Crescent Cove had been the first place I'd called home since I was six years old. Gideon had hired me on with his transient summer workers. He was a fair boss. I'd been a fuck-up with no direction. Bumming around the country doing odd jobs and learning trades with each pitstop had been good enough for a damn long time. When I got tired of one scene, I just moved on.

I'd discovered I wasn't much for city living pretty quickly. Those small boxes called apartments always made me feel claustrophobic. Unless it was a tour bus. Then again, I usually wasn't exactly sober by the time I found my bunk during those years.

I was good with my hands and learned fast. I'd built stages, learned how to be a guitar tech on the fly, and built the most unlikely friendships. Touring was backbreaking work made for the young or the hungry. I found building more interesting than the often thankless work of being on the crew.

It had been a lot of fun though.

Butch yipped, dragging me back from memory lane and into the truck. I reached up and scratched her chest. Even with the angry welts on her face, her little tongue was lolling out with happiness. I waved my hand to dispel the doggie breath. "Gotta get you a toothbrush, B."

She agreed with a slathering tongue bath.

Ruby let out a soft laugh and parked. She slid out and her long-legged stride headed for the separate barn.

Damn, she had a great ass.

She turned when she realized I hadn't moved. I was too busy enjoying the view. "Coming?" she called out.

"God, I wish," I muttered and unclipped my seatbelt. I opened the door and Butch leaped off my shoulder, then bounced from my lap to the ground. "Oh, shit."

I should have gotten a damn leash. But instead of heading for the hills, she trotted after Ruby.

I relaxed and jogged after them. Damn woman had legs almost as long as mine. She stood in the doorway with her hands on her hips. I came up behind her and she quickly moved to the side.

"As you can see, it's a blank canvas."

I reached behind my head to grip my neck. Blank canvas? It was a fucking wreck. The rafters looked half rotten and the roof was…not good. There were a few half framed out sections that held rusted farm equipment. An honest to god hoe and rake that belonged in a horror movie hung on the wall. Moldy hay was strewn across the ground with a bale stuffed in the corner from God knew when. The flutter of wings made me wince.

Probably bats.

I glanced at her. "What are you looking for?"

"I was thinking a rec room-style bottom with maybe a bedroom or two. Actually, the more sleeping room, the better. Three brothers, remember?"

"Right."

She twirled lightly with Butch dancing around her heels. "Pool table, a small kitchen kind of deal, beer cooler, electronics, and maybe a pinball machine or two." She put her hands on her waist again. "Those are my first thoughts anyway."

I walked into the musty, dust-filled space and mirrored her stance.

I could see the walls fixed up with some shiplap, which was still a fairly hot commodity these days. A big TV with surround sound, maybe a record player if she was into that kind of retro thing. The roof needed to be replaced for sure, so maybe I could raise it a bit for some extra room.

"What's my budget looking like?" Before I got more grandiose plans going in my mind, I needed to know where my ceiling was. "The bones are great, but I'll need to figure out what the structure looks like." I slapped the post in the center of the room. I could build around it and frame out the entire recreation space fairly easy. "These kinds of barns were built to last, but only when they're properly taken care of."

She tipped her head and gave me a long look. "Huh."

"What?" I turned around and walked back toward her.

"You really do know what you're doing."

I frowned down at her. "Why the hell would you look to hire me if I didn't?"

"I don't know shit about you, buddy. You walked into my shop and bulldozed me into doing you a favor. Who knows what I was going to get in return? Guys talk a good game—like all the time."

I stepped closer to her. "You must be talking to shitty guys, Ruby."

She tipped up her sharp chin to meet my gaze. "We'll see. Come on, I'll make us some coffee, and we can hash out the details."

And then she walked away from me again.

I looked down at my dog. "I hate when she does that, but I sure do like to watch her go."

Butch yipped and followed, leaving me to be the caboose again in our crazy train.

I took another minute to take some photos with my app that gave me a fair assessment of measurements. I'd do a real measure when I brought my equipment.

I made some notes on my phone as I crossed her lawn. It was more crabgrass than anything at this point. I made a few more notes about doing a till and reseeding her for the spring. Not much use doing it now, of course. Her porch needed some help as well. I wasn't sure just how much of a project she was looking for me to do, but I added it to the list of supplies I'd need.

The property was prime, that was for sure. I glanced over my shoulder at the shoreline less than an acre away from her front door. She had a rickety dock at the edge of her property line. If it were me, I'd put a wide dock instead of just a slip. She didn't exactly seem like the boating type, but I bet she'd look damn hot in a bikini, sunning on the dock.

If redheads did that sort of thing.

Hmm. Maybe in her case, it would be more like one of those flowy girly coverups and a huge hat. Either way, I saw it in my head far too easily.

I turned back to her house and paused. Was I supposed to knock?

I scrubbed my palm on my thigh.

"Get in here, Thor."

I sighed and turned the knob. The house practically echoed in its emptiness. I followed Butch's happy barks to her kitchen. It had a retro feel, mostly because I was pretty sure everything was original to the house. There was an olive green 70s stove with fridge accompaniment and the tile was a hideous muddy brown, but the walls were freshly painted in a safe neutral almond color.

It was clean—about the only good thing it had going for it.

I had to duck my head to come in. These old houses weren't made for men well above six feet like myself. The kitchen island was scattered with coffee paraphernalia. An electric kettle was bubbling as she fussed with a fancy pour over setup. I recognized the black cat on the bag of grounds.

"So, what kind of brew do you get from Queen Macy?"

Tish gave me that half smile and turned the bag. It just said Tish in Macy's slashy handwriting. "Who knows? It's just good."

"Won't tell you the secret ingredient, huh?"

"Nope." She started pouring hot water over the top basket. The rich, sharp scent of coffee hit like a hammer and instantly activated my stomach too.

"Got any food? I didn't get to take my lunch."

She nodded to the fridge. "Not sure what you'll find in there, but you're welcome to it." She spun to the cabinets next to the stove for a few mugs.

I had to fold myself in half to peek into her fridge—and found a pizza box from Robbie's with something they'd use for experiments over at Caleb's school. I pulled the box out and set it on the island. "Think we need to order a pizza."

"Why? I have a…" She trailed off when she caught a whiff of the box. "Okay, maybe not. I have to pay extra to get them to deliver out here so it might take a minute."

"I'll chip in."

"Nah." She pulled her phone out of her back pocket. "I'll call it in. Anything you hate?"

"Peppers."

"I just want to change really quick."

I looked down at my mud and cement-splattered jeans and shirt. "Hmm."

She wrinkled her nose. "I might have something of my brother's upstairs you can use."

"I'm good."

"I'll check anyway." And then she disappeared up the stairs off the back of the kitchen.

The coffee was doing a slow drip deal and I needed to distract myself or I'd eat the Formica. I wandered away to check out the rest of the house. Didn't take me long. The rooms echoed, but damn, she had good light.

I took out my phone and started plugging in a few ideas for her living space. I stopped cold when I got to her living room. A seventy-inch television was bolted to the wall and a massive leather sectional was set up with one of those raised coffee table things. A Diet Coke and massive sketchbook sat on the table.

Butch was on the arm of the couch, curled into her shrimp formation and snoozing away. I scratched the top of her head and she sighed before snoring once more.

Nosy as fuck and good with it, I turned the pad so I could see what she'd been working on. It was a series of drawings of the same car. There was one larger drawing shaded with some sort of heavy chalk in matte black with a lighter gray to show off edges and details. The matte black made the powerful car seem even more imposing. I picked it up to get a better look and realized it looked like the Batmobile crossed with something older and classier. There were various smaller drawings around it that emphasized specific details. Headlights with badass lines, wheels with stunning custom rims, and a grill that I could practically hear the growl of a high performance engine through.

"It's a Phantom Rolls I'm doing a custom body for."

I turned toward her voice and gave her a sheepish smile. "Sorry."

"I doubt it."

"It was right there." I set down the sketchbook.

"No big. I'm not precious with my drawings." She tossed me a shirt then tucked her hands into the pockets of an ancient pair of jeans with frayed holes all over. She wore a T-shirt with a zombie Care Bear holding a knife.

"Thanks." I looked down at the shirt. It was a plain navy T-shirt with an aquarium logo. "Yours is cooler."

"If my shirts fit you, I'd cry."

I barked out a laugh.

"Now if you come near my actual prototype sketches, I'll deball you before you can blink."

I cleared my throat. "Good to know."

"Bring the sketchbook. We can use the kitchen island to figure some shit out." She turned to head back to the kitchen, her bare feet silent on the hardwood floors.

I was beginning to think she liked walking away from me.

Before I forgot, I made a note about the floors. They were in good shape and probably just needed a bit of a refinish to bring them back to their former glory. I slipped the pad under my arm then tucked the bottom of the T-shirt in my back pocket.

I followed her into the kitchen and set the sketchbook on the island. She was cleaning up the coffee thing at the sink. I came up beside her. "Think I could clean up a bit?"

"Bathroom is—hey, that way, Thor." Her brown eyes were wide with shock.

I nudged her aside and pulled my tank off. "I just need a little water. You're done, right?"

She turned her face away from my naked chest so fast her ponytail whipped my arm. Damn if I didn't want to wrap all that hair around my fist and give it a little tug.

"What? You have three brothers, right?"

She stumbled into the island before scrambling around the other side.

I grinned over my shoulder. "Problem?"

"No, of course not." She picked up her mug and drank deeply.

I used the inside of the shirt to scrub at my neck. I'd need a shower to get the worst of it off me, but I was used to being dirty. I looked around for the garbage. The shirt was beyond saving.

"Under the sink."

"Right." I quickly washed my hands and my face with the Dawn on the ledge above her sink. Thankfully, there was a roll of paper towels beside me. I turned around and found her staring hard at the ugly Formica.

I hid a smile behind the towel before I threw both away.

"So, what did you have in mind? Just the barn?"

She glanced up then back down.

I had to admit I was surprised she was so nervy. I shoved my arms through the sleeves of the shirt she'd given me and tugged it on. It was tight as fuck and the bottom of the shirt barely hit my buckle. "How big are your brothers?"

She looked up and her pupils dilated. "Obviously not Thor big."

I laughed and fixed my crooked bun. Her gaze slid away again, but not before she checked out my buckle and the little strip of skin that showed. Interesting.

She pulled the sketchbook closer. "Right, well, I had a few ideas. But I know time is now a factor."

I pulled the mug she'd poured for me closer. Something spicy hit my nose before the tang of truly good coffee landed on my tongue. "So, this is what it's like to have Macy like you enough for your own brew?"

"I take it you don't have one?"

I took another gulp. "Nope."

"Maybe someday."

"I helped build her damn Haunt and still didn't get one."

She grinned behind the lip of her mug. "Too bad."

I propped my elbows on the island. "Okay, so what are we doing? And are you ordering furniture for your guests? House seems a bit empty."

"Yeah, I know. I'll put my dad in the upstairs bedroom. I'll need to order a bedroom set."

"We can check out one of the big furniture stores if you want. Unless you want something custom. That could take some time."

"Yeah, I'll look into it." She made a note. "I'm hoping to keep the animals mostly in the barn-slash-rec room."

I raised an eyebrow. "Do they know you call them animals?"

"Definitely."

"Fair enough." I nodded to her. "Tell me your thoughts and then I'll tell you if it's doable."

"I need at least one bedroom on the main floor of the barn. My brother, Cohen, is staying with me for a while. He has a busted leg, so he can't do stairs."

I pulled out my phone again and started making notes. "Okay." My brain quickly started whirling with ideas for the space.

"I mentioned toys. As you can see, I like electronics. My brothers need entertaining, and I figure once they're gone, I can use it as a space for me that isn't a garage."

"Good plan."

We haggled our way around a game plan. I made rough sketches and she redid each and every one. She had a good eye and knew what she wanted, even if she didn't know how to put it all together.

But that was my job.

The pizza came and we demolished it as the sun streamed through the windows. She could eat me slice for slice. She picked all the toppings off with her short dark nails as she talked.

I never wanted to be a piece of pepperoni more in my life.

When the slice was a pockmarked shell of its former glory, she folded it and quickly chomped her way through the remaining dough and cheese.

I fed Butch a few pieces of bacon and sausage in between slices. I flipped the last quarter inch of my crust at my dog and she neatly nipped it out of the air.

"Tell me about Cohen."

Her eyes shuttered and she crossed her arms. "Not much to tell."

Hmm. That was interesting. I didn't have the sibling dynamic to draw from, but she looked defensive. "There has to be something."

She chewed on the corner of her lip. "He's a fireman—smoke jumper, to be exact." Her gaze drifted to the floor where Butch was looking for more scraps. "You know, you shouldn't feed a dog scraps."

"I don't have dog food yet." I tossed Butch another bit of sausage.

"Fair point."

"You don't have to talk about your brother if you don't want to."

"No. I mean, it's fine. I just..." She huffed out a breath. "I haven't seen much of him for a few years."

"And now you have to take care of him?"

She played with the ends of her ponytail. "Yeah. I don't usually have to worry about him. Even with his job being so extreme, Cohen has always been bulletproof. Ezra, my oldest brother, said Cohen wasn't doing great."

I had a feeling there was more to it. Broken bones didn't put that kind of worry in a woman's eyes.

"Okay, so we need to make sure you can distract him, right?"

She straightened and her demeanor changed. "Exactly. He's super active."

"Okay. Is he a music guy or more of an action movies guy?"

"He's a sports guy. But more playing them than watching."

"Hmm." I tapped my pencil on the notepad she'd given me. "Why don't we go look at the barn again before it gets dark?"

She nodded.

I gathered the pile of sketches and followed her into the hall. She grabbed a sweatshirt out of the closet and stuffed her feet into a pair of those ugly shapeless boots women seemed to wear throughout the fall.

She shut the door then looked up at me. "Do you need a jacket?"

I shook my head. "Not until it's twenty degrees out."

"Okay then."

"How long have you lived here?"

"Three months."

My eyebrows shot up. "Decorating not your thing?"

"I keep meaning to, then I get busy at the shop."

"Yeah, I get that. My place is a wreck." More than a wreck. I had a ton of half finished projects going on at my apartment. It was a two-story house with an older couple on the bottom floor. I took care of the maintenance on the property for a bit off the rent.

In my boredom since my best friend had thrown me over for a chick, I'd started a TikTok profile. One of my how-to videos had gone viral, and I was forever chasing the next post that would get hot. I never seemed to get around to finishing the projects. I'd started a pantry, custom cabinets, a microwave stand, and a converted bench in the last three weekends.

I held the door open for the dog. Butch followed us then got distracted by a pile of leaves. Since she didn't seem to wander off so far, I let her have her fun and do her business.

Hashing out a list was my next task. Luckily, I had Gideon's contacts to get supplies, but I needed a better look at what I had to work with.

I grabbed the ladder against one wall.

"What are you going to use that for? It's an empty space."

"Yeah, just want to check a few things."

"Don't hurt yourself. I need to up my insurance before you start working in here."

"You're all heart, Ruby."

"Yeah, well, I've already dealt with one ER today, let's not go for a round two."

I set the ladder against the post at the back of the barn. It was holding up a loft with a lot more junk. "You said you have some guys coming in to do demo tomorrow?"

"Yes. I threw some money at some high school kids. They seemed excited about destruction. I have a dumpster coming tomorrow too."

"Good." I gripped the framing of the loft and gave it a good shake. The only thing that moved was dust. I'd have to do a test in better daylight and make sure it was bug free, but the strong scent of cedar gave me hope.

It wasn't cheap pine and would give me a decent base to build out a few bedrooms for the second floor. It wouldn't be a complete gut job from what I could see.

I hopped down to find the sketches scattered around the floor. She seemed to be lining them up in a certain order. I crouched next to her. "Inspiration?"

"Sort of. I really want to keep it open."

"Looks like we've got a semi-plan. I'll come back and do measurements tomorrow and supervise the guys. It's easier for me to tell them what I need torn out and what can stay."

She nodded. "Sounds good." Her gaze fell to my mouth before bouncing back up to meet my eyes. "Think you could give me a ride to Kimmie's? I need to get my bike."

"Handily, I need to clean up over there, then go dog shopping."

"Gotta get new stuff for the kid—er, dog."

I grinned at her. "Something like that."

She licked her lips, then stood up quickly. "Yeah. I'll just go get my stuff and we can go." And then she was on the run again.

It was going to be an interesting few months.

SIX

I'D PLAYED THE COWARD CARD WITHOUT REMORSE AFTER LUCKY brought me back to his worksite. It had been a damn long day, and I just needed a little time to myself. I'd hopped on my bike and headed to the shop.

The Phantom Rolls Royce at the top of my list was waiting for me in the back bay. I'd been working up the parts I needed to fabricate for weeks now. My client was a tech giant with more money than sense, but I didn't mind taking some of that green off his hands.

Gage was helping me with the remodel. He had a light hand with welding that I'd never quite managed to match. We often worked as a team on the bigger projects. This one was slated for a November finish, and I needed to score some hours on Hilda, my fabricator, to get some pieces done for him.

It was end of the workday for most of our crew. A few new mechanics were doing end of shift paperwork. Gage and Dare were holed up in the office. Dare had his feet kicked up on the desk as he laughed at something his brother said.

I wasn't ready to talk to humans, so I bypassed that side of the garage and sneaked into the locker room to change into my coveralls.

Hilda used a large water bath for the cuts I was doing, and no matter how hard I tried, shit got messy.

I snagged my headphones off the charger and headed into my section. It took a few minutes to boot up Hilda and go through my digital drawings. The Phantom was built like a tank, but the base model my client wanted updated was an older model with pristine guts. Too bad the shell was beat to hell from a hailstorm in Texas.

That was where I came in.

I smoothed my hand over the dented hood. Gage had been busy stripping the car back, which left me wide open to start building her back up.

The precise work of measurements and picking out the right sheets of metal took all my focus and evened out my rough edges. The new Billie Eilish album thundered in my ears as I tore apart metal sheets. My muscles sang with the labor as I created the puzzle pieces that would make up a new and improved vision of the Phantom.

The world and all my problems faded as I fell into the work.

My partners knew not to bother me when I was in this space. The guys had families to go home to anyway. I couldn't count the number of times I'd been left to my own devices at the garage.

And I liked it that way. Most of the time.

I shook off the twinge. My job kept me busy and fulfilled. Families and sticky fingers and having to cater to a male weren't what I was about.

Arching my back to work out the kinks, I turned my head and a photo of Gage with Rylee and their little girl caught my attention.

The girl's dark hair was in pigtails and her face was covered in white and pink frosting. Gage had one half of his face covered and Rylee the other as their daughter smushed between their cheeks.

They were a pretty cute family.

I shifted away from the wall of photos. Still wasn't in my plans. Someday I wanted a family—maybe. I still wasn't too keen on the idea of it. It seemed like a damn lot of juggling based on the conversations I heard in the garage.

A glance at the time on my phone made me wince. If I wanted to get some work done the next day before the wrecking crew of guys showed up at my place, I needed to get home and faceplant for a bit.

I locked up and sighed when I saw it was raining. I really didn't want to put my bike away for the season yet, but it was getting dicey weather-wise. I supposed I'd need to put the beater on the road sooner rather than later.

Swapping a ponytail for a quick French braid gave me a few minutes to look around the dark town. The streetlights had that vintage feel with LED lights for extra energy savings. In our last election, that had been one of the items we'd voted on. We'd even ended up with cool flickering lights for the holidays.

Crescent Cove took their seasonal decorating seriously. From Halloween—thanks to Macy's influence—to Christmas and the Fourth of July, the Cove did it up big. There was no shortage of community when it came to this lakeside town.

The diner was the only place open at this hour. The Rusty Spoon didn't bend to the nine o'clock town shutdown, and I was forever grateful. I walked across the street and found the booths mostly empty, save for Luna and Caleb bent over a stack of notebooks and binders at the back of the room.

Before I could turn around and escape, Luna waved. "Well, hey there, stranger. Haven't seen you at Brewed Awakening in a few days."

I smiled and nodded to Polly on my way by. The waitress was a staple here in the evenings since Gina Ramos had shacked up with the Chief. Call me contrary, but I enjoyed the crabby Polly. We understood each other.

"Yeah, it's been a crazy week."

"I heard." Caleb scooted over. "Want to sit with us?"

I glanced down at the paper explosion on the table. "Think it's a bit crowded."

Luna rolled her eyes. "We're still fighting over the seating charts. You'd be surprised how many teachers have hooked up at the Academy. And swapped partners. Downright scandalous over there for a Catholic school."

"You know the Catholic girls are truly the bad girls, Lu."

"What about me?"

"You're a Luna—individual in every way."

"You think you're clever."

Caleb laughed. "Just lucky."

I tried to ignore the itch along my spine. Eating with them was looking more and more like a bad idea with every second that ticked by. How was I supposed to deal with all this drippy love stuff?

He stacked up the binders in a ridiculously quick fashion. Must have been the teacher gene. "Come on, sit with us."

I swallowed a sigh and sat down. "Sure. That'd be nice."

Being polite was balls.

Luna smiled and perked up in her seat. "Yay."

Her wild lemon blond curls rioted around her stunning face. A ripped white sweatshirt had slid off one shoulder, revealing a lacy tank in eye-searing pink. She had something shimmery on her eyes and her lashes were tipped in pink even at this late hour.

I felt like a wet dog next to all her cuteness.

Polly saved me from making conversation. "Hey, T. What can I get you?"

I should've said the salad after all the pizza I'd ingested with Thor, but I really wanted gravy fries. "Silver dollars and gravy fries."

Polly shook her head. "You always have the craziest combos. Butter and syrup?"

"Just butter and lots of it."

"Gotcha." She glanced at Luna and Caleb. "Refills? Anything to eat?"

Luna rubbed her still flat belly. She was another one who'd fallen victim to the Cove baby water. "I think the baby might like those gravy fries."

Caleb grinned. "The baby, huh?"

Luna shrugged. "If you're good, you can have one."

"Gee thanks. I'll have another Coke and a spinach and egg white omelet."

Polly hiked up an eyebrow, then shrugged. "You got it." She shoved her order pad in her apron and headed for the counter.

I was pretty sure my face matched Polly's. "You're friends with Lucky, right?"

The edges of Caleb's ears went pink. "Trying to get in shape for the wedding. I've been enjoying too many of Lu's cravings."

Luna stretched her arms across the table to snag his hand. "Aww, I love your little belly."

He lifted her hand to his mouth for a quick kiss. "See? No belly for this guy, thanks."

"Dad bod a little early?" I quipped.

Luna giggled and sat back. "Not too many dad bods in this town."

"You women keep us running ragged with kids." Caleb reclined in the booth and stretched his arm along the back. "Viv is running around like a lunatic at August's house. We babysat the other night, and I'm still tired."

"She's just the cutest. We had a tea party and tried on about eleven outfits from her closet. You should see the little wardrobe August built for her. I put in an order for our baby's room." Luna gripped Caleb's fingers. "I can't believe we're having a kid."

His smile was quick and almost misty. "Now we just gotta get hitched."

"You know I don't need us to get married."

"Says the girl who proposed from my car," I muttered.

Luna laughed, then transferred her grip from Caleb to me. Her eyes went wide before her grip tightened.

I frowned at her. "What?"

Luna tilted her head. "Been a rough few days indeed."

I slid my hand out from under hers. The warmth from her touch was seriously intense. "Yeah."

"Sorry, the baby makes me even more rude these days. Empath, auras, the whole shebang is whoa—hello, merry go round. I've been working at my shields, but the baby is like nope!"

"Shields?"

Luna pressed her lips together and her gaze shifted to Caleb.

Had I asked something I shouldn't? Since I wasn't sure what she was talking about, it was hard to tell when I'd gone too far.

This peopling thing was too complicated for me when all I wanted was something to eat.

Polly came back just in time to dispel the awkwardness that had suddenly descended on the table. Maybe I needed to take my food to go.

She set down a round of waters and a soda for Caleb. I grabbed mine and drank deeply. Right now, I wouldn't have turned down something stronger.

Luna waited for Polly to leave before leaning forward. "It's okay. You don't need to talk about it. I'm around if you need to though."

I looked down at my hands. They were still red and rough from working. Even with gloves, hauling around all that heavy metal did a number on them.

The polar opposite of the woman across from me. Her skin was softly fragranced with something probably natural and herbal.

What the hell was my problem? I didn't visit Comparisonitisville often. Then again, I also wasn't used to people trying to get into my sphere.

The bell jangled over the door.

We all looked over, and Luna popped to her feet. "Lucky!" She practically ran over to him. "You made it!" She leaped at him, and he caught her around the waist.

"What's popping, Blondie?" He gave her a quick kiss on the cheek. Her Converse-clad feet dangled as he carried her back to the table.

Luna laughed and batted at him, but she didn't demand that he put her down. When you were the size of Lucky, carting women around was probably just part of everyday life.

"Wedding plans aplenty." She wiped her brow as if she was exhausted.

If that was an attempt to sound put out by said plans, it didn't work. She sounded entirely too content.

Just as I was when I was working on Hilda. Men were an optional accessory package I usually didn't shell out for.

"You've always got wedding plans on the brain." Lucky's voice was gruff but obviously filled with affection. Evidently, he was all talk when it came to complaining on the wedding stuff.

He set Luna down gently beside the booth. "Fancy seeing you here, Ruby."

"I was just going to get going." I swung my feet out of the booth.

"Aww, no. We just ordered." Luna pouted.

"Oh, here it comes." Caleb nudged my arm. "It's no use when she bats those bluebells."

Lucky took my hand and dragged me to my feet. "Nah. She'll stay." He swapped me with Luna and hip-checked me into the booth.

I landed on the bench with a bounce. "Hey."

"Hush. Did you order?"

I folded my arms and stared up at him. "Yes."

"Move over."

"Go sit somewhere else, Thor."

Lucky crowded into me until I had no choice but to slide out of the way or he'd be on my lap. He'd obviously showered. The scent of...soap hit me. But not the spicy male kind of soap I expected from him.

His hair was down and still damp. The same soap scent came from that too. I couldn't put my finger on what it reminded me of.

"Hey, Pol." The waitress looked up from her magazine on the counter at Lucky's voice. "Can you add a Big Breakfast to their order?"

"Got it," she hollered back.

Luna slid in next to Caleb, who draped an arm around her. "So, this is cozy." She drummed her fingers on the table. "I didn't know you two were...talking."

How could he make the word talking sound so salacious?

"He works for me," I muttered.

"I'm helping her remodel the old barn at the Slide farmhouse. You guys should come out and take a look. She's got a great view of the lake."

I turned to him. "It's my place. Hello?"

"What? Just being neighborly. You have the perfect spot for a bonfire. You probably need a good s'mores."

I narrowed my eyes at him. "Ass."

"Is there a better scent in the world? I love bonfires." Luna sighed.

"We've been looking at houses near there. We can't afford lakeside property obviously, but there's a new development going up a few miles from there." Caleb reached into the pile of binders on the windowsill and snatched a pamphlet. He pushed it over between us.

Lucky pulled it closer to him. "Oh, yeah. This is right behind where I was working today. Nice to see another name other than Maitland around town."

"Jackass," I said under my breath.

Caleb arched his brow. "FHK?"

"No, Maitland." I shifted closer to the window. Lucky was like a freaking furnace. "He was not happy about me buying my house. It was a private sale, and Gary Slide didn't want to sell to just anyone." I shrugged. "I got lucky."

Lucky sat up straighter and slid me a devilish smile.

I rolled my eyes. "Anyway, he keeps trying to throw money at me to buy me out."

Lucky stole my water and took a sip. "Maitland owns half of the Cove at this point. Almost every new build we see come through seems to have his name on it. I know they wanted to expand the condos around the lake."

"Yeah, well, not on my damn property." I took my water back, then thought better of it and pushed it back toward him. I didn't want to drink from it now.

He folded his massive paws around the tiny glass. "By the time I'm done with it, you'll never want to sell anyway."

"Sure of yourself, huh?"

"Definitely. Just wait until you see the plans I started drawing up."

I pulled out my phone to check the time. "It's been four hours."

"What can I say? I'm a slave to my craft."

Caleb chuckled. "Is that so? Since when?"

Lucky's brows drew down. "I don't really have much else to do, so this will keep me busy."

Caleb locked his hands behind his neck and blew out a breath.

Hello again, awkward silence. It's been several minutes since we've seen you.

Luna bridged the gap between them by gripping both their hands. "Well, let's do the bonfire thing. That way everyone can relax. I know we could use it. It's been all wedding, all the time."

"Ain't that the truth," Lucky muttered. But he softened it by patting Luna's hand. "It's up to Ruby. It's her property."

Oh, *now* it was up to me? He was making plans for everyone five seconds ago. My palms tingled. I didn't really want to have a bunch of people at my place. It wasn't suited for human consumption at the moment.

And sure, that was the only reason I didn't want to roll out the frigging welcome wagon.

Just this morning—somehow it was still the same damn day—all I could think about was how amazing it was to have my own property. Now, after looking at all the things I needed to fix...

Well, overwhelmed was an understatement.

Luna sat back and absently nuzzled Caleb's hand as he draped it over her shoulder. "It's supposed to be beautiful tomorrow night. Almost a full moon, so it should be nice and bright. We don't even have to go in the house."

I met Luna's gaze. I was eight levels of uncomfortable from the natural affection between her and her fiancé and hell, just from the buzz of happy love vibes in the room. She was so open and friendly, but it wasn't the cloying fake kind. She seemed to be genuinely happy about having an impromptu get together.

Some part of me was ready to dive in and say yes. That wasn't me. I was itchy and tempted to leap over Lucky to escape. That would be the smart, sensible idea.

I didn't want to be part of some friendship circle. Not when I wasn't sure I could keep up my end of the deal. Better for me just to jet.

Too bad Polly picked that moment to bring over our food.

"Here we go." She passed out the plates stacked along her arm.

The scent of gravy fries made me moan out loud.

Lucky glanced at me, his green eyes unreadable as he shifted in his seat. Neither of us behemoths were exactly built for a booth, especially when we were sharing one together. Our feet kept bumping and his shoulders were a damn wall, blasting out heat.

He didn't even have on a coat, just one of those thermal shirts with three buttons. The white seemed even brighter against his tanned skin. He pushed up the sleeves and again, that scent of soap wafted my way. It even overpowered the gravy, dammit.

"Where's Butch?" I asked as Polly finished passing out the plates.

"We stopped at the pet store and loaded up on dog stuff. She was passed out in my bed, even though I bought her a bed of her own."

"Typical. My cat is the same."

"Butch?" Luna paused with a fry halfway to her mouth.

Popping a sausage in his mouth, Lucky pulled out his phone and showed it to her. "We had some excitement today at my job site." He finished chewing with a sheepish smile. "Ruby here brought me to get my new girl situated."

Luna dropped her fry and took the phone. "Oh, look at her." She looked up at him. "Butch?"

"She's feisty."

I dragged a perfectly golden potato wedge through my gravy. "He thought she was a boy."

"Girls can be butch."

"With or without a capital B?"

Luna's laugh was musical. "Both. She's beautiful. What's wrong with her nose?"

"Some piece of shit tied her around her mouth to a bush."

The phone clattered to the table, sending a fork sailing into the air. With ridiculously fast reflexes, Lucky snatched the utensil out of the air before it connected with my forehead and returned it to Luna.

"Yeah, I was angry too." Lucky's tone was even, but his muscles had locked. I could practically feel the tension radiating from his big frame.

Luna tucked the fork back under the lip of her plate. "Sorry." Her big blue eyes went shimmery.

"Oh, don't cry," I said automatically. I didn't do well with all that messy emotion.

Luna sniffed. "Sorry. It's the baby. I swear, the baby's empath powers are even more intense than mine." She reached over to Lucky and patted his arm. "You're doing an amazing thing for her, and I know she appreciates it."

Lucky relaxed. "Thanks, Lu."

"You can meet her tomorrow." Lucky glanced at me. "Hey, maybe Butch and your cat will get along."

Yeah, that was going to be interesting. I shrugged. "He's afraid of his own shadow."

"We'll win him over." Lucky dug into his big breakfast.

I plucked up the cup of butter for my pancakes and slathered it on. I definitely deserved all the carbs today.

"No syrup?" he asked.

"Nope." I folded the pancake in half and lifted it like a piece of toast.

"You're fascinatingly weird."

Caleb laughed around his fry. "Way to win a lady over, buddy."

"No one is winning anyone over." I resisted the urge to cross my arms. Not that I had any room.

Luna tipped her head and said nothing.

Lucky kept glancing at my plate and finally did the butter thing on one of his large pancakes. He folded it in half and took a bite, then wrinkled his nose and dropped it back on the plate with a splat. Clearly displeased with my culinary choices, he reached across me and grabbed the syrup that had been jammed against the wall with all the plates.

"You could have asked."

"Eat your dry pancakes, Ruby."

I rolled my eyes. "Rude."

Caleb laughed. "You get used to it."

"Yay me."

Luna laughed. "You guys are so cute."

"We're not anything," I said firmly and huffed.

"Need something?" Lucky looked down at his plate. "You can have some of my bacon."

From rude to sweet in the space of thirty seconds. Probably a new world record for him.

What I wanted was a water, but he'd probably backwashed half the glass with that big mouth of his.

As if she was psychic, Polly returned to the table with a round of waters a moment later.

"Thanks." I reached for one and drank greedily, then filched a piece of his damn bacon.

Lucky didn't say anything, just kept grinning like the lunatic he was.

"So, let's make a quick list." Luna reached around Caleb for the sparkly notebook on the windowsill. She opened it and pulled a pen out of her curls. I wondered what else was in there. "S'mores, beer, some virgin daiquiris for the pregnant lady."

"You mean a smoothie?" Caleb asked and dropped a kiss on her neck.

"Shut up. Daiquiri sounds way more posh and not so boring." She elbowed him. "Oh, we should ask Gage and Rylee to come. They live right near you. Rylee has been poking at me about doing something. She's bored since Macy is in her Halloween zone."

"That's no joke. I ran into her current obsession."

Luna gave me a blinding smile. "Bats, right? She keeps trying to get everyone to put them over their door." She shook her head. "Living over the café has been eye opening."

I folded another silver dollar pancake slathered in butter. "She hung one at the garage. Dare threatened to put a boot on her truck."

Lucky snickered. "He likes his coffee too much to do that."

"Truth." I pointed at Luna with the rapidly cooling bit of

perfection. "I found it over his office door instead. His kid hates it. Wes jumps every time he sees it."

Lucky nudged me. "You have a twisted side."

I shrugged and took another bite. Wes, Dare's eldest boy, had gotten in trouble for picking on his little brother and had to sweep up at the shop every day after school. If anyone was twisted in this situation, it was Dare. Wes used his new task to avoid doing homework for as long as humanly possible, as well as an opportunity to drive his father nuts every chance he got.

Some days it was a shorter trip than others.

Luna made some scribbles with her pink pen, the fluff on top furiously twitching. "You're friends with Gage, so you can ask him. My bestie actually lives pretty close by. I'll ask her too. You don't mind, right?"

Is she human? If so, yes. If she's feline or canine or any other species, that works.

I opened my mouth to reply and swiftly gave up. Luna was already rattling off a bunch of things, and the little bonfire get-together was turning into an event.

Apparently, that was that. I was having lots of people over at my damn house tomorrow. Yippee.

I aimed a sidelong glance at Lucky, happily crunching on his bacon. He sensed my gaze and turned his head to innocently lift his eyebrows.

"Jackass," I mouthed as he grinned.

SEVEN

Lucky

THE AIR OFF THE WATER WAS BRISK TODAY. GOOD THING, SINCE I WAS sweating my ass off.

It was day two of the full-on rip out of the barn. We'd managed to get most of the building emptied out yesterday. Since this job was an official Gideon project, thanks to the sheer size and timing of it, I was able to use Charlie and Frankie from my usual crew for the early part of the day. Then a handful of kids showed up after school.

"Stone, not that…" I sighed as the muscular kid with not a whole lot of brains started swinging from one of the framing pieces to pull it down.

A sledgehammer was far easier and smarter than ripping up his ungloved hands.

The kid was just full-blown Hulk smashing everything he could. He was damn handy for the strength factor. He was almost as big as I was but seemed to have far more upper body strength than lower.

I was fairly sure he was going to fall over eventually. Damn toothpicks for legs.

I dumped my load of super gross hay into the maximum-size dumpster Ruby had delivered yesterday morning. My thigh vibrated for the eleventh time today.

Yesterday, I would have given anything for Ruby to text me. Now I was ready to block her number. I sighed and pulled my glove off to retrieve my phone.

How's it going?

Same as last time. All the destruction for all the rebuilding. Stop bugging me, woman.

I grinned at my screen as text bubbles formed furiously then stopped. Then formed again. I wondered how many times she'd stopped and started replying? Or maybe it was going to come through as a long rant. She was really good at those. I scanned back in our chat history to see the first one of the day and shook my head.

Yeah, I was freaking glad she wasn't on site.

I'm around the corner.

Well, fuck.

I looked around the site. Tyler and Win were tearing apart a few of the pallets we'd found in demolition derby today. They would be a perfect kindling base for the bonfire that night. Right now? Not at all perfect.

Especially when they were sword fighting with two of the larger slats.

"Guys!"

They both stopped mid-swing and the clack of ancient wood hitting wood echoed across the water. "I said strip the pallets, not pretend you're ten years old."

"Sorry, Lucky," Tyler shouted, swinging at his buddy one more time before he tossed the wood on the pile.

"Win, go rake that beach for the chairs we have to put out."

"You want me rake sand and rocks?"

"Works a lot like grass, bonehead."

He ducked his head, but there was no hurt in his eyes. He just loped to the truck for the large metal rake I'd brought from my place. Win—Winston Charleston, Jr.—was a good kid. Long and lanky with it, he was more bones than meat, but he was willing to take direction. Better than his buddy who thought he knew everything.

Stone came out of the barn with part of a beam over his head. He had his earbuds in and was dancing to something. Still no gloves.

I shook my head. That was a fight for another hour. For now, I had to figure out how to make things look less like chaos.

While I knew things were moving along swimmingly, to my client —and future wife—this would look like bedlam.

The wife thing just made me laugh. We couldn't be more different if we tried. But damn, her grouchy nature made me so hot.

I raced around the front of the barn where the worst of the trash lay. I tried to stack my demolition tools into semi-neat piles. Sledgehammers, crowbars, plastic glasses, and discarded gloves were scattered all over.

I tossed my Henley on the truck on the way by. The sun was high in the sky, taking the chill off the morning air. Since the client wasn't on site and we were in the middle of nowhere, Post Malone and Ozzy blasted out of the speakers I had rigged to my truck bed.

Before I could turn off the tunes, I heard her motorcycle coming around the corner. A dust cloud followed her down the bumpy lane to her house.

"Yo!" I waved at Stone frantically, but he didn't hear me. He just kept bopping his way back into the barn. "Tyler!"

"Yeah?"

"Miss Burns is here. Go grab Stone and get the trash off the driveway."

"On it." The kid let the last pallet slam onto the rocks and ran off to the barn.

I was hoping to stall for a second, but damn, her long legs wouldn't give me a break. She hopped off the bike and stalked my way, already pulling off her helmet. All that gem-toned hair haloed around her head for a moment before swinging behind her in the ponytail she always wore.

I had to have some deviant gene that got off on her anger.

"I told you we were doing fine here, Ruby."

"Fine? Is this how you run a work site?" She twirled around, the helmet practically a weapon as she took in the piles of wood I had to go through. Some could be salvaged—and should be, based on the age of the barn. Once she had half a second to think, she'd realize I was taking good care of her space.

She'd want to use some of the old wood to make benches or a table for the rec room. Or at least that was the plan I had for it. But I was only one man and wrangling a bunch of teen males. We were still in the destructive phase. Personally, my favorite time.

But to someone not in the know, it looked like hell.

"Now Ruby—"

"Don't 'Ruby' me. God, I made a huge mistake." She dropped the helmet and clutched her head as if she was in physical distress.

I'd never realized just how much of a flair for the dramatic my future wife possessed.

"Hey, this is just the start."

She kept right on talking. Her big brown eyes blazed, and anger bled in to flush her cheeks. "I figured with Gideon involved—"

"All right, stop right there." I turned her around and shuffled her around the front of the house. "I get that you're a little wound up, but this is demo day, Tish."

She did not deserve the Ruby nickname right now. That was reserved for when she was attractively pissy, not for when she was having a Miss Piggy-style meltdown.

She yanked her arm away from me and frowned, and then whatever was going on in her brain clicked back into shriek mode.

At the moment, I didn't care. I just kept moving her along. The nosy teens were already craning their necks to hear our conversation. Number one, I didn't need them to question my authority, and number two, I needed to cool her down—even if she was frighteningly sexy in her anger.

Perhaps I'd fallen off too many ladders in my day. Surely there was an explanation for my dick's bad choices.

I walked forward and she backed up with each step. Finally, we got to her front lawn. She put her hands on her hips and threw back her shoulders. A black shirt was like her second skin under her usual motorcycle jacket. "Demo? What, with the Incredible Hulk?"

"Well, I do call Stone Hulk, but that's beside the point. I'm sure your garage looks a little crazy before you—"

"No. No, it does not. My garage is neat and organized. It doesn't look like that." She flung her arm out again, pointing toward the back where my truck was still blasting music. This time, a funky, beachy version of Fleetwood Mac's "Dreams" pumped toward the sky.

"Yeah, well, I guess we just work differently."

Her chest heaved.

I rushed on before she ripped into me again. "I have it handled. There was a lot of crap in that barn that needs to be gone through. I figured since you love this place so much, you'd want to salvage some of the lumber. Not to mention the cost of tossing out perfectly good wood and replacing it with lesser quality materials."

She shut her mouth and crossed her arms. "Okay."

"Okay?"

"Sensible. And I appreciate the money angle since it looks as if I'm going to be carving out a crater in my savings."

"Not necessarily. I'd do more myself if we had time, but with the deadline, I'll need to purchase furniture and all that."

She sucked in a slow breath. "Makes sense."

"I had a thought about that too."

Her brow arched. "I'm listening."

I jammed my hands into my pockets. "Good. And if you hadn't come in half-cocked, I would have been happy to discuss things with you."

"I'm just…" She fisted her hands under her arms, emphasizing her stupendous chest.

Don't look, asshole. Eyes up.

She dropped her arms to her sides in frustration. "I've been fielding texts from Luna all day about this bonfire thing today. And I come here and see…*this.*"

I took a step closer and gently gripped her upper arms. "I got you, Ruby. Everything will be ready for tonight."

Her nose wrinkled. "I wouldn't hate it if you weren't ready, so we could cancel."

"So, you're really mad about the thing tonight and not the site."

"No. That's some chaos squared over there, Thor." She wiggled out of my hold. "I'm just not good with people."

"Cancel then."

"I can't. She did all these things. Ordered food, for God's sake. I thought it was just going to be sitting around the fire with some tunes." She nodded toward my truck. "Like what you're playing. That's cool."

My lips twitched. I didn't think a smile and a laugh would go over well with the tension emanating from her in waves. "We already started cleaning up for tonight. Don't worry."

She tucked her hands into her jacket pockets. "I don't like not knowing what's going on here."

I cracked my knuckles, considering. If I didn't give her something, she was likely to keep stopping by and distracting me. And while the idea of her distracting me in several creative ways didn't bother me one bit, the reality was I could not be trusted with that kind of situation. She was already living in my head far more than she should.

Far more than any woman had since...ever.

"Tell you what. I'll send you two daily vids of what's going on. You know, on your phone."

She narrowed her eyes. "Right. Only the pretty parts, I bet."

"No." I folded my arms. "Okay, probably one will be internet share-worthy. But then I'll give you a panoramic view of the big and the ugly."

"Acceptable."

I rocked back on my heels. "Just like that?"

"What? We hashed it out." She punched my arm. "We're good. Now I gotta get back. You can show me the barn so far though." She went around me and headed for the water.

Dealing with this woman gave me fucking whiplash.

I blew out a breath and followed her. I was always watching her ass walk away from me. I wondered what it looked like under those jeans. All firm with that little jiggle that made me want to take a bite.

Damn. *Focus, Lucky.*

I scraped my hair back and retied my bun. I would be sacrificing some time to show her around, but at least it would calm her down.

By the time I caught up with her, she was surrounded by a trio of posturing boys.

"Miss Burns, you can see how much stuff we hauled out over here." Stone was puffing out his over-pumped chest. He kept licking his lips and his gaze bounced from her wildly snapping hair to the ground.

The kid didn't have a chance with Ruby.

"You can call me Tish. Looks like you guys have been busy."

"Oh, yeah. We've been busting ass—er, butt." Win spoke up, then blushed hard.

She gave him a half grin and seemed less stressed now that we'd had our little argument. She stepped up on the pile of pallets in front of the dumpster and took a look inside, then jumped down and wiped her hands on her jeans.

"Do you need me to call them to haul out a load?"

"Handled." I slid my thumbs under the straps of my tank top, pulling them to the center where I laced my fingers loosely. "Take a look inside the barn." I nodded to the guys to scram.

"Man," Tyler muttered. "Finally got to see the hot chick and now we gotta work again."

"You don't want the hundred bucks she's paying you to work?"

Tyler clenched his jaw. "Yes, sir, I do."

"Then go help them clean up the beach. She's got friends coming tonight."

Tyler gave a deep sigh then strolled down the patchy grass to the beach.

I wasn't sure when I'd turned into the old man who gave out instructions. I wasn't certain I liked it either.

Quickly, I followed her into the barn.

She glanced back at me. "Everything good?"

"Yeah, just being idiots." I shrugged. "I've been working them all afternoon."

"Shouldn't they be in school?"

"Seniors. They have like half days of class at best."

"I know how that is. I was in shop class more than economics and all that crap."

"Better than me."

"School skipper?"

I laughed. "Dropout." I shrugged. "I wasn't cut out for school. I eventually got my GED so I could get better paying jobs."

Being on my own before I was even a teen had made school less than desirable. Homeless most of the time, I'd worried more about making cash than grades. It helped that I'd never really looked my age. Made it easy to slide in on work crews. I had a strong back, learned fast, and I had a knack for numbers.

"The stuff we know isn't exactly in the curriculum."

I didn't realize I'd tensed up until I caught her half smile and my shoulders relaxed. "Damn straight. So, what do you think?"

"It's massive."

Without all the crap that had been stored in there, it was a perfect blank canvas. She did that little twirl thing while she took everything in. I stuffed my hands into my pockets to loosen the sudden tightness of my work pants.

Hell of a thing was my chest was almost as tight. Ruby affected me in a way no one else ever had.

Good thing she didn't know the power she had over me. I'd probably have to go into witness protection.

I swallowed hard. "Yeah, we have some structural work to do, but it's really showing her bones now." I went to the large support beam in the center of the room. "I was going to try to do a different setup in here and get rid of this, but changing the structure like that would require too much time and money to change."

"No, that's okay. I like it. Maybe build around it and make it a feature? Dart board?"

I pulled out my phone and made a few notes. "I'll see if I can make it work. Or maybe build the bar around it with some large TVs making up a 3D setup. Put the game on or whatever on one side while someone's playing pool." I walked to the middle where I'd put a quick chalk outline for where I thought the pool table would go. "Could move the pool table a little."

"Hmm." She came up beside me. "Interesting. More interactive."

"And the other side of the bar could be another TV so you could watch movies on a big sectional."

"Yeah, that could work."

"Speaking of sectional." I pulled out a card from the pocket at the back of my phone case. "Since time is a factor and it keeps me working on the structure and making sure the building supplies are in order, I thought you might want to talk to a designer."

Her face went blank.

"Macy worked with her. She helped with the café and The Haunt and her apartment before Macy did the whole Gideon and house deal."

She took the card. "Dahlia McKenna."

"Yeah. It's up to you, of course, but you seem as busy as I am. Thought you might want help. I called her to see if she had any room for a new project, and she said a big job just fell through. She had put aside a lot of time for it." I stuffed my hands back in my pockets. "So, if you wanted to talk to her…"

"Wow." She tapped her nail against the top of the card.

"I don't want to overstep, but you have some stuff to cover in the house too."

"I sure do." She slipped the card in her back pocket. "Thanks. That's really thoughtful." She frowned just before pulling a pair of sunglasses out of her inner jacket pocket and slipping them on.

I wasn't sure if I should be offended or bask in the idea that I might have impressed her. Tough call.

"I'll get out of your hair." She took one last twirl before she strode out into the sunshine. Before I could trail after her, I heard the bleat of her Triumph engine.

My thigh vibrated again. I pulled out my phone.

Luna will haunt you if that bonfire doesn't happen.

It's gonna happen. Trust me.

We'll see.

I laughed and stuffed my phone back in my pocket. I followed the sound of clacking and found the guys using the handles of the rakes as weapons again.

"Come on, guys, enough with the *Star Wars* fantasies, yeah?"

Win set the rake down into the stones. *"Witcher* is far cooler."

I laughed. "Well, that's true. Let's get this done. I'll treat you to a pie at Robbie's if we can finish before four."

Stone twirled his rake, then headed down to the end of the beach. "I'll meet you in the middle."

I headed for the haphazard pile of pallet shrapnel and got to work on setting up the perfect spot for a bonfire on the beach.

My Ruby could try being impressed with me twice in one day on for size.

EIGHT

TISH

THE SUN WAS JUST SHY OF SETTING AS I TURNED INTO MY DRIVE. A Zoom meeting with a client in California had run long. I had about eleven text messages on my phone right now. Literally a record since I chitchatted with…no one.

Ever.

Now I had Luna, Lucky, and some chick named Ryan—whom I didn't even know—blowing up my phone like I lived for small talk. Even my one-word replies didn't seem to put them off. Actually, even more texts flooded my phone in response so that it was constantly pinging with annoying tones. The button on the side had gotten jammed from my repeated pressing to make it stop, so now I couldn't even turn it to silent.

My jacket pocket buzzed again. Maybe I should just toss the stupid thing into the lake.

I turned off my engine and coasted silently down the drive. I didn't want them to know I was there yet. Not that they could hear me over the ginormous speakers of Lucky's truck.

More of that funky, retro music floated out on the lake. This time, it was a different singer, but one with the same rocker-almost country sound. The song was almost like a throwback to a classic like "Sweet Home Alabama", but with more of a gritty guitar undertone.

I sat on my Triumph for a few more minutes and let the music sit in my bones. The scent of a bonfire teased the air. Not with smoke but with the crackling echoes of fall. It also smelled like maybe they put something a little extra in the fire.

Too bad it wasn't the kind of thing that would chill me out. Not that I touched that stuff anymore. It was all well and good when I was young and dumb, but I was too busy for that shit now.

Regardless, it was spicy and soothing. The wind kicked up and laughter hitched a ride on the scent. Suddenly something extra hit my nose.

Food.

My stomach roared. I hadn't had time for anything other than a questionable power bar I'd found in my desk. I could wash anything down with coffee and often did. Gage was forever trying to get me eat something healthy. I was pretty sure the bar of sawdust was his doing.

I rolled up to the top of my driveway and tucked my bike under the awning in case we got some rain. I could smell it on the air, but sometimes the clouds liked to hold onto it for a few days before giving it up.

The closer I walked, the more hints of citrus added onto the definite barbecue dinner that was brewing. When I rounded the back of the barn, I stopped dead in my tracks.

The beach I loved to distraction had been cleaned up, leaving the sand and smooth rocks glowing against the dying sun along the water. The bonfire sizzled with life, denting the cool air with a cozy heat. Adirondack chairs in muted blues and yellows were situated around the fire, but far enough away not to get roasted. Gage was chatting with some guy I didn't recognize at the top of the rocky coastline. Probably the suit who'd hooked up with Ryan.

A grill and cooler were set up at the edge of the lawn with a sturdy folding table laden with food just beside it. A large metal tub filled with ice and cans anchored the table down against the wind that came up off the water.

The flames of the bonfire flickered high, fed by a few old pallets I'd seen earlier.

Two women with dark hair wearing almost identical clothing—dark hoodies and comfy jeans—were standing in front of the fire with their hands held out for maximum warmth. They were laughing about something.

Luna, with her halo of bouncing curls, spotted me first.

"There you are." She jogged over to me, a sparkly gray sweater fluttering behind her like starlight. "I didn't think you were going to show up to your own party."

"It's not a party."

She hooked her arm through mine and dragged me toward the beach. "Close enough. Lucky has been manning the grill. I had no idea he was so handy. Caleb didn't tell me he could cook."

"News to me."

Lucky filled the space in front of the grill. A black pipe with something silver on the front peeked from one side of him. His long legs were encased in dark jeans and hugged his ass. I quickly dragged my gaze upward, and the rest of him wasn't much better for my speeding heart rate. A faded charcoal thermal shirt hugged his shoulders and arms. It had seen so many washings that it clung to his body like—okay, enough of that thinking.

Since when did I get all freaking flowery?

He turned with a massive spatula in his hand. "Hey, you finally made it." His hair was back in a tail, the curls still damp as if he'd just showered. "How do you like your hamburgers?"

"Medium."

"That's my girl." He turned back to the grill. "What do you think?" he asked over his shoulder. "Looks pretty great, right?"

I swallowed hard. It really did. Exactly like I'd dreamed about when I first stepped onto the property. I knew I'd get it done eventually but having someone do the work made my chest tight. Heavy with…regret. No, not just regret. Some relief was stirred in there like sour mix in a whiskey sour.

Guilt floated on top of the mixture like an unwanted cherry. Man, evidently, I really wanted an adult beverage. It really had been a day and a half and it was only five o'clock.

Still, I hadn't been there to help. I wasn't used to anyone doing things for me unless I was there to oversee every step.

Luna patted my arm and warmth flowed through me. Surprised, I glanced at her.

"He did great," she lowered her voice, "but he's worried you won't like it."

This woman had some weird mojo I didn't understand, but I was too tired to try to figure it out. She nudged me forward and I sighed. This polite thing was hard. He'd just done the job we agreed on—no big deal.

Lies.

He'd gone above and beyond.

And I had to tell him so. Even if I wanted to saw off my tongue.

The sun was barely a sliver on the lake, just enough to highlight his cheekbones and far too tempting mouth. I came up beside him and spotted the logo on his red apron of a guy wearing sunglasses. Under it, "Mr. Good Lookin' Is Cookin'" was stamped in bold black.

I huffed out a laugh. "It looks amazing."

"Smells good too."

"No, I mean everything." I cracked my knuckles and resisted the urge to fidget. "Doesn't look the same as when I left."

"I hope not. We busted ass to get it entertainment ready."

"Yeah." I toyed with the end of my ponytail. "I'm not sure how I ended up with so many people here."

"People want to get to know you."

"Why?"

He laughed. "You're mysterious and hot. Two definite reasons to find out more." Then he waggled his eyebrows at me. "Hope you're hungry." He nodded toward the matte black side of the grill where the pipe rose from. Upon closer inspection, I could tell it was a temperature gauge. "I started smoking a pork shoulder this morning so we could have some pulled pork too."

"And burgers?"

He let out a moan that made me think of things other than burgers. "Oh, Ruby. Haven't you ever had both together? And the bit of coleslaw with lime. It's gonna knock you out of those sexy boots."

My traitorous mouth watered. I wasn't sure if it was from the groan or the meal coming my way. "I've had a lot of things, but I think this one's a first."

His eyes glinted in the last fading rays of the sun. "I don't mind being your first."

"Please."

He grinned. "So, come on. Tell me more about how amazing I am."

I folded my arms and tried not to pick at the tray of cheese awaiting the burgers. I was freaking starving. "Not sure you need me to." I gave up and reached for a piece.

He smacked my hand. "Did you wash your hands?"

"No." I sighed. He was right. I tucked my thumb into my belt loop so I didn't lose control again.

He smashed the row of burgers in front of him before flipping them. "Now back to telling me I'm awesome."

Nerves laced his voice. Hmm. Interesting.

I pressed my lips together and swiveled to take it all in. He'd created the perfect setting. Even the dumpster had been camouflaged with a tarp to make it less offensive. He'd cleared away all the rusty tools, carted off the guts from the barn that he and the kids had pulled down, and tidied up the area. The old tractor was gone too.

The sad excuse for grass looked a little better without the carpet of dead leaves. My picnic table was also missing. What was left of it was probably in the pile of wood stacked neatly against the dumpster.

I felt a small pang that didn't make much sense.

He followed my gaze. "I'll grab some fresh lumber and rebuild the picnic table. A few of the legs were too rotten to just patch."

I jammed my hands in my pockets. "No problem."

He hip-checked me lightly. "I'll make it just like it was, just stronger."

I felt stupid for caring so much about a stupid table, but things

93

were changing really fast. I cleared my throat. "I'm going to go get cleaned up."

"Hurry up. Food's almost ready."

"You guys can start without me."

He nodded toward the table where Luna and a tall brunette were already filling their plates. "No worries with this crew." He cracked the tab on his beer then lifted it to salute Caleb when his friend waved from the other end of the beach.

The clang of metal echoed off the water.

"What's he doing?"

"Horseshoes. He wanted to try out the lawn sports pack he bought last week. I told him summer was over, but he wouldn't be denied."

A series of torches came to life at the edge of the beach, then Caleb jogged our way with Butch bringing up the rear. "I'm starving." He held up his hands. "Could use a wash up though."

"I was just going in to do the same." I stole Lucky's beer before he could get it to his mouth. "Need anything from the house?"

He frowned when I took a deep drink. Foamy cold goodness flowed over my tongue. It had been a minute since I'd had a good brew. I couldn't stop the laugh when he took the tall can back from me. "Get your own."

"Sure you don't want a new one?"

"I don't mind your backwash, Ruby." He gave me a hot look over the rim then kicked up his foot and tapped my ass lightly. "Get moving."

Caleb looked between us, his smile growing. "Interesting."

It certainly was not. *Interesting* in the Cove meant someone was about to climb on top of some hapless dude and play hide the sausage while their birth control swirled down the metaphorical drain.

"Come on, I'll show you where to wash up." Butch danced around me, jumping up to brace her little feet against my knee. I gave her a quick scratch before we headed up the lawn.

Butch trailed after us into the house.

"I heard Lucky traded some home renovation for my engagement stunt on Main Street."

"Well, he didn't know it at the time, just that he owed me. It worked out. Apparently, for both of us."

Caleb grinned then threw a look over his shoulder. "Sure did." Little heart bubbles might as well have been popping around his head. "Perfect woman and a baby on the way. I'm a lucky guy."

"If you say so."

"I sure do."

I unlocked the door and pointed to the small bathroom down the hall. "You can clean up in there. I'm going to go change out of my work clothes."

"Sounds good," he said with a cheerful whistle.

I wasn't sure what to do with all these happy people. It wasn't as if it would rub off.

At least I certainly hoped not.

I ran upstairs to my room and swapped my shop T-shirt and the bra that had been strangling me all day for a comfortable tank and hoodie with Godsmack's band logo across the front. After a quick brush of my tangled hair, I headed back downstairs.

Butch was waiting for me at the bottom of the stairs. She was staring intently at something down the hall.

"Oh, hell." I peeked around the corner and saw Dusty. They were in the middle of some sort of silent eye-to-eye showdown.

In the background, I could've sworn I heard the whistling from the "The Good, The Bad and The Ugly."

Before I had to contend with a pissed-off fur pile, I ushered Butch outside, much to her unending disgust.

There was a line of couples waiting for Lucky's grill masterpiece. He was rather adorable as he built the burgers and asked cheese preference and heat level.

Ryan and Preston were the last ones in line, and she leaned back to speak to me. "Hey, thanks for doing this. It's been awhile since I've been able to hang with Lu. Work's been madness."

I smiled. "Sure. At least I'm getting fed out of the deal."

"Damn right. I'm about to drool on my shoes." Ryan grinned as she leaned into her guy. "PMS, meet the owner of this little piece of amazing, Tish Burns."

Preston gave me a rueful smile. "Preston Shaw." He held out his hand. "Pleasure."

I shook his hand then quickly tucked my hand back into the front pocket of my hoodie. "Glad you could come."

Ryan's eyes crinkled at the corners. "We're totally barging in. Luna tends to do that. Just takes over and makes you think it's a good idea."

"Fair assessment."

I really sucked at the chitchat thing. It had to end soon, right?

"It's okay. I had to get used to all the peopling too."

I laughed. "Sure about that?"

Ryan lifted a shoulder. "Luna likes her people together—new and old. And we do what the pregnant lady says. It's just easier. Did she drag you into the wedding yet?"

"God, no."

Ryan sipped from a bottle. "Give her time. Oh, our turn." She skipped up to Lucky. "Hotter the better for me, sir."

"All right, all right," Lucky quipped with a decent McConaughey inflection.

The heavenly scents of food made my mouth water. Thank God for the music or everyone would've heard my growling belly.

Finally, it was my turn. All the couples had paired up around the bonfire, their chairs clustered close as they shared plates and drinks with naturally flowing conversation between them.

I couldn't remember a time when I'd been that relaxed in a group. I'd always moved around too much to make real friends. I could talk trash in the garage with guys without trouble. Most of the time, they didn't want more than a beer and to crack a few jokes.

Occasionally, it ended in a bounce, but that was always a fine line for me. Getting men to give me my due on a professional level was always the hardest part of being a successful woman in a field made up predominantly of males. Muddying it up with sex wasn't worth it the majority of the time.

My family was easy with little bouts of drama here and there, but even that was few and far between with all of us scattered around the country. And even less after…

Well, after Jimmy.

I lifted a beer from the tub of ice and cracked the can. I sure didn't want to think about Jimmy tonight.

"Looks good, Thor. Smells better."

"Just you wait." With a flourish, he built the Lucky-sized slider. First, the burger then pepper jack cheese topped with piping hot pulled pork. The sharp scent of lime made me take another sip of my beer to cover the drool.

Finally, he topped it with coleslaw. I almost stopped him, but he seemed to have a goal in mind. The buttered bun was set on top with a sword-shaped toothpick to hold it all together.

"I'm not really a cabbage person."

"Special recipe. Trust me."

He made another larger one for himself, though not that much different, to be honest. He was generous with his portions. A growing Thor, I supposed.

Also, I had no desire to think about Thor growing in any shape or form.

He jerked his head toward the table laden with salads. "Fill up a plate and we'll share." He lifted each of our plates dripping with barbecue goodness.

"I don't share."

"C'mon, make it easy. I see you eyeing this thing of beauty."

I huffed out an exasperated breath and did as I was told, scooping up pasta salad and baked beans. Holy hell, more of that lime scent wafted off the corn on the cob ribs piled on a platter that I had admired during late night scrolls through social media.

I filled half the plate with that and grabbed some silverware and a stack of napkins. I tucked two beers in my sweatshirt and followed him toward the fire pit.

Now that I got a better look at the bonfire, I realized he'd actually made a fire pit out of cement blocks to contain the fire. With the windy days of autumn upon us, that was especially important. No need to take out the lake with a blaze.

Unsettled by his attention to detail on all fronts, I paused outside the circle of couples.

Lucky dragged one of the chairs closer to Gage and Rylee so we made a little quartet. Luna and Ryan were chatting about wedding things, so I was more than happy to stay to this side of the nosh fest. The Adirondack chairs were oversized which let me sit cross-legged to give myself maximum lap space.

Lucky stood beside me so we could fix up our plates. We naturally divided things without much chatter. He palmed his plate with his long-fingered grip then tucked the now empty second plate under his. "See, teamwork."

I forced my lips to bend into a smile. He really took up far too much space. "So I see." I shoved my hand into my sweatshirt and came out with a sweating can. "Here."

"Ah, perfect." His fingers brushed mine, the calloused tips leaving a buzz of awareness in their wake before he moved away and dropped into his chair. "Now this is what it's all about."

The flames flickered in his sea-colored eyes. I could see some fatigue in the lines around the corners, but it seemed as if he was a happy tired.

Butch came running down the hill and flew over the rocks to jump up on the arm of Lucky's chair. She curled up, hoping for a treat or two as she kept her one open eye stationed on her owner.

"I didn't realize you were so close to us, Tish."

I turned toward Rylee. "Oh, right. I was out of town when you guys had your little housewarming thing." On purpose. I really wasn't into all these coupled up things. It seemed like every-damn-one was paired up in this town.

And more often than not, a baby stroller was included.

Gage crossed his legs at the ankle, digging his heels into the sand. "That's Tish. She isn't much for get-togethers."

"Nope."

"Why I was shocked you invited us." He bit into one of the corn ribs. "Man, these are good."

"Not ashamed to say TikTok made me do it." Lucky grinned. "I've never cooked so much until I started looking around on there. They make it look way easier than they are. Took me about five tries not to burn the fuck out of these." He lifted one and sampled it. "I finally got the right technique from Macy's chef. Decker's making some Halloween ones for The Haunt."

"Well, I'm in."

I cleared out my entire pile of them.

Finally, I went for the sandwich. Lucky watched me out of the corner of his eye. I really wanted to just put it down in indifference, but my mouth was having an orgasm. "Dear God."

He grinned and took a big bite of his own. "Hell yeah."

Rylee held up hers. "Here's to the magnificent chef Lucky."

I couldn't disagree. "Hear hear." Then I was too busy clearing my plate.

Conversation flowed around me. I threw in a comment here or there, but I was happy to just bask in the warmth of the fire and relax. They didn't make it hard on me, which helped.

Lucky hopped up and collected plates. I really should have gotten up to pitch in, but I was so damn cozy. I closed my eyes as the breeze came up off the water. The fire popped with the air pockets in the old wood just adding to the ambiance.

This was what I'd wanted when I bought the house—the quiet and nature surrounding me. I sure didn't mind the cooler temperatures to combat the bugs. Every little thing was perfect.

I must have dozed off, because the chink of horseshoes and Luna's delighted laugh dented my consciousness. But not enough for me to open my eyes. I just wanted to stay on the drift.

Then the light strum of a guitar pulled at me. It wasn't intrusive, just the kind that belonged by a fire. But the voice made it impossible to stay under.

I turned my head to find him with a beat-up guitar on his lap, sitting on the edge of the chair. The firelight turned his hair a burnished gold. It was down and hiding half his face. His voice wasn't perfect, but it suited the old guitar.

Just singing for the pleasure of a song.

I knew the lyrics vaguely. I had an eclectic taste when it came to music, but it was more that I just knew when I liked a song rather than the artist specifically.

The lyrics spoke of longing and might-have-beens. Of moving on with more good memories than bad.

I curled up my knees and tucked them into my sweatshirt, my body angled toward his. No one else was around. The clang of horseshoes down the beach told me where the other couples had gone. Butch was curled up on the arm of the chair, snoozing.

When the song ended, he glanced over at me. "Hey there, sleepyhead."

I slid my hands under my cheek. "Full belly and a fire. I didn't stand a chance."

He placed his palm over the strings. "Did I bother you?"

"Didn't you mean to?" I arched a brow at him.

"Maybe." He chuckled lightly. "You're just lucky I didn't pull out a Joni Mitchell song with this campfire."

I grinned. "What was that song you just played?"

He tucked his hair behind his ear. He wouldn't meet my eyes. "A buddy's song."

"You're buddies with a famous dude?"

He shrugged.

Interesting that he didn't want to share. Knowing a musician was pussy points for most guys I knew. "I'm pretty sure that was radio hit. I'm not sure who it is, but I know I've heard the song a time or eleven."

He strummed the guitar lightly. He was quiet for a few moments, then sighed. "Flynn Sheppard."

I whistled. "Country rocker hybrid guy? I saw one of his shows when I was in..." I had to go back a few years of memories. "Think I was in Georgia at the time. Some festival when I was still patient enough for that kind of deal."

He laughed. "I hear that. We did a lot of those. Flynn is one of those guys who lives for the road. Goes a bit batshit when he doesn't have a show lined up."

"Sounds like you know him pretty well."

He twirled the guitar and set it on the side of his chair. Butch took the opportunity to find her rightful place in his lap. Lucky automatically stroked her back, settling her on his flat belly. "I did the roadie thing for a few years. Flynn was good to me. Taught me how to play guitar, actually. There's a ton of downtime on the road."

"Wow. That had to be wild."

"It was. A lot of fun for a few years. But the endless hours of boredom then the thankless hustle for the shows eventually killed it for me. I still keep in touch with Flynn though. Probably the closest thing to a dad I've ever had." Butch inched up until she was sprawled across his chest. "Don't tell him that though."

His smile was sweet as he stared into the fire.

I couldn't imagine not having my dad around. He'd been a hardass, but I'd never wondered if he loved me. My mom had split when I was little more than a toddler. She'd wanted a different life. One that didn't include having car parts strewn all over her home.

She'd married up and I had a couple of half siblings I'd never cared to meet. Good thing, because she liked to forget we existed.

"So, when your brothers and pops come in, how long are they staying?"

"Good question." I shifted to face the fire. Just like that, Jimmy intruded. I hadn't even talked to Cohen about him. I was a damn coward. "My dad isn't great about taking time off. None of my family is, really."

"I'm shocked."

I gave him a side-eyed glance. "Yeah, well, the Burns family are hard workers. Play hard too. Why I need a space for them, or they'll destroy my house."

"In boredom," he quipped.

"Shut up."

He scratched the dog's ears. "I'll make sure the whole thing is tip top, don't worry."

"I know you will."

In no time, I'd already begun to believe that maybe this project wasn't as insane as I thought. I wasn't sure what to do with that slice of hope. It was such an abstract thing in my life.

My phone vibrated in my hoodie pocket. I contemplated ignoring it. Relaxing wasn't something I did easily, but here I was. The ringtone was on the lowest setting, but the familiar tones of Ezra's ringtone made me struggle out of the deep incline of the chair.

"Need something?"

I shook my head and hauled myself out of the chair. I pulled out my phone as I strode up the lawn. "Everything okay?"

"You answer the phone like there's a five-alarm fire every time, Ging."

"Yeah, well, you don't call me."

He expelled a breath. "Yeah. I hate when I call that I have shit news each time."

My heart sank. "What happened?"

"Nothing."

"Nothing doesn't require a call."

"Nothing happened with Cohen. Not that he'll talk to anyone anyway."

I winced. I hadn't even tried to reach out. I was the shittiest sister on the planet. "Then what's up?"

"They're holding a memorial for Jimmy. I think we should be there."

"I..." What was I supposed to say?

How was I supposed to grieve a man who had betrayed me so completely?

NINE

Lucky

I DIDN'T WATCH HER WALK AWAY BUT ONLY BECAUSE I WAS GETTING tired of being predictable. Not that I didn't enjoy the view.

Better to brood into a beer and ponder my moves.

I didn't make a habit of thinking too much. Action was my preferred MO, and honestly, I'd never had to second-guess how to behave with women. I didn't like not feeling sure of myself in this arena.

Then again, it had never mattered this much before.

Sure, I struck out sometimes. Who didn't? But this didn't feel like a normal time up at bat. This felt crucial. Urgent.

Life or death to my dick, if not to the rest of me.

At least that was a good story to tell myself.

When Caleb wandered away from the circle of women to drop down in the chair beside me that Tish had vacated, I considered it a sign. I wasn't of the woo woo variety, but my boy now consorted with witches and that had put some different ideas in my head.

I wasn't against believing the universe was working for our highest good. A lot of kismet-ish stuff had happened in my life that had brought me to this place. There had to be some sort of grand plan, right?

I grabbed the guitar again because it was easier to speak while I strummed. "So, fate. You think it's a thing?"

Caleb had been in the process of pulling the tab off his soda and managed to break it off in his surprise. He swore ripely under his breath, holding up a hand when his wife-to-be shot him a look full of reproach.

"You're not allowed to swear anymore? Did you take an oath?"

"The baby can hear. She's pretty lax about enforcement though."

"Isn't it like the size of a tadpole?"

"More like a fig. Fu—frick, I'm thirsty. Why did you have to ruin my soda with your existential crap?"

Rolling my eyes, I grabbed the can out of his hand and used the tool on my belt to take care of the pop top. "Here you go, Big Poppa."

He took it sulkily. "You need to warn a dude when you ask something like that."

"Why? You must discuss these things at home. At least when you come up for air."

"Not so much. It's not a fad with Lu. Her spirituality is as much a part of her as her hair color."

"I get that." I set my guitar on the arm of my chair and reached for my beer. "I wasn't joking around, man. I was serious."

My best friend narrowed his eyes as he studied me, the firelight shifting over his face. "I see that now. Just caught me off guard."

"Yeah." I finished off my beer before crushing the can against my thigh. "Good time Lucky doesn't have serious thoughts. What's wrong with this picture?"

"I didn't say that. I wouldn't. I know you do sometimes. You must," he added.

I had to laugh. "Yeah, so it's not my usual. But in a town like this, if you pay attention you gotta wonder. Something weird is at play here. I mean, not everyone gets knocked up right away, despite what local lore says. But an awful lot do."

"You think that's fate?"

"I dunno. What led me here? I could've gone anywhere. And I

landed in this place." I set my can down in the sand and went back to playing the guitar, my thoughts circling like the lazy curls of smoke rising into the air from the fire. "Like how we got to be friends. That had to be meaningful."

Even saying it made me feel like a Class-A asshole. We weren't the types to explore our feelings. But with all that had been going on lately with Caleb coupling up with Lu and making a whole new life, I couldn't deny things were different now.

It had to be. He was becoming a dad and a husband and all that went with it.

But what did that mean for me? I'd been at loose ends as I had so many other times in my life. Roaming from place to place, trying to see if this was where I was meant to be for more than a season or a year. But no matter where I'd gone or what I'd done, nowhere had ever fit until the Cove.

"Yeah." Caleb rolled the sweating can between his palms as he gazed across the circle of chairs to where Ryan's dude Preston was seemingly having an in-depth conversation with Butch.

I wasn't sure how I felt about my girl leaving me to sit with another man, but I supposed I was glad she was making friends. Everyone needed them.

Even Ruby, no matter what she thought.

As the silence extended, I strummed harder, launching into Don McLean's "American Pie." I'd learned that one on the road too, and our surroundings seemed made for the singalong tune.

Not that anyone was singing. Not even me.

"Look, man, I wanted to talk to you." My best friend leaned forward and set down his can in the sand before linking his hands between his knees. "I know stuff's been…different."

I kept playing.

"We used to hang out all the time. It wasn't as if I was looking for that to change. We always had so much fun."

My fingers slowed, eventually stilling. "I get it," I said quietly.

And I did. I always had. I'd had lots of friends over the years, and no matter how nomadic their lifestyle started out, in time, situations changed. Dudes found chicks and had kids and made a family. It was the goal. No one wanted to cruise the bar scene forever.

Even endless pussy got old. I know, I'd had trouble believing it too.

"Yeah. I just wanted you to know, like to say it, that it's not about you or our friendship. That's solid as bedrock. Nothing will change that." His Adam's apple bobbed with his swallow in the low light. "I promise, Luc."

I swallowed too, shocked to feel heat behind my eyes. I hadn't known I needed to hear it. Big tough guy who didn't do emotions. Why would I need emotional shit like that? I knew we were good.

"Yeah. Me too. And thanks." I took a breath and leaned closer, desperate to get back on an even keel. "So, how's witchy sex? Preston told me it's out of this world."

"He did not. Preston excels at narrowed eyed looks, which is what you would get if you asked a question like that."

"So, you're saying it's not amazing? Bummer."

Smirking, he shook his head. "Dude, you are something else. Besides, even if I said it was, you'd be shit out of luck because the only two local witches are spoken for. So, why torment you with the forbidden promiseland?"

"I knew it was incredible. The way Luna moved around that stripper pole…" I said fondly, laughing when he slapped the side of my head.

"I heard that, creeper," Luna called across the circle, making Preston glance up from his Zen moment with my chilled-out dog.

"Not a literal creeper," I informed him when he aimed the very look Caleb had warned me about my way. "I see her purely, I swear. She's basically my sister-in-law, and she's with child at that."

"He's just referring to the day I moved in across from Lu," Caleb chimed in, "and he accidentally on purpose opened her door while she was, erm, dancing."

"I was doing my stripper pole routine."

Preston did not look surprised. "You opened the door of a woman you don't know?" His voice hardened. "Didn't anyone ever teach you manners?"

Ryan patted his arm. "Down, pitbull. Obviously, it worked out okay since Caleb and Lu are engaged."

"And she's very pregnant," I added. "But you're right. I went too far, and I apologized."

"Very pregnant?" Lu peeled up her top and gazed down at her mostly flat belly. "I'd compare mine to yours any day, Roberts."

"It was just a figure of speech."

"Beware," Caleb said under his breath. "You're a vision, Lu."

She smiled at him before pointing at me. "Men do pole work too, you know. I'd challenge you to do a routine anytime you want."

I snorted so loud I could've damaged my sinuses. "Blondie, your pole would crash to the floor if I climbed on it."

"You have no idea what my pole could handle."

"Okay, okay, let's walk." Caleb stood and moved to the cooler to grab a couple more sodas. I disposed of our recyclables and followed him toward the water, mainly to keep from bantering with Lu until I got myself in trouble.

"You think she really wants me to get up on the pole?" I asked when we were safely out of earshot. I hoped. "Does she hope I'll humiliate myself? I thought Lu was a benevolent soul."

"She is, but she's very proud of her athleticism. She told me she intends to keep dancing throughout her pregnancy." He jerked a shoulder and popped the top on his can. "I reap the benefits, and she assures me it's safe for her and the baby."

"Do you do that kinky *Magic Mike* stuff for her?"

"Hardly." He chuckled. "Can you imagine me on a stripper pole?"

I shuddered. "God, no." But this conversation had rerouted my thoughts in a certain direction. "So, if you don't strip for her, what do you do?"

"Just because I said we were on solid ground didn't mean I'm going to give you sex tips."

"I don't need those. At least I don't think. I've never gotten any complaints. And I've had many wanna-be repeat customers."

"Do you mean actual customers? Like paid sex work? If so, dude, gross."

"You aren't funny." I gave him a good shove toward the lake. In the early darkness, the water placidly lapped at the rocks and the lights from houses along the shore bobbed along the surface.

Laughing, he shoved me back before sobering. "Okay, I'll bite. What are you asking?"

"I was there when you met Lu. I saw some of your fumbles in between."

"Gee, thanks."

"Can you dispute it?"

"Nope."

"So, how the hell did you seal that deal? Not physically," I said exasperatedly before we went down that road again. "I mean, how do you chip the ice enough with your dream girl to get her to see you as the ultimate god of sex?"

Caleb's eyes widened enough that the light reflected from the fire pit seemed to dance in his pupils. "Well, huh, I don't think that's happened yet. Gives me something to strive for though."

"Keep trying, Goldilocks." Lu gave Caleb an enthusiastic thumbs up when he glanced over his shoulder in her direction.

"Damn bat ears."

"It's the pregnancy. Heightens all her senses, she claims." He took a long drink and shook his head. "I gotta lay off the caffeine. It's getting late, and we have early errands tomorrow. I'm going to be buzzing."

"Oh, the wild life of a papa-in-training," I teased.

"As for the ice... I didn't break shit. I fell asleep in her bed after I mixed old rum with antibiotics and went home to the wrong apartment."

"And that got you laid? Nice, dude." I bumped my fist into his.

"You're living on the edge, my man." He pointed behind his head to where the rest of our friends were sitting.

I puffed up my chest and opened my soda. "I'm not scared."

"Right. Anyway, I don't know."

"You don't know?"

"No." He rubbed the slight scruff on his jaw. "Maybe it was fate, just like you said. Because God knows I don't deserve her. I don't have any clue how I got so lucky. I just try to be worthy of her every day."

I slid a glance toward the now empty circle of chairs. Our friends were trooping down to the other end of the beach, probably to work off dinner. My dog brought up the end of the bunch, trailing after Preston and the bun crumbs he was using as a lure.

"Out of luck, pal. She missed your lovey-dovey speech."

"Dammit." Caleb sighed as his gaze followed mine to our friends. "Well, whatever, it's all true. I worship the damn ground she walks on and I don't hide it."

"Hmm. What about playing hard to get?"

"If that backfires, you're left playing with your own hand."

"You do have a point." I clapped him on the back and decided Ruby had been gone long enough.

If she thought no one cared if she just disappeared, she was wrong. I cared.

Far too much.

"I do?"

"Yeah. Look at all you have, man. You made out big time." I gave him a quick one-armed hug. "She's lucky to have you too. You're a stand-up dude, and you'll never leave her or your kid in the lurch."

Not like mine had.

I wouldn't do that either. Not that I had kids in mind for anytime soon or maybe ever. But if somehow it ever happened, I'd do what a real man did when he had children.

He took care of his responsibility.

Caleb nodded firmly. "No. I won't."

"I'm happy for you. Truly. And I'm glad you were able to make it tonight. I'm honored to be the kid's godfather."

"About that—"

I raised a brow.

He sighed and smiled. "We're thrilled you agreed to do it."

"Agreed? I strong-armed you into it." I grinned. "And when I marry Ruby, I'll ask you to return the favor."

Jesus, what the hell was I saying? Marrying her was one thing. But needing godfather services meant...

No.

Oh, no, no, no.

Before I could incriminate myself further, I crossed the beach back toward the house to find my future wife.

And future *not* anything else.

I found her in the kitchen, her head bent as she methodically cut something with a pair of industrial-sized scissors. I didn't know if she'd still be on the phone, but she definitely was not. And she appeared to be doing some kind of arts and crafts with scissors created for a gorilla.

Her long fall of red hair tumbled forward to shield her face while she carefully cut the glossy pieces slipping to the floor like shrapnel.

I stepped forward and she swore, her head jerking up as she dropped the scissors. She flushed the color of her hair and jammed her forefinger in her mouth. "What do you want?"

"Always sweetness and light, Ruby."

"Quit the 'Ruby' stuff. I have an actual name."

Whatever progress toward friendship we'd made seemed to have been erased with one phone call.

"Let me see that finger." I came around the island toward her, caught between amusement and annoyance when she held it to her chest and backed away.

"No."

Every step forward I took, she took one back until she was edging around to the other side of the island.

"Ruby." I let out a baffled laugh. "C'mon. At least rinse it off. You're a big girl." I went to the sink and turned on the cool water.

"It's fine. I do a million things worse to myself every day. I almost hacked off a finger half a dozen times."

"Is that all? You must play it safe at work."

She marched forward and stuck her finger under the water, wincing only slightly. "It's basically just a paper cut. See?"

She wasn't wrong, but I still went down the hall to her bathroom and dug through the medicine cabinet until I found the banged-up tube of Neosporin and a Band-Aid.

When I returned, she was still standing with her hand under the water, her gaze miles away.

"Think this will help you avoid stitches." I held up my items and her head whipped toward mine.

"Stitches—oh, shut up."

"You first. Turn that off." She'd shifted the stream over to ice cold. "You're going to lose circulation in your fingers."

Shockingly, she did as she was told, although she growled when I wrapped her hand in a dishtowel to dry it.

"You're a surly patient," I told her.

With the most beautiful pair of doe brown eyes I've ever seen.

Somehow I managed not to say that part.

I ignored her grumbling while I held her in place and squirted a dollop of Neosporin on the cut before slapping the bandage over it. I expected her to knee me in the nuts as soon as she was freed, but instead, I looked up to find her smiling.

"What?" I asked defensively.

"You catch your tongue between your teeth when you're working sometimes. It's almost cute."

The back of my neck heated. What the hell? I'd had women objectify me in a hundred ways, and this one could render me mute with just a few words.

"Yeah, well, you probably snore."

I didn't know why I said it. But I definitely didn't expect her to laugh.

"The opposite, actually. I've had people check to see if I'm still breathing because I'm so quiet."

I pocketed the tube of cream, dumped the bandage wrapper in the garbage, and then hung the towel to dry. "Since I can't confirm or deny that one, I'll just say you should get some smaller scissors."

"That's my kitchen pair." She glanced toward the remnants of destruction on the island and scattered on the floor. "You're not curious?"

"I'm curious about many things."

How your lips would taste, for one.

"Thor, you're really annoying sometimes, you know that?" She didn't give me time to answer before marching over to the island and gathering up half of what I saw now was a photo. "That's my brother, Cohen." She jabbed her finger at his smiling face, his forehead partially shadowed by his shock of dark hair. "He's the one who got hurt and fucked up my life." She closed her eyes. "I didn't mean that. I love the jerk. I just didn't intend for all of...*this*. Didn't plan on it. Didn't need it."

"All of what?" I asked gently.

"The other guy in the photo," she gestured to the floor where the other pieces had fluttered, "was my brother's best friend. He died in the same accident where my brother got hurt."

"And you hate him."

"How do you know?"

Didn't deny it. Hmm. "Taking a blade to a dead man's face is usually a pretty strong clue."

She stunned me by laughing, and then I returned the favor by drawing her into my arms for a hug. She went stock still, not moving, not breathing, until I skimmed a hand down her rigid spine and urged her in against my chest.

I almost thought she'd shatter before she'd bend but she folded against me with something that sounded suspiciously like relief.

Or grief. It bothered me I didn't know her well enough to be able to tell the difference.

"That's a girl." I rubbed her back in even strokes as she trembled against me.

She wasn't crying, though I'd worried for an instant that she was. No, her eyes were dry and remained wide open and on mine. She wasn't much shorter than I was and fit so well in my arms that I knew this had been a mistake.

It was always so much harder to forget the forbidden once you'd had a taste.

"What did he do?" I asked once her shudders had subsided.

"I trusted him so I showed him my designs for my first fabricator."

I braced against what she'd say next.

"And?"

"And he took them for his own and sold them to a competitor."

I sucked in a breath as I fisted my hand against her lower back. "Your brother's best friend."

"Yes. Supposedly."

I nearly asked what he'd been to her. I could hear the current of *more* underneath the pain in her words. But she'd already given me so much, and I didn't want to ask for things she clearly wasn't ready to tell.

After a moment, I eased away from her and gathered the photo shreds off the island and the floor and dumped them in a paper towel.

"What are you doing?"

"Gonna take them out to the fire pit where they belong. Lu would approve," I added almost as an afterthought.

Even with my limited knowledge of all things mystical, I knew fire was an important way to release and cleanse. And this dude needed some serious releasing for being a fucking traitorous dick. I was sorry he was dead, but that didn't absolve him from what he'd done while he was here.

"You didn't even look at the pieces."

"Why should I? He hurt you, so he isn't worth it."

She swallowed loudly enough for me to hear. "Ezra asked me to go to his memorial in Mystic. I don't know if I can. My family doesn't know what he did, and I don't think I can look them in the eye and pretend he was a good guy when I know deep down he wasn't."

"You feel you have to go."

"Yes. Not for him."

"No, for your brothers."

Silently, she nodded.

"Would it help to have a friend with you?"

She reached up to grip her throat, her fingers digging in until I was sure she'd leave marks behind. "I don't have any friends I could ask."

"You do, and you don't have to ask because I'm offering." I wrapped my fingers around hers and carefully pried them away from her skin. With a squeeze, I released them. "Let's go on a road trip, Ruby."

TEN

TISH

W‌ATCHING THE SUN TEASE THE SKY HELD A WHOLE NEW MEANING WHEN you knew a funeral was in your future.

No one should be in the ground before the age of thirty. Hell, I'd say eighty with the whole medical advances thing. But twenty-seven? The same age as me? No.

That wasn't the way it should go.

I tucked my fingers into the oversized cardigan I wore against the biting wind. The sky was steel gray and heavy with rain. I could smell it on the air and feel it in my shoulder.

It was always my barometer. At least the old injury had been for a good cause—beating the holy hell out of a '67 Impala for a client with more money than sense. She'd wanted a replica of Baby from the show *Supernatural.*

And I'd been stupid enough to do it.

She'd found the most ridiculously rusted out piece of crap that had been wasting away in some dude's barn. It'd had water damage, frame issues, and leather eaten by God knows what. But in the end, I'd gotten that motherfucker growling as well as Dean Winchester himself.

Or so I liked to believe.

Some days were insanely fun. Some days were made to be stamped out and forgotten. I had a feeling the next two days would fall in the latter category.

The rumble of Lucky's ancient pickup coming down my drive had me turning around. My weekender was packed and a cooler with snacks, water, and sodas stood at the edge of my as yet renovated barn.

We had to wait a few days for some final permits to come in as well as roofing supplies and some lumber from Turnbull. It was the snow capital of NY and they'd already had their third snowstorm, though it wasn't even a full week into October.

I could only imagine what was coming our way this year.

Lucky and Gideon had assured me they would get the roof finished first so the rest of the barn renovation could move along.

If I had to go to a funeral-slash-memorial, at least the timing could've been worse.

I wanted to hide in the workshop and figure out the back panels of the Phantom, not face my dead lover's family. Oh, and of course my brother, who was still mourning for his best friend, and my dad, who'd thought of Jimmy as another son. All of it made me want to take my bag and hit the road for a whole different kind of destination.

I could start over again. Maybe try Canada this time.

The beige and blue battered panels of Lucky's truck as it barreled down the drive were disguised in a wake of dust. I really needed to think about improving the road with winter coming. That was going to be a bitch to keep plowed.

One more thing to add to my checklist.

He parked and hopped out. "Mornin'." He strode over to my bags. "Oh, hey. You packed snacks?" His slash of a smile made my gut twist.

Here I was, acting like nothing happened last night. That I hadn't let Lucky hold me while I shook in his arms. Never mind that I'd agreed he could join me on this trip.

He'd asked if I needed a friend, and I couldn't remember ever wanting one more.

I wrapped the edges of my sweater tighter and crossed to him. "Less stops the better."

"That's no fun. You're supposed to find shitty diners on the endless highways of America."

"Been to all of them."

"I got you a coffee from Macy's on the way."

"I could ki—um…thank you."

He grinned down at me. "What was that?"

"That's very kind of you."

His lips twitched. "What's in the thermos?"

"More coffee."

"You're so organized." He crouched down to the cooler and flipped it open. "Grapes, trail mix, nuts." He glanced up at me. "Where's the gummy bears? M&Ms?"

"Keep digging."

"That's my girl." He shoved his big paw in there and found the candy layer. "Twizzlers—you are my soulmate."

"Shut up."

He tucked the thermos under his arm, and swung both the soft-sided cooler strap and my bag over his shoulder. When my coat slipped free from where I'd looped it over the bag, I stepped forward and snatched it before he could take that too. "I can carry my own stuff."

"Yeah, yeah. Just get in the truck."

I stomped after him, my arms wrapped around my one good jacket —well, other than my leather one.

"What did you do with Butch?"

"She's getting spoiled by Luna and Caleb." He swore as he twisted his shoulders to stuff himself into the back. "They said it was mini practice for the kid."

"With your dog? No. She's cake."

"I didn't argue and neither did B. She is loving life. I'm actually worried she won't want to come home."

I came up next to him. The small backseat of the cab didn't have much room. Lucky had a ruck sack tucked in the corner and a blazer hanging from a makeshift hook in the ceiling.

"B will miss you desperately."

He glanced over his shoulder. "Are you trying to make me feel better?"

"Well, you are driving me to Connecticut."

"I can't believe that's where this shindig is. Didn't you say he was a California firefighter?"

"They both were—are—adrenaline junkies. They went where the action was." Now I didn't know what Cohen would be. Even more out of control? Or would this change the heart of him?

"Yeah, I get that." He seemed satisfied with his version of luggage Tetris, then opened up the passenger side for me. "Ready to get on the road?"

"No."

He tucked a loose piece of hair behind my ear. "Want to do it anyway?"

I sighed. "Yes."

He gripped the top of the door. "Then get that superior ass in the truck."

I hopped up and he gave me a smile before he shut the door. His soapy scent hit my nose again. He'd cleaned out the truck for me— pretty sure he'd even hit the car wash, at least on the inside.

A large to go cup was waiting for me as well as a stash of candy. I wasn't the only one who thought ahead. The truck had a big bench-style seat with the shifter on the floor, giving both of us much needed leg room.

He got in and laid his arm across the back of the seat as he backed out. I couldn't figure out why I knew his scent, but it was driving me crazy. It didn't match the kind of guy I'd thought he was.

"So, are you a rock tunes or a podcast girl?"

"You listen to podcasts?"

He shook his head. "I have brain cells too. My life isn't just smashing walls down."

"I didn't—" My jaw dropped open.

"Your face." He chuckled as he put the truck in drive. "I like that Asher dude's podcast. Murder in small towns is fascinating."

I gave him some side-eye. "Should I worry?"

He laughed and made the executive decision to go with some Keith Urban. "Don't worry, Ruby. I only give killer orgasms."

"Keep it up and I'll push you out of the truck myself."

He threw his head back with a hearty laugh. His not quite perfect baritone serenaded me for an hour before I cried uncle. I didn't want to own up to the fact that I actually liked it. That was precisely the problem.

We listened to two episodes of Asher Wainwright's podcast before stopping for a bathroom break. Traffic was light since most people were working. I knew we had snacks. I'd had all the right intentions. Then a McMuffin called my name. I'd pay for it, but right now, I didn't really care.

I got two for each of us and rushed back to the rest stop's parking lot. Lucky was sitting on the hood of the truck, tossing grapes into his mouth.

Damn, all that hair glinting in the light was giving me all kinds of very good but very bad thoughts. Lucky was going to kill me, and not the way that led to a trip into the woods.

I was supposed to be thinking about Jimmy and my brother, but just then, nothing seemed to matter but this moment.

The sun had burned through the clouds as soon as we'd left the Cove behind. He'd stripped off his shirt, leaving him in worn jeans and a black tank. His skin was burnished from the sun, and his tattoos were faded like his jeans.

He tipped his head back as he chewed, soaking in the sun.

I came to a stop in the middle of the road. I was not catching feelings for this guy, was I?

The honk of a horn made me jump as Lucky zeroed in on me. I held up the McDonald's bag like a trophy and he whistled.

"Girl, you read my mind." He stuffed the half gone stem of grapes back in the baggie and slid off the truck.

"McDonald's and a road trip go together like peanut butter and jelly." I tossed the bag at him.

"Only way better." He dug in with a groan. "Perfect." He nodded to the truck. "I've got disinfectant wipes in the glove box."

"Obsessed with germs?"

He shrugged.

Then I remembered he'd been pretty much homeless for years and wanted to kick my own ass. I got in and we cleaned up then unwrapped our breakfast sandwiches.

I held mine out to him and he tapped it with his. "Cheers."

"What do you have back there?" I asked between bites.

He looked over his shoulder. "Camping stuff."

"You know we're going to a hotel, right?"

"I like to be prepared."

"Boy Scout too?"

He waggled his brows. "Always prepared, babe."

Once the sandwiches were gone, I twisted onto my knees to get to the cooler. I pulled off my sweater and threw it on my bag. I was a bit freakish about my water being cold. I'd filled up a few insulated tumblers for the ride and grabbed one. My elbow brushed his shoulder and he stilled as my hair draped over his arm.

"Sorry." Quickly, I got back on my side of the truck. "How long do we have?"

"We're just outside of Pittsfield, so we should make it there a little after noon." He cleaned up our late breakfast then pulled out of the parking lot.

"I'm gonna blink out for a bit. I slept for shit."

"Go ahead."

I wasn't actually tired, but the closer we got to Jimmy's hometown, the less capable I was of making small talk. It had been years since I'd been out this way.

I'd tagged along with Cohen and Jimmy one summer—*the* summer we'd tangled.

Cohen had fallen in lust with a girl working in Mystic and had dragged us both with him in case the online hookup fizzled. It hadn't, leaving Jimmy and I alone. I was high on my new designs for my first fabricator machine and getting some interest from a company to collaborate. I'd been feeling reckless and happy for the first time in a while.

Jimmy was charming and there had always been something between us. Neither of us had ever thought to step over the line until we'd been left to our own devices. One hot day in July, I'd made the biggest mistake of my life.

At the time, it hadn't seemed that way. But when Jimmy asked me not to tell my brother about us, I should have run far and fast. Secrets never led to happiness. But I'd been too stupid and blind. I'd believed that he wanted me. For half a second, I'd even believed I was in love with him.

I'd been so wrong.

I didn't think I was going to fall asleep, but I supposed I wanted to escape even the memories. I woke to Lucky lightly shaking my shoulder.

"Ruby?"

Before I answered him, I pressed my forehead to the window. The sign outside proclaimed the memorial for James Devine. There were a fleet of cars parked in the lot, and a line snaked out the door.

"Ruby?" he repeated.

"I'm awake," I said quietly.

"I can head over to the hotel if you want to get ready."

Sitting up, I flipped down the visor. Going to the hotel first was the smart thing to do, but I just wanted to get this over with. I looked like death, and extra primping wouldn't help that.

I scanned the road. "Why don't we go over there? I can get dressed in the bathroom."

He followed my gaze and arched a brow. "Wouldn't be the first time I got dressed in a diner."

"I mean, we can go—"

"Don't worry about it. I don't have to impress anyone. I'll just clean up a little."

I reached over and gripped his arm. "Thank you for driving me to this."

"Don't sweat it."

I'd been pretty low after Ezra's call last night. It was the only reason I could think of for letting down my guard so thoroughly with Lucky. But right now, the idea of walking into that firehouse alone was more than I could handle.

I checked my phone. I had a few texts from Rhett and Ezra asking when I was arriving. They were saving a seat for me.

But instead of replying, I flipped my phone over on my lap.

"You don't have to do this."

I rolled my head toward Lucky. "I do."

"We can split right now. That road right there," he arrowed his hand, "can get us out of here in less than five minutes. Three if you hold onto that 'oh shit' handle."

I couldn't stop a smile.

He turned in the seat. "You can blame me. I got lost."

"You'd do that?"

"In a heartbeat. They don't know me."

Before I could think about it, I leaned into him and pressed a light kiss to his bearded cheek. "Thanks, Thor."

One of his big hands cupped my jaw. "I hate seeing you so sad. It's damn near killing me."

"It's a selfish sad." My eyes stung. "I don't want to face my brother."

He pressed his forehead to mine. "He'd understand."

"No. He'd be so hurt." I shook my head. "I can't do that to him." I slid away from Lucky and reached for the bag behind the seat.

With a sigh, he pulled out of the parking lot and did a left turn to the diner half a block down. I stepped out before he could say anything else.

The brisk wind cleared my head a bit before I went inside, bag in hand. Thankfully, the big family-style diners were all the same. I'd be able to get changed without feeling like I was in a school locker. Being tall was a pain in the ass.

I nodded to the waitress at the front door and headed for the back.

"Miss."

"There's a big guy coming in after me. He'll order some food."

She huffed out an annoyed breath, but then Lucky ducked in through the door and she and the hostess were both distracted. Six-feet-four inches of hot dude would do that.

I was mostly immune.

Okay, barely.

But at this moment, I was very glad for his charming demeanor. I could already hear him flirting with them.

I followed the sign for the bathrooms. "Bingo," I said and dumped my bag on the counter. I snapped out my handy black dress. It was the one I used for any funeral or business dinner. The damn thing never wrinkled.

I grabbed my heels. Since there were hardly any people in the diner, I didn't feel bad about ducking into the handicapped stall. Quickly, I did my business—*thanks, nerves*—then kicked off my boots, socks, shirt, and leggings. I'd worn tights under my leggings so I just had to wiggle into the dress.

It clung to my hips, but it was mostly a column of simple black from neck to ankle. I dropped the shoes to the floor and stepped into the three-inch heels.

Back in the main bathroom, I washed up, pulled my hair into a simple French braid, and put on some lipstick and waterproof mascara so I didn't look like a ghost. Damn redhead genes.

Within ten minutes, I was back in the diner, bag slung over my shoulder.

Lucky stood at the front counter. He'd swapped his battered jeans for dark-washed ones and a gray button-down. He'd tucked it in, showing off his exceptional assets.

He turned and his gaze tracked along my body before zeroing in on my face. His brows furrowed as if he wasn't sure what to make of me.

He wasn't the only one.

"I had them make us some club sandwiches for later."

"Thanks." I pulled my wallet out of my bag.

"I got it."

I gave him a tight smile. There wasn't enough left in me to argue.

"Thanks, ladies. We really appreciate it."

"Are you going to the memorial?"

I looked at the floor and nodded.

"Such a waste. He was a nice boy. He and his father were always in here. Jimmy was always such a charmer."

Charming snake who probably still had money in the bank from the sale of my machine.

I clenched my hands and said nothing.

Lucky slid his palm along my lower back, rubbing lightly. He took the to go bag and steered me out the door.

"Damn, Ruby. You're almost eye to eye with me in those stilts."

I stepped into him, grateful for the distraction. "I don't line up with that many men." I dropped my gaze to his mouth then lifted it to his sea-green eyes, the flippant flirting between us falling away. "Thanks for doing this."

"Stop thanking me." He slid his hand down to catch mine. "Let's get this done."

I nodded and let him lead me out of the diner vestibule. The firehouse was packed now so it was easier to drop our stuff off and leave the truck in the diner parking lot.

He kept his hand in mine as we walked across the street.

I meant to drop his hand before I walked in the room, but the guy standing at the podium was waxing poetic about what a wonderful man Jimmy Devine was.

Larger than life photos of him flanked the small stage. Blond and full of smiles, he oozed charisma and his eyes were blue and crinkled at the corners. One picture was of him in his full uniform when he'd first become a firefighter, and in the other, he wore his smoke jumper gear.

Murmurs filled the room. Polite laughter came from people who knew him and loved him.

Once upon a time, I'd been on that list. I'd been fooled too.

At once, my knees dissolved.

Lucky gripped my hand harder and hauled me against him. I rested my palm against his warm chest. That clean, fresh scent filled my nose and cleared out the little black spots that had been forming at the edges of my vision.

The spell broken, I glanced into the crowd. My gaze landed on a man with a scooter near the wall.

Cohen.

Mottled green bruises covered his jaw, the last ugly reminder of what had happened. They looked as if they were on the way to healing. His leg was in a cast up to the knee. He was using the scooter to stand.

Lucky followed my gaze and gently shuffled me forward.

Ezra was leaning against the wall behind Cohen, his usual dark-rimmed glasses perched on his sharp nose. He wore a suit that had been obviously made for his lanky body. He spotted me and waved me over, a frown forming on his face as he caught sight of the man beside me.

My dad and Rhett were two peas in a pod as always. I finally slipped my hand from Lucky's and went right to my dad. The tears I'd been holding onto tracked down my cheeks.

He caught me tight. Jeff Burns might have been the elder statesman of this crazy crew, but he was still a solid wall of muscle. He smelled of Tom Ford with a hint of motor oil. The old black leather jacket he wore was as familiar as his scent.

I stepped back and dashed at my eyes. I gave Rhett a quick hug. He was the dapper one of all of us in a modern suit and smelled like something expensive. I moved onto Ezra.

He crushed me close and murmured, "Who's the tree?"

"A friend."

He arched a brow, but thankfully, it wasn't the time for questions. I knew I'd have to answer them eventually.

That was a problem for another day.

Cohen was staring straight ahead, his eyes flat and emotionless.

"Co," I said softly.

He shook his head, not meeting my gaze.

The tears hit again. I tipped my head back to stop the flow. Then I felt Lucky at my back, his big hand coming to rest on my hip. All that warm sturdiness was like another blow when I felt so damn wobbly.

Cohen finally looked at me. Desolation filled his gray green eyes. They were rimmed with red, but as dry as ash. His jaw flexed and he swallowed hard.

I stepped closer to him, but he shook his head.

I dropped my arms. "Co." My voice broke. "I'm so sorry."

"It should have been me," he whispered.

"No." I didn't care right then what he wanted. I wrapped my arms around his shoulders. They were usually so sturdy and strong. He'd always been whip lean, but all muscle. Now I only felt bones.

He didn't hug me back.

I held on anyway.

Whomever was talking finished and the attendees begun clapping. They called someone else up to talk about Jimmy. The woman spoke about how amazing he was. How much he helped others. How generous he was with his time.

Each piece of the eulogy lashed at me.

When I could take no more, I stepped back. Cohen wouldn't look at me. He'd gone back to staring at nothing. Maybe at some memory we would never share.

Lucky took my arm and tried to lead me over to the wall by my dad, but I couldn't stay.

"Please get me out of here." My voice was shaky and foreign.

The whole room was too hot, too much.

People were everywhere, and it felt like I was standing in molasses.

Lucky laced our fingers and dragged me out into the sunshine. Into the brisk October breeze. I shivered, hugging myself as he urged me forward. Down a walkway scattered with leaves and then my heels were sinking into grass.

I stumbled into him, and he wrapped those huge arms around me.

"I just need a minute," I said against his soft gray shirt. I buried my face in his chest and just held on. "Just a minute."

"As long as you need, Ruby."

ELEVEN

Lucky

I wasn't sure what to do with a trembling Tish Burns in my arms. She was usually all crackle and movement. In a rush to be somewhere else as if her body was too tuned up to stay stationary.

For the first time, she felt small and fragile.

Part of me wanted to roar and slash at anyone coming at her and then there was the other half of me who wanted to run. To scrape off the feelings clinging to me like mud off a boot.

But they were here to stay.

There was no doubt in my mind that her initials were carved into my chest like an old oak. I could say with complete certainty no one had ever been important enough to scratch the surface let alone scoop out bone. Especially a persnickety female who would probably skin me alive for these hugs when she got herself straight.

For now, I'd enjoy her cinnamon and coffee scent. I also appreciated that I didn't have to bend myself in half to hug her, a true pleasure for a man nearly six and a half feet tall in work boots. But my Valkyrie, with braid included today, was perfect for me. I could barely tuck her under my chin.

Before she could get prickly on me, I took her hand again and drew her back toward the road so we could get the hell out of here. I glanced back to make sure she was with me. The silvery tracks of her tears through her makeup shredded me in ways I couldn't fathom right now.

"I'm wearing heels, pal."

I slowed a bit, but we still hurried across the street to the diner. I bustled her into the truck and slammed the door, then ran around to my side.

She gave me that almost smile. "When I said get me out of here, I didn't really mean *Avengers*-style, Thor."

I flushed. "Yeah, well, I don't do well with female tears."

She rolled her eyes. "It was a memorial."

"For a dude you hated."

Maybe. Jury was on the fence on that one.

She scrunched down in her seat and crossed her arms. "I don't hate my brother."

I chirped the wheels as I bounced over the curb to head off the traffic that was starting to come out of the firehouse. She might not hate her brother, but I'd witnessed the quick slice of pain from his indifference. I knew there was more to the story.

Guilt and sorrow had been stacked as high as my Viking princess in that room.

At least the tears had faded. I was much more comfortable with the surprise lighting her features as she grabbed her seatbelt and clipped it in place.

I gunned the engine to get out of the city traffic, turning off one of the back roads. I'd looked at maps on my phone while she got ready. It had been awhile since I'd been in Connecticut, but I'd hoped to lure her into taking a nice drive after the memorial.

Now it looked like we were going for a full-fledged escape. And I was here for it.

"Where are you taking me?"

"A little spot I know."

"We're in the middle of Connecticut."

"Remember that whole roadie thing?"

She sighed. "Is that going to be a name drop all the time now?"

"I'll ignore the catty comments since you're having a bad day."

"Big of you." She rolled her eyes. "Yes, I remember your time with the famous Flynn Sheppard."

I shook my head. "Well, he didn't like to be boxed in. We knew where to find open spaces in damn near every state."

She grabbed her sweater out of the backseat. "I don't care where you take me, just as long as it's far from here." She bunched up her sweater and shoved it against the window as a pillow then turned away from me.

That damn dress was going to end me. It stretched across her bitable ass and clung to her hips. She kicked off her shoes and curled her knees up under the skirt of the dress. A soft black cocoon created for her to totally withdraw into herself.

I'd hoped to have a little longer before she shut down, but I'd just have to rely on the views from the road.

I headed toward the water and left the music on low. Sure enough, she hadn't been lying on the soundless sleep. I kept looking over to see if she was awake or not.

But the steady rise of her shoulders told me she was sleeping off the heavy day. I couldn't blame her. The blank look in her brother's eyes had cut at me, and I didn't even know him.

The other men in her life had stared me down like I was a tick on their beloved dog. The older man with the gray hair who looked like he led a motorcycle gang scared me the most. Second only to the brother who bore the same features and temperament. The one in the suit, Rhett, was the only one who hadn't made me feel immediately unwelcome.

I didn't have all the details on her family situation, but there had definitely been shock on their faces to see me with Ruby. Was it because I was a lumberjack-looking dude or because I was simply a male? Maybe she was as solitary as she seemed.

As I drove, my gaze returned to her again and again.

I should've encouraged her to check in with them, make sure they knew she was okay, but letting her rest seemed more important than giving her family the 411 on her whereabouts.

Since she'd passed out so thoroughly, I opted for a place a bit closer to Crescent Cove. If I pushed it, I could probably get us back home, but I was pretty sure she needed the quiet time. Knowing my Ruby, she'd disappear into her workshop instead of letting herself mend. And I was pretty sure the healing view was worth it.

We were driving into the sun, my belly reminding me I hadn't had lunch. I'd already raided the club sandwiches I'd ordered from the diner. Ruby barely moved.

Then again, she probably hadn't slept well last night after that phone call with her brother.

Twice in two days, I'd seen behind the curtain. Her tough girl side was definitely her default setting. It was sexy as hell—especially when she was grouchy—but the clawing pain in those doe eyes had about done me in.

Rest and more rest was on the menu tonight, whether she liked it or not.

I rolled down the window as I sailed through the mouth of the park. It was the off-season, but there were enough people around to take in the seasonal changes that I had to check in for a campsite.

I asked for one off the beaten path. It was too late to hike up into the area with waterfall views, but we'd be able to hear the water from where we were parked.

Driving over the uneven roads should have jostled her awake, but she was seriously deep under.

I parked in the middle of an open field. Trees surrounded us in red, gold, and perpetual pine green. Leaves dusted the grass, attesting to the lateness of the season. The air had the tang of fall laced with the nearby waterfall. An achingly blue sky was already starting to darken in deference to the shorter days.

Shrugging out of my dress shirt, I tossed it into the backseat before I got out and leaped into the truck bed. I always kept my camping gear stashed in my truck. I never knew when I'd have the urge to disappear for a few days. With Caleb becoming more and more unavailable, there wasn't much to keep me around unless I was working.

I pulled out my gear from my waterproof locker. I was a big guy, so I'd had to special order an air mattress that could handle me. I rolled it out, but held off on blowing it up since that would definitely wake up Ruby.

I skipped the tent cap. A clear night was in the forecast, and the subzero sleeping bags would keep us cozy. Maybe we'd even get to share a little body heat if I was lucky.

The real star of the show would be sleeping under the stars, and maybe, just maybe, it would help get her out of her thoughts.

I glanced through the back window and saw her head suddenly pop up.

She looked out the front then the window on her side of the truck before turning around. Sleep creases marred her smooth skin, her makeup had smudged under her eyes, and her braid was coming loose.

My Ruby was too goddamn beautiful for words.

She stumbled out of the cab of the truck with a litany of suggestive ways to fuck someone sideways. I was willing to volunteer to help her out there. I wasn't sure what it said about me that I got turned on by her surly nature.

She slammed the door and gave me a menacing look.

I opened the sliding window and fished the air mattress pump cord through. "Hey, can you plug that in?"

She put her hands on her hips. "Where the hell are we?" She frowned at the line of trees before whipping her gaze back to me. "Did you bring me out here to murder me? It feels very murdery out here."

I laughed. "At a campsite?"

"Hello, Crystal Lake was a sleepover camp. Didn't stop those kids from getting killed."

"So, we aren't going to watch scary movies while we camp out?"

"Do I look like the kind of girl who camps out?"

"You look like the kind of girl who can handle anything."

Her jaw dropped for a moment, and no words seemed to form. Her dark eyes flashed confusion, frustration, and then back to anger. "Ugh." She stomped back to the cab of the truck and climbed in. She yanked the cord, looked around, then found my charger.

She backed out and whirled around. "Is there a bathroom?"

I reached into the locker and came up with biodegradable wipes. "Wherever you want, Ruby."

"Dear God." She huffed out a half laugh. "Where are the other campers?"

"I figured you'd want some privacy. We're all alone out here."

"Murdery," she reiterated.

"Nah. If I wanted to murder you, I could have done it while you were sleeping." I pressed my hands against my cheek and closed my eyes. "Sleeping so soundly."

"Ass." She shielded her eyes against the dying sun streaming across the field. Slowly, the tension rolled off her shoulders. She drew in a long, deep breath, then shifted toward me. "I'm hungry."

I grinned down at her. "We've got your cooler of goodies, and I saved you a sandwich from the diner."

"Thank God." She opened the door again and pulled out her bag. She dropped it on the grass then whipped her dress off.

I was so shocked I stumbled and almost fell out of the truck.

She raised a brow at me. "Like you've never seen a pair of tits."

"I haven't seen yours yet." Her smoky gray bra was see-through, giving me a glimpse of small pink nipples.

She yanked out a sweatshirt from her bag and pulled it on. The bottom half of her was outlined in opaque black stockings that showed every damn line of her ass and legs. She went out of view as she leaned against the bench seat to pull on her leggings from earlier.

I took that opportunity to try to breathe without attaching my mouth to the air pump for some added assistance.

When she showed up next to the truck bed again, she had on a pair of thick socks. Even those made her hotter.

I was a sick, horny puppy.

"Is this your usual seduction scene?"

I glanced at the now firm air mattress. I'd zipped two sleeping bags together for maximum warmth and movement. "I can't say I've never had sex on an air mattress, but that wasn't the intention."

She folded her arms on the side of the truck and set her chin on her arms. "I haven't had sex on an air mattress. We'll see how it goes once you feed me." She peered down at the end where the tailgate was open. "How do I get up there?"

My brain went fuzzy after she said maybe we'd have sex.

She pushed away from the truck and trailed her fingertips along the side panel as she walked to the tailgate. "Guess it's a good thing you have such a big...truck."

I couldn't remember the last time I'd struggled to catch up when a woman was so obviously flirting. Well, flirting for Tish anyway.

She pushed up her sleeves and was about to hop onto the tailgate when I finally snapped out of it. I reached the end of the truck bed in one long stride and held my hand out for her. She tipped her head and gave me a long look before we locked hand to arm and I hauled her up. She was solid and soft at the same time.

I slid my arm around her back, but she slipped away. "Food first, Thor."

Before she could escape, I hauled her right back, trapping her hand against my chest. "Are you taunting me, Ruby?"

Her lids lowered over her eyes until they were mere slits. "I don't taunt and I don't tease."

I lifted her up on the air mattress, giving her a slight height advantage. Her eyes flared to life, so dark I couldn't tell what was going on in that head of hers.

Our lips hovered mere millimeters apart. The click of a mint rattling around in her mouth made me ache for that bite of flavor.

Her tongue swiped over her bottom lip and that was all it took. Whatever patience I'd had left vanished.

My hand slid across her lower back, diving under the loose hem of her sweatshirt. Heat and smooth skin were my rewards. She shivered lightly, but her gaze was fixated on my mouth.

"Tell me you want this as much as I do."

Her gaze tracked to mine. A deluge of emotions flickered in her eyes. Surprise, want, apprehension—they all tumbled together in a kaleidoscope of frustration.

Then her mouth was on mine.

My other hand cupped the back of her neck as I tried to wrangle the inferno of passion between us. With the height of the air mattress giving her an inch on me, she snatched the tiny imbalance of power.

Her nails dug into my chest just as her tongue snaked inside my mouth. Searching and finding all the little pieces that would lead to my destruction. She tangled with my tongue, then gave a feral smile as she nipped the tip before curling around to ease the hint of pain.

I was used to being the aggressor in a kiss. The first few steps of the dance between vertical and horizontal were important to see if I needed to lead or follow.

Here there was no following. There was only surrender.

She wrapped her arms around my shoulders. The wisps of her loosening braid lifted in the breeze and curled around us like a crackling fire.

I let her have the upper hand—welcomed it because that meant I could touch her. I'd been starving for her skin, her taste, her scent. My hands slid down to grip her ass and to lightly mold and stroke.

She rocked against me, frustration and impatience humming between us. She fisted my hair, moving my head to the angles she wanted. The kisses somehow went deeper, with lashing tongues trying to fight for dominance. Her clever teeth nipped at my lower lip as her lids lifted to watch.

Her sudden smile—bright and full voltage for once—had my dick knocking against her belly. She was always beautiful, even with the sadness she'd been carrying around like a knapsack. But now with the sunset haloing the fiery and potent woman underneath the emotions that had rocked her—I didn't have a single defense.

She was the Valkyrie whose power had punched me in the chest the first time we met. Instead of irritation, there was nothing but want shimmering off of her.

For me.

"Fuck," I said against her mouth and went back for another taste. The mint got in my way and I captured it with my teeth, pulling away long enough to get rid of it. "Just your taste. I can't get enough of it."

Teeth clicked as we tore at the clothes between us. I let her go to drag off her sweatshirt and went right for the tight tips trying to blast through the flimsy bra. She pulled my hair, and I wasn't sure if it was to stop me until I let go of her hard nipple.

She growled and arched her back to get me back where she wanted me. I was more than happy to oblige. I reached around to find the snap and flicked it open with one hand. The other was too busy plucking at the nipple I couldn't get to.

I needed two mouths to take in all I wanted from her. Greed sliced at me, making me rough. The bra fell away, and my beard left red slashes across her water-soft skin.

When I backed off to let her get her bearings, she growled, "Is that all you've got, Thor?"

No bearings needed here.

I tossed the bra aside and cupped her breasts, staring up at her as I scraped my teeth over her silky skin to suck one of the tips into my mouth. I sucked strongly enough to feel my own heartbeat roar in my ears.

Her head fell back as she sunk her nails into my biceps. "More."

"Like this." I twirled my tongue around one nipple, then the other until the soft pink bloomed a deep red.

"I don't want soft kisses," she panted, fisting my hair to drag my mouth to hers. The kiss was close to violent with need. I tasted blood on my tongue. "Make me feel anything other than sad and mad."

A pang of something I didn't want to identify hit me sideways. Was she just using me? Did I care?

I hated that I was pretty sure I did.

But this was about her right now. And I'd be whatever she needed.

I tugged her off the air mattress into the slim space along the side of the truck bed. I turned her around until her back was flush with my front then nudged her braid to the side. "Like this?" I scored the column of her neck, my tongue sliding over her racing pulse.

I bit into the soft skin between her shoulder and her neck. The tendons of muscle vibrated like a guitar string under my teeth. I covered her breasts with my big hands, alternating softly cupping them with merciless pulls on each nipple.

Moving up to her ear, I sucked the lobe into my mouth, flicking my tongue along the sensitive skin there. She shook in my arms. "Think I can make you come with just this?" I plucked and rolled the tight little points of her breasts.

Her ass ground against the front of my jeans. "Can I make you come with just my ass against your cock?"

I groaned into her ear. It could happen. I hadn't come in my damn pants since I was a boy. But if anyone could drag me over the edge without an actual touch, it would be Ruby.

Her hand came up to grip my shoulder, then slid into my hair along the nape of my neck. She pulled me closer, turning her head to catch my lips in a wild kiss. She hummed her appreciation as I continued my torture. I wanted to slip my fingers down into those leggings of hers, but now I'd thrown down the challenge.

Soft and hard, rough and gentle, I changed up the combinations so fast she could do nothing but roll her head along my chest. I locked myself down, finding the strength to give her what she needed. She shook and writhed against me. I dipped my mouth to her shoulder with a tender kiss then a bite and she finally bucked against me with a keening cry of my name.

"I need—" I couldn't even form the words, but I had to know what I'd done to her.

My hand dove into her leggings, bypassing nylon and finally, a cotton barrier. She was so slick and hot. I pushed two fingers into her drenched pussy. She sucked me so deep I was willing to meet my maker just to have her once.

She pulled my hair again, arching her back so the last rays of sunshine gilded her skin as she rode my hand. I turned her toward the mattress and knelt behind her, dragging the layers of offending fabric away to get to her.

I pushed her down and she gave a startled yelp and went onto her knees. I pushed them apart and dove my tongue into her salty slit. She gripped the sleeping bags, her whole body thrumming like a bass guitar.

She pushed back against me, riding my mouth with pure abandon.

A litany of inventive swear words colored the air just before her leg started to shake.

"Yes," I said against her wet inner thigh. "Yes, just like that." I went back for more. Her shoulder crashed into the mattress as she shook around me. "Ruby, let me inside."

She cried out for my death.

"Tish," I said against her thigh, then bit down on one cheek. I couldn't resist. "I need to be inside you."

"Yes, dammit."

With shaking fingers, I wrestled my wallet out of my pocket and prayed for a condom. It had been awhile since I'd taken the time to look for a willing partner.

But there was the foiled packet, hiding behind a credit card.

"Hurry," she said and fell onto her forearms, arching her back like a cat.

"Christ." Her endless legs and perfect ass were lifted for me. Waiting for me to dive in there. I was so keyed up I was afraid I'd split her in half.

I leaned forward to drive my tongue inside of her one more time before easing back. I gripped her hip with one hand and stroked the tip of my cock through her swollen lips. The air had become crisper now that the sun was sliding away, but it didn't matter.

I eased into her, growling at how she stretched for me.

Watching my cock disappear into her perfect pussy about killed me. Then she took the reins once more and shoved herself backward on my dick.

I threw my head back at the way she clamped down on me then the ripple of pleasure was dented by her voice.

"Move, damn you."

I grabbed onto her hips and slammed home again and again. She took each stroke and demanded more of me each time. I swore my brain was going to leak out of my damn ears, but still, I held on.

I reached around and circled her clit, knowing I was far too close to the edge. She covered my fingers with her own, both of us slip-sliding around her engorged clit.

She panted out my name, then God's, then back to me. "I won't break, dammit. Stop holding back."

I wasn't.

Was I?

God, she felt so fucking good. But she was right. I wanted to mark, to slam into her until my brain settled and reset. It had been chaos since the day I'd met her, and now I was even more tangled up over her.

I kissed a pattern of freckles between her shoulder blades, then drove into her with every bit of frustration and lust that had been hammering at me for the last month.

My fingers dug into her ass and her hips and her scream echoed in the cove of trees. My knees locked as the rush of fire licked down my spine. White-hot bliss fuzzed at the corners of my vision then a cavern of darkness descended, turning into a freefall that finally, finally settled into peace.

TWELVE

I HAD A REDWOOD TREE LAYING ON ME, AND I COULDN'T COMPLAIN IN the least.

My cheek was pressed into the green sleeping bag, and all my muscles felt like liquid gold. Maybe that really was exactly what I'd needed. Except one thing.

"I'm still hungry."

He grunted out a garbled hum.

"You gotta get off me so I can get food."

Another grunt.

I lifted my head…well, kind of. More like barely two inches since he literally had me pinned like we were on one of those cheesy wrestling shows. He'd thrown a leg over me, as well as one of those superiorly muscled arms.

"Later."

I wiggled. Muscles I hadn't used in too many months to count screamed, but eventually, I managed to get free from under his arm. "If you don't want my knee in your balls, move your leg."

He sighed. "Evidently, you don't know the meaning of the word afterglow."

"My glow was delightful, and now I'm starving."

He flipped to his back. "Fine. You could feed me some grapes, I suppose."

I sat up. "With or without the palm fronds?"

He yawned hugely, all satisfied lion with his curly hair. "It's chilly enough. You can skip those."

I pounded my fist on his thigh.

He jumped, then rolled onto his side to massage his muscle. "You're pretty mean for someone who just had at least two good orgasms."

It was three, but I wouldn't swell his head. I lifted my arms over my head to stretch out my back muscles.

He reached over and ran his hand down my back. "You mark so easy."

I looked over my shoulder. "Curse of a redhead. Don't sweat it, Thor. I got exactly what I needed."

His hand dropped away. "Glad I could be of assistance." His voice was flat.

Man, he sure was touchy. I leaned back and nipped his chin. "Pretty sure it was a mutual thing."

"It could be more mutual." He grinned down at me, then brushed his nose along mine. "That was just round one."

Another round would put me in traction. I mean, I would give it a go, but I needed a minute.

Or seven.

I looked around for my clothes, but the only things near me were my tights, underwear, and leggings, which were still trapped around my ankles. I was pretty sure most of that was ripped.

Dammit, Thor.

I reached down to roll off the mess then stood up totally naked.

"Jesus."

I flipped my destroyed braid over my shoulder to look down at him. "You just fucked the holy hell out of me. There's nothing here you haven't seen."

His green eyes were lit with some serious round two ideas. His gaze tracked me from the top of my head to the tips of my black toenails.

I held up a finger. For a second, I almost said *screw it* to the cold sandwich waiting for me, but then my stomach growled. "Hold that thought. I require sustenance."

And I sincerely hoped we were as private as it seemed. Knowing my luck, some fourteen-year-old boy on vacation with his family was watching me from some campsite.

Lucky lifted his hips and hiked up his jeans, so I took a moment to enjoy the whole long, muscular line of him. I hadn't really gotten a chance to see the goods.

Now I could ogle—I mean, appreciate—them at my leisure.

He rolled off the surprisingly firm air mattress to stand beside me, then gripped my ass with one of those bear paws of his.

I stumbled into him, then pushed back. "Food."

He gave me a hot look, his gaze stalling on my lips. Personally, I couldn't believe he chose my mouth as his focus since I was buck naked. "Before someone sees you, let me go get your stuff." He released me to hop to the ground. "Be right back."

Since the idea of clambering off the truck naked wasn't in my top ten list, I didn't argue. And I needed a second to catch my breath.

Less than a minute later, his arm came through the window holding his dress shirt. "Not exactly a sleep shirt, but it will do."

I bit my lip. Did I really want to be wrapped up in his scent? Bad enough that I'd done the naked tango with him. But it was fucking cold.

Snatching the shirt, I did up a few buttons before I pulled it over my head.

I wasn't a small girl. I usually had to do some serious shopping to find things that were long enough.

This shirt was a damn dress on me.

The material was soft and warm, and that odd soap scent of his dented the chilly air now that the sun was just about set. He popped up next to the truck, dumping the soft-sided cooler at my feet and his bag along the top of the flatbed.

I crouched to open it and stuffed a few grapes in my mouth before opening the to go container. The turkey club had seen better days, but I was too hungry to care. I found my lemon water bottle under some trail mix and brought the trio back over to the air mattress.

My freaking toes were frozen.

I slipped into the sleeping bag setup he had going on and for the first time in my life, I didn't care about crumbs in bed.

The first bite of semi-dry sandwich made me moan. Without shame, I washed it down with water like a scavenging raccoon. I watched Lucky stake lights—were those Tiki torches?—into the ground. Instead of lighting them, he shoved one of his big fingers into the center and a LED light flickered on.

"Not so much for bugs, huh?"

He lit three more around each side of the truck. "It's been pretty dry. Safer to go with battery lights than starting a fire."

Surprised that he was so thoughtful, I couldn't even make a quippy reply. The truck bed bounced a little as he put a knee on the tailgate and climbed on. He flicked his boots off at the end and snapped the tailgate closed before climbing up the bed to me.

My heart tripped as he filled the space. More of that soft soap scent hit me, from his hair this time. He braced his arm around me on top of the sleeping bag and took a bite of my sandwich.

Frowning, I pulled my quarter of sandwich out of reach. "What is with you sharing food?"

He shrugged. "We shared a lot more than spit not twenty minutes ago. What's the difference?"

"There's a difference," I said stubbornly. I knew I sounded ridiculous, but I didn't care.

He laughed, then collapsed beside me.

Now that my feet were nice and toasty, I kicked them out, hoping that he'd catch a hint. He did not. He simply propped his head up on his hand and watched me eat. With the other, he played with my hair.

"Mind if I fix this?"

I frowned down at him.

He nudged me forward and sat up. "Looks all knotted." Gently, he tugged out the elastic I'd used to tie the braid then unwound the pieces.

I kept munching on my sandwich, unsure how this was going to go.

I wasn't used to people in my space. A hug here and there with family was about the extent of it. And okay, the occasional forced hug from Luna, which I didn't know how to handle.

But this was…something else. Intimate in a way that made my skin tingle. I wasn't sure if it was because I was uncomfortable or because I liked it.

Maybe both.

He massaged my neck and shoulders. "So tense. After what we just did, I figured you'd be as loose as spaghetti. I know I am."

"I am." I hunched my shoulders.

He laughed. "Sure, you are. But you will be by the time I'm done." He rummaged through his bag and came out with a comb.

"You don't have cooties, do you?"

"Just eat your sandwich." He shucked his jeans and sat cross-legged behind me.

"Why do you need to remove your pants to fuss with my hair?"

"A dude needs to breathe."

"Which dude are we talking about here? Big or little?"

He chuckled. "Both are big, honey."

I didn't know what else to do so I picked at the triangle of sandwich I had left. Bacon first because it was the best part then the tomato. All the while, he unwound the tangled mess of my hair. I shivered as he lightly combed it with his fingers before he used his thumbs to massage the base of my neck.

"So tight. I'm sorry today was so hard."

My chin fell forward as he worked his fingers all the way up my scalp. On the return trip, he used his short nails to give my skin a little extra buzz. I couldn't say I was exactly getting relaxed, but it felt delicious.

Then he brought out the comb.

The to go container slid off my lap as I braced my hands beside my hips. If someone had told me yesterday that my hair was an erogenous zone, I would have laughed.

No laughing here now though. Not in the least.

My eyes closed to slits as the gentle tugs from his wide-toothed comb drew me closer to him. Full dark had come over our little patch of the park or wherever he'd brought me. The fact that I hadn't really questioned him either made me insane or...

That *or* wasn't something I wanted to speculate about right now.

For once, I was just going to live in the moment. I'd try to forget the shattered eyes of my brother, the slice in my chest that had reopened, and the past I wasn't ready to dissect.

All of that was for another time.

It was a clean, cool night with the hearty crickets and night birds as our soundtrack. The Tiki torches gave off just enough light to push the imagined monsters away.

I tipped my head back when he found a snarl. But he didn't pull, just carefully attacked it without causing any pain.

While he worked, I took in the sky and the spray of stars above. I never really sat still enough to watch the sky at night just because.

Even as a kid, I'd always been looking toward my future to the plans I had. I'd spent my free time in the shop I couldn't stay out of, figuring out how to pull things apart and put them back together. There was no time to sit when I could be doing something.

Then here was this man behind me. From the bonfire to the plans for my house, Lucky proved how meticulous he was. And he lived a balanced life. He worked and played with equal energy.

Even as busy as he was, he'd come with me to figure out the clusterfuck of my past without a second thought. He'd understood I needed someone and simply volunteered.

Wanting to get horizontal with me didn't include this kind of bullshit. So, why was he sticking around?

I just didn't understand any of it. Truthfully, I was afraid to.

But I realized I'd dropped my shoulders and was leaning back against his knees. I couldn't stop the shiver as he gathered my hair into a tail.

His voice rumbled as if playing with my hair had affected him just as much. "I'm no expert on the intricate braids, but I can do the simple kind."

He parted the long, thick mass into three pieces then twined them together with no fanfare. Just neat and a little loose.

Somehow knowing my hair wasn't quite so crazy smoothed out some of my edges. He'd coaxed out some secret oasis of calm deep inside of me I hadn't known existed.

His fingers slid along my waist as he shifted us farther up the mattress. He tucked me back against him, his legs outstretched to cup me in his endless source of heat. "Warm enough now?"

"I'm okay."

"You were shivering."

"Not from being cold."

He slid his arms around my middle and tucked his chin on my shoulder. "Is that a good thing?"

Tipping my head closer, I folded my arms over his. His warmth and comforting scent and whatever other mojo he had created a perfect cocoon. "It's...nice."

He chuckled. "Gee, thanks." I tried to wiggle away, but he stopped me. "Nice is a good start."

"Look, I'm no good at this stuff. Fucking? Yeah, sure. I'm down for some sweaty sex to release tension but..."

He tightened his hold. "We'll figure it out together. I'm no maestro when it comes to this shit either, Ruby. I just know it's different with you." He pressed a kiss to that spot between my shoulder and neck he couldn't seem to resist. And I couldn't deny those kisses were rapidly becoming my favorite thing.

I wasn't sure I was brave enough to ask what that meant.

"I think we should curl up and watch a scary movie."

I twisted my head to look at him. "What?"

"C'mon. We're in the dark. In the middle of nowhere. It's definitely time to watch a scary movie."

"You're insane."

"I'll protect you, Ruby."

"Shut up. I'm more likely to protect *you*."

"Okay. I'll let you." He inched us farther down on the mattress and rolled us over so he was the big spoon. He reached back for his bag and pulled out a beat-up iPad. "I have a few movies downloaded on here. Let's see what we find."

When I tried to pull away, he flattened his hand over my middle. "Relax. You're as skittish as a feral cat."

I elbowed him. "I like space."

"Yeah, well, you need a good—"

"If you say fucking, I'm going to belt you one."

He laughed and tucked my braid out of the way. "I was going to say a good cuddle, you perv." His hand slid under the tail of the dress-slash-shirt I was still wearing. But instead of aiming between my legs, or even toward my boobs, he just rested his hand over my belly. "Haven't you ever spooned and watched a movie?"

"No."

"Then we need to change that." He settled behind me, twisting my ass to fit against the curve of his very hard stomach and boxers-clad dick.

Which was getting a little happy.

"Uh-huh. Cuddle. Right."

"That's just a reaction to your perfect ass. I am not a slave to my dick, Ruby. No matter what the people of the Cove like to say."

"I didn't—"

He curled his arm under his head, creating a pillow for me. "Believe me when I tell you I could easily slip inside you right now and rock this truck until sunrise." Absently, he brushed his thumb against my ribs before slipping away to set up our mini-theater.

I couldn't say I was opposed to that idea.

He propped the iPad on the side of the truck bed, then opened his movie app and flicked through a startling number of movies and shows. I couldn't even catch up, but he seemed to know just where to go.

"Do I get a say?"

"Sure. Do you like Rob Zombie-level gore?"

"God, no."

"Good. Me neither. Now a good jump scare is classic. But I was thinking of another kind of classic."

"Like what? *Halloween?*" I glanced out into the darkness just beyond the torches. Not sure I'd get any sleep with that in my brain.

"Nah." He pushed play and the old 20th Century Fox logo came up, including trumpets. Then the black faded revealing Donald Sutherland in some medieval get-up handing a blond whose name I couldn't remember a stake.

A giggle tumbled out of me. "Are you for real?"

His hand slid back under my shirt. "Damn right. Buffy is glorious." This time, his fingers inched higher to stroke just below my breast. "Watch the movie."

The campy movie was indeed just what I'd needed. I found myself drifting off with the 90s soundtrack in my head and a giant heater at my back.

Sometime in the night he did, in fact, slip inside me. The torches had gone out, and the only witnesses to our lovemaking were the stars and crickets. But the sweet, rocking climax wasn't enough.

It only whetted my appetite for more.

For a connection to someone and something. The vastness of our little spot in the middle of nowhere gave me a freedom I wasn't aware I needed.

I turned and rolled him over. His eyes shone in the darkness. The moon was close to full and gave me just enough light to be brave.

Climbing onto his thighs, I undid each button on my borrowed shirt. The cool breeze coasted over my skin like mist as I peeled it open. While he watched me, he slid his hands up my hips and his cock lengthened against his lower belly to curve slightly to the right.

Patience warred with need as he waited me out, letting me take the reins this time.

Slowly, I trailed my fingertips up my belly to my ribs and finally to tease the tips of my tight nipples. His grip on my naked hips tightened, but he didn't move. Just the harsh rise and fall of his massive chest alerted me to his response.

I lifted my arms to untie my braid. That day in the suburbs flashed in my memory. When I'd leaned over him to help free Butch, he'd reacted to my hair. Reacted to my closeness.

Here and now, I shook out my hair as he swore darkly.

I leaned over him to press a finger to his lips. I didn't want him to speak. The magic of the night was enough for us.

I brushed my breasts against his mostly smooth chest. Just a little dusting of hair along his abs led to the muscular vee ending in the thick girth of his cock. I nipped his bearded chin, then his neck as I opened my thighs wider to slide my still wet cleft along his shaft. His fingers slid farther back to cup my ass and gently guide me to rub harder.

Resting my hands on his chest, I rolled my hips to tease the tip of his cock with the hood of my pussy. My eyes closed as pleasure flared between us.

I fumbled above his head to dig through his condom stash. I should have been mad that he'd prepared for this possibility, but I didn't care right now. I just wanted him inside me.

Finding my prize, I leaned back to take him in hand.

His jaw was tight in the faint glow of the moonlight. I rolled down the latex and shimmied up to take him before I could overthink the whole damn thing. The fact that I wanted him inside me more than to ride to the orgasm I knew he could provide made me pause.

But then he was sitting up, those ridiculous arms lifting me. "Ruby."

I reached between us and guided him home.

No. Just inside. Home implied something else.

I rolled my head back, but I couldn't lie to myself. He *did* feel like home. As if he was part of something bigger I'd never known I was missing.

As if I was too. Together we were just...*more.*

He gripped my hair before hauling me against him. Chest to chest, face to face, every inch of skin pressed close. He filled me up so completely that I couldn't hold back my broken sob.

Slanting his mouth over mine, he swallowed my cries. If he hadn't, they would've echoed into the darkness. I couldn't suppress them.

He braced his other hand against my back as he rocked himself deeper inside me. We flowed together, a rushing current against an endpoint neither of us wanted to reach.

I wrapped my arms around his shoulders, then buried my face between his neck and his shoulder. The tears sideswiped me. All the pain of the day, the stress of keeping quiet about a betrayal I'd thought I buried, and this man who'd bulldozed his way into my life crashed into the wall of pleasure.

He stiffened under me, and his choked groan of release activated my own.

Even if the messy emotions tried to strangle the passion between us, they were there under it all. Refusing to be denied. They flattened me as my groan of surrender ended in a sob.

"Shh." His arms tightened around me. "Shh. It's okay."

The torrent of tears horrified me. I tried to scramble away, but he wouldn't let me. He crushed me tighter and pressed his cheek against mine. The murmur of acceptance and the comfort of his immovable strength soothed me, there for the taking.

I just had to reach for them.

"Tish, I'm not going anywhere."

My hands fisted against his back, but he didn't let go. Finally, I relaxed against him, silent tears replacing the storm.

Gently, he rocked me until the sky started to lighten. Then he simply laid down, taking me with him.

His fingers were a tender brush along my naked back. And again, I fell asleep.

Except this time, I was wrapped around him.

THIRTEEN

Lucky

THE RIDE HOME WASN'T EXACTLY WHAT I EXPECTED. AFTER THE previous night, I'd thought we were past one of the blocks between us.

I was very wrong.

She didn't say much more than five words to me. Three of them declaring her need for coffee. McDonald's saved the day again. After a belly full of coffee and tasty McMuffin sandwiches, we spent two and half hours listening to Asher Wainwright scare the crap out of us with his podcast.

I turned onto her road. We'd been halfway home to start, and she'd nudged me to leave barely past dawn. It was early enough that mist was still clinging to the lake. My eyes were gritty from lack of sleep, but my body was charged on truly excellent sex and Mickey D's.

I drove around to the barn. Before I even came to a stop, she was unclipping her belt and grabbing her bag.

"Gonna jump out before I put her in park?"

She shot me a guilt-filled look over her shoulder. "I'm tired and need a shower and a real bathroom."

I turned toward her. "I'm ready to find a shower too, but you don't think we should talk about last night?"

This wasn't my usual role. Typically, I was the one strolling away before a woman could ask if I wanted to talk about "where we are." I never did.

Overnight, I'd become a man eager to discuss feelings and crochet tea cozies.

Or beer cozies. Was that a thing? I could start the trend, assuming I could figure out how to crochet. There was always YouTube.

"It was what it was."

I knew she was still embarrassed about crying. Didn't make her words any less of a direct hit. "It was more than just a tumble and you know it."

Her shoulders hunched.

"Didn't take you for a coward, Tish."

She swung open the door and slid out. "You don't know me." She shook back all that viking red hair. "Let's just keep it business."

The jab cut deep. "You got it."

She'd barely closed the door before I was reversing and kicking up gravel in my haste. My fingers throbbed with my grip on the steering wheel, and my tires chirped as I turned onto Lake Street. I fishtailed, gunning my engine to get away from her place.

If I'd been paying fucking attention, I would have caught Crescent Cove's finest before blasting by. The whoop-whoop of a siren was followed by red and blue lights flashing in my rearview. "Goddammit. Just what I need."

Throwing on my blinker, I pulled over to the curb. I slapped open my glove box and Ruby's trail mix tumbled out. I tossed it in my backseat with a growl and dug out my registration and insurance.

When I straightened, the newest addition to Crescent Cove's police department was standing by my window.

Deputy Brady McNeill's usually affable expression had been replaced with stern lines. We'd hung out a few times on the rooftop of Caleb's place, but a job was a job. I was driving like an asshole, and that was on me.

"Any idea how fast you were going, Lucky?"

"Nope." I stared straight ahead, my paperwork crushed in one hand.

152

"Hmm." He tapped his hand on his gun, then relaxed. "Girl trouble."

My hand tightened on the wheel again.

"Definitely girl trouble." He glanced at his watch. "Wanna grab a beer?"

I frowned. "What? It's not even ten."

He shrugged. "It's a little after nine. Means I'm off shift. I pulled the overnight."

"There's an overnight shift in Crescent Cove?" Shock had me sitting back in my seat.

"There is when the hayrides have started. Not much to do in a small town but get drunk. I confiscated a twelve pack of microbrew."

My eyebrow shot up. "In my day we bought Budweiser or worse—"

"The Beast," Brady finished for me. "Come on. The rooftop is pretty toasty this time of day. Good time to get drunk."

"You're not going to give me a ticket?"

"Nah. Been there with a persnickety woman."

"How do you know my woman is persnickety?"

"Luc, the whole town knows you're gone for Tish."

I bounced my head off the headrest. "The whole town?"

If Tish figured that out, she'd probably fire me from the remodel too. But she wasn't paying me, so could she fire me?

I'd ponder it over beer with Officer Friendly.

"Luna's pretty chatty over there at Kin's shop. Talked about the bonfire. Where was my invite by the way?"

I laughed. "Was hard enough to get Ruby to deal with having two couples over."

"Ruby, huh?"

My answer was silence.

Brady grunted. "I had to work anyway. Come on, you can tell me your tales of woe."

"Am I being punked?"

Tipping his head back, he laughed good-naturedly. "So suspicious."

Cops had never exactly been my favorite people. A big kid on the street always served as prime pickings for shithead cops who just wanted a collar. Especially since I'd looked over eighteen since my early teen years. I'd never been charged, but I'd had my fair share of arrests.

"I threw the beers in my cooler. Follow me if you want some," he said over his shoulder as he walked back to his cruiser. He pulled out and passed me with a wave.

I looked down at my rumpled clothes. I hadn't been kidding when I'd said I needed a shower. Three bouts of sex and sleeping under the stars had left me pretty ripe. All the good parts smelled like Ruby.

And the thought of her had me putting my truck in drive. "Fuck it."

Day drinking sounded like a damn good plan.

I pulled out at a much more sedate pace. Main Street was alive with daytime traffic. It was a Saturday, which meant shopping in the Cove.

I found a spot a half block down from Brewed Awakening. Apartments filled the building's other floors. I'd considered moving in there at the same time as Caleb, but I was glad I hadn't. He would be finding a house with Blondie soon, and I liked my little two-family house apartment deal. Even if it was close to chaos right now with half-finished projects.

At some point, I also needed to stop by Caleb's to pick up Butch. I'd hoped to get a few hours of sleep first, but why shouldn't today be just as fucked as all the other days lately?

Might as well get my girl first. A few doggie kisses would set me back to rights.

I went around to the side entrance and buzzed Caleb's place. They'd made some upgrades to the apartments in the last few months, probably due to some teens breaking in during the remodel.

"Hello?" Luna's sweet voice came out of the speaker.

"It's Lucky."

"Oh. I thought you'd be later. Butch and I are having fun. Well, poop. Come on up."

I shook my head and opened the door when I heard the locks release. There was an elevator at the other entrance, so I had to do the stairs. I was slightly winded and damn ready for that beer by the time I got to their floor.

Luna opened the door and peeked out with my dog in her arms. A tiny pink bow fluttered between her ears.

Butch's not Luna's, but you could never be certain.

"What did you do to my dog?"

"Just because you named her Butch doesn't mean she can't be pretty." She nuzzled the dog, and the dog gave her a look of adoration in return.

But as soon as B saw me, she leaped out of Luna's arms and came running down the hall. My heart flipped as I crouched to scoop up my girl. "Did you miss Daddy?"

Luna leaned on the doorjamb. "Aww, you guys are so sweet."

"Thanks for watching her." I tucked Butch up on my shoulder, her favorite perch.

"She was a darling. I don't mind babysitting anytime."

"Good to know." I patted B's little head as she licked my cheek. "Not sure what I'm going to do with her for your wedding though."

"Oh, you should check with Bess. We had lunch yesterday, and she just loves Butch."

"Yeah? That would be great. I'll give her a ring."

"I'll just get her stuff."

"Actually. I'll stop back and get her stuff."

"Oh?" Luna cocked her head. "Got a hot date in the building?"

"More like lukewarm. I'd ask if you wanted a drink too, Lu, but I think that's off your particular menu." Brady came up behind me with an old red and white cooler.

"Well, hello there, Officer Brady."

"Deputy," Brady said with a wink.

Butch gave a happy bark, and her tail swished under my hair.

"Well, hey there, little one." Brady grinned at the dog. "Does she drink beer too?"

"She probably would." When Butch's rump wiggled at Brady's voice, I shook my head at her wanton behavior. "The cop too, Butch? Really?"

Brady laughed. "I love a woman with superior taste."

"I just bet you do." I turned back to Luna. "Is the old man around?"

"He's grocery shopping. I'll send him up to the roof when he gets back."

I arched a brow. "No problem with the day drinking?"

She shrugged. "You guys obviously need time to talk."

I didn't say a damn thing, but I was getting used to Luna knowing things even when they were left unsaid. "Do I look that bad?"

"Your aura is blasting blue." She reached up and patted my cheek before giving Butch a chin scratch. "I have clients all day today anyway. Will keep Goldilocks out of my hair."

"Thanks, Lu."

Brady nodded at Lu. "Always a pleasure, Luna."

"Likewise, Deputy."

We took the stairs up to the rooftop. The lush summer plants had been replaced with frothy buckets of mums in fall colors. A few pumpkins were stashed in corners next to happy scarecrows perched on hay bales.

Probably Luna's doing. I was pretty sure the suit who owned this place had stopped at flowers.

I followed Brady over to the table. Thankfully, he chose the one with chairs that actually fit me.

After setting the cooler down, he slid it open and popped the top on a beer with his ring. He handed one to me and took one for himself.

Silence stretched companionably between us as Butch settled in my lap and Brady sat down and stretched out his legs. He'd swapped his uniform for a worn pair of jeans and a NYU sweatshirt.

I took a long sip then pointed at him with the bottle. "NYU? Did you go?"

"Yeah, I went the criminal justice route for awhile. Being a lawyer didn't take though." He laced his fingers around his beer and set it against his stomach as he lifted his face to the sun.

"Lawyer? Huh. Well, that's way different than a cop."

"Way more different than FBI too."

I took a longer pull. The dark beer had been on the way to relaxing me until that bombshell. "What?"

Brady opened one eye. "Don't get all excited. Working for the FBI is just paperwork wrapped in bureaucracy." He took a long draw from his bottle too. "I like the Cove. Nice and quiet."

I had a feeling there was more there, but I probably wouldn't get it out of him today.

"Tell me a story, Lucky. I bet you've got a good one."

I finished my beer and jockeyed Butch as I reached for another. As soon as I sat again, Butch went back to sleep.

She had the right idea.

The sun felt good on my skin, and the warmth helped to unkink the Ruby-sized knots in my shoulders. "No story. Just a woman trying to drive a good man crazy."

"Who told you that?"

"What?"

"That you're a good man."

I laughed and clinked my bottle with his. "True that." Careful not to rouse Butch, I kicked out my legs as Brady had and crossed them at the ankle. "On a sunny September day, I met a Valkyrie."

"This is gonna be good."

"You have no idea." I drank deeply.

The beer was higher octane than I was used to, and I was already feeling loose. He wanted a story, so he was going to get one. The best one of my life—so far.

Regardless, I was on this ride until the end. Win, lose or Ruby.

FOURTEEN

AFTER TAKING A SHOWER AND THEN TOSSING AND TURNING FOR THREE hours, I couldn't stand myself any longer.

Being alone in bed wasn't what I wanted right now. And that royally pissed me off.

My dreams hadn't helped on that score. In them, I was rolling around with a certain long-haired handyman. There were no tears this time, just a whole lot of sweat and screaming.

Enough that I woke up shaking and half a minute from taking the edge off on my own.

A second cold shower later, I was heading out the door to go to my workshop. If I couldn't sleep, then at least I could work.

Always my mantra.

With Jimmy's memorial and the whole house and barn remodel, I was way behind on the Phantom project. Gage had been doing the build and didn't need any new parts from me yet, but I didn't like leaving it all to him.

Even better, it was a Saturday afternoon so no one would be in the shop but me. The nice thing about a small town was the hours we kept.

Beyond that, I really needed to get my beater on the road. There was a shit-ton of rain in the forecast for the rest of the week.

Even so, the lure of my Triumph was too much. Besides, I could finally finish tuning up the engine before I stored her for the winter.

I threw my leg over the seat and the purr of the engine settled my nerves. I had less than two months to get my house in order for my family. And after seeing just how bad Cohen had been, I was even more determined to make sure he had a bomb-ass place to heal up.

I took the long way into town. It was the perfect October day. Warm with just a hint of chill on the air. I was tempted to take a loop around the whole damn lake. Maybe even keep driving and tell the Kramer boys I'd be out of pocket for a week.

Damn responsibilities.

As I turned onto Main, I slowed to a crawl. The only bad part of a pretty day was that it was perfect for shopping. Foot traffic and cars congested Main Street. People lined the sidewalks in front of the various storefronts. Tabitha was doing a brisk business at Sugar Rush with her Halloween and fall confections. The new wine bar that had replaced a small eatery looked to be having a tasting.

I was tempted to go in to find a bottle of wine to calm down some of the chaos in my brain, but in the end, I'd rather have a beer.

After I got some work done.

By the time I finally got to the garage, I was humming for a whole different reason. I parked my bike outside and swung into Brewed Awakening for a coffee. Luckily, it was too busy in there for chitchat. Macy wasn't on duty, but as usual, her place ran like a top.

I sneaked through the doors that led to the apartments and bypassed the crush of people at the tables and waiting in line for caffeine and sugary treats. The elevator doors opened just as I was trying to escape.

"Shit."

I really didn't want to talk to anyone right now.

The tenored, imperfect voice of one Lucky Roberts came out of the elevator with a surprisingly smooth baritone pulling up the rear. The two men stumbled off the elevator singing "Sweet Home

Alabama", of all songs. I almost didn't recognize Lucky's drinking buddy.

Deputy Mc…something was looking decidedly un-cop like. Brent? No, I was pretty sure it was Brady. I'd only talked to him in passing a few times.

We took care of the cruisers when they needed a tune-up. Not like there were a whole lot of car crashes in this town. Hot pursuit usually included a duck more than a resident of the Cove.

There were some slurred words and then a third guy hiccupped his way off the elevator, singing very off-key. And there was the third Stooge.

Caleb came teetering off the elevator with his hand wrapped around the neck of a beer bottle like his life depended on it.

It was barely two o'clock in the afternoon.

I took a fortifying sip of my coffee. I was well-versed in dealing with happy drunk boys as my brothers often started out that way and ended up throwing punches five minutes later.

"Tissssh!" Caleb toddled my way like a drunk baby. "Hey, we missed *yoush*." His face was sweetly soft after consuming what I guessed was far more beer than was wise this early in the day.

"Does Luna know where you are?"

"*Pshhh*. It's fine. She's working. It's fine." He bumped into the wall. "Hey, where's the cooler?"

"You left it on the elevator, dumbass," Lucky said then started singing again. He walked toward me in an almost straight line. "What are you doing here, grouchy?" He poked me.

I blinked at the combined scents of sweaty male and beer. Wow, that was rough. "I was going to work."

"Hey…no. No, you should drink with us. We're going to get more beer to party it up on the rooftop."

"Pretty sure you partied it up for three, Thor."

"Ha. I like when you call me Thor."

He kissed my forehead and I tried to step back out of fume range. "All right. I'm fairly sure you don't need any more."

"Oh, we do. Don't we, buddy?" He stepped back to slap Brady on the back. "This is my friend, Brady. He was really nice to me today. Didn't even give me a ticket."

Brady stumbled forward. "It's okay, man. Girl trouble."

"Yeah." Lucky's face went from happy to sad. "Girl trouble sucks." He stepped to the side and leaned on the wall. "These beers are really strong. I can usually drink a twelve-pack on my own."

"Micro brewskis," Brady said with a squinty grin. "I confis—took it from some teens at the hayride last night."

I took the bottle from Caleb.

"Gimme, that's mine."

I held up a finger and read the label. "Fourteen percent. That's not your average beer, boys."

"Def not averageee," Caleb slurred and took it back. "So tasty. We're gonna get some more."

I took another two gulps of my coffee and set it on the small table by the door. "All right. Time to put you idiots to bed."

"No. It's sunny out. There's no bed." Caleb tipped the bottle back then stuck his tongue out when nothing came out. "Damn. All gone."

"Thank God." I took the bottle and turned him back toward the elevator. "Come on, you too, Thor."

"No."

I hung my head for a second. Luckily, the other two were a little more helpful. Brady was singing "Dream On" by Aerosmith now, but at least they were in the elevator. Caleb was trying to help out, but he just sounded like a howling hound dog.

Lucky waved. "Imma just sit here." He slid down the wall and thumped to the floor. His legs were too long, so he looked more like a collapsed giant in a dollhouse.

"Hey, is he okay?" Caleb stuck his head out of the elevator.

I palmed his face and pushed him back inside. "He's fine. Come on, let's get you guys settled." I propped up each of them in a corner and said a small prayer of thanks that the elevator was finally finished. If I'd had to get them up the stairs, it would *not* have been fun.

While the boys serenaded me with a very butchered version of "Dream On", I pulled out my phone and texted Luna.

I have your husband to be.

Why?

They tried to escape the apartment for more beer.

Escape? I don't understand.

I sent her an audio clip of their cat shrieks. How long did it take for us to go up three floors in this freaking elevator?

Oh, goddess. Where are you?

Elevator.

I stuffed my phone away and held the door open. "All right, ladies. Let's go."

"*Pfff.* I'm not a lady. *You're* a lady." Caleb crowded into me.

"Not generally. Remember that and follow direction or I'll knock your ass out." He swayed and I lifted him up by the arm. "There we go. Straight ahead, buddy."

Brady straightened his shoulders and walked out on his own steam. "If you knock my ass out, I'll arrest you."

"You couldn't arrest a baby right now, buddy."

"Of course I could. Not that I would. Babies are cute. This town is full of babies." Brady shook his head sadly. "It's nuts. Imma go fall down now."

"In your bed, please," I called after him.

He did a little wave and bumbled his way down the hall.

Luna flew out of their apartment, a flowy robe with moons and astrology symbols all over it trailing behind her. Her blue eyes went huge. "Goldilocks, what did you do?"

"Hey, Lu." He leaned hard on me. "I can't feel my lips."

"Not again."

My eyebrow rose. "Is this a regular thing?"

Luna laughed. "Goddess, no. But our first...date if you will included a little sauced Goldilocks." She came over to hook his arm around her neck. "It's a long story. Come over tomorrow and I'll tell you."

"Uh, that's not—"

"Nope. We're going to be friends, I just know it. Come on over tomorrow. We're going to play poker with Bess and Ryan. We're teaching Tabitha."

I blinked. "Poker?"

"Yes."

Caleb leaned into Luna and kissed her cheek. "I love you. Do you know that?"

She rolled her eyes. "Yes, I know."

"You're so pretty." He buried his nose in her hair. "And you smell so good."

"Oy. I better get him in bed."

"Good idea. I gotta deal with Thor."

"Hmm."

I lifted a finger. "No. He works for me. That's it." And I would not think about the fact that he'd fucked the holy hell out of me less than twenty-four hours ago.

"Right now, your aura is hot pink, Tish."

"I don't know what that means."

"I do." But she didn't say anything else. "C'mon, Goldilocks, it's time to get you to bed."

"Bed sounds like an *esssslent* idea."

"Doesn't it just?" They shuffled their way to their door.

I stepped back into the elevator. When I got back to the lower level, I found Lucky in the hallway where I'd left him. A ripping snore filled the room.

I put my hands on my hips. "Awesome."

What the hell was I going to do with him? There was no way I could get him on my bike like this. I stepped over him and went out the door. "Of course your truck isn't out here. I don't even know if there's a parking lot for the apartments."

I thought about texting Luna, but she had enough on her plate. I rotated my tense neck. My only option was Lucille. Dammit, I didn't want his drunk ass in my pristine Caddy.

I turned back around and kicked his boot.

He snorted, sat up for a second, then his chin lolled back onto his chest.

"Perfect." I slammed out the door and stalked over to the garage. I dug out my key and turned off the alarm before I went through another door to the main garage.

Gage had on his welding helmet and was slowly working a bead of welding rod down a join. It looked like it was the bat template we were using on the rear brake lights. I waited until he was at the end of the join and his torch went out.

"I hate to interrupt."

Gage flipped up his helmet. His head was sweaty, and flux and metal shavings dusted his apron. "Hey, Tish. Where you been?"

"Family stuff."

"Dare said your brother's friend passed. I'm sorry."

My chest tightened. That wasn't even half of it. "Yeah. It was not how I wanted to spend a few days away."

"No shit." He pulled off his gloves. "You here to work? I was only going to finish this up then get home."

"It's fine. I had plans to do just that, but I have another thing to deal with now instead. Can I borrow you for a second?"

He dropped his gloves on the bench. "Yeah. Let me just put this shit away."

"Thanks."

I headed over to the back of the garage and flipped off my covering. The smooth gleam of a deep smoky lavender Cadillac El Dorado gave my heart a little jolt.

Lucille was my first rebuild. Every piece had been salvaged and brought back to her former glory. And the parts I couldn't find, I replicated based on the exact specs. I loved this car more than anything.

And if Lucky threw up on my white leather interior, I'd toss him onto the side of the road and leave him for dead.

I got in and flipped the visor down to find the keys I'd stashed there. Since it was probably easier to put a six-foot-four male into my car with the top down, I hit the hand releases.

Thank God it was a nice day. Besides, if he froze his ass off, it was his problem. That damn man wasn't ever cold anyway.

"Oh, taking your baby out?"

"Yeah. Part of the favor. Can you open up the bay for me?"

"Yeah, you got it." Gage jogged to the chains on the door. We'd tried to convince Dare to upgrade to automatic doors, but he was stubborn. It would take a blowtorch to get through the locks, so I couldn't really fault him.

I maneuvered my car through the empty garage and slowly eased down to the road. I had to go around the block to get to the front of the apartment building. The idiot I was going to collect lived up to his name, and I was able to slide into a space right in front.

Gage was standing in the open bay door. I climbed out of Lucille and waved him over.

"So, about that help."

He put on a baseball cap against the sun. "What's up?"

I sighed and aimed for the door to the apartments.

Gage followed me and peered in the doorway. He had to cup his hands around his eyes to see in. "Fuck."

"Yep."

"Is he okay?"

"Define okay."

His eyes danced. "That looks sauced to me. Or did you knock him out?"

"Tempting. But I would have left him there if I knocked him out."

"Taking him home? That's big of you."

"Yeah, well, his best friend is just as drunk. They decided to take a twelve-pack of micro brew for a test drive."

Gage laughed. "Yeah, they sneak up on you. Especially if you drink like Lucky does. Some of the guys from the garage play pool with him down at The Spinning Wheel. He usually has quite the tolerance."

"He helped me out yesterday so looks like I'm returning the favor."

Gage folded his arms. "Huh."

"Shut up and help me get him in the backseat."

"What would you have done if I wasn't here?"

"He'd have a lot more bruises." I held the door open. "Now help me get him up."

Gage and I stood side by side in the small hallway.

166

"He's really big."

"Yep." I sighed. My lady taco could attest to that on a personal level. "One arm and one arm to start? Maybe we can drag him like we did Dare that one time."

Gage snorted. "Pretty sure Lucky has a good fifty pounds on my brother."

"You're a strapping guy."

"Yeah, but—"

"I can handle it."

"If you say so." He crouched down. "Hey, buddy. How are you feeling?"

Lucky just mumbled something about Ruby aka me. Good grief. All I needed was a drunk Lucky telling all our drama to my business partner.

And yes, Gage was one of my best friends on the planet. I still didn't want all the crap I'd confessed to Lucky over the last few days to come spilling out of his loose lips.

I stepped over Lucky and gripped under his arm. "All right, we're gonna get up now."

"Mmm. No. I'm good." Lucky nuzzled against me. "Unless you want to get naked. I might need a minute though," he said with a snicker.

Gage took off his hat and spun it around the back. "Naked?"

"Shut up."

Gage grinned and went for Lucky's other arm.

It took us three tries, but we finally were able to haul him upward using the wall and a lot of swearing. Thank God no one else came down the stairs or through the door.

"Holy shit, what does this guy do? Live in the gym?" Gage looped Lucky's arm around his neck.

I did the same and wrinkled my nose. He needed a shower and a bed. And right now, I didn't really care which order it happened in. "What do they say? Muscle is heavier than fat?"

Gage grunted. "Jesus."

We stumbled our way down the single step and almost lost him to the cement sidewalk.

I wrapped my arm around Lucky's back and gripped his belt. "Would be nice if you helped," I growled at him.

Suddenly, Lucky stood up straight. "What's going on? Hey." His green eyes went all glassy and happy as he peered down at me. "Did you change your mind?"

My chest went tight. Dammit, why did he have to be so adorable? I didn't do adorable. "Get in the car, Thor."

"I love when you're grouchy. Did you know that?" His smile was wide and soft as only a drunken male could be. "Not sure what that *sezz* about," he hiccupped, "me." He shook his head and squinted at Lucille. "Hey, the car." He swiveled his head so fast Gage had to catch him.

"Okay. I can't pick you up off the ground, big guy."

Lucky weaved a bit, but he stood on his own for a second. "Where's Luna and Caleb? The proposal. Edward!" He lifted his arms up as if he'd scored a goal and almost fell on his face.

I grabbed his arm then gave Gage a look. "Don't ask."

"Gotcha." He put his arms on Lucky's shoulders and steered him to my car.

Rushing after them, I opened the door and shoved the seat forward. "In we go."

"Oh, look at that." Lucky patted my head. "It's big enough for me."

"It sure is."

We twisted him into the backseat. I folded his long-ass tree trunk legs into the back, then sagged against the side of the car to catch my breath.

"Holy shit." Gage bent at the waist. "I think I pulled something."

"Really?"

He grinned and waved me off. "No. Well, maybe a little, but nothing a hot shower won't cure. Think *he* needs a cold one."

"Icy."

Gage dragged me in for a hug. "He's a good guy."

I stiffened. I was beginning to see that, and I didn't know what to think about it. "What's that supposed to mean?"

"Oh, nothing." Gage peered into the backseat. "Think he's safe back there?"

"Safe enough to get to his place." I dragged up my hair into a messy bun. "Speaking of… You wouldn't know where he lives, would you?"

"As a matter of fact…" He held up a finger and pulled out his phone. "We worked on his truck so we should have him in the computer." He flicked through some screens and tapped a few things, then my phone buzzed in my pocket. "Texted the address to you."

I tried not to feel guilty about using his personal information. It was a deep sore spot for me. But in this instance, it was simply to dispatch him to a bed. One that I wouldn't be in. "Thanks."

"No problem." He scratched under the ball cap before pulling it around the right way. "Do you want me to follow you?"

"Nah. If he doesn't wake up, I'll just put the top up and let him sleep it off in the car."

"You're a cruel woman."

"Yeah, well, he's an idiot."

One I didn't want to develop feelings for, but I didn't seem to have much choice in the matter.

FIFTEEN

Okay, so I wouldn't leave him in the car. It was supposed to be near freezing tonight. That was even too cold for the human heater.

I shoved the car seat back and nudged Lucky enough that he woke up. Wonderful.

"Ruby. Ruby." His voice was a singsong tenor crossed with a warbling bird. "Ruby of the finest beauty."

I shook my head and slowly pulled into traffic. Handily, it was early enough that the sun should keep him from freezing his ass off. I looked at the text Gage sent me. I wasn't exactly sure where Lucky lived, but that was what the maps app was for.

God bless Apple products. The address had turned into a hyperlink and popped open the app.

I set the phone in the cradle and turned on the radio, hoping it would drown him out. Unfortunately, Lucky was a human jukebox and seemed to know every song.

Didn't matter the channel I changed it to, he knew them all.

When I got the urge to sing along with him, I stifled it just long enough to pull into his driveway. I was obviously losing my damn mind.

I turned off the car and he slumped in the back, pressing his cheek to the window like a forlorn very large boy. "You took the music away."

"Time to go to bed."

"Oh, I like that idea." He sat up, but he got his big feet tangled and fell back again. "I might need help, Ruby."

I slipped out of the car and glanced up at the two-story house. It was tidy with the lawn freshly mowed, and two brown bags set on the curb for pickup. The bottom level had a cheery array of fall flowers, pumpkins, and the twisted gourd things. A wreath on the door was obviously handmade with a set of small hands in the mix. The second floor had a wrought iron railing that gleamed in the late day sun. A heavy rocking chair with a sunny yellow pillow was the only decoration there.

Probably Lucky's part of the house.

Which meant stairs. Yay me.

I glanced back at the car. Lucky was staring at me, those green eyes seeing far too much. I had a feeling most of the beer had worn off. He probably had a metabolism like a steam engine.

I pulled the lever for the seat to flip forward. "Think you can make it up the stairs, Thor?"

He held out his hand to me.

I gave him a flat stare. "You think I can pull you out?"

"You can do anything."

"You're literally the worst." I leaned in to grab his arm, but he hauled me on top of him.

"Oops."

I planted my hands on his chest and rolled my eyes. Not *that* sober, evidently. "Very funny."

His hands slid down to cup my ass. "I wasn't laughing. Just wanted to feel you on top of me again, Ruby." He brushed his nose along mine. "I really liked when you rode me this morning."

"All right. Enough of that." And I would not focus on the fact that everything below my waist went liquid.

Even drunk, he was potent. Especially now that I knew what he was capable of.

"I always wanted to make out in this car. So rare for them to fit me."

"Truck bed wasn't enough for you?"

His eyes lost the glassy drunk gleam. Instead, they became painfully direct. "I'll never get enough, Tish."

He rarely said my name. Just when he was disappointed in me, and when he was slipping inside me with that ridiculously adept cock of his. I swallowed hard, my gaze dropping to his full lower lip. The top was a slash that gave his face so much character. From a grin to a snarl, his expressions always made me want to kiss him to shut him up.

Before I could lean in and do just that, a screen door slapped.

My head popped up, and I smiled at the older woman who came outside. "Can I help you? Oh, Lucky." Her wrinkled hand went to her neck. "Who's your lady friend?"

Lucky sighed quietly, then he craned his neck so he could see the woman. "Hey, Mrs. Newsome." He moved his hand up to my waist. "This is my...Ruby."

As I struggled to get off him, my knee slid a bit too close to the very happy Lucky Jr.

He hissed and lifted me off him. "Well, that'll ruin the mood."

Mrs. Newsome's eyes danced. "Ruby. What a lovely name."

"Tish."

The older woman looked at Lucky then back at me. "You don't know her name, Lucky?"

I pushed my hair out of the way. "He just insists on calling me Ruby. It's fine."

"Oh, already at the love names stage? How nice is that? Probably because of that gorgeous red hair of yours." She patted her short, stone-gray hair. "I had red hair once upon a time. From a bottle though. Yours looks real."

I slid onto the seat as Lucky finally maneuvered himself in a semi-seated position. It didn't really work with his size.

"Oh, crap." His eyes went wide. "Where's Butch?"

"Why are you asking me? How the hell am I supposed to know?"

He clamped a hand on the back of his neck. "Fuck, I left my dog. I got drunk and left her and she's probably wandering the streets, crying for Daddy."

"That's quite a picture," Mrs. Newsome offered.

I bent until Lucky looked me in the eye. His eyes were wheeling a bit from panic. "When did you have her last?"

"On the roof. Drinking."

"The dog?"

"No, me. Us. Though Bess came in the middle, after Caleb." His rapid breathing slowed to a more manageable level. "My baby is with Bess. She has to be." He started patting his pockets. "Where's my phone?"

It took him a minute, but he found it and texted Bess with his clumsy fingers. A moment later, he dropped his head to the back of the seat with a loud exhale. "She has her. She knew we were out of control and took her to her apartment to eat goldfish crackers and watch daytime TV."

I couldn't help laughing. "Corrupting a young mind as we speak."

"It's not funny. I'm a bad dad. Bad dad," he repeated sorrowfully enough I almost felt sorry for the oaf. "I'll make it up to her. I'll stop drinking and change my ways."

"Fat chance there," I muttered.

"I've only been a dad for a short time. I'll fix it." He reached outside and opened the door, clambering out and nearly landing on the bag of leaves. He missed it and hit the grass on his hip.

I peered over the car door. "Are you okay?"

"Fine. Just my dignity." He flipped his hair back.

"So, I can go?"

"No. I need your help upstairs."

I squinted at him. "You look fine."

"Upstairs, woman."

"That's not how you get help." I turned to Mrs. Newsome. "Sorry about this. He and his best friend decided day drinking was a good idea today." I didn't know how the cop fit in. I probably didn't want to. "He hasn't been a pet parent long either."

"Oh, child. I've seen far worse from my Henry. You two go on up. We'll take out our hearing aids." She was surprisingly spry as she hurried into the house.

"Hear that? We can be as loud as you want." Lucky laughed and dropped onto his back. "I'm too fucking old to drink like that."

I got out of the car and stood over him. "If I help you up, are you going to pull me down there?"

He sighed and flung his arms wide as if he was going to make a snow angel in the very *unsnowy* grass. "No. You can leave me here. I'll make it up there eventually."

I crouched beside him. "C'mon, I'll make you my hangover specialty—depending on what you have in your fridge."

He opened one eye. "A bottle of tabasco sauce and eggs?"

"I can make do with that."

He lifted his hand to a lock of hair that had slipped out of my bun. "Damn, you are beautiful."

My chest tightened, and my belly did a little flip. Damn him. People didn't say those kinds of things to me. I wasn't ugly, but men often found me intimidating.

Not this one, and I couldn't figure out why.

I sighed. "What am I going to do with you?"

"I vote for keep me."

"Incorrigible." I stood and dragged him up. Kind of. He really was a damn redwood. But between us, we somehow managed to get him upright. And when he wrapped an arm around my shoulders, I caught him trying to cop a feel.

Before I could kick his ass about it, he tightened his grip and squashed me against his chest. I pinched his side. "You stink."

"Sorry about that. I didn't get to go home before I went over to get Butch." He rubbed his face with both hands. "I can't believe I abandoned my dog. What will she be like as a teenager now?"

I snorted. "I'm sure she'll be a delinquent. C'mon, let's get you all cleaned up."

His shoulders hunched as he climbed the steps to the wreathless door. I held the screen door open for him. It was an old house with a narrow staircase to the second floor, and he still pinballed his way up the stairs. I resisted the urge to grip his ass and keep propelling him upward.

It wasn't the time for that.

"C'mon, Thor. Don't feel too bad. You're still new at the dad thing."

"I know. But I went over there to pick her up and I did, but then I got drunk and left her behind. Oh, and I almost got a ticket except Brady took pity on me and my girl troubles. *You* troubles," he said over his shoulder.

I winced. "Now's not the time to talk about that."

"When are we going to talk about it?"

"After the barn is done?" *Never? Please?*

Couldn't we just enjoy it for what it was? I didn't want to think about how good it was between us. I had so much more to worry about right now.

At the top of the stairs, Lucky shouldered open the door, then dragged me through it and up onto my toes before he closed his mouth over mine. He tasted of beer and sunshine. The feeling of overwhelm slid right on into want.

I'd thought the first time was a fluke. It would be so much easier if it was. An itch to be scratched and then we could just move on. That was how it usually was when I finally let myself get naked with someone. Once the initial flash happened, the glow soon burned out like a cheap candle.

Nothing was the usual with Lucky.

I sighed into the kiss. He knew just what to do now. At first, forceful and hot, then sleepy soft. Keeping me off balance until I shut off my brain.

I looped an arm around his shoulders. His hair dripped over my arm, the wild frazzled curls just as delicious as his talented tongue. He crushed me closer, deepening the kiss until I really didn't care about keeping it just about business.

As if I'd ever had a chance.

He twisted his fingers into the bottom of my T-shirt, dragging it up and over my head, then his mouth was back on mine.

"I'd strip you down, but you'd probably knock me out with that smell," I said between kisses.

He laughed into my mouth. "Niceties are nonexistent with you, Ruby."

I shrugged.

His gaze dipped down to the Batman logo bra. "That's hotter than it should be."

I grinned. "I like big bad boys. Guess that works for you." I tapped a nail along his chest. "You take a shower and maybe I'll let you take off the bra too." I slid away from him. "I'll make us some food."

"Damn, I do like watching you walk away."

I tossed a smirk over my shoulder and gave my walk a bit more of a sway.

He growled something under his breath and headed for a hallway that I presumed included a shower.

I found my shirt and slipped it back on. I might've been comfortable with my body, but I needed to cool things down with him. Showing off a half yard of skin was probably a little too much to keep things businesslike.

Ha, as if.

I distracted myself by looking around his space. The layout of the house reminded me of my dad's place. An older house with small rooms and lots of wood paneling. A half wall cut up the room between living space and galley kitchen.

His place was a maze of half done projects. A gorgeous corner unit was half stained. The details on the drawers drew me in to take a closer look.

It was definitely no cheap prefab kit from a box store. I ran my hand over the wood. It wasn't my medium, but I could tell it was solid art in furniture form. Hell, August Beck might have some competition if Lucky let people know he could do this kind of work.

Another handmade bench was in a similar state of finish. This one was stained, but he seemed to be working on another treatment other than a simple varnish. Maybe apoxy. Hmm. Interesting choice.

I crouched and noticed he'd put different woods together in a pattern that reminded me of a beach. Like something I'd seen on social media. He seemed to take kernels of ideas from viral videos and put his own spin on them.

I lifted the tarp on another piece. It was nosy as hell, but I couldn't resist. This one was a bit more farmhouse style. It looked like something I'd find in a foyer for shoes and kids crap. Three intricate knobs in classy versions of Marvel logos were screwed into the tall backboard. The bottom had a lid set into the storage as if he wasn't done measuring something.

I wanted it.

The need was sharp enough that I flipped the tarp back down and headed for the kitchen. Every time I thought I had Lucky Roberts figured out, he proved me wrong.

I opened the fridge and sure enough, there were a dozen eggs, tabasco, and generic brand butter. The veggie drawer was about as questionable as the pizza in my fridge the other day.

Slamming that drawer, I snagged the eggs, butter, and tabasco, dumping them on the small counter. He had an air fryer, toaster, and a blender jammed into the small space.

Surprisingly, the sink was sparkling clean. And I had to admit I was surprised there wasn't a crumb in sight. I was almost sure I could eat off the floor too.

However, the pan situation was not ideal. The cupboard contained a mishmash of pans, cookie sheets, colanders, and plates. I shook my head. My organized soul wanted to rip it apart and force it into making sense. I grabbed a fry pan and quickly shut the door against the avalanche of cookware.

As much as I enjoyed spice, I needed a few more items. The cabinets were chaos.

I gave up and headed for the hallway he'd disappeared into. "Thor?"

"Yeah?"

"Where's your spices?"

"What?"

"Where are your spices?"

"I can't hear you—open the door."

I paused at the doorknob. Showering was intimate business—hell, the whole bathroom deal was.

"Ruby, you've seen it all too, remember?"

I blew out a breath and opened the door. He was far too large for the bathroom that hadn't seen an update since the 70s. His head lifted over the top of the shower curtain ring around the claw-footed tub.

I laughed at the soapy hair he'd piled on top of his head.

He opened one eye. "Can I help you?"

"Spices? Salt and pepper? Possibly other things."

"Oh. Over the stove. Top cabinet." He turned around and crouched so he could get under the spray.

That super clean soap scent filled the steamy room. Obviously, I didn't have any resistance to this guy today. Or since we'd rescued the dog, to be honest.

I couldn't help looking around. Evidently, nosy bitch was my new name tag today. Again, the space was freaking spotless. It was a hideous green tile, but the sink, commode, tub, and shelves were gleaming white.

He was such a weird mixed bag of puzzle pieces that didn't seem to fit. But that didn't mean I didn't want to see how they lined up.

Even if I didn't *want* to want to.

"Just gonna watch?"

"Sorry." *I'm trying to figure out your psyche while you shower?* Yeah, that wasn't going to go over well. "I was trying to figure out what that scent was. You usually smell like soap, but not like guy soap."

Uh huh, that sounded way better. What was wrong with me?

He held up a blue bottle with a duck on it. "Good enough to get crude oil off a duck, good enough for me."

I busted out laughing. A deep belly laugh that came from my toes. When was the last time I'd even been that amused? I really didn't know. "Yep, that's the one. You are so weird."

He shook out his wet hair and whipped the curtain open. "You like it."

I was aware my mouth had dropped open, but I couldn't stop it.

Under the cover of night, I'd gotten a good handle on things—at least I'd thought so. Nope. That was a whole lot of man. His skin was golden and darker tan through the shoulders and arms.

God, universe, the divine...they'd all been involved in granting some serious blessings to this man.

Lucky raked his hands through his hair to get out the water then grabbed the towel off the bar. He didn't bother cinching it over his hips. Instead, he just swiped away water from his chest as Lucky Jr. increased in muscle mass. "Enjoying the view?"

I nodded. "Actually, I am."

He ducked under the curtain frame then stepped out. I couldn't stop laughing at gigantor crammed into such a small bathroom.

He gave me that eyebrow raise that did sinful things to my libido.

I backed up to the door and gripped the doorknob. "Okay, get dressed and I'll make you that—" My brain went offline as he tied the towel around his waist in a way that only showcased his ridiculous cock. "Going."

"Coward," he yelled after me.

The insult didn't start a fight this time. About this one point, I wasn't in denial. I was very much a coward when it came to just how completely this man was wedging himself into my life.

And I wasn't sure I hated it.

Contemplating my changing feelings was dangerous in ways I didn't know how to handle just now. Eggs I could handle.

Ten minutes later, I did, in fact, find his spices, which were plentiful, and made a big batch of scrambled eggs. It took a few minutes, but I finally found a large plate that we could share since the man didn't know what personal space was when it came to food, and I was tired of looking for dishes.

Two forks and two ice waters would have to do.

His dining room table was covered in papers, but the carpet was freshly vacuumed. A cute pink-striped dog bed sat on the floor under the TV along with a pile of toys, several bones that were bigger than Butch, and the freshly laundered Harry Styles towel.

Lucky ambled in with his hair blown dry. His curls shouldn't be *that* perfect from using dish soap. It seemed as if only men could get away with that crap.

Though it was hardly fair, damn, did he clean up well.

He wore a pair of faded jeans, no socks, and a deep green Henley. He pushed up the sleeves as he walked toward me. "Smells awesome."

I nodded at the table. "Find us a spot and maybe you'll be able to eat some."

"Oh, right. Sorry." He stacked up the pile of magazines and swatches of fabric, stain, and paint samples. "I was pulling some stuff together for the barn actually."

"When did you have time?"

He shrugged and tugged out a chair for me. "I don't sleep much."

"Really? It's my favorite thing in all the world." I set the plate down then pushed a fork over to the place he'd cleared for himself as well.

"In all the world?"

I sat down. "Pretty much."

"We gotta fix that." An involuntary shiver skated down my spine as he loomed over me. "Smells amazing," he rumbled in my ear before sitting at my side.

The fact that he didn't even question us sharing a plate probably said something deeper than I was prepared to dig into. Instead, I forked up some eggs.

He plowed through more than half of the eggs then pulled down the sketchbook from the pile. "I was thinking about the barn."

"Handy since that's your job."

"You think that waspish tone is going to scare me off. It won't." He slid the notebook in front of me.

"I—" I huffed out a breath. "Sorry. I'm just used to doing all this alone."

"Yeah, well, you don't have to. Now look at what I want to do."

I frowned down at the page. "Did you draw this?"

He lifted one shoulder. "Makes it easier for me to visualize. I'm learning a program on the iPad and I'll mess with it a bit there to make sure the measurements are right. But this is a rough outline of what I think we should concentrate on. And what we can leave for future projects."

"Future?"

"With less than six weeks to go, some things won't even get here in time. A few things need to be special ordered. But I'll make sure to have the foundations set—the bedrooms, furniture, wall treatments."

My head swam. "Treatments?"

He tapped one wall on the drawing that looked different than the others. "I figure a feature wall in reclaimed wood. I was able to salvage a lot of it. I also have a buddy who has lumber from other barns built around the same time. I also figured some sliding barn doors like Doc Thorn had at the clinic. I think it would be a nice way to section off a bottom floor bedroom for Cohen. Then I'll put three upstairs. Could also be a cool place for kids' sleepovers or whatever in the future."

"Kids?"

His gaze tracked to my mouth, then up to my eyes. "Sure. You don't want kids?"

"I..." I'd never actually thought about it other than as something that might happen in the future. I cleared my throat. "I figured I'd be Aunt Tish more than Mom."

He coasted a hand down my ponytail and tugged at the end. "A little girl with all this red hair? Seems like that's something this world needs."

A brief flash of a freckled girl zipped through my brain before I firmly pushed it back. "I really don't have that mom gene. Didn't really have one myself."

"Makes two of us." He reached down for my hand. "We don't have to echo our pasts, Ruby." His long, thick fingers tightened around mine. "That's what we come from, not who we are."

"You want kids?"

"I never thought about it until..."

I didn't want him to finish that sentence. Before he could, I dropped his hand.

Hell, I didn't even want to think about that kind of permanence with anyone, let alone someone who would rely on me for eighteen years at minimum.

I pushed my seat back and gathered the dishes. "I'm going to clean up. We can go over the plans, and then you can get your dog."

He circled my wrist with his fingers, effectively stopping me from escaping. "Do you think running will make things between us less intense?"

I didn't look down at him. I couldn't, because I really wasn't sure what the answer was. If I ignored things—*men*—long enough, they usually lost interest. There was always a willing woman looking for a good man. I wasn't that woman.

I liked being on my own.

Dammit, I had a plan. And those green eyes and that long wild hair wasn't in it.

Proving yet again I was the coward he'd called me, I fled.

SIXTEEN

Lucky

"DAMMIT." I STOOD UP AND FOLLOWED HER.

She was standing at the sink, her fingers gripping the edge as if her life depended on it.

I came up behind her and she stiffened. *"Shh.* I'm not good at this stuff either, you know. I'm a bad bet from every angle. I should let you run."

"But you won't."

It was my turn to lock my muscles. Did she really not want me? "If this makes you that miserable, I'll back off. I don't want to be an idiot puppy who doesn't know how to control himself. Even if that's how I feel every time I'm around you, for fuck's sake."

She relaxed against me. "You know we don't have any issue when it comes to sex. I'm not going to deny that."

"But you don't want it." My voice was resigned.

She raised her arm to slip her fingers along the back of my neck. "I like neat, orderly checkboxes."

"Life isn't a checkbox."

"The last time I leaped, I—"

"No. Not his name here." She still hadn't admitted the rest about her brother's best friend, but inside, I already knew. The muscles

185

between my shoulder blades were so tight I was afraid they'd snap. "I'm not him."

"I know. But all that shit got dredged up." She twisted around in my arms to face me. "I can't *not* feel like I'm in the middle of a hurricane when we're together."

"They say to get up against a big, sturdy wall when they come through."

Her eyebrow spiked. "I take it you're the wall?"

"I can't say I'll never hurt you, Ruby. I just know I'll never mean to." I cupped her face, dragging my thumb across her cheek. "But I know I've never felt like this about anyone."

Her gaze dropped to my chest.

Even without her spelling it all out, I suspected she'd loved someone else before. Maybe more than one person, though I had my doubts. "It doesn't matter if I'm not the first."

Her gaze snapped to mine. "First?"

"C'mon, Ruby. I'm gonna be the love of your goddamn life. At least from here on out."

Her dark eyes widened. "Stop saying that. We barely know each other."

"All it takes is a moment." I drew her closer.

She slapped her hands on my chest, pushing back. "No, it doesn't."

I lowered my mouth to hers. "I'll wait for you to catch up." I kissed her before she could make another excuse.

I might not have been what she had in mind, but I was hers—whether she was ready or not.

Bending, I lifted her. At least her body knew she could count on me. She instinctively twined around me. Arms around my shoulders, legs around my waist.

God, she was magnificent. I didn't have to worry that I'd break her. She was made for me, I was convinced of it.

I gripped her ass and stalked through the kitchen, out and around to the hallway that led to my bedroom.

"This doesn't change anything," she said against my mouth.

"Right."

"It's just sex."

"Sure." I kicked my bedroom door open and tossed her on the bed.

She bounced and fell back on her elbows. "Is this supposed to be a seduction scene?"

"This is supposed to be fun." I grabbed her foot and flipped off her Converse sneaker. I dragged her down to the end of the bed and took care of the other foot. The Incredible Hulk socks made me laugh. "Mixing your comics."

She rested her foot against my belly. "I'm a rebel."

I reached under her pant leg and scrapped my nails over her calf as I dragged off her sock and tossed it over my shoulder. I repeated the move with the other leg.

She was trying so hard not to grin at me, but I knew this was exactly what we needed.

The truck had been overstimulation with a side of grief. My goal had been to take her mind off things. This was two adults learning what made sex fun for each other.

I had a feeling she didn't allow herself to have too much fun these days. She was independent, headstrong, brilliant—a hell of a combination with art in the mix. Even if I'd bet my truck she didn't see herself as an artist.

The whole package made her endlessly fascinating. Add in the warrior steel under her porcelain skin, and I was so damn sunk.

The sun was streaming through the window, making her hair look like fire. Goddamn, she was so beautiful.

Leaning over, I flicked the button open and whipped off her jeans. They were loose and well worn enough that I didn't have to struggle for what I was looking for. I wasn't disappointed to find matching Batman cotton panties.

I nibbled my way along her yard of leg before I knelt on the floor at the bottom of my king-sized bed. I pulled her forward for a repeat taste of what I'd sampled last night.

The truck had been madness and darkness. I'd felt my way around to find exactly what she needed. Now this was for me.

Sunlight slashed across her skin from my blinds, letting me see every inch, every curve, and every freckle on her water-soft skin.

I hooked her knee over my shoulder and licked her inner thigh.

"Lucky." Her voice was sharp with hesitation. I knew there as a difference between the reckless comfort of yesterday and a sun-filled today. But I wanted to show her that both were okay between us.

Both would be amazing.

I tucked my hands under her ass and lifted her hips to roll off her panties. Instead of letting her think things through—which was always dangerous with this woman—I widened her legs with my shoulders and sent her into a tailspin.

No part of her went unexplored. I wanted her taste and scent buzzing in my head. Her hips lifted so she could undulate against my tongue. I followed her lead, finding the correct combination to her lock. This lock anyway. Her heart was a much more fortified area.

But here, we were compatible in every way.

I pushed up her shirt to flip her bra up and out of the way. She arched off the bed as I held on through each buck and twist. My Ruby liked a rough hand sometimes, and today that seemed to be where we were headed.

I wanted to keep it light. To hear that husky laugh as I made her come. But as always, the desperation set in. My entire goal was to hear her crash and burn in my arms.

I drew one hand between her legs to stroke her lightly with my thumb as my tongue circled her hard clit. My beard was abrading her skin, but it only seemed to enhance her tension.

She was as tight as the strings on my guitar, vibrating on the knife's edge of pleasure. I held her there, held back until her fingers fisted in my hair.

She lifted my head and our eyes locked. Hers were near black with temper. "I'm going to kill you."

I laughed against her soaked slit then twisted my hand to thrust two fingers into her swollen pussy. She clamped down on my fingers, and her surprised cry nearly shook the windows.

Hearing her say my name so urgently made me stone hard. I'd tucked my own needs into a box as I focused on her, but now there was nothing but my lust fueling me as I stood and bent her knees toward her chest.

Her thighs shook and her lids dipped to half mast as her chest heaved for oxygen.

"Fuck, you are so damn beautiful."

She reached her arms above her head in a feline stretch, her skin pink where I'd pinched her nipples and scraped at her skin with my rough hands.

Then she grabbed two fistfuls of my my hair and dragged me over her.

"Ruby, I'm too heavy."

Instead of arguing with me, she rolled me over and straddled me, ripping at my zipper. "While I enjoyed the one-sided trip to O-Town, I'd really like to go for another round. You up to it?"

That smile I'd been looking for hit me like a punch. Sly and drunk on her own power, she curled her fingers into my boxers to draw out my cock. "There we are." Her touch was one pulse point away from too tight.

My hips lifted in reaction. Most women were too gentle, thinking we were as fragile as their sweet softness. I let out a tortured growl as she licked her palm and stroked me hard.

"Tell me your Boy Scout tendencies are intact here in your bedroom." She flipped off her shirt and finally reached behind herself to unsnap her bra.

My hands went right to her tits as if they were a siren's call. Her head fell back for a moment as I caressed and cupped her.

"Distracting me," she moaned.

"Yes."

"Condom, Thor."

I reached over to the bedside table and fumbled. My hands weren't steady.

All her fault.

Impatiently, she slid off me to stretch toward the drawer to do the honors herself. "Well, well. There's a lot more in here than a box of condoms."

My neck heated. "I'm open-minded."

Her eyebrow lifted when she came out with a pair of black steel cuffs. "Are you now?"

I swallowed. "Damn, girl."

She dropped the cuffs back into the drawer. "I'll remember those."

"Yes, please."

She snatched a condom out of the mess of lubricants, oils, and whatever else ended up in there. The women I'd been with in the past weren't exactly the shy types—mostly.

She rubbed her breast across my arm before she lifted her leg to get on me like her motorcycle. She dropped the condom on my chest, then braceleted my wrists in each of her strong hands to drag my arms above my head.

"So, do you like to be the cuffer or the cuffee?"

"Take down your hair for me, Ruby." The plea was nearly a groan. I didn't even care. I was close to begging at this point.

"That's not what I asked."

"I don't mind being under your control."

Her eyes flashed. "Hmm." She lowered her face to mine. When I lifted my head to kiss her, she moved out of reach. "You don't mind being under my control, right?"

I swallowed. "I probably shouldn't have said that."

"Too late."

She let my wrists free. "Don't move."

I groaned, but I left my hands where they were. Suddenly, I wished I'd taken the time to get a proper headboard, because I had a feeling I would need it.

She shimmied down my belly to lower her mouth just above the straining shaft of my cock. She smiled at me as she reached back to tug out her hair tie. All that fiery softness slithered around my belly as she pushed up my shirt, scraping her teeth over my skin then easing the bite with a soft kiss.

I was about ready to jack off into the air, but this time, she hauled my thermal over my head, only to leave it trapping my hands together. She positioned herself on my lap and found the condom that had fallen onto the bed.

"I didn't get a chance to enjoy all of this the first few times we did this."

I groaned. "Enjoy all you want."

"I intend to." She ripped the foil and took me in hand to roll the latex down my length. Inching forward, she rose up to her full height on her knees. And I was so very grateful for those Amazonian legs right now.

She rolled her hips as she took me. Her head fell back as she slowly lowered herself onto me, inch by torturous inch. Then she tipped her hips forward to take even more.

I struggled out of the shirt binding my hands to reach for her. She didn't even bother trying to tell me to stay still. I sat up and wrapped my arms around her. I was too far gone to play games as we raced to the sweaty finish. She gripped my shoulders as our bodies synced up, pushing and pulling, accepting and giving.

My hand slid up her slick back to fist her hair. Her eyes flew open and our gazes locked as she rocked against me faster and faster. Sunlight haloed her hair, turning it burnished gold. I lifted my hips to meet her. All my muscles burned, but I couldn't stop. I wouldn't let go until she was with me.

She circled my neck with her arms, her lips fusing to mine as I swallowed her groan. She quaked around me from the inside out. I lifted her and flipped her onto her back at the other end of the bed. Nothing mattered but driving into her slick, clasping pussy.

She gripped my hips and took each punching thrust, her hair a wash of flame around her as she accepted everything I offered. Again, we locked eyes, and again, she tried to hide in a biting kiss, but I reared back to watch her.

I cupped the back of her neck, lowering until we were forehead to forehead, my strokes short and tight. "Tish."

Her gaze burned into me as she twined herself around me and held on for everything she was worth.

I couldn't wait another second.

I groaned into her neck, pouring myself into her. *This* was what I'd been looking for all my life. A peace that had always been just out of reach.

Her arms fell away as she starfished across my bed. "I think you killed me."

I grinned against her skin. "What a way to go."

"What a way indeed." She pushed at my shoulder. "Okay. Now I need real food."

"Seems to be a focus in your life lately."

"Gotta say I'm not used to working up such an appetite." After sliding out from under me, she stood up and twirled around. "Jeez, did you have to throw my clothes everywhere?"

I rolled onto my side to enjoy the view. "They were in the way."

"At least I know they didn't land in a dusty corner. You are very clean, Thor."

I shrugged. It was the second time she'd mentioned it. Living on the street where I never knew where I was going to lay my head left me very aware of my surroundings. I might've had too much shit all over the place, but everything was spotless.

She tugged on her jeans then leaned onto the bed to give me a quick kiss. "I like it."

I drifted the back of my fingers over the Batman logos cupping her breasts. "And I like this."

She laughed. "My brother, Rhett, sent me Batman boxers from this place. I loved them so much I joined a subscription. You should see my Thor ones."

I growled and tried to drag her back into my bed.

Nimbly, she leaped away. "Nope. Food. A gallon of water. We can go get Butch too." She strode down the hall. "Chop, chop, Thor."

I rolled onto my back with a sigh. Damn, she was my perfect woman.

Maybe I'd even get her to watch some action movies with me after we went to get my dog. I missed her.

One day, she might even be *our* dog. I grinned. A guy could hope.

SEVENTEEN

Lucky

RUBY NEVER TOOK THE EASY ROUTE.

Formulating our game plan and starting to execute it was what we did for the next month. More than one delay hampered our progress, but she was determined to get things moving for Cohen and her family's arrival. She was running me ragged, but I knew this was important to her.

By day, we were both working our asses off. She'd nixed the idea of a budget, and I realized just how freaking rich the love of my life was. I knew her reputation was impressive in the car business, but she was literally a genius.

The ideas she came up with for the space bent my brain. But they also excited me into changing things up. We'd nixed the idea of a bar around the post in the center of the room. Instead, we decided to use it as a table by the pool table for drinks.

But not only that, she'd designed a control center that would be built into that post. I could run electricity through there and wrap it with her fancy hub. In her business, there were a lot more modifications available than to the average homeowner. Her extra upgrades would take it all to the next level.

As eager as I was to make serious progress on the project, she wanted everything to go at the speed of light. And remodels just weren't fast-paced in this era of lumber shortages and staffing issues, no matter how much money you tossed around.

Something she was going to learn the hard way.

I threw my phone onto the makeshift table I'd made out of leftover plywood. The blueprints and notebooks I used to keep notes and receipts together were scattered. I'd been on the phone all damn day, trying to find another crew to do the roof repairs.

"Everything okay, chief?"

I turned to Joe. He was one of the four guys Gideon had lended me for the job. He was in his late thirties, as lanky and strong as an ox. He'd become my right-hand man when it came to working long hours.

"Just got a call that the roof repair is being delayed again. Fucking weather."

Joe pulled off his ball cap to bend the brim, his typical thinking pose. "Did you try Davey over in Syracuse?"

"Yep. I tried every contact Gideon had too. Oh, and the flooring has been backordered."

Joe winced. "The cork floor you convinced her to get?"

I raked my fingers through my hair, dragging out my hair tie out in the process. "Yeah. One in the same."

He whistled and settled the hat back on his head. "Not sure those kisses you distract her with are going to work this time."

Butch trotted in with her battered avocado squeaker toy in her mouth. She wagged her tail and stared up at me until I picked her up. I set her on my shoulder where she happily curled up against my neck, her beloved toy tucked under her chest. I didn't mind. Her warmth chilled me out a little.

"Don't say that out loud, for fuck's sake. She's already going to skin me alive."

We weren't exactly secretive about the fact that our relationship was a bit more than foreman and client. But Ruby didn't really like everyone knowing our business.

And I was okay with making sure I kept my hands to myself until after work hours. Most of the time. Now and then, I couldn't help myself, especially when she got frustrated with timelines.

Ruby didn't know the meaning of nine-to-five. We spent most evenings working on the barn after she'd already worked a full day.

Most nights, I spent in her bed. Sometimes after a tumble, sometimes we just passed the hell out. We were both pulling twelve-hour days. Butch and I had pretty much moved in, at least for the duration of the job.

I was tempted to buy a king-sized bed for her damn bedroom. My freaking feet hung over the edge. But in the end, it didn't matter, since I woke with my Amazon curled around me most mornings.

She kept telling me she liked her space while sleeping, but she always found her way on top of me in the night. I hoped it was because she wanted to be close to me, not that her bed hadn't been made for someone who was six-foot-four.

Oh, and a cat and a dog. Couldn't forget them.

Joe let out a long exhale. "Well, we finished the reclaimed wood treatment on the feature wall. It'll be ready for the shelving units, surround sound, and electronics by the end of the week."

"How's the upstairs looking?"

"We had to redo the second bedroom because it got wet." Joe pointed at the ragged hole in the roof. "Want me to send Frankie up to tarp it?"

I sighed. "Yeah. Tell him to weatherproof it as much as possible." I picked up my phone again. Now I had to find an alternative for the floor and hope it wouldn't take more than two weeks to come in. This delay meant I couldn't bring the furniture in either.

Fuck me.

"I'm going in the house to make some calls." I pinched the bridge of my nose. "Text me if something else goes wrong."

I lifted Butch off my shoulder and tucked her into the inside pocket of my jacket. Being this close to the water in November made for cold working conditions, even for me.

After gathering my stuff, I headed for her house. My phone buzzed with an incoming text from Ruby and one waiting from Dahlia, the decorator. I couldn't take any more bad news today so I skipped the designer's text in favor of my girl's.

"Shit," I muttered and quickened my step. She was already on her way home for the day. I'd wanted to have some answers before she showed up.

Quickly, I texted her back to bring food, hoping that would give me a bit of a buffer. I opened the front door then juggled Butch out of my pocket, and she scrambled into the living room with her toy in her mouth. Probably to terrorize Ruby's cat.

They had a love-hate relationship. Kinda like her mama and I.

I had one ace up my sleeve, but I wasn't sure it would be enough to combat all of the less than awesome news I had for Ruby.

I dumped my things in her brand new breakfast cove. The table was small enough for when it was just Ruby and—God willing—me in the future and could be modified with inserts for larger gatherings. The bench-style seating along the wall was where I'd hammered out the bulk of the details of this renovation. And it was where I sometimes had dinner with Ruby when I managed to get her to stop working.

At least the design improvements in her house were moving along with less drama. Dahlia McKenna was a wonder. She'd come in with her own crew to paint, decorate, and hash out furniture with Ruby. A full kitchen remodel was in the plans, but we had more important things to worry about first.

For now, Ruby was happy to fix up her space so they could eat dinner as a family, along with making sure her dad had a place to sleep when they arrived for Christmas.

Before I could even get another phone call in, Ruby sailed in with a bag of takeout from a nearby sub shop.

"Why is there still a hole in my barn roof?"

I flattened my palms on the table and took a breath. I was used to her sharp tone in the best of times, let alone now when our stress levels were rising.

Straightening, I turned to face her. "Sit down, Ruby. We need to talk."

She crossed her arms over her chest and leaned on the kitchen island. "I don't need to sit. And I don't need to hear excuses about this freaking remodel. It's been one thing after another, Lucky."

"I know it has." I gritted my teeth together. "This timeline is tight, let alone doing this in late fall in Central New York. Weather is hit or miss."

"It's been clear for days."

"Yeah, now it is." I moved to the kitchen window and flipped open the curtain. "See that ice and leftover snow out there? It makes roofing a little more dangerous."

Her face went impassive. "You said you could get it done."

Frustration rippled across my shoulders. "I know what I said."

"So, you aren't a man of your word?"

I stalked over to her. "I've been busting my ass for weeks to get this done for you."

"It's your job."

I reeled back and straightened my shoulders. "You're damn right it's my job. And as the foreman of this operation, I'm going to tell you that it's going to take more time than you'd like to get it done right."

"Then just hire more people."

"You can't just throw money at it, Ruby. That's not how this works." She opened her mouth and I cut her off. "I need a good roofer to make sure all of that is sound. What I don't need is to go on fucking Craigslist and hope some crap operation can come and screw it up. We're waiting the extra week to get it done right. You, of all people, should know how important that is."

She drilled a finger into my chest. "I appreciate that you want it done right. And you're correct—but we don't have time for this. Half of the things in that barn remodel are more intricate than needed. And that's on you."

I caught her finger, then flattened her hand on my chest. "It *is* on me. I want that space to be perfect for your family. I know how important it is to you."

"I don't need magazine-ready work, Thor. I need it done."

"Yeah, well, you're not going to like my additional bad news." I stepped back. "The flooring is backordered."

Her brown eyes went shark flat. "The floor *you* wanted, when I said laminate would work just fine."

"Yes. The sustainable cork floor I wanted is backordered. It wasn't when I made the decision. The supplier is having unforeseen issues." He'd clearly over-promised, but it was too late to deal with it. "I'm trying to find an alternative, but it's going to take time."

"I don't have time." She whirled on her heel and headed for the door.

"Goddammit." If she thought she could run away from me every time we had a problem, she was mistaken.

I followed her out into the sunny day. She went right to the barn. My crew scattered like Malificent herself was coming through. Ruby on a rampage was a sight to behold.

Normally, I would've chased her down and cajoled her into accepting my shitty news, but I was out of placating platitudes. It was a setback neither of us could control.

She fisted her hands into her hair.

I came up behind her and set my hands on her shoulders. She shook me away and twirled around, looking at all the half done things. We were working around all the setbacks, trying to get everything done in between.

"I should have known better. This looks like your place. Everything half done like some ADHD child. Just like you."

"That's not fair." I steered her over to the finished wall. "My crew worked on this wall for three straight days."

"Wasted time. Could have just painted it."

"Oh, right. Like you'd do that with one of your cars. It's like painting it flat white. Don't give me that, Ruby."

"There's pallets of furniture just sitting there."

"Yeah, because it just came in this afternoon." I urged her up the stairs to the second floor. "You helped me paint last night. This is almost done. The doors are going on tomorrow after we patch up the roof enough to finish up here."

Three simple rooms were framed out, and the wet sheetrock was sticking out of the bin we used for trash. The new one was up and taped out, but it needed to be primed and painted.

"What happened? We had this done last night."

I pointed up at the roof. "Leak got worse. Why we need the roofers."

"I'm going to have to put my family up at a hotel. Maybe I can talk to Sage."

I wasn't touching that one with a ten-foot pole. Sage's B&B had been full for weeks. Ruby's family was coming in for Christmas. Not exactly ideal.

"At the very least, we'll have the room ready for Cohen downstairs. It's already framed out. We even used the leftover reclaimed wood to make a feature wall in there. Plumbing is finished, and the walk in shower is all tiled. We're getting there. It's all set to keep him comfortable."

"Not fast enough."

"I'm not a miracle worker, Tish. This kind of job would normally be two to three months minimum. I'm doing the best I can."

"I'm not trying to be difficult."

"Oh, is that so?"

"Between this and Luna dragging me into the wedding…" She looked ready to scream. "I just can't."

"You love Luna."

"I didn't have a choice."

"Sure you did." I moved to her and took her hand. "You're just a little overwhelmed."

She twisted her fingers away and crossed to the pile of furniture all perfectly labeled. "I don't get overwhelmed."

"Hate to break it to you, but you're human. And this has been a lot of changes in a short amount of time. You're overwhelmed."

"No, I problem solve."

I sighed and came up behind her. This time, she leaned back against me. I relaxed as I looped my arms around her middle and tucked my chin on her head. "I had a thought."

"Oh, great."

I laughed and turned her around to face me. "The floor is cement, so we can do a treatment on it. Probably better anyway considering foot traffic, sand, and weather. It's not ideal, but it will cover us."

She scratched her chin as she thought it over. "Why didn't you say that before?"

"Before or after you ripped my head off?"

"Sorry. I had to take half a day for the dress fitting. I've been pricked a whole lot today."

"Not the right prick."

"Believe me, I'm not looking for that one either." She tried to back out of my hold.

I pulled her in tighter and just wrapped my arms around her. She was stiff as a damn board, but finally, she melted into me.

She laid her cheek against my chest and sighed. "Okay, maybe this doesn't suck."

We swayed a bit in the cold barn before I let her go. "How about I show you something good?"

"I told you I wasn't in the mood for another prick, Thor."

"So says the woman reaching for me at four in the morning." I slid my hand down to clasp hers. "C'mon, you'll like this."

She laced her fingers with mine. At least we were making a little progress when it came to her dealing with my need to touch her all the time. She only wiggled away when she was feeling extra thorny.

I drew her out of the barn and over to her detached garage. The matte black steel doors were down, but she also had a side door access.

Her usually long stride slowed until I had to practically drag her to the door.

"What's wrong?"

"You didn't do anything to my garage, did you?"

I braced my arm across the door. "Why?"

"My garage is exactly how I like it. *Exactly.*"

My stomach sank. Well, I was too far into it now. I opened the door and accepted my fate. Not much else I could do.

I turned on the light switch and she rushed in.

"What did you do?"

I leaned my shoulder against the doorjamb. Her garage had been cluttered, which was weird since she was so organized in the house. I waited for the creepy music from *Sleeping With the Enemy* every time I opened her cupboards. All the cans were face out and in alphabetical order.

But in here, she had tables lining every wall with tools. How the hell did she find anything?

"I kept it all in the same order from each table, just put them on a peg board so you could see everything. I replaced the rickety tables with tall, thin ones that you can use to organize all the parts you have everywhere."

She did her usual twirl. I was convinced that was how she took things into her brain for processing. The problem was, it usually resulted in her blowing a head gasket.

"But that's not how I like it. I won't be able to find anything." She stalked back to me. "Why would you do this?"

"I did it to make your life easier. Because I know you're an organized freak who likes order. Except here for some reason."

"I didn't ask you to touch in here."

"No. I did it because I care about you. But you wouldn't know how to say thank you even if someone yanked it out of your tonsils." My chest heaved and hurt hit lower than the anger. Which pissed me off even more. "You know what? Me and Butch are staying at my place tonight."

"What?" The squeak in her voice mollified me a little, but I was too mad to shake it off.

I left her in the garage. Butch was running around Joe's feet as they played keep-away with her beloved avocado.

I gave a sharp whistle and her fluffy white ears perked. She immediately zipped my way with her toy in her mouth, her tail wagging like a feather duster. I scooped her up and set her in the truck. "Looks like it's just us tonight."

As the tightness in my chest eased a fraction, I shot a look over my shoulder. Tish was waiting in the doorway of the garage, her arms tightly folded over her breasts.

Stubborn pain in my ass.

When I got into my truck, Butch gazed up at me with adoring eyes. At least one female in my life looked at me as if I was her favorite.

As if I had a purpose besides dispensing orgasms and doing favors for people who didn't even appreciate them.

And this time, I was the one who took off.

EIGHTEEN

So, IT TURNED OUT EXCELLENT SEX WITH AN ENTIRELY TOO SWEET MAN with a massive...*thruster* turned me into a shrew.

Who knew?

It wasn't entirely my fault. I refused to accept all responsibility. I had my brother to worry about and my family's upcoming visit, and most tragically of all, I had been yanked into a wedding party against my will.

Who could blame me for snapping at Lucky? Besides, I sort of was learning to trust the guy. I knew he could take my spewing.

Or maybe not, since he'd bolted. But he was probably overdue.

In any case, even if I'd been wrong to lash out at him, this was still partly Blondie's fault.

From the moment I'd received the pretty invitation with fancy lettering and rows of pine trees stamped on the bottom, I'd known I was fucked.

I didn't know how fucked, exactly, until I was in my bedroom trying to shimmy into something called a shaper so that I could fit into the bridesmaid dress I'd been fitted for just last week.

Bridesmaid material? Me? Let's be real. I was hardly the type to be a wedding guest, never mind in the party. I found ways to skip weddings whenever possible. My friends were dudes. Pre-Crescent Cove, I hadn't had many girlfriends at all.

Fine, none.

Somehow Luna and I had become friends, I supposed. But I hadn't expected her to ask me to not only come to her shindig, but to be part of it.

The dress I'd been fitted for was nice enough. It was a long column of deep wine red and flowed down into a slight flare around my calves. The plunging bodice was just a shade away from scandalous, even more so with the current condition of my tits. I'd never been an overly endowed chick, but this shaper was making me look like a porn star-in-training.

And the worst part? As I skimmed a hand down the side of my rebellious breasts, my first thought was that Thor would just love this getup on me—assuming we could have a civil conversation. He would've come in handy right about now as I reached back to tug up the dress's zipper.

I was far more winded than I should've been. Jeez, it was winter, and I always tended to put on a few pounds watching my guilty pleasure Christmas movies on cable, but never this early. We hadn't even reached the holidays yet. This was not a good sign for slipping back into my leathers once the weather turned enough for me to go riding again.

In like half a year or so. Gotta love upstate New York.

I'd managed to yank up my zipper and huff my still partially wet hair out of my face when my phone started bleating like the National Weather Alert system. I'd never heard so many frantic buzzes at one time.

I dug it out from where I'd tossed it in my tangled sheets and scowled at the readout. Now what? Wasn't I already doing my civic duty by shimmying into this dress?

And there were heels to go with it. Not flats. Oh, no. Just because the bride was a shorty, she wanted the entire bridal party to teeter around on matching stilts. Hadn't she gotten the memo that I would loom over almost all the women and a good segment of the men?

At least Lucky held up his end of the bargain there. I almost felt small around him.

Why did I keep thinking about him? So what if I'd be seeing him soon? I saw him all the time. He was my contractor. He went in and out of my house more often even than the mice he'd hired an exterminator to shoo out into the cold.

Cute little things. Old house. Stuff happened.

I hadn't tucked one into my hoodie pocket after one particularly active construction day while they leveled the cement floors. No proper lady would do such a thing.

I snorted. Proper was definitely not the word for me. But I hadn't kept the little dude, adorable as he was. He was probably outside casing the joint at this very moment, trying to find his way back in.

A quick swipe of my thumb over my phone, and Blondie's tear-filled bluebell eyes filled my screen. I started to ask her what her damage was when an ear-splitting screech pierced my eardrums.

"Damn, look at those knockers! Go Tish!"

I released a baffled laugh as I glanced down at my chest. A weird sense of pride filled me, probably a holdover from when I'd been too tall and skinny with it. Knobby knees, elbows, and braces for the junior high spring formal had set me on my path to social awkwardness early.

And now my big accomplishment was that I'd somehow grown breasts—or at least the appearance of them in this too tight dress.

Yay me.

"Yours are climbing high too. Is that a wedding dress or are you trying on your honeymoon lingerie?"

"Neither. This is my slip." She hiked it up higher and her jugs threatened to overflow like Mount Vesuvius. "You don't remember my wedding dress?"

"Uh, it was light-colored..."

Shaking her head, she laughed. "It's gray. Not white because I'm super preggo." She reached down to cup her noticeable baby bump, and something rippled through my midsection. The feeling wasn't uncomfortable exactly. Just...weird.

What was it like to have one of those in there? Just cooking away and getting bigger by the hour.

Not that I wanted one. My life was work, work, and more work. Family would be part of the mix soon too. And yeah, Thor tried to get me to see there were other things in life, but babies? Not so much.

"You're beautiful." I swallowed over the unexpected dryness in my throat. "Except for those tears, Blondie. It's your damn wedding day. Chin up. Unless Teach did something he deserves a steel-toed boot in the junk for, and if so, I can shed these fancy threads in a nanosecond." I grimaced and shoved up my breasts. "Well, maybe a full minute. Good thing I have an assortment of wrenches available to get this zipper back down."

She let out a watery giggle and ducked down long enough for me to see her entirely too crammed dressing room. There was a handsome blond dude in a tux and a pair of society types who probably were her parents—and the parents of Mr. Slick if the resemblance held true.

A few other random women milled about whom I assumed were in the wedding party. Luna had assured me it was small, but I was pretty sure my idea of small and hers were very different.

"I'm sorry to call this late. I know you'll be leaving soon."

I checked the time on my phone. "I am? Hippie Acres isn't far from here."

The wetness in her eyes dried in a blink. "Happy. And um, have you looked outside today? It's a mess out there."

I went to the window and groaned at the blanket of white outside. Dripping from the trees, thickly coating the grass, stacking high on the banks of the shore.

Great. One more complication for my day. Now I'd have to find my way to some apple farm on the back roads of Turnbull in a damn blizzard.

I shut my eyes and debated pretending I'd lost cell service from the storm. But that was low even for me. It was Luna and Caleb's wedding day. That meant joy and happiness and fa-la-la-the-fuck-la.

"You know, maybe you shouldn't have skipped doing a wedding

rehearsal? That way, at least some of us would have a clue how to get there."

"There's a map on the back of your invitation," she said primly. "And I didn't want to have a rehearsal because—"

"You wanted it to be all natural and for events to unfold without scripting. I can guarantee they will since you're having your freaking BFF marry you. Is she even legal?"

"Of course. Our handfasting ceremony will be as official as any other."

"Says the witness in your belly," I muttered. "Anyway, I'll figure it out. If everyone else can find the place, I can too."

"That's just the thing." Her chin wobbled. "Some of the family and friends can't make it because of the storm. The wedding started out small and now it's even smaller. And..." She took a deep breath, clearly trying to keep it together. "My bestie can't be my maid-of-honor because she's on the way to urgent care with her grams."

"What the hell kind of excuse is that? Wrap up grandma and get on the road."

Truth be told, I was a little jealous of this so-called bestie for having called in the spilled blood excuse before I'd thought of it.

Slow on the uptake, Burns. You snooze, you lose.

But no, I wouldn't bail on a friend, even a new one like Lu. Besides, she was important to Lucky because of the whole Caleb deal, and that mattered because no one wanted a rift with the man who held the fate of their home's foundation in his hands. Any more of a rift in this case, since I'd already created a deep enough one with my mouthing off.

That explanation was as good as any other, so I was running with it.

"She fell, Tish, and April's freaking out. Her grams is basically like her mom to her. She offered to send her guy in her place. He's smokin' hot, but you know, I didn't think he'd fit in her dress."

I grinned. "Probably not. But what does this have to do with—*no.*" Horror dawned. "I just shimmied into this dress with considerable difficulty, and now you want me to wiggle into another?"

"Please? I can't ask anyone else, and the vibe will be all off. And the pictures will be uneven. Besides, you and Lucky are like such matched bookends."

"What's that supposed to mean?"

"You're both so tall, and you look amazing together. Not that I'm insinuating you are together. Or have been together, probably amazingly. Which might be why you try not to stand too close to him so no one else gets burned by the sparks you two keep throwing off." She coughed delicately into her fist. "Or something."

I wasn't blushing. In fact, I was almost sure I didn't even have the capability despite my hair color. I was immune to such shows of embarrassment.

"You're seeing things, Blondie."

Yeah, yeah, so he'd been spending most nights here until we'd had that stupid fight. Not a fight exactly. Dammit, he shouldn't have touched my sanctuary.

"Even that. You adopted his nickname for me. You two just fit. Everyone says so. But Caleb says—"

"Who is this 'everyone', and what does Caleb say?"

The polished blond dude who was probably Lu's brother or cousin twice removed moved forward and laid his hand on her shoulder. "Caleb says you're lovely in that dress, so why have you exchange one lovely dress for another? Right, Lulu?"

She mumbled under her breath before brightening. "You're right, X. He's right. Why not buck tradition? Every part of this wedding is different from the norm. I'd be honored if you would stand up for me and not only because you and Lucky belong together—"

"She can't help matchmaking." X put his hand over her mouth and she giggled. "Damn these in love people who assume all the rest of us should be as happy."

She pried off his hand. "I haven't given up on you, X."

"Tell me about it."

Watching their sibling teasing made me hunch my shoulders. My brothers would be here soon, and normally, I'd be excited. I was now too, but I was also worried. Seeing Co when I was keeping stuff from him about his best friend made everything so much more difficult. But I didn't want Jimmy to cause me to lose anything else.

Like, oh, your sense of trust? Your faith in men? Your belief that a man could just want you for you and not for some ulterior motive?

"I'll do it," I said suddenly. "I'll even wear the stu—stupendous maid-of-honor dress. Assuming it fits me. Is April short?"

"No, she's almost as tall as you. *Ish.* It's perfect."

"Sure, if you don't mind me flashing some leg at a family event."

"Don't worry. Caleb's sister-in-law is attending too, and she's already here so she can't get stuck in that snowbank like the others. She'll make any needed alterations."

"What others? Snowbank? My beater car can't make it through any heavy-duty snow, Lu."

She waved me off. "Already taken care of. Your chariot awaits. Just hurry up and finish getting dressed. Thank you, love you, see you soon." The screen went black.

"What the hell? What kind of chariot could make it here in this weather?"

Since I was alone, I did not get an answer.

With a sigh, I clomped over to the window, hiking up my dress so it didn't drag across the floor. I hadn't put on my torture device heels yet. Why did women insist on tormenting poor innocent toes that were so much happier in Chucks or my perfectly broken-in boots?

Outside, white obscured my vision. There was so much snow that it was starting to cling to the windows themselves, never mind pile up on the sills.

Normally, on a night like this I'd be curled up, remote in hand, watching something schmaltzy I probably wouldn't admit to in mixed company. Or any company.

Hell, it was the holidays. I was allowed to watch some cute 90s teen queen meet her small town's mysterious innkeeper who was the only one who could help her make five-hundred centerpieces for the Christmas charity craft fair in two days.

More than that, I was entitled. Holiday spirit, dammit. I had it too. Sometimes.

Out of the swirling snow, a pair of headlights appeared. The truck swung into my driveway, and my heart went wild, fluttering in my chest.

Apparently, I was no better than the 90s teen queen without the cute factor and with an additional half a foot of height.

"Chariot indeed."

Something dangerously close to excitement and pleasure hummed along my skin as I hurriedly finished getting ready. I gave my hair the quickest blowdry known to man while I worked my kind of magic with a curling brush and hairspray. Good enough. The storm would wreck it anyway, and no one had invited me for my wizardry with hair styling tools.

God help them if they did.

I went to grab my leather jacket and realized a girly furry stole thing would probably work better with this getup. Whatever. Like I had one of those. If they wanted Tish Burns, they were getting her, leather and all.

I stuffed the damn shoes in a bag and put on my most ridiculous snow boots. Ezra called them my moon boots because of their shape, but hey, they kept my feet toasty and I wasn't ruining my regular boots with this crap.

How could snow come down so fast? It had only been a few hours since I'd looked outside. Flurries were one thing, this stuff quite another.

Then I opened the door and faced the mountains of snow between me and the truck waiting patiently in my drive.

Too late to rethink my plan to dress before I got to Dippy Acres?

I shut my eyes and prayed for patience. I was going to have to take this dress off again and put on some freaking snowpants. Fuck my life.

My phone went off and I slammed the door, leaning against it as I read Lucky's text and sent one of my own.

Open your door, Ruby.

I have to change.

Open your door, Ruby.

"Open your door, Ruby," I mimicked, doing a quick sweep for Dusty just to make sure he wasn't curious enough to dart outside. My cat wasn't dumb enough to go wading in snow, but before today, I would've said I wasn't dumb enough to get myself roped into a wedding.

It took all kinds.

The cat was nowhere in sight, so I had to assume he was curled up somewhere and enjoying himself far more than I was. He had a full bowl of food and fresh water so he was set.

I yanked open the front door again, ready to march outside and yell at Lucky that he could hold his ass while I changed into something that wouldn't cause immediate frostbite to my lower limbs.

But I didn't expect him to be standing *right there.*

The sight of him in an eggplant purple tux and a sweeping dark coat with his hair long and loose and sprinkled with snow like confetti took my breath and my irritation away.

So, his massive height and the breadth of his freaking shoulders had something to do with it too.

"You opened the door." Plumes of frosty air streamed from his lips, oddly fascinating me.

I blamed them for being distracted enough that he managed to lift me straight off the ground, pull the door shut, and cart me across the snow to his truck before I marshaled the wits to scream.

Either that or my lungs had frozen. Holy crap, it was cold.

He muscled me into the front seat and something about the action reminded me I was in motion not of my own doing. I brought my leg up and jammed my knee hard into his inner thigh, dangerously close to where his prized possession rose up like a hungry beast.

Such a shame it was caged in those restrictive tuxedo pants.

"You nearly nailed me," he panted in my ear.

Which did not remind me to be mad, gotta say. I hadn't had my hands on him in days now. His warm breath and soap scent and huge arms clamped around me made me feel decidedly fond of him actually

"Remember that next time you get handsy." I poked his insanely broad chest, shaking loose a moderate snowstorm in the cab of his truck.

"Oh, yeah?" Daring me now, he slid his big bear paws down under my ass and cupped me against him. My fault for not disabling that armed menace in his trousers when I'd had the chance. "What are you gonna do when I make you come all over my pants?"

Say thank you, I needed that?

No. Wrong answer.

Brain, come back online. Anytime now would be awesome.

"You absolutely cannot do that. There's no...dry cleaner at Hoppy Acres."

He lifted his head, his green eyes dancing with mirth in the low light. "Happy."

"No, not particularly, but it is what it is—" He started to laugh and I thumped him in the gut, not checking my strength one iota.

He only laughed harder, the ass. And then I was laughing too, and he was kissing me and I sort of forgot to be cold when we were generating a massive amount of heat.

This was a very unwise idea. We were already probably behind time-wise to get to this shindig and now I was Lu's main squeeze in the wedding party. I probably shouldn't be late.

I definitely shouldn't be writhing and moaning as he let out a sound of torment while he filled his hands with my breasts.

"Fuck, I've missed you, Ruby. Let me look at you in this dress."

"Please don't," I gasped. "It's not truth in advertising."

His laughter was loud and baffled but it didn't stop him from trailing hot, wet kisses down the side of my throat to my cleavage. "Says who?"

"Me. It's the damn shaper. I'm not built like...this." I was rapidly losing oxygen in this cramped front seat, which didn't make sense considering he was still hanging out the open door. I wasn't sure he could fit on top of me if he didn't, but it didn't seem right for his ass to get frostbite for his trouble.

"Too late. Already did." His long fingers spanned my cheeks as he tilted my face upward. "Now I want to look at you out of it."

"We're outside." Speaking was getting harder by the second. "Your ass is going to freeze if you pull down those pants."

"Aww, worried about me, Ruby?" He licked his way up my throat and then found my mouth, sinking in with a primal noise that made me try to clench my legs around his tree trunk thighs.

"Just because I have a use for you."

"That so?"

"Oh, it's so." I grabbed his backside and hauled him more onto the seat, dragging his hard cock over my cleft just the way I needed.

We both groaned and laughed when the sudden forceful movement rocked the truck.

I sucked on his lower lip and skipped the formalities, shoving my hands down the back of his pants so I could cup his truly bitable ass. "Gotta say, Thor, I appreciate your control."

"Control?" He gasped out a laugh as his icy fingers delved into the stupid shaper to caress my needy breast. My yelp made him laugh harder as he found my nipple. "My dick is an icicle. I'm not entirely sure I can thrust."

"Let's find out." I pinched his cheeks and he jerked against me, proving he could just fine. "See, I had faith in you."

"That was just the feeling returning. Fuck, look at this thing. Your tits are sky-high." His reverence as he jolted up to get a better look made me snort, then choke on a laugh when his head bounced off the ceiling. "Ouch, Jesus. You're killing me, Ruby. Literally." He rubbed his head and grinned down at me with pure joy in his eyes.

My belly rioted, heaving in a way that did not entirely match the situation. I hadn't eaten much today. A sandwich at lunch with some chips. Probably needed to cruise by the dessert table before the ceremony and see if I could steal a damn cupcake or something.

Then he slid his hand up my thigh and found the rest of my foundational garments—also known as the thong I'd had no choice but to wear to avoid panty lines. His reaction was a litany of swear words uttered with a devotion I hadn't known he possessed.

"I want to eat you. Have to." He was already sliding backward. I wasn't entirely sure his legs hadn't folded beneath him. "Can crouch on the—"

"What? No. No. No eating. If I can't, you can't either. Pussy or otherwise." I was giggling like a maniac. "Get up here, you oaf."

I scrambled backward across the front seat, bumping and scraping both my limbs and my pride, then I pulled him upward all the way into the cab. He managed to shift enough to get the door closed behind him and fit himself between my thighs, rutting against me hard enough to send my head into the driver's door. He immediately grabbed my head, muttering apologies between kisses as we writhed against each other.

This time, he sucked his fingers into his mouth, warming them, before he slipped his hand into the shaper to tug on my painfully hard nipple. Pure need speared through me, landing between my legs so that I couldn't do anything but arch against him and beg.

Nonsense words. Pleas. Vague threats and ones that weren't so vague when he made me wait.

His mouth replaced his fingers on first one nipple then the other. I almost couldn't take the infusion of pleasure from his tongue and the razor skim of his teeth. Mindlessly, I ran my hands through his long hair, laughing again through my sighs when I hit the crunchy, frozen part courtesy of the snowstorm. Then his wet fingers slipped over my pussy and I exploded. Just one brush against my clit and I was gone, shaking against him and holding on as if the parts left of me would disintegrate if I didn't.

"Missed that sound so much." His big hands framed my face until my heavy lids lifted and focused on the world captured in his green eyes. It was cold as hell beyond the bubble of heat between us, but when I was trapped in his gaze, I couldn't feel it.

Nothing else existed except him.

Except us, and the me I became when I was with him. I fought it with everything I was even as I rushed toward it again and again.

I turned my head and nipped the pad of his finger, tasting myself there. That same twist in my belly had me swallowing hard, but he didn't know of my internal struggle. He yanked down his zipper, fighting through layers of fabric to get to my favorite part of him.

Well, only one of my favorites of his. There were many. I just wouldn't admit it.

My head revolved. I didn't know if it was still attached. That was a new aftereffect to an orgasm, even an incredible one. Add in the touchy stomach and I didn't know if I wanted more or to cross my hands over my lady business.

Was I hungry or nauseated? Lovesick? Was that an actual thing? Probably not. And I wasn't that anyway.

I hoped.

He lifted his hard, heavy cock and circled the tip over my clit. I forgot about my belly and my head and anything but yanking the dress up my thighs to give me enough room to wind my legs around him. I couldn't get close enough. I was a vine around his big body, touching whatever part of him I could reach and begging for things I couldn't name.

No matter how he sated me, it was always temporary. And when the need came back, it was ten times as intense.

Drowning me just like he was devouring me with his hot, urgent kisses. His tongue lashed mine and I moaned, bowing up into him until his cock dipped into me and he surged forward to the hilt in one slow roll.

Heaven, perfection, destruction—all at once.

"Fuck, shit, dammit. No condom." His agonized expression hit me down deep, and I started to laugh the laugh of someone who had lost their mind.

Or really wanted another orgasm.

I rocked against him, urging him on. Telling him without words he better not fucking stop anytime soon. My nails sank into his ass, and he drove forward with a long groan, letting loose in a truly spectacular fashion considering the confines of the front seat. His head hit the ceiling more than once and mine hit the door and the

215

pain only made the torturous need climb higher. My thighs were shaking with it, my nipples diamond points that throbbed against his tongue when he sucked them deep. I dragged my hands through his hair, pulling with enough force that my nails scored his scalp. His grunts were like liquid kerosene poured on the fire inside me, and his desperate strokes pushed me closer to that edge from which I'd never come back.

I knew it like I knew my own name.

Yet when I reached the pinnacle, I still pinwheeled into the dark, arms out, as if I believed I couldn't ever fall. Not when he was with me. On me. *In* me, filling up all the spaces and gaps down deep that no one had ever touched before him.

Or would after.

He panted my name into my ear. His version of it, the name that had become mine as much as my own.

"Ruby. My Ruby."

And as he stilled before that last mad thrust inside me, spilling himself into my depths, I clutched my arms around his back and shut my eyes.

Just like that, I knew something else too. It didn't matter that we hadn't used a condom. Didn't matter that we were reckless together because it had only taken once to change everything.

I knew.

NINETEEN

Lucky

FOR A LITTLE WHILE IN THE TRUCK, I WAS SURE I HAD FINALLY REACHED her.

It wasn't the first time. We always had pockets of understanding and laughter in between the petty arguments and sniping and insanely hot sex. But she always locked down. Sometimes I could even physically see it happening. The shields dropping to block away any emotion she didn't want me to be privy to.

But not only me. She hid them from herself too. That was the only way a woman as responsive as she was could only play half the notes on the guitar and pretend she covered the whole damn G clef.

Leticia might be her first name, but Denial was her middle.

I had to assume Jimmy was a big part of that. Sure, she'd told me about his betrayal. But she hadn't told me the rest. The most salient part.

He'd broken her heart by abusing her trust. And I was clearly a heartless bastard, because the only reason I wished he was still alive was so that I could kick his ass for what he'd done to her.

What he was still doing, even if she'd never admit it.

The ride to Happy Acres was slow and by inches rather than miles due to the endless snow slanting down from the gray sky. She was quiet through the trip, lacing and unlacing her fingers. She wasn't the chatty sort normally, but this was a lot of stony silence even for her.

She'd been there with me. I was damn sure of it. So, there could only be one explanation.

"If you're worried about the condom thing—"

"I'm not." She stared out the side window. "Not an issue."

"Are you on birth control?"

"It's not an issue," she repeated.

I gripped the wheel tighter and forced myself to stay focused on the blur of white out the windshield rather than her profile. I loved looking at her, and I sneaked greedy glances whenever I could. I wanted to see her willingly soft and vulnerable after sex, to glimpse her with her shields down. Not because I'd pushed beyond them, but because she finally understood she didn't need them with me.

That was probably a fantasy.

"Look, I'm not just bouncing on you just because it feels good."

"Oh, no? You interested in my designs too?"

The arrow struck deep, as intended. I sucked in a breath and wished it really was a physical arrow so I could reach down and make the bleeding stop.

She swore under her breath. "I'm sorry. That wasn't fair. Neither was me leaping on you about the house delays. I was way out of line then and now too. I just—I can't do whatever you're aiming for right now."

"No kidding." There was no keeping the bitterness out of my tone. "My fault for thinking this time, you were with me and not him."

"What?" Her head whipped toward me although I refused to return her glance. Petty maybe, but I had my pride too.

"You heard me."

"You don't know what you're talking about."

"Don't I?" I asked quietly.

"Before we go to Holy Acres, I need you to stop somewhere for me."

I couldn't even laugh about her mistake. "Need a morning after pill? Can't take one fast enough, I'm sure."

She locked her jaw with an audible snap. "You can't outdick me, but I can tell you're ready to try. So, just get it out of your system so we can be rational about this."

"I'm fucking in love with you. Be rational about that." I slammed my hand on the wheel, and the truck swerved on a patch of ice, careening off the road and hitting a snowbank with a soft thud. The impact reverberated, rattling the metal enough that I instinctively shot out my arm across the passenger seat to keep Ruby safe.

That was all I wanted. Her safe and happy.

And most of all, I wanted her to be mine. Warts, cracks, strengths, smiles, and all.

I blew out a breath and took stock. Everything was still in one piece. From the looks of things, she was fine too—physically at least.

Her crazed gaze swerved to mine a moment later, but I didn't remove my arm from in front of her. I hoped like hell she couldn't see how it was trembling. "So, that was the snowbank."

I frowned. "What?"

"Just something Lu said earlier. But there aren't any cars here, so I guess they dug their way out of it. Or were towed." Her voice pitched higher. "Or maybe freaking aliens swooped down in their spaceships, because I don't see any damn vehicles, do you?"

"Actually, there are two just around the bend. Maybe the people got picked up, and they left their cars for when the weather clears."

"Or maybe they're human popsicles as we speak."

"Are you okay?" I kept my tone as even as possible. "Did you hurt something?"

"No. We're just fine. Burns are made of stronger stuff than that." She dipped her head and stared pointedly at my arm. The muscles there were bulging with enough tension that even my coat barely obscured them. "Besides, you'd throw yourself in front of me to keep me safe if necessary."

"Doesn't work in a car accident." My voice was strangely thick, and I didn't know why.

She scoffed. "That wasn't an accident. More like a tiny bump. And that part of the road already caught a few drivers today. Damn storm."

I reached out to grip the wheel, wrapping my fingers around it one at a time. The truck was still running, the motor purring away just like normal. The old thing was strong and sturdy and as reliable as the tide. But concern for the Ford wasn't what had me holding on as if I needed the support.

"You said *we*."

"I'm sure you can just reverse out of this. Big ol' truck probably didn't even get dinged."

"Tish."

She continued as if I hadn't said anything. I would've thought she was just having a normal conversation if I hadn't heard her teeth chattering in between the words she forced out. "Bet you don't even have a scratch. Nothing to remember this by except a fond memory."

What she was saying didn't match what had just happened unless you read between the lines. But I'd become an expert at it the last couple months.

"And hey, if you do have a dent or a ding, I know a good body shop. Fix you up in no time. You'll go on as if this never even happened."

I unclicked my seatbelt and reached over to undo hers.

"What are you doing? We have to go to the wedding."

"In a minute." I drew her into my arms, holding on even as she bristled.

Her resistance barely lasted a minute before she softened against me and pressed her face against my chest. Right over my heart where it was thundering like the fiercest summer storm just before the rain came and washed everything clean.

"I don't know for sure."

I stroked her hair. If she could tell my hand was shaking, she didn't mention it. It hadn't stopped from the crash and wouldn't be anytime soon.

"I didn't even think about it. Never considered. We weren't in town. I mean, we did it a lot in town too, but it probably happened the first time. Maybe. I don't know. Of all the luck—"

I stopped her right there and tipped her face up to mine. "From where I'm sitting, my luck finally came in."

"You don't know what you're saying."

"Try me."

"It's shock. It's because you got off. It's because Caleb is getting married, and you're high on love fumes and don't want to be alone."

"You're right. It's all of those things. But none of those change the fact that I wake up in the morning and I want to see your face. I want to hear your voice. Hell, I even can't wait to see what snarky insult you'll toss at me next."

I brushed her hair away from her mouth and realized I wasn't the only one shaking. I pressed my forehead to hers. "We're in this together. You'll never be alone again. I promise you, Leticia."

She released a sound caught between a laugh and a sob. Pure relief drenched me as she eased back and stared up at me with achingly dry dark eyes. "I wasn't even sure you knew my real name."

"Of course I do." The corner of my mouth lifted. "Ruby."

"Jackass." But she grinned.

Inside me, it was as if the sun beamed down after the storm, although the thunder still raged in my chest. I had a feeling it would for a while.

I lifted her hand. She was so cold. I kissed the tips of her fingers, my gaze roaming her face. Soaking in every detail from her freckles to the little divot in her upper lip as if I'd never seen her before. In a way, I hadn't. This moment was unlike any that had come before or would come after.

"Let's go take a test and find out."

Immediately, she shook her head.

"Ruby, we have to know."

"I know."

"So, let's just make sure."

"No need." She set her chin. "I know."

Laughing was the only option I had left. "Fine, you know. What harm does it do to check the boxes?"

"I can't deal with this now. I have to go be the maid of honor to a woman who checked out my tits and thinks we look like perfect bookends."

"You haven't seen your tits in that dress. Anyone who didn't check them out is missing a pulse."

"Somehow this isn't sinking in. Do you get the gravity of this situation, Thor? This isn't just a chaotic winter and back to normal. This is late night feedings and mopping up drool and changing diapers. I don't do those things. I have no idea how. And how the hell am I supposed to raise a kid and do my job and make sure my brother is okay—"

"First, try taking a deep breath."

She glared daggers at me, and my heart rejoiced.

She would be just fine. *We* would be fine.

"I don't appreciate you being calm while I lose my mind. But hey, you don't have to carry the kid. You just did your part and walked away whistling."

"Any man who whistles and walks away from you is asking for a kick in the ass."

Something crossed through her expression that had nothing to do with the specter of a baby. And I hated that even now in this moment that should belong only to us, *he* intruded. There was no place he couldn't enter.

She'd engraved an all-access pass for him, and it was valid even after death.

She started to slide across the seat, but I gripped her arm, softly yet firmly. "I had no one to rely on growing up. No one. The only person I could count on was me. If you think that I'll make my kid feel that way for even one second—even when he's in your belly—you tangled with the wrong man, Ruby."

Her eyes closed and when she spoke again, her voice wobbled. "I'm sorry. I'm doing this all wrong. But I only realized like half an hour ago. I should've figured it out when my damn tits exploded out of the shaper, but I was too busy appreciating them to think it through."

"Me too."

"Your tits are exploding? Here I didn't even know you wore shapers."

I wound a handful of her hair around my fist. "Smart ass."

"Better than a dumb one. How the hell am I going to get through this wedding?"

"With me by your side. He's important to me, Ruby," I added quietly as her gaze swung to mine. "He's my family, and by extension, so is Blondie. I have to do this for them. I want to. I would appreciate if you'd be by my side through it too."

Her lower lip quivered so she bit it to make it stop. "So not fair."

I shrugged. "Did it work?"

"Moderately. But I can't take a test yet. I just can't and act like a functioning person in front of all these people."

"After?"

She hesitated. "Isn't seeing my belly grow to match the giant boobs answer enough?"

"Kinda takes longer than my patience would allow."

"Not really. They're growing by leaps and bounds already." She heaved out a sigh. "Fine. After."

"Thank you." I cupped her still cold hand in mine and kissed her knuckles. "Together is a word you should try to get used to."

She gripped her stomach with her other hand. "One thing at a time, Thor."

"Are you sick?"

"Hell if I know. I just need some food. Or maybe to puke. I can't really tell."

I blew out a half laugh. "We'll start with food and go from there."

"We're so late—"

I rubbed her knuckles and shifted in my seat. Time to see if I could dig us out of this snow mess. "Better late than never, and they can't start without me."

Turned out they could, in fact, start without both of us. Or they would have if we hadn't shown up precisely when we had.

We parked as close as possible in the half full lot. There weren't a ton of people here. I knew Lu had said it was a small wedding, but women tended to underestimate. I had no doubt the weather had kept some away.

That snowbank right in the middle of the rise that led to Happy Acres probably hadn't helped. If I didn't have a wedding to be part of myself, I would've gone down there and tried to make a dent in the snowpack.

The physical exertion would've helped to clear my mind and the assortment of thoughts whirling through it like the snow pelting our faces like little chips of ice.

Such as...

Did you really fuck Ruby without a condom?

Holy shit, best ever.

But she could get pregnant...nope, guess what, she can't!

That barn door is already housing a horse—if her feminine vibes are right about the occupancy of her uterus.

Judging from the way she kept covering her mouth with her gloved hand—not that she had brought any of her own, but I kept an extra pair in the truck—and squinting as if she was trying to figure out if she could make it to the front door of the main building, I had to think she had a good read on her own body. Women's intuition or some shit.

Besides, she'd been hanging out more with Blondie. Maybe that extraterrestrial sense rubbed off or something.

Not extraterrestrial, dumbass. Extrasensory. Did that slide into the snowbank knock something loose?

My messed-up thinking probably had more to do with my major life changes in the last hour, but anything was possible.

I grabbed her bag, then helped her out of the car.

Dear God, a baby. Mine. Hers. Ours?

Why did you tell her you were in love with her? Want her to have more ammunition against you?

All I wanted was for her to have the truth. She needed to know how I felt.

Period.

We tromped through the snow coming down faster than the

proprietors of the apple orchard-slash bed and breakfast-slash event facility could keep the snow cleared away. There was a literal team out there working with plows and shovels. If anything, it was snowing harder here in the little hamlet of Turnbull than it had been in the Cove, which was saying a lot.

I gripped her arm and steadied her as we neared the walkway that led to the wide porch's front steps. "Are you okay?"

She didn't growl at me, which proved she was in rough shape. "Do you know where the bathrooms are in this joint?"

Uh oh.

"I'll find out." I yanked my phone out of my pocket and texted Caleb with my clumsy, half frozen fingers.

Where's the john here?

Caleb's reply was surprisingly swift since I was pretty sure he should be busy right now.

Dude, you are late. So late. And your 1st concern is your bladder?

Not mine. Ruby's. And not her bladder. Need a br. Where do we go?

Is she ok? Right off the entrance to the left.

Thanks. Sorry. Cya in a min.

Or ten depending how bad the spewage was, but I didn't add that. The guy had enough to deal with. He didn't need to find out his replacement maid-of-honor was on the verge of tossing her cookies upon arrival.

"You know," I said over the rising wind, laying a hand at the small of her back, "you would basically make my life if you'd be okay with me carrying you again."

"Thor, I'm at low ebb here. Weakened state."

"That wasn't a no. It would be my honor. Really."

"Um, not sure if you're aware, but this is someone else's wedding. Added to the fact," she rubbed her belly in frantic circles, swallowing hard, "I'm pretty sure if you lift me up right now, you'll be wearing this afternoon's ham sandwich as part of your wedding attire."

"Okay. No carrying."

I rushed up the steps and drew open the door, the warm, homey scents inside immediately washing over me. Rich winter smells like roasting chestnut, the tang of apples, and something like sugary vanilla made my stomach growl as I turned back toward Tish and opened my voluminous long coat.

It had been an inspired choice, especially considering my current use. "Here, duck under here."

"What? Duck? I'm almost six foot tall."

"And mouthy with it too." I shrouded it around her and ushered her inside, pleased when she ducked her head against my neck as people swarmed toward us. Many people. Far more than a pregnant woman about to have her first episode of baby-induced throwing up should have to contend with before she…expelled.

"We'll be right back." I used my most booming voice and smiled brightly as I drew her to the left and down the hall to the women's room.

I was almost sure some of the guests gasped in our wake.

I'd need to come up with a good cover story for this one. It didn't seem likely Ruby would be okay with me announcing we were expecting.

Lord help us, we were expecting an actual human baby that we would have to take care of for, like, eighteen years.

I'd be how old by then? Quickly, I did the math. Hopefully, I'd still have all my hair. I didn't want to be the pity dad at graduation. That whole patchy on top and long in back look never did anyone any favors.

"Thor." Ruby pounded on my chest. "You're blocking the damn doorway. Move."

I opened the door and she charged inside, aiming straight for the toilet. The setup was for one person with no separate stalls, so she was in my full view when she dropped to her knees, swore ripely, and emptied her stomach.

The sounds she made were not pleasant.

Rushing to the sink, I dropped her bag, then soaked a couple of paper towels. I moved to her side and wiped her brow with one hand and drew back her hair with the other, trying to keep it out of the way. I yanked the old scrunchie off my wrist I'd picked up somewhere—hey, the silky fabric was less damaging—and tugged the long mass into a loose ponytail.

She flushed then grabbed the towel and wiped her mouth, her dark eyes lasering onto mine. "Why are you in here?"

"Um, you're sick? I'm helping."

"You can't see me this way."

"Why the hell not? I put that baby in you."

"*Shh*, for fuck's sake." She reached up to thump me in the general thigh area, but I could only imagine how it looked when the bathroom door swung open, and an older lady shrieked for Jesus.

"It's not what you think," I began as Tish jerked to her feet and stumbled over to the sink to wash her hands.

She glanced at the mirror and let out a string of expletives. "What in the fuckity fuck did you do to my hair?"

I stepped forward to poke at the droopy side ponytail. "I got it out of your way, right?"

"With an *orange* Casper the Ghost scrunchie? If I had my steel-toeds, you'd be in trouble."

The bathroom door slammed shut behind the horrified woman.

Well, this wedding was off to a rip-roaring start.

I crossed my arms. "You already got your use out of me, now you want to maim me. Typical."

"What use was that exactly? Your best use is at swinging a hammer, not your dick." She dragged off the scrunchie and started teasing and fluffing her hair at warp speed. Then she hissed out a breath and tied her hair on top of her head, securing it with the hated scrunchie. "Fuck it. Fuck it sideways."

A knock sounded at the door approximately sixteen seconds later, then my best friend stuck his head in. If he'd heard Ruby, he didn't let on, though he did cock a brow at seeing me hanging out in the ladies' room.

She started wildly spraying something floral.

"It's not helping," Caleb informed her.

She ignored him.

"Look, I hope everything's okay, but my bride is flipping out so I hope one of you is ready to be her maid-of-honor. I don't care which. She'll take any friendly face at this point."

Ruby pointed at me. "Take him. He can play both roles. Leave me in peace. I beg of you."

"I'll do it. I'll stand up for both of you."

"Oh, stop being so upstanding. It's seriously annoying." She nudged me out of the way and marched out, leaving Caleb staring after her. "Teach, let's go," she called when he didn't move.

"She's a lot." My buddy scratched his chest. "You sure about that one, brother?"

I grabbed her bag. "Never been more sure of anything in my life."

"Always knew you were a contrary sort." He grinned and clapped my arm. "I'm happy for you, man."

"How much did you hear?"

"Doesn't matter what I heard. I can see just fine. Lu's convinced you'll be married by this time next year. I was sure she was high on marital bliss, but now I think she's spot-on."

"She just snarled at me."

"Right. She also looked at you like she didn't know if she wanted to climb you like a tree or karate chop your junk. Definite marriage material."

My laughter dislodged something in my chest. Probably the big block labeled *baby* I still couldn't quite breathe around. "I fucking love her." I frowned. "Someday I'll say that without the fucking in front of it."

"Yeah, but definitely not in the first year."

We laughed like the cheerful perverts we were.

"Teach! Your wife is going to skin you, and I'll help."

"Aye, aye." Grinning, Caleb turned to leave, but I stopped him and pulled him in for a long hug.

"Glad for you, man. You're an inspiration to me, you know that?"

He hugged me back and then eased away, his brow furrowed. "Yeah?"

"Yeah. You didn't expect to have a kid, and you still took it on like a champ. I know you're going to be an incredible father. It's good to see." I swallowed over the block that had now moved from my chest into my throat. "Some dudes won't ever let their kids down."

"No, I won't. Absolutely not. And when the day comes, you won't either." He smiled as he backed away. "Thanks, man. For everything. Especially for being at my side when I do this thing."

"I wouldn't be anywhere else."

After he left, I grinned. Today was a good day.

Until I drew a deep breath and decided I needed to breathe somewhere else. Quickly.

On the way out, I tossed a twenty on the sink. Maybe the tip would help make up for the baby stink.

I walked out into bedlam. Sweetly smelling, festively decorated bedlam, but bedlam nonetheless.

Festooned Christmas trees and glittery decorations were everywhere, mixed with the subtle magical hints that had to be Luna's idea. Stars and crystals and shimmering snow dripped from stark birch branches in heavy pots, adding extra sparkle in every corner.

A sandwich board sign announced the Beck-Hastings nuptials were taking place in the chapel on the property, so I turned to go back outside. I bumped into a tall, lean dude with Tish's lush mouth heading in. Not that I made a habit of noticing guys' mouths, but even with the big puffy jacket pulled up to his ears, I recognized him as one of her brothers immediately.

Fuck. Another unexpected change of plans.

Tish would be ecstatic.

TWENTY

Lucky

My mind spun. What was he doing here? The Burns weren't supposed to be in the Cove yet—or here in Turnbull at all.

Tish's place was not done, and she wasn't one for alternative routes. Ever. To say she had a plan and she lived to execute that plan about summed it up.

Rhett's gaze zeroed in on mine as if he was seizing the last life raft. His smile was quick and easy as he pushed a hand through his thick dark hair. It was longish on top and short in back, and snow flew in my face as he patted his jacket pockets then unzipped and did the same with his shirt pockets.

"Hey. You're a familiar face. Lucky, is it? How the hell are you?"

I couldn't help my grin at his clear confusion as he searched for something. She'd referred to him once as Mr. Wanderlust.

Right now, he looked scattered and as if he was three steps behind.

"It *is* Lucky, isn't it? If I messed up your name, man, I'm sorry. I'm running on little sleep. Traveling, you know?"

"Yeah, that's me. Rhett, right?"

Should I introduce myself as Tish's baby daddy? Probably not. She'd likely deball me in front of the wedding guests. Besides, we should wait for the official test before we announced anything.

Or was it better to wait until after the first trimester passed? She was two months in, assuming it had happened the night of the memorial.

We hadn't even been in the Cove. Once we lived here, did the whole baby thing cling to us like cologne?

Water, dummy. Remember, she brought a ton with her?

That couldn't be it. No way. People just joked about the water in the Cove.

But she was pregnant…maybe. Probably. And we had been careful. But I'd been careful with plenty of other women. I was just glad local lore hadn't kicked in before now.

Maybe that was the whole point. It only happened once it was meant.

Tish's older brother was staring at me, probably wondering when I'd keep the conversation going. Problem was, I had like three going in my head.

"Sorry. A lot on my mind."

"I hear that. I didn't even know I was going to a wedding today. I had a gap in my schedule so I figured I'd dip into the Cove, see if I could hit up Ging. I found my way to the coffee place in town and they pointed me this way, said a lot of people would be here, even Tish. Seemed dubious, but hell, I've got some time to see what's what. So, where's my best girl?"

"I'm not exactly sure. I'm guessing at the chapel changing into a maid-of-honor dress. Then again, maybe not. She wasn't real keen on swapping dresses."

Rhett laughed. "I imagine not. She's not much of one for dresses anyway. Maid-of-honor, huh? She consented to that? What kind of bribery was involved?"

I had to laugh. "A little guilt, I'm sure. It's for my best friend's fiancée. His wedding." I cleared my throat. "*Their* wedding."

"So, she did it for you." He rubbed the light scruff on his chin then popped on a pair of glasses from the pocket of his flannel shirt. "You two serious? I have to assume it's a thing since you were at the memorial and now she's wearing dresses for you."

Now that was an image—my Ruby in a dress for me. Maybe for *us,* as in a wedding of our own.

Not that she'd need to wear a dress. She could wear anything she wanted. I wasn't particular, as long as she showed up.

Knowing her, she'd alter her vows to call me a jackass. And I didn't much mind.

"Deadly. At least on my end." I slipped my hands into my coat pockets. "You didn't hear me say that."

"No, I didn't, but you might want to let my brothers know. If you're dating Ging, they'll be ready to read you the riot act. They're even worse than our father."

"I'd tell everyone if she'd let me."

"Sounds like Ging. Friendly piece of advice—don't let her rule the roost. Push back. Sometimes she needs a nudge toward where she doesn't realize she wants to go. Her first reaction is defensiveness. Started young with her. Being the only chick in a bunch of guys can do that."

"Yeah. I can see that."

"It wasn't only that though," he said after a moment before blowing out a breath. "So, where the hell's this chapel?"

The senior citizen from the bathroom wandered by at that moment and *tsk-tsk*ed under her breath. She was weighed down with paper shopping bags, so at least that probably meant she wasn't a fellow wedding guest.

I hoped.

"Let's find out." We headed out, falling into step side by side down the stairs to the snowy walkway.

An older couple was shoveling with big smiles wreathing their faces as if it wasn't coming down at a steady clip. "Hey there." I returned their smiles. "Nice day."

The older man laughed and leaned on his shovel. "Pretty usual for this time of year around here. You folks looking for the wedding? Chapel is around the side here and straight through to the back. Glad we enlarged the lot once we fixed up that chapel for my Leelee and my son-in-law."

"Oh, they were married here? That must've been cozy." It was hard to speak when the howling wind was chapping my lips with every word.

"Actually, it wasn't their idea to marry here. Nick just horned in on his best friend's wedding. Fred always gets the story wrong, although Simon worked with him to fix up that chapel. It was a dreadful mess. I'm Laverne Ronson, by the way, and this is my husband. We own Happy Acres." She stuck out a purple gloved hand while her husband went back to shoveling.

Laverne's halo of white hair fluttered as she pumped my hand enthusiastically before she moved on to Rhett. "And you are?"

"Rhett Burns. I know Nick. He's a character."

She laughed. "That he is. Are you in the music business?"

"I dabble." He smiled. "I'm sure I'm terribly late in asking this, but you probably don't have any rooms left, do you?"

I frowned. "What about Tish's? We're not quite done due to some delays, but if your brothers give us a few more days as planned—"

"My brothers do nothing as planned. Besides, with this weather, I imagine many of the wedding guests will be bunking down here tonight." He tossed back his hair and sprayed me with snow yet again. "I'd hoped to attend the wedding with Ging, but it looks like I'm late there too."

"We don't have a room, and we'll be driving back."

"Not if that weather forecast is accurate." Laverne chuckled and patted our arms. "We'll get you all in here, don't you worry. We have room in the main building, plus the separate bonus building for the inn to boot."

"This place is huge. I heard there's a winery too?"

"Sure is, and a performance space as well. Along with gift shops and a café and more apple products than you could shake a stick at." Laverne winked at me and dusted snow off her gloves. "Luna already requested a *special* room for you and Leticia, Lucky."

Hmm. She hadn't known who I was, yet she knew Tish. Was everyone around here all-knowing or what?

"Thank you, ma'am. I'll need to discuss it with Ru—Tish," I corrected. "She may have other ideas."

"Of course. You just let us know. And we'll set one aside for you, Rhett. Enjoy that wedding now. I may just pop my head in if I can get away. I'm just a sucker for them."

"Thanks so much," Rhett said with a smile, skidding his way down the rest of the walkway as Fred pushed his shovel in the opposite direction. Even the area he'd just cleared was already filling up again.

"Nice meeting you, ma'am."

As we walked down the long winding walkway that led to the chapel—not so much a walkway now, as the snow was falling hard and the team of shovelers had seemingly vanished—Rhett nudged my arm. "Hey, don't suppose you can pretend you invited me here?"

"Me?"

"Yeah, Tish is gonna have a kitten. She'll be like, why didn't you tell me you were here early? A guy goes off the grid for a month to write a song with Oblivion and misses some calls and it's an issue. Truth be told, I wasn't sure I'd make it back in time."

"I'm glad you're here. Tish needs family around her with all the changes."

"All what changes?"

"Her place. Cohen's injury. You know."

"No, I don't know, but I have a feeling she's keeping something from me. Just in case you doubted it, two out of three Burns brothers know martial arts and the third is just an all-around supreme athlete."

I swiped a hand down my face to get rid of the snow and smothered a laugh. "Noted."

"So, are you going to say you invited me to this wedding? Because I technically don't know the bride or groom. Who are they again?"

I laughed and waved at Dare and his wife Kelsey heading into the chapel. They were squabbling about something, but Kelsey immediately brightened and waved, her gaze lasering in on Rhett.

"New blood?" she mouthed before her husband ushered her inside.

"Groom is Caleb Beck, my best friend. He's a teacher at the Catholic school—"

"Oh, right, he knocked up the witch." Rhett wiped off his glasses on his shirt. "Yeah, I'll just let you do the talking until I get the lay of the land. Not that I'm landing long. But maybe I'll get a song out of it."

"You're really a songwriter? That's cool. And for Oblivion? They're massive."

"First time working with them. I work with a lot of people though. I've kind of been under the radar for years under a pen name."

"What is it?"

"I am not telling you."

"C'mon."

"Hell, no. Banging my sister doesn't get you those kind of privileges. Marry her and we'll talk." Grinning over his shoulder at me, he yanked open the chapel door and some kind of mystical decidedly non-religious music poured out. It seemed to be a combination of wind chimes, Tibetan singing bowls, and harps.

"This must be a non-denominational chapel."

"I guess?" I had no clue.

"Does she have any other witchy friends?" he asked before we walked inside.

"That's a very popular question." I fell silent as I noticed the cluster of people at the front of the small chapel.

Caleb had his hands folded in front of him, looking like a Zen master befitting the music. At his side, his older brother, August, was smoothing Caleb's tie and speaking in low tones before he strode away to take his seat beside his wife, Kinleigh, in one of the pews.

And like a fire goddess out of mythology, my tall, striking Ruby shot out of the back in a column of white, the color setting off her hair like flames. They matched her blazing eyes as she noticed me— and the man at my side.

She conferred with Caleb for a moment before she marched over to us, brandishing her cluster of winter flowers tied in a velvet bow as if she intended to use it as a projectile.

"Why are you here?" she demanded, and for a moment, I wasn't sure she didn't mean me.

Since I was currently struck dumb by her staggering beauty, I had no answer. And when my powers of speech returned, things went in an unexpected direction.

"You're going to have to marry me."

I'd assumed if I ever said those words, I would at least get a response. But my intended bride was too busy jabbing pointy stems into her brother's chest to hear my proposal.

Was it a proposal? I wasn't even sure. After today, I had no clue what would come out of my mouth next.

"You're early, and you never even actually said yes. Not definitively. It was a lot of 'I'll try, Ging,' and 'you know, my schedule is rough, Ging.' Regarding your own brother. Your own flesh and blood. I know you can't commit to anything more intense than all you can eat breakfast, but maybe try just once?"

"I'd like to point out I'm here." He smoothed a hand down her back and drew her against him, crushing the bouquet between them. "Hi. You look amazing. I missed you. Also, did someone say all you can eat breakfast? I'm starving."

"It's late afternoon," I pointed out unhelpfully.

Ruby sniffled against her brother's chest and then turned her narrowed eyes on me. "You came in with him."

"He invited me to the wedding." Rhett flashed me an innocent grin when I glared.

"Figures." Hurricane Ruby spun away from him and into my arms as if she'd been propelled there.

So, I did what any man who'd just been ignored after a proposal did—I kissed the holy hell out of her in front of some of our friends and family and God and country.

Her sound of protest changed into a moan before she wound her arms around my neck and pressed her recently fuller breasts against my chest. Heaven. Her tongue coiled seductively around mine, and she tasted like cinnamon and sin. *Mine.* My hand was on its way down her back to cup her ass when a cheer rose up around us.

Whoops.

She drew back to breathe lightly against my lips. "I sort of hate you right now, but I'd bang you like a screw if we were alone."

"Nail. Why let that stand in our way?"

"Nail what?"

"You. Let me take you into the confessional and make you praise Jesus."

She snorted out a laugh and jerked back to glance at her brother. "What?" she demanded. "I slipped." Then she grabbed a handful of her dress and swished away, gorgeous long hair swinging.

Noticing everyone had turned to look at us, she made a revolving gesture with her fingers. "Face forward. The bride's about to appear. C'mon, Thor. Get in position."

As if she'd hit the music herself, a New Agey version of the wedding march begun as she flicked a look at her brother. "I'll deal with you later."

"That sounds positive," I muttered to Rhett before he slunk into the nearest pew.

"That's Ging. Hey, did you really just propose to her?"

"Ask me later. Still working on it." I dropped my coat in Rhett's pew and walked toward the front of the chapel toward Caleb, who only now looked the slightest bit nervous.

I decided to do him a solid and make him feel less antsy as I took my place at his side.

"Tish is pregnant," I said under my breath as a look of pure astonishment replaced his worried expression. "You didn't hear it from me."

TWENTY-ONE

Lucky

As the music swelled louder, Caleb jammed his fingers in my ribs. "I'll get you for that later," he whispered, "but wow, congrats, man."

"Thanks. You, too. Don't tell anyone. Secret."

Also, not confirmed, except by afternoon sickness. Whatever. I was excited. I wanted to tell people.

Maybe possibly I also wanted to see what Ruby's style of punishment consisted of. Either or.

I caught the eye of Caleb's parents and Caleb's little sister, Ivy, and her husband, Rory, and gave them a quick salute.

The bridesmaids finally began filing out at just about the same moment Luna's bestie, Ryan, appeared with Preston. Ryan was dressed in a red, official-looking robe, though she was currently kissing her guy in a way that didn't belong in a chapel. But hey, I couldn't exactly talk since I'd just done the same.

After Ryan joined Caleb and I, I leaned in close. "Hey, officiant, can I marry you and the suit? I'll take notes today. Unless there's some kind of course I can take."

She choked, flushing the same color as her robe.

Caleb started laughing. "Same way I reacted when he said he was going to be my kid's godfather."

At my sharp look, he cleared his throat. "From joy, I mean."

The short parade of bridesmaids swept to the side of the front of the chapel, and Tish walked out, tugging at the front of her dress as if she had an itch. Then she realized all eyes were on her and straightened up to her full height, moving slowly and regally down the aisle.

Our gazes connected. For once, she didn't shoot mental darts at me. If anything, she almost looked...tender. Her cheeks were rosy with an internal glow, and her smile felt like it was just for me.

And when she took her place on the opposite side of Caleb and I, I almost forgot I was at my buddy's wedding. It felt like this was ours. Like I could open my mouth and say I do and it would be real and last forever. How could it not when I was so utterly mad for her?

But then Luna appeared at the head of the aisle, and gasps sounded around us. I was pretty sure even I did, and I know Caleb did. She was glittering, her gray dress glinting with faceted crystals that shot off light with every step she took. Her hair was swept back from her face and topped with a circlet of flowers and more crystals. But her wet blue eyes were all for Caleb, as his were solely focused on her.

When she joined him, he pressed his forehead to hers, whispering something that made her giggle and a tear to slip out of the corner of her eye. Then he lightly touched the swell of her belly and she gripped his fingers, holding him there as she turned her teary face toward her best friend. Ryan was crying openly too, and I was shocked to find my throat was too tight to swallow.

On the other side of Luna, my girl stood tall and proud, but her dark eyes were damp as well.

Ryan let out a sniffly laugh and started to speak about the bonds of love. I kept my gaze on my Ruby the entire time.

Luna and Caleb each had written vows for each other, and laughter and tears flowed in equal measure. Rings were exchanged after they both said, "I do", and then it was time for the big celebratory kiss before officiant Ryan pronounced them married "as hell."

Whatever worked.

Caleb lifted his bride to spin her around, but the minute he put her down, I gave him a big hug and a smacking kiss that made everyone laugh. Then I aimed for Tish, who must've sensed my next move and was already backing away.

"Lucky," she warned, waving her finger. "Haven't we created enough of a spectacle for one day?"

"Have we?" I pretended to think before I bum-rushed her off her feet and tipped her over my shoulder. "Nope. Guess not," I said cheerfully as she laughed and pounded on my back.

But I didn't leave her suspended for long. With a laugh, I let her slide down my body to the floor, fully expecting her to make me pay for my hasty decision.

Instead, she worked her fingers through the snarls in my hair from the wind. "Were you serious about the confessional?"

"No, but I could be." My dick was intrigued already.

The devil danced in her eyes as she undid my jacket and slid her hand beneath the patterned vest I wore underneath. "Any closet or alcove will do. Preferably one indoors, so nothing important freezes."

"That's a sound plan." I traced my finger over the worry lines between her brows. "How are you feeling?"

"Horny."

I slid a surreptitious look around to make sure no one was paying attention to our conversation. "You know what I mean. Can you eat? Do you want a snack? Or if everything is still sloshing around, I could get you some ginger ale from the general store in the main building. Or how about—"

"How about you rail me into next Tuesday, and we'll think about dinner after that?"

My lips curved. "I think that could be arranged."

But alas, it was not to be. At least not right now.

Rhett appeared behind Tish and slung an arm around her waist. "So, sis, let's chat."

She rolled her eyes. "Can't you let a girl get laid in peace? Especially a girl who has spent months getting my place ready for you heathens, and now you're here early to wreck everything?"

"I have wrecked nothing." He rubbed his scruff. "Yet."

Tish frowned and I clamped a hand on her hip, keeping a hold on her in case she decided to bolt. I didn't know what Rhett intended to tell her, but I could tell from the tightness of his jaw that Ruby wouldn't like it. And if she wouldn't, neither would I.

"What are you talking about? Why are you here?"

Rhett slipped his hand in his pocket and glanced over his shoulder where our friends were still milling around, talking and laughing. "I hate doing this here, but somehow I got nominated. Ez is a damn pussy."

I cocked a brow. "Watch it, dude. From where I'm standing, dicks aren't too awesome right now."

Tish shot me a grateful look as I moved my hand from her hip to her shoulder. It felt good to be standing at her side when it seemed like she appreciated the support.

Rhett shot me a rueful glance before aiming it at his sister. "Yeah, yeah, you're right. I'm sorry. This is a damn wedding, so I should've known better than to intrude. I just didn't think it would be *this* cozy. And here I am, swinging in here like Captain Pecker, the wedding party wrecker."

I didn't get that reference, but it wasn't pertinent right now.

"Tingle, stop dilly-dallying and get to the point."

"Seriously? Why do you have to call me that in front of non-family members?"

"Oh, you'd be surprised how much family he is. Now get to the freaking point before I tell every one of your secrets with glee."

I considered it a victory that I managed not to bruise her shoulder with the pressure from my fingers. She'd called me family. It had to be the baby. Maybe it had to do with hormones, or that she wanted more sex and what the hell, she was already knocked up. We obviously had heat and affection between us, and we worked well together as the house project proved.

And I was in love with her. No doubt there.

The doubts portion of our program belonged solely to Ruby. But if she was calling me family, that meant something. Talk about a weighty word.

I was part of Caleb's family because he'd been gracious enough to invite me into it. But I'd never had my own space just for me. I'd never imagined I could have a family period, never mind be the head of one. Well, joint head.

I was now a parent. Possibly. Probably.

Whoa.

Someday I'd get used to the concept. I hoped seeing those two lines on the pee stick would nudge me along. Or did they use actual words more often now? I'd prefer that. I wasn't steady enough to trust myself to not see lines that weren't there.

Lines I might want to will into existence, now that I was starting to wrap my head around the idea of fatherhood.

Tish and Rhett had not stopped their conversation while I pondered the meaning of family and my actually having one of my own, holy fucknuts.

"Look, it's not my fault he doesn't want to talk about this shit, Ging. The guy is hurting. You know how he gets. Add in Ezra being Ezra and probably having the subtlety of a bulldozer, and can you really say you're surprised Co opted to stay home rather than do some big crazy Burns holiday scene?"

"I've been working for months to make that scene happen." Tish's voice broke at the end, and I had to fight every urge that demanded I tug her behind me. I'd face every threat for her. Battle anyone that might do her harm—even if it wasn't intentional.

But that wasn't what she needed from me right now. I had to stand with her and wait to see how I could help.

Rhett shoved a hand through his hair. "I know you have. Ez does too, which is how I drew the short straw to tell you about Co. He didn't want to hurt you. None of us do. But our brother is frigging stubborn as hell."

"Which one?"

"All of us and you too and Dad. It's a Burns trait." Rhett glanced between us, his brow sliding into a lazy arch. "Back to that thing about this one being family too. Did I miss something? Though he did propose back there, but he seemed as surprised by it as anybody."

"He what?" Tish sent a look over her shoulder, her expression a mix of confusion, shock, and annoyance. Those were probably three of the ingredients in her special blend coffee from Macy, along with an extra dollop of snark topped with a little sweetness.

"We'll talk about it later."

"So, no one is gonna tell me—"

"Tish might be—"

"Nope, no one is going to tell you." Tish's expression could've killed me where I stood if I wasn't well used to her dynamic death rays. "Some things need to be verified before people go around telling people stuff."

"Some people already told some people because some people think they should have a right to since the stuff is theirs too."

"Who did you tell? Ugh, damn motormouth. You're lucky you're cute."

"Is that what the name comes from? I assumed it was a nickname for scoring with chicks."

I had a moment's gratification when my girl turned her irritation on her brother.

"You are not funny or cute and I'm mad at you."

"Why? Because I'm the messenger of bad news?"

"No. Because I don't see you enough and I miss you." She tugged on a lock of his dark hair and he drew her into a hug that apparently signaled the skirmish was over.

As we were trudging back to the reception room in the main building, I realized it was over between the siblings but not with us.

She waited until Rhett walked ahead and was busy on his phone to dip her hand into the back pocket of my trousers. And not for a celebratory ass rub either. More like a reproachful pinch.

Which my traitorous dick didn't mind.

"Who did you tell?"

"Just Caleb."

Her look of pure horror couldn't even be obscured by the fat flakes drifting down in the oncoming twilight. "*Him?* Why not take out a freaking billboard? And if Luna starts groping my belly—"

"Can I watch?"

"You are such a male."

"Guilty as charged." I puffed out an icy breath when Ruby sped up despite the snow-covered sidewalk. I gripped her elbow to make sure she was steady, maintaining my hold even as she flashed me a stare cold enough to grow icicles on the tip of my nose. "Stuff should be verified soon is all I'm saying."

"I know that. And I will."

"We will."

I expected her to argue. "Yes, we will. I want you there."

"You do? I mean, of course you do." I took advantage of the rare almost warmth in her voice and moved closer to kiss the top of her head.

"People didn't know we were dating."

"Is that what you call it? Me at your house almost every night?"

She ignored me. "Now look at us. Everyone keeps winking at me and congratulating me and saying that I landed the biggest player in town, har de har. I didn't try to land you."

"Exactly why you did. You act like you'd rather clean gum off your shoe rather than be seen in public with me."

She came to a halt on the sidewalk and crossed her arms over her chest. She was shaking slightly from the cold, and I immediately started to remove my coat so I could drape it over her shoulders.

"No, wait. I'm fine. And that's not true. I'm not ashamed to be seen with you. I'm not," she insisted at my silence. "I just didn't know where this is going, and if it wasn't going anywhere, then we shouldn't —Tingle, scram."

Rhett flashed the peace sign over his shoulder and continued walking. Not very fast in my opinion, but I was curious what she'd say next too, so I couldn't blame him.

"How are you feeling about that whole 'where this is going' thing now?"

She gazed up at me in the near darkness with snow gathering on her thick lashes and dusting her pale cheeks and my heart raced as if

I'd just run a two-minute mile. So much hinged on her giving us a chance. Now more than ever.

"I like being with you."

"Sorry, can you speak up?" I made a show of leaning toward her and cupping my ear. "Didn't quite hear you."

The corner of her mouth kicked up. "We have fun, Thor. But it's all moving so fast. I don't want you to regret anything when reality descends, and you see the stretch marks. Because they are coming, dude, and my cocoa butter cream can only do so much."

"I will never, as long as I live, regret a single second I will spend with you or our baby. The only thing I'll regret is the ones you won't let me share."

Lost in her dark gorgeous eyes, I almost missed how her lower lip trembled. But I definitely couldn't deny the rush of relief as she stepped toward me and circled her arms around my waist. "I'm trying," she whispered. "You probably can't tell that I am, but I swear it's true."

I wound my arms around her so tightly that she gasped. "I love you. And I kinda love saying it. So, maybe let me love you tonight, and we'll see how we both feel about it in the morning."

She tipped her face up to mine and for an instant, I would've sworn a tear glimmered on her cheek. I smoothed my thumb over it and came back with a snowflake instead.

Nodding, she gave me a tentative smile. "I can do that. But I still want that railing."

It was so easy to return her smile. "I can do that."

TWENTY-TWO

Everyone was having a darn good time at this reception. Other than me, and I was fully aware that was probably my own fault.

I wasn't much of a drinker other than at social events where I was expected to talk and be friendly, usually with people I barely knew. Then a beer went down smooth and also gave me something to do with my hands other than tug at my hair like a girl on the sidelines at a junior high dance.

But that whole puking thing earlier along with the recent recognition of my enlarged breasts and absent period—*a bit late there, Burns*—had squashed my desire for a drink. Well, not the desire, but I wasn't having one. I wasn't taking any chances.

Sure, I might've just put on some early winter weight. Maybe my period was late due to stress. I could have the flu.

One that also made certain things smell really strange—like frosting.

"Here, have a cupcake. Look at the tiny Caleb and I." Luna poked the little plastic figures atop the frosting and beamed so brightly that I didn't have the heart to tell her the smell of that gooey white confection was going to make me hurl.

Then again, if I could avoid doing it on her wedding dress, that would be a win for us all.

"No, sorry, thanks. I'm dieting." It was a miracle I didn't pinch my nose. I could still smell it even if I turned my head.

What was in that thing? Had Tabitha flavored it with preggo lady repellant or what?

"You, dieting? Why? You are perfect just as you are. Especially in these dresses today. Lucky must be having a hard time keeping his hands off you."

"Again with that stuff? You didn't even see the kiss."

"No, but I saw him holding you and rubbing your—" She stopped, her eyes widening.

"Rubbing my what? Because I definitely don't remember anything like that. Hey," I said when she set aside her cupcake on the tray it came from and cupped my belly as if it was a crystal ball she could peer into and see her fortune.

And peer she did, staring right at the approximate place where my bellybutton was on the other side of the silky ivory fabric. Figured that the bride wasn't wearing white but I was, though I was no more virginal than Luna.

"Oh, pardon me." Luna closed her eyes in apology. "I didn't ask to touch, but I was drawn. Please forgive me."

"To my belly?" My spine went to liquid to match my suddenly shaky knees. "Was it growling that loud? Sorry. Lucky foisted some finger foods on me, but apparently, they weren't enough."

She lifted her face to mine, her cheeks shining. "You know, don't you?"

I tried to swallow the sudden grittiness in my throat. "Know that I'm starving? Sure."

"Tish, you know. But if you had any doubt, your aura is very clear. Usually, you're more of a pulsing red. Today you're more like a tea rose. You're sick with it, aren't you?" The sympathy in Lu's tone and in her expression made me feel as if I wanted to weep.

I so badly needed someone to stroke my hair while I cried. I wasn't usually that woman. Sometimes tears escaped at appropriate times, like after Jimmy's memorial. But at a wedding reception? That didn't make sense.

Except of course it did, because my hormones were going haywire, and I didn't have any clue what I was doing. And I was already so afraid I was going to break this kid I didn't even have the balls to find out if I was carrying.

"The other aura is blue," she said when I didn't speak. "That doesn't necessarily mean a boy but..."

I swallowed. "It could."

"Yes, it could. You're not arguing with me?"

"I don't have enough energy to argue with a gnat right now."

"But what a conversation it would be, huh?" Her sweet laughter made me smile instead of snarl.

This whole potential pregnancy thing was building a kinder, gentler Tish. Or a more exhausted one, which basically translated into the same thing.

Discreetly, I drew her hands away from my stomach. Despite Lucky telling people right and left—God only knows how many he'd informed since I'd gone off in search of a sweet snack I couldn't even eat—I wasn't ready for everyone to know.

Heck, I didn't even know for sure, no matter what Luna and my twitchy belly believed. This train was going far too fast, and I wanted to get off.

"Sorry. That was a definite boundary crossing. I feel terrible. Especially since I know how violating it can feel when someone you barely know is feeling you up." Lu shuddered.

"We still talking about bellies here?"

Her laughter made me smile again. "Yes. I don't mind when my husband feels me up, and he'd bite anyone else who tried." She grabbed her abandoned cupcake and licked off a dab of frosting. "Probably literally. Oh my goddess, this is delicious. Sure you don't want a bite?" She corrected herself before I could. "No, I see you're off. That's fine. Why don't we order you some tea?"

"Yeah, because no one will notice I'm sipping some Earl Grey while everyone else is getting loaded in this joint. Blizzard outside, so not like there is anywhere else to go." I pursed my lips and made myself focus on her instead of myself for a change. "This weather T-boned your honeymoon. I'm sorry."

"Nah, we aren't going to Florida until after the first of the year. Gotta do the first blended family Christmas thing. My mother is practically spinning her top that I married a Catholic school teacher. She keeps hoping I'll renounce my heathen ways."

I snorted. "You, a heathen? You have the most loving energy of anyone I've ever met."

Immediately, she stopped nibbling on her cupcake. Had I insulted her somehow? "Thank you. That's so sweet coming from you."

"From me?"

"Yeah. You're a total badass. I sort of figured you'd think I was a wimpy soft female who only wanted to be married and make a home with someone."

"Is that a bad thing?"

"No. It's not. It's an amazing thing. But you're so incredible and have this fascinating career to boot."

"And you don't? I just play with cars. You're ten times more fascinating than I am, and you're going to have it all."

"So are you, Tish," she said softly, her eyes sparkling in that all-knowing way I found comforting tonight rather than irritating. "If you let yourself."

I took a deep breath to stop myself from hunching my shoulders. Not immediately going on the defensive was so much harder than I'd ever guessed. "Can you see your own baby's aura?"

She shook her head. "Too close to him or her." She rubbed her growing belly with the hand not holding the cupcake. "But I've tried. A lot."

"You don't want to know officially? Or it still too soon?"

"To be honest, I was hoping I'd be able to tell and then could test the accuracy with the result. But none of my research has allowed me to find a way."

"What about Ryan? Isn't your bestie witchy too?"

"Auras aren't her thing."

"Hmm."

"I know it all sounds crazy. I just appreciate you being so patient about it. Some people are not." She went back to eating her cupcake in an avaricious way I completely envied.

I'd be lucky if I didn't end up making friends with the porcelain throne again before this night was through. Though some of that could have been due to nerves.

Fuck me sideways, I'm having a baby.

Maybe.

"Caleb isn't one of those, I'm assuming."

"Goddess, no. He's curious about everything and is always encouraging me to talk about my practice. Even when I come up with ideas that we can try that some might consider…unusual."

"Like?" I couldn't resist. Plus, talking to her was distracting me from my queasiness.

She glanced around conspiratorially and lowered her voice. "Like seeing if I could tease out the baby's aura during Tantric sex. I mean, as Tantric as I can get with this body right now. It gets harder to hold certain positions. And you have to pee a lot."

"Yay." My tone sounded vaguely like Daria's from that 90s era comic sketch on MTV. "The fun factor of all of this sounds enormous."

"Some women love being pregnant."

I stared at her dubiously. "Do you have proof?"

"Well, I'm not in the habit of handing out lie detector tests, but yeah, I have it on good authority."

"Do you?"

"Most of the time, I really enjoy it. It feels special. Like you and this other person love each other so much something beautiful came from that love. And of course, it's not always that way. Some situations aren't nearly as happy, unfortunately. But we feel really blessed that ours is."

"Hmm. I mean, that's sweet and all…"

"But you're thinking I'm full of crap."

"Not full of it."

She tried not to smile. "Pretty sure you're not going to be one of the women who loves pregnancy?"

"I don't know. Right now, it sort of reminds me of an alien invasion without the anal probe."

"Oh, it's early yet. That happens too." Her giggle at my horrified expression somehow made me laugh too.

When Lucky strolled toward us with a plate of food, I nearly salivated. But before I could praise him for his manly hunting and gathering skills, his jaw went slack as he realized Lu and I were giggling together.

Oddly, I felt proud. As if I was a weirdo little kid who had somehow learned how to make a girlfriend.

Lucky stopped at my side. "Are you okay?"

"Yes?"

"Are you unsure?"

"No?"

Luna shook her head, laughing at us. "You two are so cute I literally cannot stand it. I need another cupcake, and then I'm going to find my husband. It's time to get jiggy with it."

"There aren't any poles on site." Lucky's expression was entirely serious.

"I'll see if I can manage to dance without one, Luckster." Luna patted his chest before plucking another cupcake off the tray and dancing away.

Speaking of plucking, I stole a cube of Monterey Jack from Lucky's plate and popped it in my mouth. I moaned as if he'd dropped down to the floor and lifted my dress to go to town.

His eyebrows hiked toward his hairline. "That was nearly pornographic."

"Nearly? I can do better." Without moderating my volume, I let out a breathy moan that had him dragging me against him with a look of consternation.

My giggling fit was epic.

"Now I really think you're not okay. Tish Burns, giggling?"

"Well, this is a day for firsts. By the way, Blondie says we're having a boy."

Lucky had picked the wrong time to bite into a pickle spear. His eyes blew wide as he choked. I whaled on his back until he was breathing normally.

"What?" he wheezed.

I couldn't help laughing again. "Sorry. I'm not great at picking my moment."

"Says you. I think you're absolutely incredible at everything. Including growing babies."

I narrowed my eyes at him as a dangerous glow spread in my chest. I didn't know what to make of it so I ignored it. "Is this because your possible offspring could be male, thereby fulfilling some adolescent penis fantasy of tossing the old pigskin with your progeny?"

"All those words equal yes to me."

Grinning at him was faintly ridiculous at this point. After all, Rome was burning, and Rome was actually in my midsection.

Ugh, acid reflux too? This whole pregnancy thing was already a sham.

That didn't stop me from consuming more cheese. I'd never been so fond of a dairy product in my life.

"Why don't we go sit down? You can eat—wow, you're on that already."

So what if I was plowing through his plate at a speed that defied logic? I'd decided if I didn't have time to process how the food was landing inside me, I could enjoy it just fine.

"I am, and I don't want to think about anything heavy right now." I lowered my voice. "I know we have stuff to discuss and to—"

"Find out for sure," he interjected.

I lifted my finger to his lips. Getting him to be quiet was basically my life's work these days. He never did what I expected him to and he never acquiesced easily. That was probably why I lo—

Liked having sex with him. Yes. Much better.

To give myself a second, I chewed on a cracker. My belly was granting me a momentary reprieve. "How do you feel about dancing?"

He bit into a little sandwich that wouldn't do anything but make someone hungrier. "I'm okay with it. Not a native skill of mine and I move sort of like Frankenstein, but yeah, it's all right."

The man did not move like Frankenstein.

I'd known he wouldn't. He couldn't possibly be that sexually skilled and not know how to dance enough to get by. But he was far from some beginner. Oh, no, this dude had clearly had lessons at some point. The kind that came with learning dips and flourishes that should have made me fear my stomach's rebellion.

But nope, my belly didn't balk at my sudden movements as I was whirled around the dance floor that had been set up in the reception area. My stomach was probably as shocked as the rest of me.

I wasn't sure what it said about me that my biggest surprise of the day was that Thor could cut a rug—or whatever that old term was.

I didn't officially know about that other bouncing surprise yet. So, it didn't count.

We danced for a long time, breaking occasionally to hydrate and fuel up. They finally served a real dinner later in the evening including toasts for the happy couple. Lucky grabbed the microphone and regaled the remaining guests with tales about Caleb's not-so-checkered past, usually concerning his regrettable drinking adventures. Since one of them had led to his landing his wife, he seemed pretty damn smug.

When Lucky ran out of steam, Ryan shared some tidbits about how she and Luna had met and gave the couple her best wishes. Preston did similarly. His speech was far quicker than Ryan's, though he had genuine affection on his face for Luna.

Ryan offered to do a tarot card reading for Lu and Caleb's marriage so long as she could snag the audio for their podcast. Luna declined, so that was that and the dancing resumed among the few people left.

They were winging everything at this point since the place was clearing out due to the blizzard. Not that most of the people left wanted to chance driving home, but there was some hardy sorts with their versions of monster trucks willing to go for it.

I had a feeling some of them would be hiking back up the hill in due time. Laverne and Fred, the older couple who ran this operation, assured everyone they had plenty of beds, but that remained to be seen.

"Hey, Tabitha's cupcakes were here, but not Tabitha." I frowned and spoke loudly enough over the music that others could weigh in. "She was invited, right?"

"Flat tire on the way here." Caleb shook his head from where he was dancing beside us with his jubilant bride.

Who said she needed a stripper pole? She seemed to be doing just fine on her own—and in super high heels, no less.

Mine were currently tucked in a bag with my moon boots. I was dancing barefoot and not ashamed in the least.

"That sucks." Lucky frowned. "Is she okay? Does she need some help? I'm sure Dare and Gage have everything covered, but I have my truck." He shot me a quick grin. "It already survived one snowbank today."

"No, she's good. Brady caught the call and summoned the Kramer cavalry. Dare was already on his way back from here."

Lucky angled his head, spinning me around slowly so he could talk to Caleb when his friend swiveled in the other direction. "Caught the call? Since when do cops do tows?"

"When the vehicle involved jackknifes into a tree." Luna sighed. "A small one. She's fine. But that old sedan of hers is toast, I think. I feel so bad for her. She was more worried we had enough cupcakes than she was about herself."

"How did the cupcakes arrive if she didn't?"

Caleb smirked. "The fine officer delivered them."

Slowly, I shook my head. "How do you get that service?"

Caleb released Luna long enough to raise his hands, palms out. "Don't ask me. I'm just the messenger."

Soon after, they danced across the room, Lu's musical laughter trailing after them.

"He took lessons." Lucky inclined his chin toward his best friend. "Me, I'm all self taught."

"No way."

"Yes way." He grinned. "It was fun surprising you."

"Let me guess, you learned so you'd have another tool to charm the ladies?"

He jerked a shoulder. "Maybe. I didn't want to just be a street kid forever. No class or manners or, I don't know, breeding."

My belly trembled for a whole new reason.

I slipped my arms around Thor's neck, forcing myself to look at him when his gaze dropped to mine. "You'd really charge off into a blizzard if someone needed you, wouldn't you?"

No questions asked. He was just a fundamentally decent dude.

"Depends. If I'd have to leave you, no. But I figured you'd come with me." He aimed a frown in the general direction of my belly. "Although I guess things are different now. Can't have you helping to pull cars out of ditches when you're traveling for two."

Even as my feminist heart squawked, I couldn't help laughing. "That's not a thing. Also, may I remind you I work at a garage?"

"Yeah, but you aren't out there towing cars. You're not, right?"

He looked so adorably worried I had to smooth away the wrinkle above his upper lip. His beard was growing in fuller, but I could still see his worry line under the scruff. "Not my area. Not going to say I never pitch in if needed, but rarely."

"That's good." I'd put up my hair in a ponytail post-ceremony and he slid his hand down it possessively. "I know you're gonna say you can take care of yourself. I know that. I just like taking care of you." His Adam's apple jerked. "It's important to me."

"Why?" I hated how uncertain I sounded. I wasn't like that. Or I hadn't used to be, pre-baby invasion.

Really, pre-Lucky. Developing feelings for him had messed with all my shields, and I was still trying to figure out how to be me and maybe possibly have him in my life.

His face softened. "Aww, Ruby, don't you ever listen to a guy when he tells you he loves you?"

TWENTY-THREE

Swallowing suddenly got very difficult. "It's so fast."

He rubbed his fist over his chest. "It feels like forever in here."

"If you change your mind—"

"I won't." He kissed my forehead, his big hands coming up to massage my shoulders. "You can depend on me. I swear on my life."

We'd stopped dancing in the middle of the decidedly uncrowded dance floor. Caleb and Luna and Laverne and Fred were the only couples still swaying to the Michael Buble tune.

Outside, snow fell in fat flakes thick enough to drown out even my objections. Because I wanted to fucking believe him.

I wanted it more than anything.

On the next break from dancing, I made excuses about needing to pee. I could tell by the look on Thor's face that he assumed that too was due to the baby. All functions in my body were now in support of new life.

Assuming there was one. And I supposed if I was thinking about next steps and making room in my life and what that meant, I needed to take this test so I knew exactly what I was dealing with.

So *we* would know.

Turned out stopping by the bathroom was a good idea. After I finished and washed up, I wandered down the hall past the reception room into the lobby of the main building. I strolled into the handily located general store, hoping upon hope they carried things for a truly fun romantic night.

Who needed condoms when you were on the hunt for a pregnancy test?

While glancing over my shoulder about sixteen times as if I expected to be brought in for B&E, I roamed the aisles. I grabbed a bag of old-fashioned ginger candies since they supposedly helped with nausea, a package of Doritos, and the jumbo size package of peanut M&Ms. Soon, I had so much food in my arms of a non-nutritive nature, I couldn't see over the pile.

"Here you go, dear. Take a wheelie."

I looked over to find proprietress Laverne pushing a wheeled basket-style cart at me. "Oh, thanks." I dumped everything in the cart then shifted and realized the pregnancy tests were right in front of me.

Serendipity? Or just potential embarrassment when I had to grab one and toss it in the cart next to my king size roll of Rolos?

"Weren't you just dancing a few minutes ago?" I kept my voice chirpy while I turned sideways and tried to bump the package off the shelf into my cart. Crap, I'd probably need a couple for accuracy.

Then again, the contents of my cart were probably all the accuracy I needed. I hadn't considered consuming so much junk food since... ever. I was freaking starving. My stomach was in an empty itself then immediately fill up again cycle.

Somehow I'd become Dusty with a hairball except mine would grow for nine months and be much larger.

With Thor involved, I didn't want to contemplate *how* much larger. Why didn't I think ahead and have sex with a much smaller man to balance out my own giant genes? It was the Cove, for pity's sake. No one with a vagina escaped unscathed.

And with Lucky as the papa, mine would be so scathed I was wincing even now.

"Yes, dancing is so much fun. I love weddings. All those

possibilities in the air." She smiled mistily and patted her snowy curls. "But our night cashier had a migraine so she's upstairs resting. By the way, Luna reserved a room for you. I put you in a very special one." She winked in a way that made me wonder where the television crew was.

"Oh, um, great. Special how?"

"The room has a bit of lore. Although upon second thought, I may have jumped the gun there. Or didn't fire soon enough." Her denim blue eyes twinkled as she reached for the pregnancy test I was bumping against as casually as possible. "This is a good brand. I recommend it. This one too." She plucked the one beside it and added both to my cart.

I cleared my throat. I was speechless for the first time in my life.

"Nothing to be ashamed of. With a strapping young man like yours and with your coloring, you will have the most beautiful babies. You'll send me pictures, won't you?"

I blinked. "Um, ma'am, you'll excuse me because I don't have a mom, and I'm new to small towns, but do you do this with everyone?"

"My Leelee would say so. My daughter," she explained. "My only child." Her laugh was melodic as she nudged me toward the café tables set up on the other side of the cash register. "How do you feel about peppermint hot cocoa?"

"Very fond," I admitted reluctantly, gripping the handle of my cart as if it would float away otherwise. "I can order—"

"Fred," she called. "Two large mints. Candy canes included. Croissant sandwich for Leticia." She glanced my way. "Ham, turkey, or roast beef? American, provolone, muenster, swiss?"

I nearly moaned in anticipation. How could I be hungry again? Or still? "Turkey and swiss, please. Thank you."

She called out the rest of my order then indicated I should sit at one of the small tables and took a seat opposite me. "Deli meat isn't the best for the baby, but we all need a last hurrah."

"Ain't that the truth. Besides, maybe I'm not—"

"If you're not, bottle that glow. You'll be a millionaire in a month."

I rested my cart against the wall and slapped my hands to my cheeks. "I'm just flushed."

"Glowing."

"Hmm."

"My Leelee has twins," she said conversationally while I stared at her in abject horror.

"Two? At the same time? Why? How?"

"C-section at seven months." Her tone was matter-of-fact. "She was on bedrest for much of her pregnancy due to complications."

"Is—is she okay now? And the babies?"

Babies. That required literal *months* of rest to grow in a bed.

I would lose my ever-loving mind.

I was afraid to touch my stomach. It now felt like a volatile missile, no longer under my dominion.

"Leelee's just fine and those little girls are so smart and fun. Well, Charlie is fun once you peel her off the ceiling. Too much like her father, that one."

"Oh."

"He's a rockstar."

"Like..." I thought for a minute. Who would she consider a rockstar? "Burl Ives?"

"No, not quite." Her laughter was rich and ripe and made me feel like a fool with pregnancy brain.

"Or Corey Taylor?"

"Closer. He's in Oblivion. You might have heard of them."

"What? No." I could've sworn Rhett had mumbled something about working with them when he pulled me into a dance earlier before claiming he had "calls to make" and disappearing.

Which had been convenient for me, since seeing my brother reminded me how spectacularly I'd failed with Cohen. I hadn't been the one to decide he shouldn't come here, but it felt like I'd screwed up by not finding the words to get him to the Cove.

Thinking about the "oh, fuck" factor of those tests in my cart was preferable to drowning my sorrows over Co in Rolos-covered Doritos.

Hmm, that was an idea.

"No, you haven't heard of Oblivion?"

"Oh, no, I have. Of course. Everyone has. Which one is he? Hopefully, not the mouthy blond guitarist. He's always starting shit."

Laverne's smile was beatific. "That's the one."

"Does this floor have a trap door? Maybe it could suck me down into the netherworld? If not, I know someone who could add on that feature for you."

She positively giggled as her husband brought out a tray with two steaming mugs of hot cocoa piled with mounds of whipped cream and crushed candy canes and my croissant sandwich, neatly arranged on a bed of lettuce. I fully intended to eat that too.

A child needed a full serving of vegetables hourly, right?

Fred set down the cups with a flourish then presented my sandwich to me while I wondered if leaving him my Visa card would be tip enough.

"I have never seen anything so beautiful," I told him sincerely. "Bless you."

"You're quite welcome. I hope you enjoy it."

"Oh, I will. I'm going to enjoy it so hard this whole damn wedding party will know about it. Oh, shit. Dammit." I stopped unfurling my napkin and cast a glance at the doorway of the general store. "I forgot my—Lucky."

"He's rather large to lose, dear."

"Tell me about it. I'm the one possibly bearing his firstborn." I wrinkled my nose. "I left my damn purse in there. I don't have my phone." I shot a glance at the guilty pleasures in my cart, pregnancy tests excluded. Those were testing for proof of previous other pleasures. "I don't have any money." I gazed forlornly at my sandwich. Parting was such sweet sorrow. "I'll go get my purse and my—Lucky and be right back."

Laverne pursed her lips against a smile as she lifted her gaze behind me. When it went up and up, my spine tingled.

Late again, Burns.

"Your Lucky wants you to keep this on you at all times." He dangled my purse over my head and I snatched it with a sigh.

"I just forgot, okay? I didn't go far, obviously. Hey, look at this sandwich." I hoped I wasn't drooling.

He didn't look. Instead, he stroked his big hand over the top of my head and down my hair, and everything just...smoothed out inside me. Calmed right the fuck down as if I was a jumpy horse and he was my master.

I mean, fun game for later with those handcuffs, but not my usual scene.

"Thank you for finding her for me," he said evenly. "She's precious."

Even as my neck went hot, I frowned at Laverne. "I thought you said the night clerk had a migraine."

"She does. But I can never resist the request of a handsome, worried daddy-to-be." She smiled and stood, then she motioned for Lucky to take her dollhouse-sized chair.

I just waited for the legs to give out under his bulk, but nope, things around here were built to last.

Looking at the faint creases of concern fanning out around his green eyes, that seemed to be true about him too.

"Have a nice night, you two." Laverne gave a little wave as she strolled away.

"Wait, your cocoa." I called.

"It was never for me." She sent a smile over her shoulder before she disappeared into the back.

Rather than apologizing for my unintentional screw-up—my life in a nutshell—I made the ultimate sacrifice and gave him half my sandwich. "Saved that for you."

His laughter teased out a smile of my own before I dug in and didn't speak for like, three-and-a-half minutes. He sipped his cocoa silently and just watched me until I sighed. "I'm sorry I freaked you out. You probably thought I did a runaway preggo."

"I didn't want to think that."

"I wouldn't do that to you, Thor. I might walk away, but if you've been paying attention, I always come back." I swallowed hard and chanced looking into his eyes again. "I can't seem to stay away."

He nudged my heaping mug of cocoa toward me. "Drink it before it gets cold."

I wrapped my hands around the warm cup and took a deep breath. "Yeah. Then I'll—*we'll*—take those tests." I tipped my head toward my cart. "I got a couple. For accuracy."

"Yeah." His exhale made the tower of whipped cream on his cocoa shiver. But it was melting now, and when he drank, a little coated his upper lip.

I couldn't resist swiping my finger along the whipped cream and popping it into my mouth. The green of his irises seemed to deepen as he tracked the movement.

"After, we can check out that room Luna got us. The *special* one." I narrowed my eyes. "Wonder if it has a mirror on the ceiling?"

He chuckled hard enough to spew a tiny bubble of whipped cream at me. Shamelessly, I swiped it off my cheek before sucking that off my finger too.

"If so, don't get too used to those actions, pal. Soon, all mirrors will be covered with brown wrapping paper."

"You wish, Ruby. If you're—if it's real…" He sucked in air. "I want to see every bit of you every minute of every day."

I didn't know why I was suddenly so congested. Must be the canned air in this place. "Going to be hard for you to work if you're ogling my growing tits every second."

"Luckily, one of my main projects at the moment happens to be conveniently located near your bedroom." His eyes were strangely bright.

Damn seasonal allergies, affecting both of us. Odd we hadn't seemed to have any before this very moment.

"Drink your cocoa before it gets cold," I said, echoing him from earlier.

We finished our drinks and paid for my purchases and then we went up to our suite. My hands were shaking for some reason, so I kept rubbing them on my hips so he wouldn't see and freak out that I was freaking out.

Not that I was. I was super calm.

Right.

"We, ah, don't have any pajamas."

"We'll get by somehow."

He sat on the edge of the lake-sized bed, and the twinkling colorful lights on the Christmas tree in the corner of the room flickered over his face.

Gathering my courage, I moved closer and leaned over him, resting my hands on his massive thighs in his fancy tux. "If I had to pick a baby daddy, I'd probably pick you."

One side of his mouth rose and the heaviness in his eyes lightened as he cupped my cheek. "If I had to pick a baby mama, I'd definitely pick you."

I dropped my forehead to his then gave him a chaste kiss before slipping away. "So, I'll just get this done."

Flashing him the brightest smile I could manage, I grabbed the paper bag with the tests. Nestled inside with them was chocolate-peppermint "intimate" lotion.

"How did you sneak this in here?" I held up the tube.

He wiggled his fingers. "Magic."

It made me grin even when I would've said I was far too scared. But the weird thing was I wasn't anymore as I closed myself in the small bathroom with the pedestal sink and cheerful lighted snowman sitting on the back of the commode.

I faced myself in the mirror. I looked tired, worse for wear, maybe a little bedraggled. But I didn't look frightened.

And I wasn't alone. However this went, I wasn't alone today.

I wouldn't be tomorrow either. I had to believe that.

Taking the tests was pretty straightforward. I'd also consumed enough liquid to make it easy. I set the two sticks on the sink and opened the door, leaning against the jamb.

Thor was sitting on the edge of the bed with his head in his hands, but he lifted it immediately as I came into the room. He jumped to his feet, prepared to do any kind of battle I needed.

Even with a duo of preggo sticks.

There was no way I could tell myself that any part of this man was anywhere else right now but here in this room with me. He'd been by my side every day since I'd had the fucking wisdom to come to him for help with my house.

Sometimes I was a damn near genius.

"Waiting." I tucked my hands under my arms and didn't object as he drew me close and rested his chin on top of my head. One of us was shaking.

Possibly both.

Hell, probably both.

His voice was thick when he spoke again. "Uh, you think we should check now?"

"I guess."

"Do you want me to?"

I drew in a breath sharp enough to make my ribs ache. "We can do it together." Biting my lip, I looked up at him and held out my hand.

He clasped it with his own and lifted it to his mouth, brushing a quick kiss over my knuckles. "Whatever happens, it's you and me. You and me, Ruby. Got it?"

The lump in my throat made it impossible to speak, but I nodded. I nodded like my life depended on it. In a very real way, it did.

This was everything.

We crowded into the doorway together, laughing a little as we made ourselves fit. He nudged me through first, but I hung back so he could pick up the tests. First one, then the other.

Wordlessly, he showed them to me. One had two lines. The other said pregnant.

His large fingers shook as he grabbed some toilet paper and wrapped them in it. But rather than tossing out the bundle, he set it on the edge of the sink. Then he drew me into his arms.

The best place in the world for me to be while I sniffled and shook like a...well, like a damn girl. But he was shaking too, and his eyes were wide and damp when they met mine.

"Congratulations, mama," he whispered, framing my cheeks with his hands before he kissed me, soft and sweet.

I could do this. I could.

I wouldn't fuck this up. Not when it was so important.

"Congratulations, daddy," I whispered back, burying my face in his chest.

He rubbed my back, his hand circling like a metronome. Back and forth, back and forth. The gentle motion comforted me and excited me and made me itch to get out of these damn wedding clothes into something more comfortable.

Being naked sounded good, with the added weight of Thor's long, naked body on top of me.

Then my gaze drifted over his beefy shoulder to the sink. "You're going to throw those out, right?"

"What?"

"The tests."

"Of course not. They're our baby's first hello."

I snorted. "I peed on them. Not quite sure you're getting that."

"I'll sterilize them later and put them away in a box for the baby." He scratched his jaw. "Make that a box *about* the baby. He probably won't want his mom's pee sticks."

"He?"

"Luna," he reminded me as I took a few deep breaths at the fact now I was someone's mom.

Me, the girl who'd never had one myself. I could be that for a baby.

I glanced down at my flat belly and tentatively pressed my palm there. Lucky cupped his hand over mine as our eyes met. God, the timing was all wrong and it shouldn't have been perfect but it just was.

Somehow everything was perfect.

TWENTY-FOUR

Lucky

"You know you don't have to keep driving me places, right?"

"I know." I chucked my phone on the dash as I turned onto her road. I knew it as well as my own at this point. Better, even. Since the wedding, we'd been back to the sleepovers and making plans for a baby.

Christ, it was still was insane to think that, let alone say it out loud.

"I can—"

"Ruby, I'm about to be in your driveway. Quit trying to do everything alone. I'll see you in a minute." I reached for the phone and hung up on her. I loved her to distraction, but her independent streak threatened to send me to the bottle some days.

We'd managed to get the whereabouts of Cohen from Rhett before he escaped Happy Acres. The Burns family was a protective lot, but he'd seemed to finally get that there was something more than grief going on.

And I wasn't letting her go deal with that alone.

Road trip to her dad's place to the rescue. God help me.

I glanced at the dog bed behind me. Butch knew we were close to her second favorite human. She scrabbled up and over the seat to my shoulder. Her tail was wagging madly, her little body vibrating with glee. She sniffed the top of the truck and batted at the half dozen lights I'd crisscrossed on the roof inside.

Our first Christmas wasn't going to happen without some cheer, dammit. Even if I had to go face the reality of just how much pain Ruby had been dragging around with her for the last few years.

When I arrived, she was standing at the edge of the beach. Her red hair was in her typical ponytail, but this time, she'd shoved it through a gray hat with a makeshift hole for such things. She wore my favorite jeans and those stupid boots she loved. Instead of a jacket, she had on an oversized sweatshirt.

She turned with a mug between her gloved fingers.

Snow still covered every surface, but it had been plowed aside by the guys on my crew. The snowbanks were as tall as the dumpster shrouded in a tarp. We'd given the guys the rest of the week off for Christmas since there wasn't any reason to rush anymore.

I parked and climbed out to meet her as Butch leaped down to get to her mistress.

Tish trudged up the slope with a bright smile on her face. I reached out for her hand, helping her up the last bit that had turned to ice.

Damn, I didn't get to enjoy her mega-watt smile that much. Though I had to admit, she did it a lot more since Caleb's wedding.

Her full-on killer smile made my chest tight.

She crouched to give B a scratch then shielded her eyes against the blazing sun. "What did you do to your truck?"

I pulled her in close, then turned toward the truck. "Well, since you have to sacrifice your beloved Hallmark movies for the next few days, I figured I'd bring one to you."

She huffed out a laugh. "You weren't supposed to see that."

I stroked my hand down her ponytail. "Couldn't sleep last night."

"I tried not to wake you."

I kissed her temple. "I can tell when you're not next to me. Especially since your bed is made for midgets."

"Shut up. It's a perfectly respectable queen-sized bed."

"I'm not a respectable man."

She snickered then lifted onto her toes to kiss my cheek. "There is that. I love the truck." She scooped up B and rushed to the door. "Oh my God, a tree too?"

Her eyes sparkled as she circled the back of the truck. Her delighted husky laugh made every hour of setting this up worth it.

She opened the tailgate and hoisted herself in. "There's a freaking train!"

I went around to the side of the truck and peered in. The tabletop tree was small and probably wouldn't make it past the ride to her dad's house, but it had the intended effect. I'd nailed the crisscrossed wooden base of the tree to an apple cart I'd snagged from Happy Acres, then jury rigged the whole damn thing to a piece of plywood.

I'd found a kids' toy train set at one of the big box stores—where I'd also snagged the tree and some cheap ornaments. Well, all but one ornament. The one that had given me the whole idea.

"Is this what you were doing when you said you needed to go to the store?" She was crouched in front of the tree, touching the star lights and smoky red balls that reminded me of her hair.

"Maybe."

"It's utterly ridiculous." She looked up at me, her eyes wet. "I love it."

I sniffled a little. Seeing her happy was going to take me out. The difference between the woman I'd met a few months ago and this smiling one seemed huge.

Baby glow?

Maybe some from me?

Right then, I didn't care.

"Check out the ornament near the top."

Her gaze skimmed the gaudy garland that I'd clumsily wrapped around each branch. My damn bear paws weren't made for tiny things. Though that would be changing soon.

She tugged off her glove and cupped the crystal couple. "Our First Christmas," she said with a little hitch in her voice. Then she flicked it off the branch and tucked it in her pocket. "I don't want it to get ruined on the drive."

Then she hopped down and launched herself into my arms. I caught her against me and was surprised at the heat in her kiss. She wrapped her legs around my waist and nearly knocked us both into the snowbank.

Staggering, I laughed and spun her around, Butch yipping and jumping around my ankles.

"I can't believe you did this."

"Someday you'll figure out that I'd do anything for you, Ruby."

She buried her face in my neck. "I'm starting to believe that."

I wrapped my arms around her tighter. Good thing I was a patient man. Well, not generally, but I was learning to be.

Keeping things light, I set her down. "Wait until you see inside."

"Oh, yeah?"

I opened the passenger side door, and Butch bounced inside with the springs that seemed to be in her damn feet. After exploring from the wheel well to the bench seat, she turned to face us, her tongue lolling out.

"Oh, wait." I opened the glove box and took out the pint-sized red jacket I'd gotten for B. I came out with a pair of antlers and handed them to Tish.

She gave me a bland look. "I'm not wearing those."

"C'mon." I found the little switch on the top of the headband and tiny twinkle lights blinked.

"Not in this lifetime."

I shrugged and put them on. "I'll go get your bags."

"They're on the porch."

"On it." I clomped my way to the porch, then hurriedly made sure the door was locked. When I got back to the truck, she was fussing with the lights all over the interior of the truck.

I opened my door. "What are you doing?"

She snorted. "You can't drive with those."

"Watch me." I slid inside and the antlers bent forward. Not exactly a lot of headspace for my giant self. "Okay, so maybe not."

She plucked the antlers off my head and threw them in the back.

Butch attacked them with glee and curled herself in the curve of the headband.

"This is insane. How many... Never mind." She saw the banded battery packs I'd tucked into the front corner of the dash. "That's a lot."

I shrugged. "Made you smile."

"Might not make you smile when it's dark and all you see are the interior lights."

"Don't get all pragmatic on me, woman."

She giggled and leaned in to kiss me again. "I wouldn't dare."

A few minutes later, we were all packed and heading for Buffalo. It wasn't going to be a long trip, but as usual, weather wasn't on our side. I was almost certain our route was following the storm. It wasn't going to be a bad one, just would slow down our progress.

"We can wait to go after Christmas."

"No. I know you want to see Cohen. And your dad."

She slipped her feet out of her boots and tucked one under her butt. My Amazon liked to pretzel herself whenever she did manage to sit her ass down. Today's socks were all the Marvel hero logos. From what I could tell, they were knee socks.

That shouldn't be hot. And yet, as usual, when it came to Ruby, everything seemed abnormally attractive.

She reached in the backseat to give B a scratch. "I do. We should probably do the whole doctor thing before we tell my family."

My stomach went leaden. "If you want to wait, we can."

"I don't want to." She reached over to cover my hand on my thigh. "I want to tell them. I just don't know how all of this is going to go."

"Are you going to tell Cohen everything?"

"I don't know. Part of me thinks I should, but then I don't want to hurt him any more than he's already hurting."

I wanted to ask if she would be telling *me* everything, but I could tell she was too lost in her own thoughts.

On the trip there, we killed time with our favorite murder podcast. About half an hour outside of her dad's place, the conditions had turned white-out dangerous. I was white-knuckling it every mile. Normally, I'd be a helluva lot calmer.

I'd spent three-quarters of my life on the road. This was nothing compared to a few of the blizzards and hurricanes I'd been through.

This time, I had far more precious cargo.

When my rear tires slipped for a third time, I swore. A sign for a truck stop made the decision for me. I flicked on my blinker. "I think we should pull over and wait this out a bit."

She nodded. "I think you're right."

"Sorry. Can I get the time and date of that one?"

"Ass." But the tips of her fingers were bone-white as she held onto the dash. B had climbed into her lap after a bathroom break and stayed there ever since.

A line of cars had the same idea, including half a dozen tractor trailers. I eased behind a Bronco and put it in park. An army of plows were making short work of the rapidly falling snow, but as soon as they cleared it, more was there waiting.

The sun had been missing for the last hour, leaving the sky an eerie iridescent orange full of snow. It wasn't even noon, but it looked more like dusk.

She flipped open the cooler on the floor and found B's little bottle-bowl contraption. She squeezed out some water and offered some to my shaking dog.

"*Shh.* It's okay."

I couldn't help smiling at her as she crooned to the dog.

She looked up. "What are you smiling at?"

"Not maternal, huh?"

"Shut up." She tucked the bottle away then cuddled B. "Dogs are easy."

"I'm onto you, Miss Burns." I unclipped my belt, then hers and dragged her and my dog over. I stretched out my legs on the bench seat until she had no choice but to lay on me.

"This is not comfy."

"Sure it is." I lifted her hips until she straddled my legs with one of hers. "There we go. Why don't you try and take a little nap? Not much else we can do here."

She laid her head against my chest as B curled up in the small space between us and settled down.

Having both my girls in my arms wasn't a bad thing. I smoothed my hand down her hair. She'd taken off the hat during the drive, and the cinnamon scent of her hair filled the cab of the truck.

"Did you grow up in Buffalo?"

She played with the button on my shirt. "We moved there after my mom left. So, yeah, most of my life."

I pressed a kiss to the top of her head and let her talk if she wanted to.

"My dad needed help from his family. Three boys and me—yeah, we were a bit of a handful as you could imagine."

I smiled against her hair. "Bet *you* were a handful."

She tucked her cheek against her hand on my chest. "I'm wondering if the universe is going to give me a hellspawn in retribution, let's put it that way."

I tugged her ponytail. "Well, there is red hair involved."

She rested her chin on her hand and grinned up at me. "Did you know your family at all?"

I shook my head. "My mom dumped me on my grandmother when I was a baby." I slid my hand under the hem of her sweatshirt to make little circles on her lower back. "She was thrilled as you can imagine." I looked out the windshield. Snow was piling up, and the windows fogged. "She died, and I got gone."

Ruby stared at me. "Died? You didn't tell me that."

"It didn't really matter. She fed me because she had to. I hustled enough to buy clothes, and thankfully, school was tolerable. After she died, I escaped before CPS found me and put me in the system." I cupped her cheek. "I'm a survivor, Ruby. Just like you." I hated the sadness in her dark eyes. "Our kid will never think I don't want him or her."

She leaned into me, her kiss soft and caramel-flavored from her candy. Butch decided she wanted in on the action and climbed up to give us both a tongue bath.

Tish laughed and pushed the dog away enough to get her arms around my neck. She wrapped herself around me tightly and my chest eased.

I didn't talk about my past because I would rather forget what happened. It wasn't horrible, just a series of lonely stops. At the time, I hadn't thought so, but I always moved on before someone else could.

I tightened my hold on her, and we stayed like that for a good long while.

Finally, she scrunched back down to rest her head on my chest. "You know, we aren't that much different. I had my brothers, but Ezra took off as soon as humanly possible. Rhett and I were the closest in age, but he was always dreaming up ways to get out of Buffalo too."

"And Cohen?" I didn't want to ask. Part of me wanted to know all the details, but another part of me didn't want to hear about it. To know she'd loved so hard that the scars had lasted years.

She laughed softly. "Our daredevil. He was always looking for a high. Not the kind in a bottle or pill or whatever, but his drug of choice was always adrenaline. One time, he actually broke his arm— like full bone sticking out of his damn skin broken." She trailed her fingers down my arm to catch my hand and laced our fingers. "He got up off the track and was so damn excited about the jump. Of course then he got a look at his arm and passed out in the middle of the dirt trail."

"So, you held that over his head for…"

She snorted. "Forever."

"Shocking."

"But then there was a field trip for school. He was seventeen when he got his first glimpse of a firehouse. Then bikes and motorcycles seemed tame compared to fighting fires."

"A new high."

She toyed with my fingers, her thumb drifting across the calluses on my palm. My breath backed up in my lungs. I was forever touching her, but this was the first time she'd relaxed enough to do the same.

Well, when it didn't have something to do with sex. She was plenty touchy then.

But this was different, and my chest ached at her words and touch.

"Yep, you got it. He went from a volunteer firefighter to part of the main crew in Buffalo. But even that wasn't enough. He entered the California program and went through training to be a jumper."

"And met Jimmy," I murmured.

"Yeah. At first, he was just another dumb boy in my house for the holidays. I was too interested in the garage. If it had an engine, I could pull it apart and put it back together. It was the only way me and my dad knew how to communicate."

"Sounds pretty amazing to me."

"It was. I loved the puzzle of it. I started working on the custom jobs my dad didn't have the patience for. Then people began asking for me. Fast forward a bit, and I was the one who was traveling all over. I had a knack. Even when I'd butt up against the boys' club, they eventually had to let me in."

I chuckled. "Because you were better than them."

"Damn straight. Then I started learning about fabricators. The ins and outs of them, their pros and cons. Nothing could do exactly what I wanted. So, I came up with one on my own. I was so excited about it, I went home and told my family."

My gut twisted as she tensed in my arms. "It was early summer. We tended to hang out as a family in those few weeks before fire season. Jimmy and Co would land exhausted from their brutal training programs. They loved it, of course. They played just as hard as they worked." She relaxed and smiled against my neck. "They drank me under the table. There was always a little something between me and Jimmy, but it was weird with Co. So, we never did any more than flirt until that summer."

I swallowed against the acid streaming up from my gut. "And you hooked up."

"Yeah. It was fun. He was always fun. And I was high on the deal I had going with this manufacturer out of Georgia. They believed in my drawings. I didn't have capital then, so I was looking to hook up with a company. It wasn't even a good deal now that I look back on it. But at the time, I was too stupid to know any better."

"You're far from stupid."

"Yeah, now. Then I was just cocky. I knew I was good, knew I had a good product. And I should have gotten a lawyer. Should have paid more attention to my paperwork. Then there was Jimmy. I babbled all my details to him. I was trying to impress him. I wanted to dazzle him with my awesomeness."

I didn't know what to say just then. Ruby had always been so put together. I couldn't imagine her starstruck by anyone. And maybe that was why it hurt so much to hear her talk about him.

"He said he'd help me with the paperwork. I didn't need to waste my money on a lawyer taking my money." She huffed out a bitter laugh. "I should have been looking closer to home with where my money was going." She sat up. "I was dumb enough to trust him. He was my brother's best friend. He fucking snowed me. Put both our names on the paperwork and when the check came in, it went to him in California. He was gone. And so was my money."

"What the fuck. You couldn't fight it?" I sat up with her, outrage bellowing through the car.

She leaned over and kissed me. "No lawyer, remember? And with both our names on the paperwork, he could cash the check. It wasn't like we had a partnership."

"You could have fought it."

"I could have. But then I'd have to drag my whole family into it. Drag Cohen—"

"And you don't think he'd choose you over this piece of shit?"

"It didn't matter. I was so mad at myself for being so stupid. For getting taken in. I thought I deserved it."

"Fuck that." Rage left me seeing red, and it wasn't my Ruby's hair this time.

She launched herself at me. "I love that you're so offended for me, Thor." She pressed her forehead to mine. "I love the way you see me."

I dragged her back onto my lap until she straddled me. Butch yipped at all the activity and leaped into the back to put herself back into her bed with a huff.

Ruby laughed as she threaded her fingers into my hair. "I love that you are here for me, expecting nothing."

My throat tightened. "I'll always be here for you."

"I thought I loved Jimmy. But now I know it wasn't love. It doesn't come close to how I feel about you." She covered her belly with her hand. "Or how I feel about this crazy thing we're doing together. I mean, a baby? It's just insane. But I want it. I want you both so much."

I cupped the back of her neck and covered her mouth. The kiss was wildfire-hot, and we were both breathless when we pulled apart. "You can't get rid of me, you know."

"Forever seems like a really good word when it comes to you and me."

"Forever?" I gripped her ass, dragging her harder against me.

"Yep. You're stuck with me."

The bleat of a truck horn had us both jumping. While we'd been talking, the snow had let up. I hit the windshield wipers and laughed at the line of brake lights merging back onto the highway. "Well, I guess forever includes talking to your dad about all of this."

"Yeah. And Cohen. Maybe I'm better off just keeping it to myself." She slid off my lap to her side of the truck.

"Whichever way you want to go, I'm with you."

She leaned back to me and cupped my face. "God, I love you, Thor."

"Holy shit." My heart thudded so loud I couldn't hear the wiper blades over the rush of blood in my ears.

"What?"

"You said it."

She punched my arm. "Oh, stop. I just told you a bunch of ways how I feel."

"Doesn't matter." I dragged her back over to me. "Say it again," I said against her mouth.

"I love you, you idiot."

"Close enough," I said and kissed her brainless.

TWENTY-FIVE

I DIDN'T EVEN REALIZE TALKING IT OUT WITH LUCKY WOULD SETTLE ME. Then again, I wasn't used to leaning on anyone, let alone someone outside of my family.

Ha.

Well, he was family regardless at this point. Even if the baby was the size of a kernel of corn. Which was just mind-boggling. I laid my hand on my belly again. Well, not really a belly yet. Unless I kept eating candy and salty snacks at the rate I had since finding out. Then I might start showing even before the little corn nut grew into the next fruit size, according to the book I'd downloaded on my phone.

The storm had eased, leaving a blue sky and eye-searing sun bouncing off the snow.

Lucky was singing with Christmas songs as Butch howled along. I hung the ornament he'd gotten for us on the crisscrossed lights tacked to the ceiling of the truck. It swung merrily, the colored lights refracting in each facet.

I wasn't sure how I'd ended up with such a romantic...*what?* Boyfriend? That seemed lame and not even close to how I felt about him. And hoo boy, did that sneak up on me.

I glanced over at him. He'd put the antlers back on, bending them to look more like floppy ears than bone. Bonus points that it pushed his wild hair back.

His wild fistable hair that made me crazy. A good kind of crazy. Maybe a tiny bit more intense than the annoyance levels he brought out in me with the renovation.

A renovation that didn't even need to happen.

Then again, I might not have Lucky in my life if I hadn't had to move the project up. Maybe things happened just as they were meant to.

I pointed to the exit we needed to take to my dad's place.

He turned down the radio. "You seem a little…thinky."

"Astute observation."

"And snarky with it."

I reached across the seat and squeezed his hand. "Yeah. I'm a little nervous about talking to Co. Maybe forcing this on him wasn't a good idea."

"Maybe. Or maybe it's just what both of you need to start talking again."

"Stop being so annoyingly smart."

"I keep trying, but then you have a problem and I gotta help."

I rolled my eyes. "Ass."

His face lit up with a smile. "I just realized that every time you call me an ass, you really mean I love you."

"If that makes you feel better, Thor," I pinched his rock hard middle, "then you can keep your delusions." But I was smiling just as widely as he was.

"Did you give anyone a heads up that you were coming?"

"I figure Rhett did. Though he can be a freaking coward, so maybe not." I pulled out my phone and flipped it around in my hand, then stuffed it back in my hoodie pocket. Too late now. "Take your next left."

My dad's ranch-style house came into view. When my brothers had moved out, he'd turned part of the house into an extension of the garage. My dad had two full bays. One for his precious Stingray and one to tinker on whatever project car he was doing on the side.

One of the bays was open, and my dad stood up straight as we came up the drive. He wiped his hands on the red rag he always had at the ready.

"So, does your dad have a vest or anything?"

"Vest?"

"You know, motorcycle club."

A laugh rolled out even with my stomach in knots. "No, my dad isn't affiliated with a club. He's a grease monkey more than a bike guy. He'll probably like your truck actually. My dad's all about American made."

"As he should be." He cleared his throat. "He's not going to kill me or anything though? You know, for putting a baby in his little girl or some shit."

"Probably not," I said as I slid out.

"Hey, wait. What do you mean, probably not?"

I closed the door on him and ran up the walk. "Hey, Daddy."

"Hey, Ging. I didn't know you were coming in." He scratched the back of his neck and put his glasses in his shirt pocket. "I didn't decorate or anything."

I went up on my toes and gave him a kiss on the cheek. He was a few inches taller than me and still as fit as my brothers. He'd gone on a workout kick after he hurt his back a few years ago. "You look good."

He shrugged. "Started running with...a friend."

My eyebrow rose. "A *female* friend?"

"Maybe. What are you doing here, kid?"

I turned to see Lucky hovering by his truck. I held out my hand to him and he straightened his shoulders, then strode over to me. He took my hand, lacing our fingers. "Well, we kinda did a drive-by with the memorial."

"We were surprised." My dad gave Lucky a once-over. "Jeff Burns," he said and held out a hand.

Thor rubbed his palm down his thigh, then clasped my dad's hand. "Lucky Roberts, sir."

My dad's eyebrow rose. "Sir? Wow. More manners this time than the last time you came running through with my daughter."

Lucky slid his arm around me. "I was a little more worried about Ruby at the time, sir."

"Ruby?"

"No one likes to use my given name, what can I tell you?"

"Hmm."

I resisted the urge to smile. Thor looked like he was ready to pee his damn pants. Then again, I got my intimidating face from my dad. "I was hoping I could talk to Co."

My dad's smile slid away. "I don't know, Tish. He's been really hard to talk to."

I sighed. "Let me at least try. Then we'll take you over to Bob's diner for dinner. How's that?"

"I could go for an open-faced sandwich."

I pulled down Lucky to kiss his cheek. "Behave."

His eyebrows snapped together. "You're leaving me alone?" He swallowed. "With your dad," he said under his breath.

I slapped him on the arm. "You'll be fine." I turned to my dad. "Hey, can you check Lucky's truck?"

"There's nothing wrong with my truck."

I knew that if my dad had something to do, Lucky would be better off. "We had a little bump into a snowbank the other day. It's been making a noise."

"I'll check it out." My dad took out his glasses and set them on the end of his nose. "You keep her pretty nice."

Lucky tucked his hair behind his ear. "Yeah. First truck I bought when I settled in the Cove."

"Well, let's open her up."

Lucky gave me a helpless look. I opened the passenger door and scooped up Butch. "I'll just take Butch in to meet Cohen."

My brother loved dogs. I'd use any way to get him to open up, even if it was a little underhanded.

I curled B up against my neck. Maybe Butch would help me too.

I wove my way through the living room to the hallway that led to the bedrooms. The walls were full of photos from Ezra's various shoots. Some published, some just for his family.

Co and Rhett mugging for the camera at Christmas. A family portrait on the lake when I graduated from high school. One of Jimmy and Cohen when they finished their first training.

The frame was crooked, and the corner of the wood was chipped. I frowned as I straightened it.

Finally, I reached the spare bedroom. A room I'd crashed in a million times. Butch seemed to feel my nerves. She burrowed into my neck and licked my jaw. I nuzzled her and kissed her head. "Thanks, girl."

I lifted my hand and knocked.

"I told you I wasn't hungry." The door swung open. Cohen was leaning on a cane. A plastic boot encased his leg up to his knee. His eyes shuttered, then his gaze dropped to the floor. "Ging. What are you doing here?"

"Checking on my big brother since he decided not to show his ugly mug at my place."

He hobbled back to the well-loved brown recliner in the corner. "I wasn't in the festive mood."

"I get that."

He put up the chair's footrest. "No need for it to be a downer for everyone."

I sat on the edge of his bed. Like the angel she was, Butch curled on my lap. "You're not a downer. What happened was shocking and horrible."

Stark, red-rimmed eyes met mine. "I watched him fall."

I set Butch aside on the bed and went onto my knees next to the chair, gripping his arm. "Oh, Co." Butch jumped down and hid behind me.

All of his muscles were tight, his shoulders ramrod straight. "The whole thing was a shit show. The flight into the flames. We were just supposed to Phos-Chek and get the hell out of there. But then the perimeter was a mess."

He didn't see me as he was talking. I could tell he was back there again.

"We'd been fighting all day. Me and Jimmy."

I frowned. "You guys never fight."

"We were packing up the day before. Jimmy left the packing to me, as usual. Asshole never wanted to do the hard stuff. 'You'll take care of it right, Co?'"

His voice slid into the cajoling charming tone that sounded so much like Jimmy that I shivered.

"'You like organizing. It's not for me, bro.'" Cohen swiped his hand through his overlong hair and pushed it away from his face. Clearly, he hadn't been eating. His face was all sharp angles and his skin looked pasty. "Why should he do anything that had even a shred of responsibility?"

All I could do was hold onto his hand. "It's okay."

"No, it's not okay. It's never going to be okay. He broke protocol and geared up to jump. It wasn't safe, but he wanted to anyway. Our captain ordered us back, but he wanted to be a goddamn hero. Or just get away from me."

"Co." I pulled him down to me, but he stiffened. I let him go and just held his hand.

"He couldn't face me, Ging. Why didn't you tell me?"

I stilled. "What?"

"Why didn't you tell me he hurt you?"

I looked down at his hand. "He told you?"

"No. He definitely didn't tell me you guys were together. I figured it out a long time ago. You guys weren't exactly subtle."

Butch sniffed my leg and crawled in front of me "It's okay, B. I'm fine." I sat back on my feet and cuddled the dog close to me. "It didn't last long. I didn't want to come between you."

He let out a rough laugh. "Come between us? Is that what you call this?"

It felt like he meant more than just a breakup. "Co—"

"You didn't tell us he stole from you?"

I stumbled back and landed on my ass. Butch scrambled away. "I didn't want anyone to know."

"My best friend stole from my sister almost four years ago, and you didn't tell me? You let that man stay in our lives?"

"It was just money, Co." It wasn't just money. I didn't even have an excuse. "I'm sorry."

"You don't get to be sorry. It was his fault. He's the one that made you go away."

"I didn't go—"

"You did. You took off to what? Colorado then somewhere else. You didn't come back for almost a year." He shoved down the footrest. "You didn't tell us."

"I was ashamed." I stared down at the scarred wood floor. "I was so stupid. I didn't want anyone to know that I could be that stupid." The shame rolled over me as if it was that day so long ago. "I practically handed him the check."

"No. You trusted him. You trusted him like I did. He was family." Cohen's eyes were bright red with anger and pain. "I knew he took shortcuts. I was always cleaning up after him, but I thought we were best friends. You take care of your own. But I let you down."

"No. No, you didn't." I crawled toward the chair, pushing into his space though he held himself at arm's length. "No. It wasn't like that."

"Why didn't you come to me?"

"We were sneaking around and then I was just so…embarrassed that I let him have that much control over me. Over my money. He kept telling me he was helping me. Saving me money." I gave a harsh laugh. "But then you guys were in the middle of wildfire season and I just couldn't." I leaned upward to wrap my arms around his shoulders. They seemed so frail. So unlike my big, strong brother.

We stayed like that for a long time. I wasn't aware I'd started crying in there somewhere. When I eased back, I saw Cohen was as well.

I pressed my forehead to his. "I'm so sorry."

"I hate him. Hate what he did to us. Hate that he stole from you. That he could do that to my baby sister. That he dared to touch you to begin with, but that? No." He dashed at the tears then tipped back his head to inhale a deep breath. "I just want to bring him back so I can throttle him myself."

I cupped his cheeks. "No. It's not important anymore. It was a really shitty lesson." I barked out a laugh. "Really shitty." I sniffed. "How did you find out anyway?"

He stretched out his booted leg. "Moving, remember? Jimmy was such a fucking slob. His papers were everywhere. I found the residual check. Is that what it's called? I don't know. There was the check stub and some report." He drilled his fingers into his hair. "Now that I think about it, every year he would spend a lot of goddamn money."

I settled back on the floor and tucked Butch in the middle of my crossed legs. "Yeah, part of the contract was that I would get a percentage of the cost of using the machine."

He scrubbed his hands over his face. "So he stole from you yearly. That's great."

I leaned forward and patted his knee. "About that. I made a new machine and made like…way more." The number seemed rude to give him. But I'd improved on my design and kept the copyright. "People pay *me* for the use of my machine now. No one else." I dropped my voice to a whisper. "I charge a lot."

He laughed and the heaviness in his eyes lightened a bit. "A lot, huh?"

"I don't want to make you cry again with the number."

Cohen laughed and slumped back. "Just like you to rub his nose in it."

"Yeah, well, you know how much I hate to lose."

"That I do." He nodded at Butch. "Who's your friend?"

I lifted up B and set her on Cohen's good leg. "Meet Butch. She's my feisty fur baby. Well, my guy's baby, but she's mine now too."

Not our only baby, but one thing at a time.

"Well, hey there, Butch." He gave me a raised brow. "*Her?*"

"Long story. My guy is sorta odd sometimes, but I like him." I propped my elbows on my knees and tucked my chin in my hand. "Actually, I love him."

B burrowed into my brother, her tail swishing against Cohen's track pants. "Whoa? Love him?"

"Yep."

"The big guy who came to the memorial?"

"That's the one."

"Well, if you're happy..."

"I am." It almost seemed like tempting fate to say it, but I was learning to let myself enjoy whatever this was between us. Trying to anyway.

Kinder, gentler Tish was still a work in progress, but luckily, my guy was patient.

"He seems pretty protective of you. That's kind of interesting."

My palms were now officially sweating. "I've got a little more news for you."

"Uh oh."

"You know, since I kept the other thing from you."

He narrowed his eyes. "Yeah."

Time to just go for it. "You're going to be an uncle."

"What?" He set Butch on the arm of the chair and scrambled to his feet. "Oh, shit. Fuck. Shit. Ow."

I laughed and sat up straighter. "Careful."

"Dammit, I haven't been doing my exercises." He hissed and rubbed his leg. "Uncle?"

"You should be doing your exercises."

"And you should know better about birth control."

"Yeah, well, that's a story too. I live in a strange little town that seems to be a tad baby-crazy."

"It's gotta be if you got knocked up."

"Hey."

He laughed. "Can you grab my cane?" He grimaced. "I can grab it myself but—"

"Let me help."

"You sure, preggers? You don't need to strain something."

"I'm not *that* pregnant." I rolled to my knees and had to admit I was a tiny bit winded. "I have been eating a lot of candy though." I laughed and got to my feet then crossed the room to grab the cane.

I passed it to him and Co used it to take a couple of steps toward me. I hoped he hadn't hurt himself with his sudden movement. As per usual, Butch circled around us, excitedly barking.

Then my brother tossed the cane against the chair and dragged me in for a hard hug.

My eyes went damp all over again as I hugged him back.

"Does Dad know?"

"You're the first."

"Ezra is gonna shit."

"Nice." When I stepped back to open the bedroom door, B charged down the hall as if she'd been imprisoned. Probably heading right back to her daddy. "You know you'll have to clean up that firefighter language around my kid."

"Like your kid won't swear."

"I'm trying to clean up my act."

"Sure."

I leaned into him and rested my head on his shoulder. "Are we okay?"

"We will be."

"That's good enough for me." I felt as if a whole car had been lifted off my shoulders. Cohen still looked haunted, but nothing like he had been when I walked in the room.

"So, how do you think Dad will react?"

"Eh, he's getting old. He might be excited about it."

"I hope so."

Cohen slung his arm around my shoulders, and we staggered down the hall. I noticed he left the cane behind, but I didn't call him on it. With my brother, progress came in fits and starts.

He was like his sister that way.

"Uncle. Man."

"*Shh.* I didn't tell Dad yet."

"Tell Dad what?"

I winced at my father's voice. "Hey, guys," I said as we came out. My dad's head was in the fridge.

Lucky was sitting at the dining room table, a sweating beer in front of him. Immediately, he rose. "You need help?"

Cohen waved him off and hobbled to the table. "I got it. So, you knocked up my sister, huh?"

A crash came from the kitchen.

"What?!"

I kicked Cohen in his good foot. "Way to go, jerk."

"Ow." He dropped into a chair. "I'm injured, remember?"

"Yeah, keep talking, and you'll have another broken leg."

"Such a brute." He crossed his arms and aimed a look at Lucky. "You going to make an honest woman out of her?"

"Are you kidding me right now?" I whacked him in the back of the head as I passed him to check on my dad.

"I plan on it," Lucky answered.

So, I wasn't going to think about *that* right now.

I rolled my eyes as I entered the kitchen. "Oh, Dad."

He was crouched down, cleaning up a jar of hot dog relish. "There's glass."

"I think I can handle it." I grabbed a roll of paper towels. "So, you heard."

"Baby? With him?" My dad gathered the yellow and green mess into a towel.

The scent of mustard made my stomach roll. "Yep." I nodded to the counter. "Yeah, evidently, relish is on my not a good idea list."

My dad frowned.

"Don't think you want to clean up two messes."

"Oh. Right. Yeah, I got this."

I opened the cupboard under the sink, grabbed the cleaner, and handed it to him.

"Thanks."

I leaned on the counter and craned my neck to make sure Cohen wasn't messing with Thor too much.

My dad threw everything away and came back to stand in front of me. "So…"

I stepped into his arms. "Grandpa."

"Wow."

The scent of motor oil and sandalwood evened me out the rest of the way. "I love him, Dad."

He relaxed. "He seems like a nice guy. I won't hesitate to put him in Connolly's compactor if he hurts you though."

The last bit of tension I'd carried drained out of me as I grinned against his chest. "I'll help."

My dad laughed as we went back to the dining room.

Lucky got to his feet. "Sir."

"Stop calling me sir."

Lucky cleared his throat. "Mr. Burns."

My dad sighed and drew him in for a hug. "Welcome to the family, Lucky. I expect a wedding before the baby comes."

"Dad!"

He let Lucky go and grinned at me. "What? You're not going to marry him?"

"Oh, she's marrying me." Lucky grinned and looked unbelievably happy.

He wasn't the only one, but I had my rep to consider. I'd still be a badass biker babe, just a badass biker babe toting a snuggly.

"You think so, Thor?"

He walked around my dad and stood in front of me. His gaze tracked over my face, then he curled his arms around my waist and lifted me up off my toes. "We're totally getting married, Ruby."

I cupped his cheeks. "Your proposal needs work."

"I love you."

"I love you too, you idiot."

He swung me around, and miracle of miracles, my stomach didn't protest. "Someday you'll drop the idiot part."

I grinned. "Probably not."

He was right. We were totally getting married. But I wasn't squeezing into another freaking dress.

Next up is Brady & Tabitha's story!

As a hardworking cop in small-town Crescent Cove, I occasionally indulge in some harmless fun with the occasional badge bunny. Then I sampled Tabitha's special ingredient frosting. Now the only cookie I want is hers… even if she's not sure our one-night-stand baby can lead to forever.

If you missed Lucky's bestie's story, you can grab **Caleb and Luna's** book, WRONG BED BABY, now available!

Maybe you'd like to take a trip into Kensington Square as well? **Preston and Ryan's** story, HIS TEMPORARY ASSISTANT is live!

And there was a cameo with **Gage and Rylee** during the bonfire. Did you miss their story, PIT STOP: BABY? It's now available as well!

We appreciate our readers so much!
If you loved the book please let your friends know. If you're extra awesome, we'd love a review on your favorite book site.

Turn the page for a special sneak peek of DADDY ON DUTY now!

 **BRADY**

DADDY ON DUTY

CHAPTER ONE

Valentine's Day was a pisser under the best of circumstances. And my skill at viewing situations as "the glass half full" depended how crappy my day on patrol had gone.

Today wasn't looking awesome, which meant neither was my outlook on the big love shindig.

If you were single, you searched around for a date and then hoped they didn't have excessive expectations. Though the high-quality pickings weren't usually plentiful by then, since a lot of people were so desperate to be coupled up, no matter how dubiously, that they snagged whomever was still available in early February.

If you were seeing someone, then you had to evaluate what level the relationship was at. And God forbid if you realized you were at different levels.

Oh, the horrors.

Then there was always the horniness factor to consider. I was better than a teenage male in the sense I didn't let my pointer dog lead me up all the wrong trees—usually—but I enjoyed sex to a level that had caused unnecessary drama in my youth.

As in before my last birthday. I'd matured since then.

But Valentine's Day fucked with even the most responsible among us. Especially when you were on patrol with your commanding officer who happened to be the chief in our small, sweet, heavily coupled up and baby-infested small town. And *he* was about to split because he was heading home to get some from his Salma-Hayek's-younger-sister-lookalike fiancée.

Bitter? Who me? I was the moron who'd decided to embrace the single life several months ago after the last chick I'd considered dating had decided *casual* meant fifty-five texts per day.

Sixty-five on weekends.

But man, why had I drawn a line in the sand before the holiday that literally celebrated sex?

"I don't foresee you having any issues tonight other than the snow. Christian's headed in with the new recruit and he's well versed in dealing with crowd control for the Fest. But this snow is making things tricky."

"This?" I snorted and gestured out the windshield. A family hurried across the street at the crosswalk, ducking their heads against the slashing white flakes as they tugged along their small child. "This is a day in the park."

Jared slanted me a sidelong glance. "Don't discount it. You've been away for half a dozen years and aren't familiar with recent Cove winters."

"Yeah, but I lived here for over twenty-five years. I think I know central New York winters, Jared. I mean, sir."

It was Jared's turn to snort. "Respect is a rough pill to swallow."

"Not when I have a special Macy's blend in my cup." I grinned and lifted my to-go cup of heavily lightened and sweetened coffee. My little secret since Christian made no bones of the fact he took his black and probably added Pennzoil to the brew to prove the size of his balls.

We were patrolling in twos tonight on account of the Valentine's spectacle—I mean, wholesome holiday event—taking place on Main Street in the Cove. Crowd control wasn't much of a thing for us, especially in the middle of winter, but big annual events like this drew out the townsfolk and tourists alike.

Especially this particular one, because the day of romance had become a week of romance, plus all the attendant festivities. Romance meant getting out to shop and eat broiled meat on sticks and buying candy for your beloved so she'd have sex with you later. Even if, statistically, you were more of a morning wood sort of guy.

I was only a little cynical.

"Rub it in. Besides, I do too. Though I had to cut back and now my special blend is more the green tea matcha variety." He winced and tapped the lid of his own takeout cup. "The terrible twos are killing us right now. Sami's cutting saber teeth instead of the standard baby variety."

I laughed and patted him sympathetically on the shoulder. "Wise move you decided to hire on that part-timer."

Jared's lips twitched. "Wiser than you can even imagine."

I didn't know what that meant, but Jared always thought he was a comedian. "Any line on the other one you wanted to hire?"

"Still interviewing potential candidates. We have another few interviews scheduled for this week and next. One coming in from Turnbull, one a recent city transplant." Jared growled and picked up his megaphone. "Camden Connolly, get that skateboard off the road in this weather!" He shook his head as his blasting voice nearly blew Camden right off the board. "Damn kid's going to kill himself with that thing when it's this icy out. I swear, I'm not ready for teenagers."

I chuckled. "Think you have a while yet."

"True. Thank God. But I still won't be ready."

"Maybe you should go back to the coffee beforehand? Help settle your nerves some."

Jared sent me a sly grin. "Oh, I have other ways to soothe myself, don't worry."

I officially hated the chief with a fiery passion.

"No one likes a braggart."

"Who's bragging?"

"You are. And are you going to hurry up and get married already so you're in misery and having no sex like the rest of us?"

He laughed. "Son, that will never happen, although gotta say, I never expected such woe in that department from you. Didn't you used to have a handful of girlfriends at a time?"

"Not a handful. Just casual dating isn't so casual anymore when you're past thirty. Never mind living in a town where every single woman has an egg timer in sync with the sale season at the baby shops on Main Street." I shuddered as the chief signaled onto a side street and weaved around a cluster of tourists admiring the endless heart decorations and ignoring traffic.

Admittedly, I wasn't much for babies, but in recent months I'd discovered kids weren't so bad. My little sister had hooked me up with a volunteer opportunity at the learning center and now I played basketball a few times a week with little kids, along with helping with some light tutoring here and there. I could handle reading and homework assistance. But these kids were way beyond diapers, unlike the chief's kid. I shuddered again.

Jared heaved out a breath. "Snow's starting to make a mess. Maybe I should tell Bee we'll have a later dinner. She's always my busy bee, she's used to juggling. A delayed meal is nothing."

"You can't put off Gina. She'll skin you alive."

"Nah, it won't be that much longer. I can spend a few more hours on patrol with you, get through the worst of the Valentine rush while the snow's snarling the roads."

"Chief, I'm fine. You honestly think I can't handle this? Do you remember I used to—"

"Work for the FBI. Yes, I remember. But tonight's a busy night, and this ice and snow isn't helping."

"No, but Christian's on patrol too with the new dude. I can always call for backup if I need some help with crowd control or an errant duck."

The errant duck wasn't an idle concern. This wasn't their usual time of year to be around, but our ducks were especially hardy and attached to this area. I wouldn't put it past them to steal a fried brisket out of some unsuspecting toddler's mouth.

They'd done odder things.

Not that I would need Christian's assistance to handle a rogue swarm of ducks, but if it made the chief feel better that I had help, good enough.

"Listen, Bee is making her famous chicken and biscuits on Sunday. She decided it's time we start our own Sunday dinner tradition. You should come over. Bring…a friend."

Did I seem that pathetic? That lacking in feminine company that my boss felt the need to set up a situation where I could invite someone over for home-cooking? And his fiancée Gina—the Bee nickname was solely Jared's for her and probably referred to some weird sex thing I didn't need to know—was one hell of a cook since she worked at the diner, so that would be a pretty thick carrot to tempt someone with.

"Hmm, we'll see. Or maybe she could make me a plate to take home?"

"You're a dyed in the wool bachelor."

I shrugged. "Third wheel isn't my color."

"So, find someone to bring. Bee worries about you."

"Sure she does. Not you though." I shook my head with a smile as Jared swung over to the curb behind my parked cruiser, his radio going off with reports of a power outage in town. Before he could insist he would put off going off duty, I pointed at him. "Go. You're off the clock. You trust your men, don't you?"

Jared's jaw locked. "Low blow, McNeill. Yes, I do. And I'm going."

"Glad to hear it. Have a good night."

He started to issue orders and I shut the door, pointing at the tree beside us listing in the wind with a helpless gesture. Not my fault the gust slammed it shut. He shook his head at me and pulled away as I climbed into my own car and indicated I was available to dispatch.

"McNeill, power on Main Street and in the surrounding area is out. Power company's ETA is thirty minutes. They suspect a weather-related cause."

"What was their first clue?" I frowned at our dispatcher Bonnie, who just happened to be Gina's mom. She also couldn't see me frowning through the radio. Good thing too. My general Valentine's malcontent was getting harder to stifle by the moment.

She ignored me. I supposed when a woman birthed five children she learned to tune out a lot. She also was very particular about doing things her own way. She used standard police codes when she wanted to and skipped them when she did not. Since Crescent Cove wasn't exactly a big city, things were often more informal here than they would've been in a more urban area.

Only partially due to the high rate of duck nuisance calls.

"Two minutes ago, a distress call came in from Sugar Rush, the bakery on the corner of Elm and Main."

Immediately, the long, wavy reddish-blond hair and guileless smile of Sugar Rush's owner Tabitha swam into my mind. And possibly her incredible rack and equally stunning hips. She was curvy in all the right places.

So I'd noticed. Sue me.

I'd been into the bakery a few times picking up donuts for the station and discovered Tabitha made treats for dogs too. Better yet, she catered to a wide range of dog allergies. Apparently, her mom had a dog allergic to wheat flour, which was beneficial for me since my Daisy was allergic to half the foods in existence.

Possibly three-fourths.

Tabitha hadn't said much to me the first few times I'd visited the shop but she'd smiled a lot. After the last time, I'd found a white bag outside my apartment filled with blueberry banana dog cookies—and my dog had nearly mowed me down to get at them. I hated how limited Daisy's food options were and really appreciated Tabitha's sideline business, but when I'd tried to thank her, she'd waved me off and practically shut her apartment door in my face.

Because, oh yeah, we were also neighbors.

Other than chatting at the first rooftop party I'd gone to last summer, saying hi as we passed in the hall was as good as it got. She rarely even made eye contact with me.

But man, her donuts were a wonder. And her eyes were insanely blue. And I was really fond of watching her walk back into her apartment since her rear view was just as stunning as the front.

Might as well make the best of her reluctance to talk to me for more than a moment or two, right?

"What was the call, Bonnie?" I was already signaling into traffic to do a U-turn. Sugar Rush was just a few blocks away in the opposite direction.

"Multiple calls, actually. One about the power outage. And..."

"And?" I prompted.

"She requested someone to help take care of a puppy."

"Help take care of a puppy? Does she think that's the job of the police department?"

"She found the puppy in the trash. It's very young and she requested veterinary assistance."

My known weakness toward dogs made me roll my shoulders. I would not be suckered by a wet nose and a pair of doe eyes—neither the pup's nor Tabitha's. I was in a vulnerable sexless state tonight and had to shore up my boundaries. "From the cops?"

"Brady, she's flustered and she's never dealt with babies before. I suspect not human or canine. Give the girl a break. Eat one of her cookies and chill out."

I narrowed my eyes. Bonnie was using that tone I recognized as a motherly matchmaking voice. My own mother's career in law enforcement had given her a different occupation when it came to her two sons and her daughter—mainly to encourage us to choose any career *but* law enforcement—but I was sure she could rouse that particular tone if needed.

Besides, I had enough trouble picking my own dates. How could someone else do any better?

"Chill out in the dark with her and cookies and a crying dog? Sounds relaxing."

"The power won't be out long. As for the dog, I don't know what to tell you. Tabitha said the two emergency vet clinics near town are full to the seams right now."

I sighed. "Did she call Grant?"

Grant was Daisy's vet and the vet of many of those who lived in the Cove. He was technically located in nearby Kensington Square, but he was close enough and had a good enough reputation to draw clients from all over the area. Not to mention the man would keep his clinic open until all hours if there was an animal in distress. He would help Tabitha's puppy, even on Valentine's Day. The man was a widower and I was pretty sure he hadn't had a night off in ages.

And I did not feel the least bit guilty at throwing him under the bus—also known as shoving my problem off on him. Even if it wasn't my problem anyway because I was a damn cop, not Officer Friendly of the small and furry division.

"I don't know if she called Grant. She indicated the two places she did call were full. I thought you could do community outreach." The next bit she said under her breath. "Not like you have any other plans tonight."

"Hey, Valentine's shaming is a thing."

"Hmm?" Bonnie asked innocently as I swung into Sugar Rush's small corner lot with its attached parking area. Small was an optimistic term for the size, but due to the obvious power outage—I'd never seen Sugar Rush's neon sign with its pair of huge plump lips dark before—no one was here except for the small aging sedan I recognized as Tabitha's.

"You know what I'm referring to. Just because all your children are pairing off and producing grandchildren for you at a rapid fire rate is no reason to be smug."

"I most certainly am not smug. Nor am I shaming you for being single on the holiday designed for love. I just want to help."

I'd just bet she did. She must've had a gap in her baby booty knitting schedule and wanted to get me and my future progeny booked early. "I'd ask why you didn't send Christian to Tabitha, but I know why."

"You're newly on shift. Christian is at the tail end of his and is dealing with the new recruit to boot." She coughed loudly. "He's a handful, like someone else we know."

"Mmm-hmm. And I suppose it has absolutely nothing to do with Tabitha and I living across the hall from each other. Easy access."

"Your access is your business. Though you both have connections to special needs dogs—"

"Daisy isn't special needs. She just can't have rawhide or wheat flour. I hate peas. Does that mean I'm special too?"

"Yes, and not for that reason. Go in there and do your damn job." She clicked off.

Shaking my head, I slammed out of my patrol car and promptly slipped on the ice and had to grab the damn roof to keep from ending up on my ass. Mid-flail, I glanced up at the back door, narrowing my eyes at the woman huddled under the awning and cooing to what I assumed was a dog in a plaid blanket.

My annoyance crackled and melted into a puddle that centered somewhere in my chest. It was warm and spreading and nearly made me forget the sleet pelting me in the damn face as her red hair unfurled in the growing wind and her big damp eyes lifted to mine.

I wasn't one to be fanciful—as shown by my irritation that anyone really believed Valentine's Day was anything but a racket—but maybe Bonnie had put a bug in my ear. Or it could be due to the town's love vibes that seeped into everyone's pores like some kind of happy gas. More likely, my sudden good feelings had a simple cause.

I hadn't gotten laid since last summer. *Officer Horndog, reporting for booty.*

Whatever the reason, as I stared into Tabitha's eyes while she cuddled that sweet homeless dog, a buzz hummed under my skin. My regulation pants shrunk half an inch in the zippered area and the organ in my chest I didn't give much thought to started beating just a little faster.

And then my soul mate opened her mouth.

"About time you showed up. I was about to drive down to Dunkin' Donuts to interrupt your break."

Now Available

For more information go to www.tarynquinn.com

Have My Baby

Claim My Baby

Who's The Daddy

Pit Stop: Baby

Baby Daddy Wanted

Rockstar Baby

Daddy in Disguise

My Ex's Baby

Daddy Undercover

Wrong Bed Baby

Lucky Baby

Daddy on Duty

Cop Daddy Next Door

Protector Daddy

CRESCENT COVE STANDALONES & SHORTS

CEO Daddy

Fireman Daddy

Mistletoe Baby

For more information about our books visit
www.tarynquinn.com

MORE BY TARYN QUINN

OTHER SERIES

Happy Acres

Kensington Square

Afternoon Delight

Deuces Wild

Wilder Rock

Walk on the wilder side with these stories

After Dark

HOLIDAY BOOKS

Unwrapped

Holiday Sparks

Filthy Scrooge

Bad Kitty

Saving Kylie

For more information about our books visit

www.tarynquinn.com

ABOUT TARYN QUINN

USA Today bestselling author, *TARYN QUINN*, is the sexy and funny alter ego of bestselling authors Taryn Elliott & Cari Quinn. We've been writing together for years, but we have decided to pull the trigger on a combo name just for fun.

And so…Taryn Quinn was born!

Do you like ultra sexy small town romance full of shenanigans? Quirky office romances full of steam? Okay, look…we pretty much just love writing steamy stories. If you're all about that, we're your girls!

For more information about us...
tarynquinn.com
tq@tarynquinn.com

QUINN AND ELLIOTT

We also write more serious, longer, and sexier books as Cari Quinn & Taryn Elliott. Our topics include mostly rockstars, but mobsters, MMA, and a little suspense gets tossed in there too.

Rockers' Series Reading Order

Lost in Oblivion

Winchester Falls

Found in Oblivion

Hammered

Rock Revenge

Brooklyn Dawn

OTHER SERIES

Tapped Out

Love Required

Boys of Fall

If you'd like more information about us please visit

www.quinnandelliott.com